Also by Warren Adler

NOVELS
Residue
The Womanizer
The David Embrace
Flanagan's Dolls
Funny Boys
The War of the Roses
Random Hearts
Trans-Siberian Express
The Children of the Roses
Banquet Before Dawn
The Henderson Equation
The Casanova Embrace
Natural Enemies
Blood Ties
Twilight Child
We Are Holding the President Hostage
Madeline's Miracles
Private Lies
The Housewife Blues
Cult
Mourning Glory
Undertow

MYSTERIES
American Quartet
American Sextet
The Witch of Watergate
Senator Love
Immaculate Deception
The Ties That Bind
Death of a Washington Madame

SHORT STORIES
The Sunset Gang
Never Too Late For Love
Jackson Hole, Uneasy Eden
The Washington Dossier Stories
Warren Adler Short Story Contest Winners
New York Echoes

AVAILABLE IN ALL FORMATS AS EBOOKS AND PRINT ON DEMAND
WHEREVER BOOKS ARE SOLD ONLINE AND OFF.
VISIT WWW.WARRENADLER.COM FOR MORE INFORMATION.

Empty Treasures

by Warren Adler

For Sunny

ISBN: 1-59006-025-3

ISBN: 978-1-59006-025-4

Inquiries: www.warrenadler.com

STONEHOUSE PRESS

I

Elly had deliberately chosen the table in the first row of the café. From there, while they sipped their Campari and sodas, they watched the Venetian dusk descend on the elaborate relics of the lost empire.

The light disappeared softly, blurring the contrast between the pink and the white marble of the Doge's Palace directly across the wide promenade that fed into the Piazza San Marco. With little neck strain, they could see the last gasp of the faltering light play on the bronze hide of the four horses over the central doorway of the Basilica, the clock tower, the boat traffic on the Grand Canal and, of course, the most compelling exhibit of all, the human throng.

As they passed, people's faces lit with smiles. Without embarrassment, couples kissed, squeezed, and hugged each other.

Behind them on a small bandstand, a quartet of strings played lush romantic music. People stopped to listen and smile as they gazed beyond them to the musicians. Joy seemed catching here, she thought. Everyone is happy.

"Am I?" she asked herself, reaching out for Al's fingers, entwining them. With his free right hand, he lifted his glass in an all-inclusive toast.

"Wonderful," he said, nostrils flaring, which was his way of showing that his senses were open. She puckered her lips and tossed him a kiss in the soft air. The place, she decided, called for such a gesture. After all, they had come to Venice to search for renewal.

"I vote for making love before dinner," she said. Was it the place that made her moist and tingly? Or Al? Or the imagery?

"I second that motion."

They had always regarded that part of their relationship as candy, treats. Good. No hang-ups in that department, she thought, wondering how much beyond that was going bankrupt. Giving into lust, however, was not a bad thing, and they both knew the value of enhancement and surprise.

"With the windows open," she whispered, "so that we can hear the music and the human symphony, and after we can watch the lights and the reflection on the Grand Canal." She moved her leg so that it was between his, rubbing her knee along his thigh.

"A long way from home," Al said.

"*Horas non numero nisi serenas,*" she said, proud that she had memorized this legend from the sundial.

"I count only the happy hours," he translated. He, too, was working hard on renewal.

"I feel new, Al. That's what I feel."

They had been in Venice for two days—before that, Cap Ferrat. In Nice, they had hired a car and driven along the coast on the *péage* through the seven hundred tunnels carved into the mountains, then across the boot of Italy to Venice. In two days they would take the train to Rome, then fly back to Washington.

"Well then, mission accomplished," Al said, adding tentatively, "I hope."

"We work too hard, Al," she said, avoiding an answer. No, she thought, sorry she had injected this old note of contention. Did they work hard to avoid each other or themselves? They had indulged in endless rationalizations, infinite images. One she liked was that Washington was a racetrack on a sunny day with a crowded, thundering, high-kicking field on the flat. It was not a city for laggards or falterers, and the ante was always mysteriously raised. Someone was forever moving the finish line beyond the measured distance.

For Al the track was well defined. He was a lawyer who moved in and out of administrations, depending on the party in power. The field was loaded in favor of lawyers, who winked at each other under their blinders and kept the pack sniffing at their rumps.

For her, a journalist on "the" Washington daily, the tactic of the race was to be ever alert, looking for the openings in the field ahead. Fall back and someone would whip themselves into the place in front of you. Being an also-ran in the big race was a gnawing reality, which only increased her hunger. For what? She knew, vaguely, but when she tried to explain it to Al, especially now that she was thirty-four, with the deafening and relentless ticking of the biological clock pounding in her ears, he turned away in frustration.

It was too late for either-or. He had other things in mind for their future. And doing both meant cheating on both. Other women do it, he had argued, have kids and careers. I am *not* other women, she would scream inside herself. Now. His chant was, Family now! It was the Greek chorus of their seven-year marriage. There is still this mountain to climb. Now, she insisted.

She upended her glass, hoping to abort this unproductive and repetitive introspection and recover what seemed to have been a promising lost moment. Forcing herself, she turned to her natural stance—intense observation. "It's one helluva big world."

She meant that the faces on parade reflected all shapes, sizes, races, countries, and classes. It made her feel almost provincial.

The hawk-eyed waiter, apparently watching for signs of empty glasses, came up to their table.

"*Due*," Al said, lifting two fingers.

"*Grazie*," the waiter said.

She acknowledged, finally, that the moment was illusionary

and continued to look out at the people, the happy faces, hoping to find her own among them. The waiter came with their drinks. Then she realized that the music had stopped, which, she told herself hopefully, may have also accounted for the sudden change of mood.

"It's still very beautiful," she said. Across the canal she could see the island of San Giorgio Maggiore and its landmark cathedral, cast now in subtle electric lights. Still? She wondered if he had caught the inference.

Across the table she watched him, his high handsome profile under his longish hair, which fell neatly in two black half-moon waves over his forehead but continued to partially cover his ears. In old photos it had been long and sloppy, shoulder length. Now, strand by strand, it was crawling up the sides of his head.

Last flickering light of the sixties, she sighed, knowing that it wouldn't be long before his ears began to show. And yet, they had both arrived chronologically too late for that era. By a hair, she chuckled to herself.

Sitting here in the Piazza San Marco sipping Campari and soda, she felt the old longing and envy for that missed moment. She would have been good at it, a willing recruit, a true child of the sixties, smasher of icons, a soul in rebellion, like her late father, except that he had never needed an excuse to bloody establishment noses. Alas, ten years too late. It hurt to think about it, as if she were telling herself that life had passed her by.

"Good to get away," he said.

She had forgotten where her knees were, and now he was returning the pressure, squeezing her bent leg between his thighs.

"Although the nearer you get to the end of it, the more you start thinking of what's waiting for you back home."

"Stop that," she admonished playfully. "We promised." I, especially, she thought.

"That we did," he said with his mock Irish lilt.

His parents, the Brians, although born in this country, still carried around the apparent genetic pull of the old sod. The music began again, which helped put her back in the mood, at least partially.

"We'll finish these, then we'll go," she said, smiling, feeling better. "I love your leer."

"I was hoping you would."

"Think we can do it in a gondola?" she asked suddenly. "Like in the movies."

"Not in any I've seen."

She noted that the gondoliers stood in the stern of their boats working their oars and that the passengers were separated by a partition. There was surprise and danger in the idea—anything to take life out of the norm.

"Then we'll make our own."

She detected in him a slight case of reluctance, a Washington hangover. He was deep into dignity and image these days—three-piece suits and his Phi Beta Kappa key hanging from his vest. Once he had thought it pompous, then quietly it had reappeared about two years ago. She supposed it would be good for his practice. Irreverence, she had observed, seemed to peter out in men at about thirty-five. Al had just passed that Rubicon.

"We could ask him to take us somewhere remote, away from the tourists," she said.

"Whatever turns you on," he said, smiling.

In a salvage operation one had to be creative, and he was giving it his best shot.

"You, too. Once you fancied the nautical." They had done it

once in the paddleboat on the reflecting pool adjacent to the Jefferson monument.

"But old Tom was facing the other way," he said, brushing his fingers through his hair.

"Wouldn't have minded it if he peeked," she said, feeling girlishly wanton again, liking the feeling.

He paid for the drinks and they walked arm in arm, she leading the way through the narrow *calles*, searching for some off-the-beaten-path *fondamenta* where the gondolas were moored. Finding one, he negotiated a price while she lounged in the gondola and waited, stretching out on the soft pillows and partially covering herself with a light blanket.

"One-hundred-thousand lire," he said, smiling as he got in beside her.

"What are you smiling about?"

"For what we have in mind, it's double."

"How did he know what we had in mind?"

"He knows the turf, the lascivious bastard."

"Good for him."

The gondolier pushed off, and the boat glided away from its mooring.

"I like this," she whispered, nestling close to him, looking up at patches of sky visible through the dark cliffs made by the villas that lined the *rios*. The gondolier moved the craft softly through the water away from the tourist routes, and soon they could hear only the lapping of the water against the stone siding.

She had slipped off her panty hose, and he had matched her in kind, although the tops of his pants were only to midthigh. Occasionally as they caressed each other, they would pass people walking on the *calles*, talking softly, laughing.

"Good to break the pattern occasionally," she whispered.

"That's what vacations are supposed to do."

He had, she knew, assured himself that getting away would erode her resistance. With the beginnings of success—his definition—had come the beginnings of arrogance and, consequently, a growing belief in the power of his persuasiveness.

Weren't all the arguments on his side? Family now! She was thirty-four years old, for crying out loud. Not yet! That was her battle cry and slogan, but it was beginning to lose its credibility.

Soon "not yet" could become "never." In a fit of compromise, a rearguard action, she had offered to hyphenate her name, a major concession, since keeping her own name continued to bother him. He was too shrewd and secure to accept that sop, and she had remained the unhyphenated Elly Fox. But it had been an important, even seminal concession. Her father's name—a giant chunk of herself, a commitment beyond even marriage.

He had rejected the offer contending, wisely for him, that it was not important enough. Not like family. Thus, the argument, the issue, the "heart of the matter," children, family, like a snake, slithered around them, squeezing and choking off air.

"I don't want to miss the big one, Al," she insisted, whatever that was, except that she knew it was coming, would come at any moment. It was more like a primal scream than a battle cry. His response was always the same:

"And then?"

At the moment the big one was nowhere in sight. Staleness was in the air.

"It's good to be married," she said, at that moment, sincerely. "Good to do this."

It was like making a statement that they were still willing to take chances. She felt the exquisite stirrings. At least they understood their bodies. Perhaps it was only that which held the whole thing together.

What he could not understand was that, for her, children signaled an end, not a beginning. It was not conventional wisdom
and, therefore, to say it aloud sounded cruel and inert, not life
enhancing. Nor was it enough to tell him "not yet."

"This part is always the best, Elly," he whispered, which implied
a vast wasteland elsewhere. Sometimes during these moments, he
added, "But I get tired of shooting blanks."

"Soon," she would reassure him, an idea that increasingly
challenged her sense of ethics. Yet, she had not the heart to say
"Perhaps, never," the real truth probably being somewhere in
between.

They'd been married since 1983, weathering nine years as a
couple, counting the two they'd been living together. There were
ups and downs, of course. Why hadn't they made peace? Because
there was an obvious conflict of priorities.

At that moment, of course, their priorities were in perfect sync,
although to achieve them required an effort of contortion. Their
change in position shifted the balance of the flat-bottomed boat.
The gondolier deftly compensated for the changes.

She wondered if he was peeking, but it was only Al, in the
missionary position, who could really tell. She had patches of sky
to watch and the canopy of stars in the soft clear air.

Then she watched nothing, holding tightly, letting the pleasure roll over her, sensing his simultaneous spasm. This mutuality,
which rarely misfired, had become an irony.

The blanket had slipped from his rear. She heard nearby voices
and the grunt of the gondolier as he tried to slow his craft's course.
Still she held Al in a tight embrace.

Then, just above her, on the higher elevation of the stone walk,
she saw two faces peering down at them. They seemed colorless,

almost ashen. An older couple, Italian faces.

"*Buona sera*," she said aloud, slapping Al on his exposed buttocks. Under her, she felt the surge of the gondolier's thrust as his oar moved the boat swiftly forward.

Al scrambled to her side, and they both quickly dressed, none too soon, since around the bend they could see the lighted hump of the Rialto Bridge.

"For good measure," Al said, handing the gondolier additional lire as he stepped onto the *fondamenta*. She saw his wink and the gondolier's playful gesture of kissing his fingers and raising them to the sky. "Well worth it, my man."

They crossed the bridge and got a canal-side table at a trattoria, where they toasted themselves again with Valpolicella, and ordered *baccalà* and anchovies and *cicale di mare*.

"What is that?" Elly asked.

"Something they call squill fish," Al said.

"How do you know that?"

"There's English subtitles," he said, pointing them out.

They ate ravenously and finished the bottle, ordering another.

"I feel so decadent," Elly said.

"I feel very Hemingway," Al said. "Remember *Across the River and into the Trees*?"

"No," she said, saddened suddenly by her lack of knowledge, suspecting that perhaps this later Hemingway was a male thing. "Only *Death in Venice*." She sighed, watching him roll pasta around his fork. While his mouth was full, she continued, "About a man with an obsession about a young boy. His whole life focuses on the boy, with whom, in the story, he barely exchanges a single word."

"When it comes to human behavior, I guess anything goes," Al said, washing his pasta down with wine. He lifted his glass. "Like doing it in a gondola."

She wondered suddenly who really had initiated that little caper. Was it an act to placate on her part or persuade on his? Had she meant by it, let us be daring and unique and prove that we are above the traditional conventions? Or had he said, you must give me what I want, when I want, where I want? It was an idea with too much spin, and it caused her attention to drift. She spilled some wine, which made a red puddle on the tablecloth.

It broke the sudden tension and she laughed loudly. People turned around to look at them. She hoped that they were thinking of them as youngish lovers on a holiday, selfish for each other, oblivious to other cares, other burdens. Not as they were in real life.

Washington images began to assault her, the thundering hooves of the sweaty-hided herd on Capitol Hill, the greedy grunters climbing over each other on the greasy pole of ambition at the paper, her journalist colleagues, who were the secret enemy, and Al, dear Al, who wanted heirs and a wife, as he might be imagining she was at that moment.

Maybe he was right, she wondered. Why all this angst on her part? Creating progeny was the reason for marriage. Wasn't it? Motherhood was a woman's function, a female imperative, an evolutionary necessity. Not ambition or revenge. Revenge? She shivered.

"You see," Al was saying. He had refilled their glasses. "A lot of it took place in Harry's Bar, where we had a drink last night. But I forgot. Imagine that." Her mind lurched to catch up. He must be talking about the Hemingway book. "An old soldier, an officer, tries to recapture his youth by falling for a woman less than half his age." He shook his head. "Now why did I forget?"

"And did they get together? Live happily ever after." Have

babies, she thought, contemplating the cruel irony of gender. She knew that such an idea would not have occurred to him.

"How old were you when you read it?" she asked, hoping to redirect her own thoughts.

He shrugged.

"Fifteen. Sixteen. When I read all Hemingway."

"See. You came to Venice and recaptured your lost youth." So the old soldier also came for renewal, she thought, wondering if he had succeeded.

"I'm more inclined to look to my future than my past," he said pointedly.

"I'd say I'm more into the now," she said, deflecting any attempt on his part to get heavy. She looked at him and forced a giggle. She could tell from his supercilious expression that he was getting drunk.

"In a gondola," he chuckled.

It was an experience, of course, that would last them a lifetime in memory. Already in her mind, it had become a kind of symbol. Of resistance or surrender. She wasn't sure. Yet she believed in symbols, signs, foreshadowings. Often, she forgot them. Sometimes she remembered.

The night before she was interviewed for the job at the paper, she'd awakened from a nightmare, but couldn't remember what it was. That morning she had spilt salt and walked under a ladder.

Another harbinger of doom that morning was that before the interview with the executive editor, Charlie Carruthers, had barely got under way, one of her contact lenses had popped out, and they had both spent nearly a half hour on their hands and knees looking for it, only to find that it had fallen into her shoe. Adding insult to injury, Carruthers had gotten a nasty bump on his head as he tried, during the search, to move out from under his desk.

"Nothing but investigative crap," he had muttered when the interview finally got under way. With a sour expression, he had looked through her sheaf of clippings. Some of her earlier ones from the old weekly where she worked for her father were yellow.

"In Wilkes-Barre, we knocked over the police chief."

"Big deal."

"He was corrupt. A monster. You see—"

"I can read, kid."

He continued to shuffle the clips, shaking his head, as he scanned her series on the city council.

"We don't issue hunting licenses," he sighed, and looked up to study her. "Not any more."

"I just want a job," she had told him.

Again, he had shuffled through the clips and reread her resume.

"Wish you were blacker, older, and walked with a limp," he croaked, relishing his performance. "One thing we don't need is another female barracuda with brass balls."

"Mine are gold," she shot back, not actually offended, just picking up his smart-ass rhythm. It got a rise out of him, and he smiled.

"Why gold?"

"It's the brightest metal on earth," she said, toe-to-toe. "And the most valuable."

He had tapped his teeth and scrutinized her. Then he stuck out a roughhewn hand, and she grabbed it.

"Just keep them out of my soup, lady."

They decided to take a vaporetto back to the Piazza San Marco from the Rialto. They bought their tickets and waited at the dock. It was getting late, and the crowds were growing sparse. They held hands. When the vaporetto arrived, they crossed the threshold and took seats near the window, she on the aisle.

As the boat moved away from the dock, her gaze washed curiously over the occupants. A familiar profile suddenly froze her survey. No, she thought, distrusting the recognition. Couldn't be.

He was sitting a few rows ahead of her, lost in thought—oblivious to her scrutiny. She hadn't ever seen him from that angle, jowls spilling over the side of his neck, large horn-rims with lenses that looked like the bottoms of bottles, thin strands of hair pasted over a bald pink pate.

During their interview, she remembered, he had removed his glasses from time to time to wipe them. Without them, he looked like a pudgy baby.

Short, with a waddling walk, he tried to compensate for his roly-poly image by wearing perfectly tailored pinstriped suits and white-on-white shirts and blue ties with white polka dots tied in a Windsor knot. Her reporter's eye was remembering now. He also wore elevator shoes and short lisle socks, with legs that showed naked pink above them.

Bending low, she tried to get a glimpse of them, but it was impossible. He was too far up front.

"You getting seasick?" Al asked.

"This is the way I ride vaporettos," she joked. He shrugged and turned to look at the Venice lights sliding by.

The boat sailed smoothly to its first stop after the Rialto. People moved on and off. The man sat frozen in his seat. He had turned his head so that she no longer saw him in profile, but the back of his head with his double rows of upper-neck fat was also familiar.

Still she distrusted the recognition. Irving Leopold. Was it?

No. She offered herself a mild protest. It was the spell of Venice, the wine, the sense of illusion. Nothing was as it seemed. Besides, Mediterranean people resembled each other. She shrugged it away, deciding not to dwell on it.

The vaporetto docked at its next stop. It was getting more and more crowded with people heading toward the piazza for the last gasp of the Venice night.

But she could not dismiss the idea of it, the coincidence, and her eyes seemed to take on a life of their own, their gaze fixed on the familiar head. Ahead she could see the globe of reflected light from the Piazza San Marco and the *piazzetta* with its two granite columns.

Passengers stirred, stood up, and moved toward the double doors as the boat slid past the Gritti Palace into the station dock. A brief surge of people blocked her view, but she remained seated. Al had begun to rise, but she pressed his thigh with the flat of her hand, and he sat down again.

"But it's San Marco—"

"I know."

"What is it?"

"Please, Al. Wait."

She could feel him follow her gaze as the man she had been watching rose, turned, and headed toward the door. Waddled. And as he passed her, she caught something else vaguely familiar. A scent he wore. She remembered writing something about lilacs in the air.

The pulse beat in her neck as she glanced briefly toward the heavy, departing, well-tailored back. No question, she thought, comparing the face and body against the matrix in her mind. She watched him waddle through the double doors. It's him. Irving Leopold.

"Come on," she said, grabbing Al's hand. But after they had moved out of the vaporetto, she pulled back, slowing them. Ahead, she could see the rotund figure move in its distinctive way across the *piazzetta*, past the base of the two columns.

Al walked beside her in tandem. She moved with obvious stealth, walking behind clusters of people heading over the Ponte della Paglia. As they moved with the crowds, she saw him veer off to a dock where a speedboat taxi waited. The driver tipped his hat, his body bent in what struck her as an obsequious gesture. Probably paid him inordinately well, she thought, noting that the driver held the boat steady with his foot, taking the man's uncertain hand as he assisted the clumsy body onto the deck.

Elly moved to the rail at the hump of the bridge and watched the water taxi glide away into the darkness.

"Irving Leopold," she muttered, shaking her head. "Imagine that."

"Leopold?"

She did not take her eyes off the boat, which headed into the channel, picking up speed.

"Remember him? The man with the briefcase," Elly said. "A month ago."

The police had picked up a thief, who had burgled a number of apartments in this posh building on Massachusetts Avenue. Seems the man was a former night attendant on the reception desk. The police had picked him up at his own apartment, where the loot that had not yet been fenced was stashed, including nearly a hundred thousand dollars in cash. The cash was in a rococo leather briefcase clearly labeled in gold leaf with the name Irving Leopold, who kept a small apartment in the building but had not reported a burglary. Grist for the mill. Irving Leopold was a well-known celebrity groupie, jeweler to the stars, a kind of court jester to the rich and famous.

Others among the burgled were also newsy types, a senator from Colorado, an assistant secretary of state, the head of the Democratic National Committee, and some local well-heeled businessmen. It was the cash that titillated the public. None of the victims stepped forward to acknowledge the cash as stolen. The thief claimed it as his own, saying that he had simply stored it in the briefcase.

The police, of course, felt differently. They impounded the cash with whatever else seemed like stolen goods. Mary Hobbs, editor of the Style section, assigned Elly to do a tongue-in-cheek piece, which made the thief, a surly well-dressed young man named Newton Parker, the Washington celebrity of the moment. Dutifully, she had interviewed all the crime victims, including Irving Leopold, who had a cute little Viennese accent.

"Me? I got credit cards. Who needs cash?"

"But you're in the jewelry business."

"So the thief didn't get no stones, just my briefcase."

"Which you didn't even report."

"Report a briefcase? I got apartments in New York, Vienna, and Tel Aviv. I leave things. Sometimes I have all my jockey shorts in Vienna and all my T-shirts in Tel Aviv. Sometimes I have my brown socks in New York and my blue socks in Washington. How should I know where I put my briefcase? I got three, just like that one."

It was a funny story. Even Charlie Carruthers sent her a note. "Real rib tickler. Not bad."

Not bad was as close as he got to superlatives. As for the money, Newton insisted it was his own, that he didn't trust banks and challenged anyone to prove that it wasn't.

When she interviewed him, he was out on bail awaiting trial, and the police still hoped that someone would step forward and make a claim for the cash. Elly suspected the senator or the head of the Democratic National Committee. Hot political money. What else?

"So?" Al asked with annoyance, standing beside her on the bridge. "Why are we here?"

"I'm not sure," she acknowledged. For some reason, she hadn't suspected that it was Irving Leopold's hundred thousand. Not then. She wondered why she hadn't simply stood up and reintroduced herself. There had been no hostility between them. He had been rather charming and fatherly and had offered her a cup of coffee and cookies, which she had taken along with the chitchat and self-serving anecdotes.

"Are you sure it's him?" Al asked.

"Is the Pope a Catholic?" She started, pointing. "Look." She squeezed Al's hand.

"Ouch."

The speedboat grew increasingly hard to see, although she imagined that she could see its wake in the distance. Following the wake, it seemed to arc toward a ship anchored in the canal. She had noticed it earlier from the balcony of her hotel. It flew a flag she did not recognize, although she had noted the half moon of an Arab country, and painted on it's stern under a name she could not read, the word *Iraq*. It had seemed vaguely threatening. Iraq. Hussein, the mad butcher of the Middle East.

She squinted into the darkness. The wake seemed to form a path, drifting to the port side of the ship. She could no longer see or hear the boat. Her mind began to toy with the shred of an idea, a tiny juxtaposition of images.

"What does it mean?" she asked aloud.

It was obviously not a question directed at Al. Yet she saw his shrug. He had been holding her hand. Suddenly, he released it, the act a statement of frustration, of disengagement.

Her hand, she noted, had begun to sweat. She continued to peer over the side of the bridge watching the ship. A number of water taxis passed, churning the dark waters, making the gondolas and other craft tremble in their moorings.

"How long are we going to stand here?" Al asked, covering a yawn.

She ignored the question, her gaze fixed on the ship. Suddenly Venice had disappeared. The romance and sense of abandon shattered. The vault in her reporter's mind had swung open, and the interrogatory beast was unleashed.

"Where do you suppose it went?"

"Guess it slipped around the other end of the ship."

"Do you think he got on the ship?" It was, she sensed, an idea catching hold, a personal antenna suddenly alive to strange and distant signals. Irving Leopold, who mixed with the high-and-mighty of America. Venice. An Iraqi ship. The unrepentant enemy. Saddam Hussein, the butcher of Baghdad. The war in the desert. Tiny shreds of information suddenly connected.

"I don't get paid for this," Al said.

It was his inevitable coy signal of withdrawal. Her work, the continuing bone of contention between them had, once again, intruded. This vacation had been a temporary truce, a time to exchange prisoners. Now she had violated the truce, trounced on the white flag.

But it hadn't been her fault. How was she to know that Irving Leopold would suddenly appear, take a water taxi toward a ship flying the flag of a renegade country? She continued to remember: photographs of Leopold with the president, with members of the Cabinet, with stars, all of them movers and shakers.

"I smell a story, Al."

"You always do," he sighed, dead sober now, showing irritation and truculence. In Washington she could counter with her own accusations. His work was equally absorbing, and he traveled frequently, was often self-absorbed. Let he who is without sin cast the first stone. It was always her bedrock retort.

"It's what I do."

"I'm tired, kiddo."

"Could be more to it."

"Yeah, I know. Another Iran-Contra. Maybe even another Watergate."

His sarcasm was thick, always a prelude to nastiness. No, she thought, she would not be baited into a confrontation. Not now. Not after this good day. His recalcitrance made her curiosity more intense.

"But why would he board this ship, an Iraqi ship?"

"You didn't see him board it. And if he did? So what," he said smugly.

"Leopold knows everybody—important political types. It's his stock in trade. He bragged to me about it." Part of the chitchat with coffee and cookies. She had not written it into her story. At the time it seemed too self-serving and name-droppy. He was, after all, a known publicity hound.

Her mind was filling now with an avalanche of reminders from their interview and what she had read about him. He had defined himself as a jeweler to the stars. But was he more? A confidante?

His cute little Viennese accent echoed in her mind. She remembered that she had thought it charming. He did, he said, a "holesell" business, rings, brooches, bracelets, necklaces. He knew stones. Nobody knows stones like Irving Leopold, he told her.

It wasn't exactly a secret that he sold jewelry to politicians, lobbyists, the high-and-mighty, past and present. Ronnie bought a five-carat ring for Nancy, top secret, of course. Jerry bought a necklace for Betty, sapphires. Even George had bought a "little something" for Barbara.

But who talks about it? It's private, off the record. Go to any Washington party—the discreet little dinner parties, of course—here's Irving's work: half the Cabinet. Didn't even have to be rich, Irving sold "holesell."

Even to some of the most important ambassadors. The Arabs? Why not? Stones have no bias. Why shouldn't the ones that run America and the world get the best? Hollywood? Chiselers, the bunch of them. In Washington they don't chisel. They get the best price automatically. When he spoke, the words had the air of satire. But there he was in the photographs, on the scene where the big shots gathered. Good old Irving.

The crowds faded, the lights of San Marco slowly disappeared, the traffic on the Grand Canal thinned. Still, she peered into the darkness, watching the ship's deck and cabin lights. Beside her, Al grew more restless.

"There's a story there, Al. I know it," she said.

"But how will that affect the price of tea in China?"

It was another of his ploys to indicate his unhappiness with her work, her concentration on things outside his orbit, her world without him, prodding his determination to take her out of the game, to put her on ice.

This was proof positive that she was not ready for that, not now, perhaps not ever. His question, of course, was rhetorical, requiring no answer. Peripherally, she saw him stare at her for a long moment, then move away toward their hotel, leaving her alone on the bridge.

II

"You think they'll have valet parking?" Terry Silver asked. She had just put the finishing touches on her hair.

"Doubt it," Harry mumbled. He was lying on the bed, eyes closed, trying to catch five before they went. "Too cheap."

"They have budgets. It should be part of their entertainment expense." She was inherently practical, everything judged against the old Midwest-farm-girl standards gone slightly awry from too much Washington.

Raindrops clattered against the windowpanes. In the distance there was an occasional burst of thunder, then a flash of lightning.

"Maybe it doesn't look good to be too lavish, considering the recession?" she asked.

Ordinarily, he might let her critiques pass into oblivion. But tonight he was tired, edgy, too quick to respond. When she turned from the bathroom mirror to look at him, he closed his eyes.

"It's dress-up for crying out loud. Formal. Everybody will be dressed to the ears, jewels and all. Besides, the Italians—the *Italy* Italians—like all that display." He paused for a moment. "Greedy guineas," he muttered. But it was not in the context of her remarks. It was the other thing, the payoff to the ambassador.

"I wish you wouldn't be such a bigot, Harry," Terry rebuked, meaning that all God's creatures were part of the grand, divine design. Everything that was inside her was still there, expressed differently, translated—he supposed—into the language of lost innocence.

He didn't respond, surrendering instead to a hopeful hint of drowsiness, suddenly remembering his father, whose method of escape was similar. But Harry was not having the desired results.

He heard her moving around the room, opening closets. From downstairs came the sound of television. Bobbie, his ten-year-old daughter, was watching the perennial reruns of *Mash*. Sometimes, when he was home at the right time, he would have to elbow her away so that he could catch the network news.

For the past week he had deliberately avoided it, although he had gobbled up the newspapers. Every day that passed without him seeing his or Billy's name in the paper was a bonus day. Like reading the obituaries, knowing you were alive when you didn't see your name. The hardest part was to maintain the facade of calm. "Show the bastards nothing," Billy had said. "When they come at you, pull the curtain down."

"You think I should wear the red or the blue?" Terry asked, tweaking his naked big toe. He opened his eyes and saw her there in panty hose and bra, holding the gowns draped in front of her. He remembered when she had made her own clothes out of store-bought patterns and her mother's old Singer.

"Go with the red," he said.

"If I remember, there were a lot of red things in the embassy. This could clash." Clash?

"Then go with the blue."

"You really think so?"

After fifteen years and his zero credibility in the realm of fashion, she still asked him. There was still the jewelry to go. Leopold had been generous with the discounts on her adornments, too generous. Considering their involvement, how could he not be? He wished she wouldn't wear any baubles at all, but he didn't want to call attention to it.

Not like Millie, Billy's wife, who could display her wealth of jewelry with impunity, wear it on any anatomical part. Harry half expected her one evening to wear something in her nose, perhaps a diamond-encrusted bone. Besides she could get away with it. She was rich and her well-honed public image was steeped in extravagance. Even her tart tongue was like an adornment.

But Terry's sense of thrift came out of *Poor Richard's Almanac*, and she had to be convinced that anything Harry purchased for her was both practical and affordable. "Damn it, it's an engagement ring, Terry. I never gave you one." It had also needed a reason. Three carats in a Tiffany setting for fifteen hundred dollars—how can you beat that? You couldn't, of course. Leopold's offers were nonrefusable. Even for Terry. But once the dike was breached, he gave her a pearl necklace and a diamond wedding band. Who turns down champagne on a beer budget?

At least Harry did not have to put up with the likes of Millie Tucker. She had really dipped into the Leopold coffers, wanting the big rocks to enhance her public flamboyance. Did she have any idea of the real cost? The emotional cost? The risk? Harry wondered, feeling his gut tighten and the first tiny hints of heartburn.

"What about white?" She still hadn't made her choice of dress. She poked in the closet searching for her white gown.

"White's always good," Harry said wearily.

"I'll go with the blue," she said. If she was insecure, she had reason to be. His ambition had made her an alien in a strange land.

Again, he closed his eyes. He was, of course, happy she was happy or seemed happy. But then, she had always seemed happy. And, he suspected, that even the corrupting influence of Washington's social life had not robbed her of her essential innocence. She still made the family say grace at mealtimes and made love in the dark on Saturday nights and led them to church on Sunday.

She would not, under any circumstances, understand what had been going on between him and Billy and Irving Leopold, except that it would be all Billy's fault. Billy, to Terry, was the tempter incarnate. She hated being in his debt. It had not, after all, been her choice. Poor Terry. Yet, above all, she did believe in appearances and, he knew, she secretly liked the dressing up, the social stuff, and the prestige of being the wife of the commissioner of customs.

He expelled a burp and wished he could go to sleep instead. Vain hope. In ten minutes, she'd be at him to get dressed, and he would perform his old Army routine—shit, shower and shave, and jump into his Washington uniform, his trusty tuxedo. He wondered vaguely if she had given it to the cleaners. The last time he wore it was at a garden party, and the weather had been suffocating. He had sweated like a horse, and his tux probably stank under the arms.

"Is it a dance?" he asked superfluously. He knew what it was. A charade.

"No. Just a sit-down. About forty, I think."

"Good."

Billy would be there with his end. They had jointly agreed to the idea. As everything connected with the Leopold thing, it seemed bizarre enough to be appropriate. A payoff to the ambassador proffered on—to stretch a point—the soil of his fatherland.

Billy had gotten the word directly from the ambassador via the telephone, a perfectly pedestrian and straightforward code. "All your friends are welcome in my country, Mr. Secretary."

Discussing such transactions, they rarely used the phone,

which made Billy paranoid on principal and Harry nervous. The real conversations wer e always held outdoors, sometimes walking in Lafayette Park across the street from the Treasury Department or, if they were at home, at some ball field halfway between their respective homes.

It didn't look out of place, was perfectly natural. Everyone knew that Harry Silver and William Tucker were boyhood friends. And it was certainly not untoward for the secretary of the treasury and the commissioner of customs, which came under the secretary's authority, to have business conversations wherever they chose.

Nor would it seem strange for them and their spouses to be simultaneously invited to an embassy party. Washington was a party town. Indeed, it seemed a fine time and place to pass cash, which would buy the ticket for Irving Leopold's forced exile.

"Better move it, Harry," Terry said.

He did not wait for a second call. Since he was not sleeping, he did not want to just lie there and think. Thinking had become a painful business.

He shaved, took a quick shower, and dressed, posing, as always, for Terry's last-minute inspection. She patted his lapels and smoothed the front of his shirt then stepped back herself.

"How do I look?" she asked.

"Like a million."

It was something his father had always said to his mother, a statement tossed away, never sincerely meant, an acknowledgment to facilitate escape from further conversation.

Oddly, he thought a lot about his father lately. Perhaps nostalgia was a side effect of danger and uncertainty. Andy Silver, his Dad, had married into a family of screamers, talkers, and achievers, a fatal association for a failed, quiet man.

Harry's mother, always assertive and dominating, wasn't

exactly a beauty, and Harry always suspected that his uncles had used guile and intimidation to get his father to marry their only sister. His father was thirty-seven when they were married and his mother thirty-five.

Because of this, Harry always felt, his conception was rushed to get him in just under the wire.

His father was no bargain, not in that family, but at least he was a white-collar worker, a bookkeeper, a role with a reasonably respectable facade. It wouldn't do to have any blue collars in his mother's family of lawyers and doctors. They always referred to him as an accountant.

He had been very handsome, black hair, straight nose, good features, slender build, a good dresser. He had all the outward accoutrements for general acceptance. They could take him places. Who would know that he could not earn a living? Also he kept his mouth shut, which was different from being inarticulate, although his mother and her family believed he was.

Harry knew better, although the knowledge was intuitive, never proven. It was the quintessential mystery of Harry's life—the father who withdrew, escaped. Harry's most potent memory was of a man sleeping on a couch in the living room, rarely speaking, eyes closed, mouth slack.

What did he really think? What did he know? What was in his mind, beneath the surface, as he slept? Or, as Harry suspected, merely pretended? Even now, Harry begged in his heart for his father to speak, to break the lifetime of silence. Dad, tell me what you really think—of *everything,* of *me.*

What are you hiding? Why hide it from your son? Tell me. Always, in moments of crisis, Harry seemed to pose this question, and it always frightened and angered him. After all, the man had died more than a decade ago.

Bobbie gave him an obligatory farewell cheek kiss. Then he went into Paul's room and looked over the boy's shoulder. He was doing his math homework. Touching his back, he kissed his head and watched for a moment as his pencil sped over the paper.

"Don't know what it is, but it looks pretty smart," Harry said. He was proud of his fourteen-year-old who rarely ever brought home less than an *A*, although his seriousness sometimes concerned him.

"Simple stuff, Dad. You'd pick it up in minutes."

"Think so?"

The boy nodded without turning, and a wave of sadness rolled over Harry. How would Paul react to their exposure? He hoped the boy would never have to find out.

He helped Terry on with her evening cape and put on his trench coat, although the September evening was not as chilly as he had hoped. Washington weather was never much for cooperation and had made disasters out of public events. In this case, it was barely cooperative, since their plan necessitated that Harry wear a coat with large pockets, trench-coat pockets.

He felt the heft of the weights, the tightly packed currency bricks. Fifty and smaller, Ambassador Manelli had insisted, which meant that he and Billy had to carry four bricks in two coats. It had been the biggest problem from the beginning. Stashing cash.

"Crazy," he had told Billy when the matter first came up, just after that absurd story in the paper. Talk about luck. Who could have predicted that Irving's apartment would get robbed? The hundred thousand, Irving's ten percent for that run, had been in his briefcase. Imagine if it had been the other end, the nine hundred thousand? Best that Irving take a long trip somewhere where he couldn't be traced.

Like Italy. Irving insisted on a civilized place. Yes, Venice would be fine. Ambassador Manelli had obliged, no questions asked, for a price. Especially since the FBI might see fit to take a look at the case, not to mention the Washington police. As always, Billy was Mr. Anonymous.

"It was our best shot," Billy had explained. They needed safe passage through any foreign customs and a safe country.

Guaranteed. And Manelli had done them, Harry, on Billy's behalf, small favors before, always on Billy's behalf. But this was the first time that outright bribery was involved.

"It's over the edge," Harry had warned.

"Better than Irving spilling beans," Billy had countered.

"Yes, better than that."

"But you're the fucking secretary of the treasury," Harry said.

After that remark, Billy had turned away, hiding his face.

Would this be the end of it? Harry wondered.

Harry and Terry got into their Mercedes in the garage, and he pushed the automatic buttons, waiting for the door to rise. Terry's perfume filled the car with its scent.

Peripherally, he watched her while he backed the car out, gray eyes peering from behind high cheekbones covered with a creamy complexion. Peaches and cream. She was peaches and cream all over. Always it was startling to see her shiny jet black hair sparkling below her smooth white belly.

Odd, what his thoughts were becoming. Such images belied her lack of interest in things carnal. Then why was he suddenly dwelling on it? Actually he had dwelled on it only during the two years of his courtship. Then, as partially now, it was the forbidden Valhalla.

Benchmarks—that was what he was searching for, certain signs that anchored his life: love, marriage, fatherhood, friendship, loyalty, and honor. Whatever.

He compared his situation to what soldiers must have felt facing enemy fire in Vietnam. They understood the danger but weren't too sure about the cause. In the end, they probably put camaraderie and honor at the head of their list. There didn't seem to be anything else with more meaning. He'd have to think about it more, he decided. Justify it to himself.

They cut into Foxhall Road from Spring Valley and then up Nebraska past American University, around Ward circle, toward Connecticut Avenue. The Italian Embassy was, like most embassy residences, an old mansion formerly owned by a multimillionaire dowager. It sat on the edge of Rock Creek Park on ten acres. A long sweeping driveway led through wrought-iron gates, past old stables now used as garages, to the house. It was still raining when he pulled the car up to the entrance under a portico.

"See. No valet service. But you're in luck."

She let herself out while he parked the car along the circular driveway, dashing through the rain to the entrance. Inside the large hallway, standing beside a table on which the seating arrangements were displayed, was the ambassador and his wife. He was a dark-complexioned balding man with thin lips that offered the barest hint of a sardonic smile.

"*Benvenuto*," he said, using a two-handed grabber, his inside grip reaching to the elbow. His wife was a tall woman with an alabaster complexion and a squint. Her handshake was limp and cold.

After the initial greeting by the ambassador, their eye contact ceased, although Harry felt the ambassador's gaze as he carefully removed his coat. A small lady in a black maid's uniform took the coat, hesitating as she felt the heft then shrugging, hung it in a cloakroom to one side of the hall.

A group had begun to gather in the large drawing room beyond the reception room. He could hear their subdued voices. He looked over the seating arrangements displayed on a velvet board in the foyer, leather circles with little cards jutting out like cogs on which were written the names of the guests.

There were to be three tables of ten guests each. As the ranking Cabinet officer, Billy was sitting to the right of the ambassador's wife, and Millie, Billy's wife, was to the right of the ambassador. Other guests, Harry noted, included two senators and their wives, two congressmen and their wives, a female network correspondent and her husband, a social columnist and her husband, two corporate executives and their wives, and two lobbyists and their wives. He noted that he would be sitting next to the social columnist and the wife of one of the senators.

He took it all in quickly—the place, the guests, the ambiance, a typical gathering of the power tribe—assessing it first with his now well-honed Washington eye for status, which indicated a good mix, and second for its use as a cover for the passage of money. This latter observation induced a natural tremor of anxiety. Who needed it?

He moved forward and stepped down into the reception room, a long impressive place two stories high with a balcony across its length. In Washington, a country was often the reflection of the houses its nationals officially inhabited. He passed through the reception room to the drawing room.

Many of the guests had already arrived. He saw Billy Tucker chatting with one of the senators, a Democrat from Missouri named Sam Baker, and a couple of the wives who were vaguely familiar. In Washington, he noted, all "wives of," those without labels or working titles, looked vaguely familiar. Like Terry, he decided, who chirped away with a congressman's wife and the old battle-ax of a social columnist. He remembered that the woman was hard of hearing, which made her normal testiness reach an inordinate level of arrogance as she barked "what" when she could not understand.

Millie wore her familiar turban, her voice always two decibels higher than those around her. Her currency, in Washington terms, was to be "refreshingly outspoken" and "her own person," which accounted for her flamboyant "creative dressing."

She was always hatted in some way and wore what she called antique clothes, most of which looked as if they had been gathered from a Salvation Army fire clearance. She always wore three or four rings, a couple of bracelets on each wrist, and a heavy necklace. Harry, of course, knew their real worth. They were, after all, Irving Leopold's best. On Millie, thankfully, they looked like costume jewelry.

Her eccentricities were a contrived strategy to set her apart, at least publicly, from her husband, to whom she was irrevocably tied by her own soaring ambition, which did not fall short of her husband's. Harry wondered if he, too, suffered from the same affliction. Worse, he wondered if he resented sharing the stage with Millie.

Billy's tolerance of his wife's excesses was, among other things, a never-ending source of personal irritation and puzzlement to Harry. Probably could be explained by guilt, Harry had decided, since it was Millie's father's firm on Wall Street that had started Billy off. Millie and Billy, the press called them.

Billy thought that it was probably good for name identification. He had the uncanny ability to reverse all negatives in his mind. Yet Billy's repeated assurances that Millie knew nothing about what they had concocted with Irving Leopold could ever truly assuage Harry's fears. If Millie knew, God help them all.

"Well, Harry, where next?"

He turned and saw Nell Harris, a correspondent for one of the networks; he forgot which one.

"Up to the boss," Harry said, meaning the president. He knew that he was being considered for a White House slot, close to the real action. Actually, he would be a trusted ear for Billy, who would need it when the jockeying started for the presidential sweepstakes. Wasn't that what all this hocus-pocus was really about?

"I'm not knocking Customs, Harry. But a guy like you wants a bigger stage."

"Yeah. There's one leaving in an hour."

The joke sailed over her head. Press, Harry thought. If it doesn't get spoon-fed into their brains they rarely get it right. Then the irony of the humor tightened his gut. Maybe he should catch that stage after all. Take it as far as it went. Her hand swept the air in Billy's direction.

"He's got to get in line fast. Beat the rush."

He knew what she meant. Her perception, like everybody's, was that he was Billy's man. And with the president a lame duck, the jockeying for power was accelerating.

Of course, the word was out on Billy. To Harry it had always been out, and the moment of commitment was fast approaching, although obfuscation was still the order of the day. Perhaps. Maybe. Depending. Billy, William Hewlitt Tucker, the Wall Street wunderkind had fastened his tail to the president's kite from the beginning.

He, Harry, had come aboard in the first campaign, which gave him loyalist status and tied him to the president's team, of which he was a loyal, card-carrying original member. And Harry was Billy's man. Good old Billy, to whom he was now, and perhaps had always been, irrevocably tethered.

"I like it where I am, Nell," he said. He had met her in the first campaign, which gave him enough insight to avoid her in the second.

"Come on, Harry." She bent over to give him a whiff of her scotched breath. "Greasing the skids for VIP wives bringing in undeclared contraband."

This impression of his job always angered him. His record on drug interdiction was one of the jewels in the administration's crown, and he was about to launch a narcotics sweep that would make people stand up and take notice about what this secretary business was all about.

"There's more to it than that, a lot more."

"Pound for pound, you've been a runaway coke buster," Nell smiled. She had blushed. He could see she hadn't meant to be harassing. She patted his arm. "You're a good soldier, Harry." He hated the sobriquet. Is that what they thought? What he really was?

He loosened up after she moved on, passing him along to one of the titans of industry in typical Washington fashion. The game at a Washington party was to stay mobile.

"You know Harry Silver," Nell had said before shifting. It was never a question, always a fait accompli.

"Not really," the man said.

He was, Harry saw, tight assed and intense, with thin grim lips and eyes that burned like hot ash. He put out his hand and gripped Harry's, squeezing the bones together and pumping. "Bart Finacre from Allied."

"Harry Silver," he repeated. "Customs."

"You got one tough job," Finacre said. "Keeping everybody straight. Last week we got hung up for three hours coming into Kennedy."

"It happens sometimes. Might even get worse when we do a sweep," Harry replied.

"Jeez, I hope not."

"Price we pay," Harry shrugged.

Peripherally, he saw Billy break off his conversation and move through the room toward him. Billy had the touch when he worked a room. He moved past the ladies with a smile, patted men on the arm and maneuvered his way to Harry's side. Unchanging, Harry thought.

The youthful look was still there from far. Closer, his skin would be leathery, all bones and angles, his sandy hair expertly cut in a tousled look sprinkled with gray. He gave the impression of boyishness grown wise. A born leader was the tag he lived with.

Harry had met him, of all places, in the Boy Scouts back in Omaha, when Billy was sixteen and an Eagle Scout, and he was a tenderfoot. That ranking seemed to define their relationship since. In college at the University of Nebraska, Billy was captain, it seemed, of everything, and Harry was, as now, a kind of lieutenant.

He followed Billy to Yale Law. As always, Billy, a senior, had cleared the way, and Harry was instantly in the right circles. Still there, he thought sardonically, still searching for benchmarks. Hadn't Billy said from the beginning that they were going to the moon? And beyond?

There was a decades-long gap. Billy went to New York and became a Wall Street shark, married the boss's daughter and soaked up a lifetime's worth of money. Harry went back to Nebraska to practice law, married a nice Midwestern virgin, a rare item in 1970, and settled down to the approved lifestyle of his mother's family.

But distance did not dim their loyalty to each other. Billy threw lots of law business his way, and Harry ducked in and out of national politics to help Billy in the Midwest. He joined Billy in the presidential campaign, set up a year before the president's first election, which meant they were now together on the big-time political scene going on seven years.

Harry broke off from Finacre in preparation for Billy, avoiding all circling and breaking eye contact with others in the room.

"Done," Harry said, his face wrinkling with smile lines.

"Lucky Irving.

"Everybody deserves a vacation," Billy said. "Stashed in the Lido in Venice. Worth every penny."

"And now?"

"Now nothing. Irving takes a long vacation. Home free."

The words lightened Harry's load somewhat, although not completely. Things were always going wrong. Pesty little unforeseen blips intruding, as Leopold getting robbed, and the culprit turning up with the cash. It was ludicrous.

"Things go wrong in funny ways," he had told Billy. "Remember Watergate? Mickey Mouse stuff."

"There's risk in everything," Billy had admonished. "Silver and Tucker haven't gone wrong yet."

Not yet. The idea had been to declare then fund-raise. But this, Billy had argued, required some shortcut, big money fast. Ready to go. Credible, quick viability, the president had told Billy. Your own money or your family's won't do, Billy was advised. Not at first. Not if he wanted the endorsement of the president himself. The president had to go with someone who looked like a winner from the go. Harry hadn't quite understood it, certain that pieces were left out, but he had not probed further.

Then Irving, quite out of the blue, had come up with his

incredible suggestion. It might even have been coincidental, a theory expounded to the wind. But Billy had caught the scent, savored it, tested it on quivering nostrils. Show me, the president was asking.

"You only get one ticket," Billy had told Harry. Irving told him how it could be done.

"Diamonds are small and clean," Irving had said, a prelude to his scheme. "It's the prime currency of our South African friends."

"And what in exchange?" Harry had asked.

Administration favors, Billy had explained. Always within reason. Apartheid was, even the Afrikaners agreed, a curse that had to be modified in due course, perhaps taking as long as a century.

Only two or three individuals, at the most, knew how the diamonds were to be passed and for what purpose. Irving assured them that they would never know for whom. Every step was at least once removed, arranged through third, sometimes fourth parties. Irving Leopold was the converter, diamonds for cash, and only the three of them knew how that worked.

"The president knows that?" Harry had asked from the beginning.

"Of course not."

"All he wants is verbal receipt."

"For how much?" Harry had asked.

"Minimum ten million, something to get the ball game rolling fast."

So now there was ten million in cash laying around, for crying out loud. When Harry thought about that, his adrenaline surged to counter his fear. So much? Just thinking about how it was stashed boggled his balance.

Billy moved away, circled then stopped to chat with one of the congressmen. Suddenly a voice boomed his name, like a karate chop, in his left ear. Millie's.

"Nice pad the Eye-ties have here. Cost two mil, someone said. Signora Manelli thinks it's full of ghosts. I said the whole town's full of ghosts."

She stared at Harry with big brown eyes flecked with yellow, her most interesting feature. Always, she wore a little yellow to call attention to it. Tonight it was in a large tigereye pendant that hung on the thick gold chain around her neck. Why had one of her weaknesses been for jewels, of all things? This had been the divining rod that led to Irving Leopold in the first place. Harry noted that she wore a big emerald-cut rock on the forefinger of her right hand, the deliberately showy finger. Was she taunting him with it?

"Haven't seen one yet, Millie."

"Like Lincoln's which is supposed to walk the White House. Whose do you suppose walks here? Al Capone?" She laughed a loud throaty guffaw, enjoying her joke.

"Not all Italians are mafioso," Harry said.

Years ago he had developed a triggered response to her little shocks, a kind of pedantic put-down, his only effective defense against her attempt to play the intimidating wife-of-fearless-leader role.

"They should be. Maybe add a dash of stability to their governments." To someone else, Harry thought, it might pass for profundity.

"I'd stow that until after dinner. Long after."

"Oh, loosen up the tush, Harry. It's all right."

What's all right? he wondered, sucking in a deep breath. Surely Billy wouldn't be fool enough to confide in Millie, of all people. The old fear.

"I was just thinking of Liz Halloran over there." He nodded lightly in the direction of the columnist. "Oh, that free-loading antique." She grimaced and finished her glass of white wine. "People read her," Harry snapped, knowing it wouldn't make a particle of difference in reshaping her conduct. Millie had reached the stage in which she believed that outrages were expected of her.

"Thank goodness most of Washington is illiterate," Millie said, flouncing away from him toward an oncoming waiter carrying a silver tray of drinks. She seemed to Harry to be sloshing more than usual. Was that a clue?

Millie Tucker had already become a national figure of sorts, the reigning lovable Washington eccentric. The city apparently had been ready for it and, miraculously, it hadn't hurt her husband politically. Not yet. Harry, however, worried that she could overplay her hand.

A social secretary suddenly appeared and, offering discreet instructions, started the guests toward the dining room. The group strolled across the large reception hall. The men who arrived first stood behind their predetermined places waiting for the ladies to be seated. That done, everybody who hadn't met was introduced and the dinner settled into the traditional formal ritual.

To Harry's right sat a tiny close-lipped wife of a congressman, a Mrs. Catucci, awed by what seemed to be her first embassy dinner, which somewhat explained the reason for her invitation. No one in Washington ever invited anyone to anything without a reason.

"Do you like Washington?"

"Yes."

A long pause.

"Does your husband like Congress?"

"Very much."

Another long pause.

"How many children have you?"

"Two."

In the prevailing pause Harry turned toward his smoked salmon. Time to duck inside himself, he thought. Better the inarticulate than the overarticulate. At Washington dinner parties, it was always the luck of the draw.

Tonight he had been unlucky. What did that augur, he wondered? He got through the fish without having to confront Liz Halloran, a practiced Washington star fucker trying valiantly to pry something out of the senator on her left, who was making every effort at tolerance and charm.

During the beef, she turned toward him.

"So you think the secretary will make his move soon?"

"What move?"

"Now let's not be coy," she said.

"Decoy," he whispered, expecting her loud "What?" which came on cue. "You'll have to ask him," he said coherently.

"But I'm asking you."

He turned toward her, amazed that people could overlook her hoary ugliness and arrogance and do handstands not to offend her. In a way, he was thankful that Millie was not sitting within earshot. Not tonight.

He noted that Mrs. Halloran's wig was crooked, which took the edge off his tension. Yet her manner was so forbidding, it triggered an odd fear that the little maid who took their coats would suddenly come rushing into the room, money bricks in hand, yelling her hedeedad off in Italian. Ease up, Harry, he urged himself, remembering Billy's words: *Home free.*

"Knock on any door in this town," he said, offering a smile. "Everyone wants to live at 1600 Pennsylvania Avenue." And you've known most of them, he thought.

"That's being evasive."

"Of course, it is," he said pleasantly.

"And what about you, Harry?"

"Me? I'm a happy contented man. I like my job."

"No, you don't. It's just a stepping-stone. You know it. I know it."

"Knock on any door—," he began.

She shook her head in despair, and he watched with secret delight as she grew more irritable and finally turned back to the senator. By then, the dessert had come then the toasts. The ambassador talked of Billy as if he had walked all the way to the embassy on water, and in his response, Billy praised the ambassador for a catalogue of virtues so profuse they took ten minutes to expound.

Harry felt his dessert congeal in his stomach. He looked toward Millie who winked and mouthed a clear resemblance to "bullshit." Typical Washington party, Harry thought, wondering if the ambassador had emptied the pockets of his coat. Harry was certain he had ducked out at an appropriate moment and done the deed.

Watching him, looking pink and satisfied, beside Billy's standing figure, bathing in phony adulation, Harry felt only the briefest sort of relief. Was he home free? Really? "

III

She must have dozed. The edges around the drawn draperies had lightened. There was this sensation of climbing out of a strange parallel world… a character in some spy novel. This character had seen something… something odd, and it triggered some outlandish scenario, a mystery built around a potential conspiracy.

Her awakening self tried to brush it out of her consciousness, like a silly dream remembered then dismissed. Unfortunately, reality put a different spin on the fictional scenario. She had seen Irving Leopold in the flesh moving in another landscape, oddly out of place and context. The revolving antennae in her mind had picked up strange signals that were irresistible to her trained reportorial mind. Something was happening, she concluded, that shouldn't be happening, and she felt suddenly duty bound to find out what.

She deliberately cleared her throat in an exaggerated way to prod his attention. Then she said: "I can't leave it alone, Al."

"Damn," he muttered. "Can't you unhook yourself?"

She had turned long enough to see his smirk of displeasure as he burrowed his head into his pillow.

"Case closed," he muttered.

"But it's not. That's the point."

"There is no point. You're on vacation."

"It's like being an off-duty cop in your own hometown. You're never off." She moved toward the bed and sat down beside him, wanting him to participate.

"You're not a cop," he muttered.

"But don't you see the implications? Here is this fellow, Irving

Leopold, the court jeweler, the jester. All the power mongers, the president, some of his Cabinet, the rich and the famous, the power people all buy their jewels from him. He moves around in their circle, a court jester. Ubiquitous. Everywhere. Then suddenly—"

"Then suddenly a spy," he mumbled with disinterest.

"A something."

"You're fantasizing."

"An Iraqi ship?"

"You didn't see him get on it."

"Well, then, where did he go?"

"I don't know. And I don't care."

"There's something here. I know it."

"Shit."

She reached under the sheets and pulled out Al's arm, reading the time on his wristwatch.

"You're not?" Al mumbled. She noted the sudden alertness in his voice. He turned, sat up, rubbed his eyes then looked at his watch.

"It's only six."

"One in the afternoon in Washington." Charlie would be out to lunch. This required hopscotching her immediate editor. She would wait until two.

Al got out of bed and walked to the bathroom. She heard the familiar male tinkle. Was there anger in the force of the stream? It was an odd idea, she knew, but frustration and exasperation were often expressed in bizarre little tics. She heard the flush and then he was in the room, again confirming her suspicion.

"I don't think I can handle this, Elly."

"You're being unreasonable," she snapped. No way for her to stop. Not now. "It's what I do."

"Why must I always be the heavy? There is still time for salvage. Let me advise you. Leave it alone. It endangers us. Do you understand that? Today we are to go to Torcello. We are in beautiful romantic Venice." He seemed caught somewhere between anger and sadness.

Although he was being emphatic and forceful, his argument seemed trivial. Visiting Torcello and its lost past was increasingly irrelevant in her scale of priorities. He paced the room now in his sky blue bikini underwear. It struck her as an incongruous costume for a display of indignation, which partially accounted for his message having little teeth.

"It's a question of values," he was saying.

Or had she simply tuned in somewhere in the middle? Because somewhere along the way, he had grown pedantic.

"I don't want to sound nagging or resentful. But I don't think it's wrong for a husband to demand the undivided attention of his wife when they're on vacation." He paused, swallowed. "And vice versa." He paced the length of the room and looked out of the window. "I don't really give a shit about Irving Leopold."

She realized that he was hiding the mist in his eyes, spouting euphemisms, evading the truth of this dilemma.

"It's what I do," she said, gently, sensing too late that she was feeding the fire. Back to the endless pattern of parry and thrust.

She had wanted to avoid it. Now she let it happen. The endless argument of clichés, when the real answer was that he was ready to plant and harvest, and she was not. It was even beyond love and caring. She let him talk, listening.

"You can't just put it on that basis, Elly. It's not fair. I work hard, too. I love my work. The problem is that I can shut off my work at will and you can't. Time for wife. Time for work."

"I am what I am," she muttered, having heard the masked

argument ad infinitum for years now. It wasn't that he underval-
ued what she did. And she knew that he feared being considered
immature or unreasonable in both his demands and his definitions. Nor did she have any doubts about his faithfulness, love
and devotion. Was it really because their areas—*her* areas of compromise—were too far apart?

Above all, this frightened her the most. She could imagine
herself on the outer ledge of loneliness. This part of her life, she
knew, was essential to her well-being, her peace of mind.

Was it time, once again, to invoke the image of Daddy and
the one-horse weekly, his crusade against power and corruption
in the jerkwater town of her childhood and early youth, loss, and
bitterness? A story, repeated so often, it was too scratchy now. Al
would barely hear the melody. Lately his theme was that she was
trying to get even, to score for Daddy, for Daddy who charged
the windmills and got impaled on his own spear. And that it was
time to stop it forever.

"Wrong," she had shouted. The defense of herself exhausted
her once again; she felt her thoughts spiraling into infinity.

"Haven't I been understanding? Reasonable?" There was that
word again, meaning she was being unreasonable to devote her
life to her vaunted work, her passionate ambitions, the paper,
the world outside of his, of theirs. "Can't you just render unto
Caesar—?"

"Not that, Al. Not again."

"It's the nub of it, Elly."

"I think you're making a federal case out of it."

"But it *is* a federal case."

She wondered if he was expressing one of his subtle ironies
and, when he smiled suddenly, she realized that he hadn't recognized it at first.

"Just one lousy call, Al."

She had moved closer to him until there was barely a wisp of distance between them. Bare-breasted and still wearing the skirt of the night before, she knew from experience that arousing his libido invariably led to a temporary truce. It troubled her sometimes that this resort to biology was merely a palliative. It probably defined their relationship now. Well, then, it would have to do for a while.

"You can't just fuck it away, Elly," he whispered, as she closed the gap between them. She felt the hardening in the pouch of his briefs.

"Better than nothing," she said, boiling it down in her mind, yet once again. So he wanted kids and a mommy waiting by the fire ready with his slippers, open, available, loving, adoring. Wasn't that exactly what she wanted? Daddy waiting with love and comfort. So what else is new, she told herself, as she circled her pelvis around his. By now, his arousal was obvious. As she dropped slowly to her knees she looked at her watch. Plenty of time, she thought, wondering if she should like herself.

***

While Al was in the shower, she called Charlie Carruthers. Her pulse pumped in her neck. His sandpaper voice barked hoarsely into her ear. As always, perfect casting, she thought, his macho pose secularly endearing.

He treated all human beings, talk aside, as without gender, although he was predictably inconsistent and unfair in language but consistent and fair in deeds. That was what the people around him, his minions like her, perceived, although they were never dead certain that they were right. At least he allowed himself to be approachable.

Myth or not, he still got away with most of his verbal ethnic, racial, and gender outrages. Of course, he held their careers by their short hairs. That was the reality of all his relationships with his staff, all fifteen hundred of them. Since he always demanded quick takes, she gave him a hurried and slightly encapsulated version of what she had seen and postulated.

"So he's a mover and a hustler on his way to the forbidden East. Big deal." His reaction disappointed her.

"But the implication is obvious. Considering in what circle the man moves."

"You think he's a spook?" Charlie asked, faintly interested.

"Ours or theirs?"

"You got a point."

"I mean the man deals in high places. He's a confidante. Like a hairdresser—only more so," Elly pressed. "I just feel there's something there. In my gut."

"Gut? Give me facts. Give me story."

"When I did my piece, I researched the guy. Look in the files. He sells diamond rings to the president's wife—for crying out loud—to half the Cabinet. Then suddenly his briefcase turns up in the apartment of a thief along with a hundred grand in cash. Put it all together."

"If I remember, the burglar said the cash was his."

"And Nelson Rockefeller died reading an art book."

He snickered. She knew he liked that line.

"So go ask the CIA?"

"Not a bad idea."

"And if they call me and dance me around about national security, you'll think you had something."

"Wouldn't I?"

"Maybe."

She could tell she was getting to him. Time to press on.

"Maybe that hundred grand he disowned was for secrets. Suddenly he shows up in Venice, slips aboard an Iraqi ship. *Slips.*" She emphasized the word, not without a tinge of regret. In its way it was a journalistic violation. She didn't see it. Not directly. "In the dead of night." Have no regrets, she begged herself. The symbolism was too strong, the logic too compelling.

"You're getting my attention."

"Maybe the FBI is already on it."

"If he was such a big spook, why would he have consented to be interviewed?"

"That's just the point, see. You're answering questions with questions."

"You know guys like that. Ego. Maybe he likes the publicity. Some people want to be part of the action—inside, close to the power. It turns them on. This town's full of people like that." She waited through another pause.

"But suppose it was just a plain old act of God."

"Leave him out of it." His joke was leaden.

"Remember what started out as a simple fuck-up?"

"And ruined the field of journalism for generations. Everybody wants to be Woodward and Bernstein. You know what it means to have to work with a bunch of salivating shavetails."

"Shavetails? What's that?"

"You're too young."

"Not too young to smell a scam out there, Charlie. All I'm asking is that you keep an open mind."

"On a hunch," he said with surprising gentleness.

"Isn't that what Watergate was all about?"

"I don't ever want to hear that word from you again. It's haunted me now for two decades."

At this distance, it seemed to her like a genuine rebuke. He'd been there, the quarterback. Times had changed now. He was gorged with it, bloated. In front of him was always a full plate of investigative stories, possible exposés, developing scandals.

Every reporter on the paper had heard his speech about limited resources, the effective use of manpower, and timing for maximum impact—balanced, of course, with the shrinking definitions of the laws of libel and slander. And every reporter that came to him with the hint of a political or international scam burned with the zeal of the reformer.

"The courts are on our ass," he would tell them. "They think we've got a blood lust for kicks. Read the recent decisions." He would stop short of the clincher, but the unsaid words echoed and re-echoed. "Time to lay low for now."

It was the moment for her to test him—and herself. Time to see how blue the flame was, just how hot. For her, too, it just might be the big one to lay it all to rest once and for all. Only then could she consider that other role, Al's dream.

"I was just calling to whet your interest."

"From Venice, that's a helluva pun."

"Is it wet enough for a go?"

"Now you're talking funny. You're our ace on the Style section, the soft stuff. What you're asking is for another slot."

"Okay then, I'll give it to the competition."

It was a local joke. There was no real competition. Not in Washington. Al came out of the bathroom wrapped in a towel, beads of moisture on his back. His hair was flat and wet on his scalp. He gave her the finger.

"I don't know what I can do here," she said, turning her face to emphasize the confidentiality. Even her voice had lowered to a whisper. "But I'll be home in two days and—"

"One," Al shouted. "You'll be home tomorrow."

"What was that?" Charlie asked.

"The man I live with. He's pissed."

"Listen to his message," Charlie said.

"I've heard it before."

Now she was growing hot, balancing on the razor's edge between two examples of the other species. "I'm good, Charlie," she said. "I know I have a scent. You know it's a story. Don't let someone else have it. Give me my shot."

She wondered suddenly if she had built it too large in her mind, had overreacted. Was there a touch of hysteria in her voice? Or was Al pressing a choice on her. And what was that other thing ticking in the background? The biological clock?

"We'll talk when you get back," Charlie said. "Gotta run."

"Please, Charlie. Give it a more positive ring."

"See you when you get back." She heard his click at the other end. She was silent for a long time, sitting on the bed, staring blankly at her hands. Was it worth it? she wondered. Al, fumbling in the closet, still in his towel, had pulled out their suitcase.

"What about Torcello?" she asked.

"Fuck Torcello."

IV

Beside him, Terry slept, her lips pouting slightly, her hands folded across her stomach over the covers, a quiet, peaceful, contented sleep. He supposed this sense of calm meant that she was happy, satisfied. Her sense of well-being was always an important consideration for Harry. Making her happy had been the principal consideration of their contract, an important measure of his own success.

She was the anchor of his life, the mother of his children, the mirror of his well-being. He lay beside her telling himself these things, wondering how and why she had become more of an appendage than a participant.

Had he ever really confided in her? At the beginning, perhaps, he had, as is the case of all moonstruck young men, told her of his plans and ambitions. Of course, he had colored it for her approval and respect.

She was a big dark-haired doll with breath that smelled like milk and values and verities that came from her stoic farm parents. Coming from town people, Harry believed, then as now, that farm people were the salt of the earth, the last real Americans.

Subconsciously, he probably had cast around for a farm-reared lady and he had found her, quite appropriately, at the University of Nebraska. The old-fashioned and completely traditional manner of their courtship and marriage always amazed him in retrospect. It was as if the so-called revolutionary spirit of the sixties had sailed right over their heads.

A practicing virgin until marriage, she was still somewhat reticent about sex. He suspected that her mother had instructed her, and her mother's mother—a matriarchal figure who had crossed the plains in a covered wagon—had instructed *her.*

The bottom line apparently had been that sex was a necessity of a man's nature, important to his well-being, to be administered on Saturday nights and sometimes on Wednesdays. All attempts to break the pattern had failed. But wasn't life, after all, a compromise? No. An accommodation. He knew the difference. In a compromise, both parties moved toward each other.

She still did "chores," although she had succumbed to the lure of Washington ways, the heart of which was to appear the proper appendage to her husband's position. He, the husband, did "man's work," a throwback to her farm upbringing.

Still, Harry knew, Terry resented that he was "Billy's Boy," a sobriquet never quite expressed in quite that way. His traditional defense was that Billy's strength and formidable talents had hacked through the thickets, made it possible for him to follow. He had tried to explain that there was always a role for "best friend," "trusted adviser," especially an alter ego, and sometimes a devil's advocate. Such roles had rewards and compensations; for example, his present position and, therefore, her present status. As the song went, he had hitched his wagon to a star.

From her perspective, Harry surmised, he was more of the "hired hand" than "best friend." But then she was not privy to their discussions and machinations, although she certainly knew that Billy wanted, yearned for, worked at, and was obsessed with becoming president of the United States. And what was more evident that such a position was attainable than his being appointed secretary of the treasury?

It was exactly the job he had aspired to, the stepping-stone he needed in this economically overheated environment. The president had made him point man in unraveling the mysteries of America's economy. More important, the country was in a prosperous phase.

As always for Billy, the stars had converged to shine on him. And what was wrong with being, at the very least, "trusted adviser" to a man that had what seemed like the inside track to be the next president of these United States. In simpler terms, as they put it on those television cop shows, nobody climbed any career ladders without his rabbi.

No, it wasn't farm logic, where hard physical work and trust in providence was the key to success. But then all Harry needed from his wife was her toleration, her cooperation, and evidence of her occasional enjoyment. She gave him, at various times, all three and kept the rankling to a minimum. Of course, she didn't approve of Millie, especially her flamboyance.

"She'll cost him some day," she warned Harry, who defended Millie's style as colorful and unique.

Harry wondered if her tolerance would stretch to forgive the Leopold enterprise. He knew better, of course. It would shake the foundations of her inner vault, where the old verities were locked for safekeeping.

It was not a question of her being appalled but of how wounding it would be. Yet she would stick by him through thick and thin, stoic and sacrificing, playing out the role of brave durable woman following her man across the plains in a Conestoga wagon.

Raising himself on one elbow, he continued to watch her face, a good Anglo-Saxon face, a little Swede, a little Scotch-English, a dab of Irish. No flighty Mediterranean shit to heat the blood, like the heavy dollop of dago on his side—his father's mother.

His mother's side hadn't known that until later, and then it was treated like some genetic defect. She had died years before, and his grandfather had remarried a flinty lady from Kansas City. Stop, he rebuked himself, getting his head back down on the pillow. Life passing before one's eyes was for drowning men.

***

In the beginning he had argued against the concept. Not argued. Just a little change of costume to red and a pitchfork and some articulate advocating of the worrisome negatives. It was during the president's first campaign, and Billy Tucker was not quite in the inner circle but working on it, number two on the finance committee, Harry, his assistant.

A hotel room in Kansas City, they were in the candidate's party, his entourage. Billy was working the businessman types for contributions, making speeches to small groups, hitting panic buttons, giving them his very effective shy-boy routine.

They did have these laws on the books that required listing the source of all political contributions, and even these had an individual limit of one thousand dollars. Billy usually got the maximum. To get around this, someone figured out political action committees, or PACs, which gave the power of the buck to causes of every stripe as well as individuals who wished to exercise power. But that was all, as they say, above the line.

Billy did even better with the PACs than he did with individuals. But the constraints became frustrating. What Billy Tucker decided was needed was a private cash fund, outside of the reporting system, a swift source, to be used as necessary when it was essential.

"You're talking slush fund, Billy," Harry had argued. The idea seemed laughable, naive. "Read history. Remember Checkers?"

"Cash has no memory. No records. No identity. It is intrinsic."

"Kid's stuff," Harry told him.

"Cash makes things happen. Cash means more than mere money."

Billy was, Harry knew, testing the waters. Beating the idea around. Mental fencing. In political campaigns, the savvy vendors took money up front. No TV or radio commercial, newspaper or magazine ad, piece of printing, bumper strips, balloons, all the paraphernalia of election hoopla, reached the public without money up front. It was the watchword, a biblical incantation—money up front.

Sometimes the pipeline got choked up and quick injections of cash had to be applied, especially for people on the road, the bush beaters, the advance men, the skid greasers, the grunts doing the shit work. No records needed here. Just cash.

"Where is the line between the records and the void?" He had bent over to whisper in Harry's ear. Evidence enough, Harry thought, but he did not call Billy on it. He wanted to hear what was about to be said. "Candidate himself needed a quick hundred thou."

"What for?"

"I didn't ask."

"It came to you? Direct?"

Billy nodded, offering a sly wink and his crinkly smile.

"He's not going to account for it?"

"His option."

"He doesn't think it's dangerous?"

"It's cash, you see. No eyes. No ears. We didn't discuss where it came from. It's from the campaign as far as he's concerned and I'm the deputy finance chairman."

"How come he didn't ask Struthers?" Struthers was the finance chairman.

Billy shrugged, raising his eyebrows, showing innocent eyes. Harry knew how he had done it. A suggestion here. A nuance there. Any special financial problems? I'm the designate, the troubleshooter.

"Call it building a relationship," Billy told him. "The man's fabulous. He has the right stuff. Views on target. Knows how to use the tube. Why not tighten the knot of the tail we put on his kite? I've done the Wall Street gig, Harry. I'm ready for a bigger stage."

Harry did not question that assumption. For Billy Tucker, as always, the sky was the limit. Maybe president some day. In Billy adolescent dreams never died.

It was to this end that Billy Tucker had carefully cultivated his public image. Most important, he had done it so cleverly that it appeared effortless. The facade was so smooth, the seams so faultless, you couldn't see the inner works. Not unless you were as close as Harry.

"Where did it come from?"

Billy smiled and winked.

"Funny money," Harry had harrumphed. "These things have a way of boomeranging."

"Chances you take, Harry," Billy said, perhaps tongue-in-cheek. "I'm very much aware of the dangers. Also the benefits. I'm taking a shortcut. The candidate knows he can trust me. That's important. If he's elected, he's the man who hands out the plums. I've got credentials, connections, and ambition. Time to put the building blocks in place for what I have in mind."

"Bigger the risk, bigger the prize. Is that it?"

"In a way, Harry. The point is that I've chosen another path than most. I don't want to submit myself to any of the filth and humiliation of the preliminaries. I don't want to be senator or governor. I want a shortcut. First, I need national visibility where it counts—a Cabinet post, something like Treasury, where my credentials fit. Then maybe move out to foreign policy. There are things that you know about yourself from the beginning, Harry. I've got something worth parlaying. I've made my pile. I don't want to be one of these guys who climb the mountain, then look around them and say: Is this all there is? I want it all, Harry. Money is fuel. Power is fire. One comes before the other."

Harry had listened, watching Billy's face. His eyes sparkled with inner light. His face glowed with the force of it, whatever *it* was. Some people had *it*. Some didn't. Billy was one of the blessed, the lucky, the charmed. The promise was not lost on Harry. He had his own dreams, his own point to make. Not quite as grandiose. But hadn't Billy always led the way. Up to then his moves and judgment had been infallible. But the cash thing was still bothersome.

"Mark my words. You'll have the press on your ass. If not now—someday."

"Cash is anonymous."

"Someone always talks. Or something goes wrong. What is least expected happens. Always does. Like early Nixon and the Checkers' speech. And late Nixon and Watergate. A lousy little burglary. In the end it was the funny money that tripped them up."

"You can give me a hundred yards of examples, Harry."

"The risks don't square with the dangers. Take the advice of the guys that went before. The consequences of their folly are laid out like a smorgasbord for all to see. You start taking other people in, you've exposed your flank. I thought you were smarter than that, Billy."

The rebuke, Harry remembered, had become quite heated. He

had paced the room like a caged animal, making point after historical point. By the time he was finished, he felt drained and a bit silly. He was merely mouthing the obvious.

Billy had lain on the bed listening intently, making no effort to counter the arguments. Finally, he had said: "But the money part. The cash part. If the source was, well, exclusive."

"Like from a printing press?"

"A single source."

"No such animal."

"Maybe." Billy had slapped Harry on the shoulder and had poured out two scotches from a bottle on the hotel dresser. "Fret not, old buddy. I did give the man his hundred thou in cash. But it came from my own coffers. Little private loan. No sweat."

Harry remembered he had glowered at Billy. But the relief took the heat out of his anger.

"You made me go through this song and dance on a line of bullshit."

"Sort of."

"What does that mean?"

"The idea still has teeth. Cash is always king, if handled judiciously, mixed in. How much would I need to start the ball rolling? Say ten mil."

Harry remembered he had smiled and upended his scotch.

"Pipe dreams," he had said, but not with sarcasm. He knew better than that. Pipe dreams had been what Billy had started with. Now look at them.

At that moment, Harry had looked into the mirror across from the edge of the bed where they were seated together. There they were, the two of them. Was he waiting for Billy to ask? "Come on, Harry. Let's see what's on the other side of that mirror."

***

On the other side of that mirror lay Irving Leopold. How he had appeared it was difficult to say. Even Billy couldn't pinpoint it, although he had some vague idea of meeting him at the White House during a State dinner. Irving was not one to stay in the background. A cherub, his round rubbery body swathed in thousand-dollar suits, a fresh boutonniere always in his lapel, Irving Leopold was an incarnation of his own imagination. Nobody could have thought him up but himself.

"Everytink in my life," he had said, dozens of times, in the lisping Viennese accent which made his thick lips pink and slightly moist, "I owe to my tiny markup and my nose's ability to sniff out stones to die for."

He had other talents as well. He affixed himself to people before they reached whatever pinnacle they aspired to. He was, therefore, automatically "in" when they arrived. Because he seemed both innocuous and without real gender, he was able to move freely among groups of both men and women. With the former, he could appeal to their sense of manly obligation to their wives or mistresses. (His discretion was often described as immaculate.) With the latter he could play the fawning fag, raving with superlatives, courtly and confidential. He made them feel as if his jewels in their settings had their name on it. "It says *you*, dahlink."

"People tell me thinks," he led them to understand, although no one was quite sure how he did it. "They trust me."

Harry, because of his relationship with Billy, found himself on the edge of Irving's most exotic circle. More of an observer than participant, he found it amusing that this simpering jeweler never referred to people except by their first names.

Often, when the president was mentioned, he told whoever was within earshot. "Talked to first lady on Vensday. osing too much vate, I told her."

Sometimes at a party, finding himself next to a member of the Cabinet, a Supreme Court justice, or any number of Washington movers and shakers, he would put his moist lips to a bent ear, and say something like: "Zelda looks depressed, boychik. You should buy her a bubble."

His "bubbles" were more than "strictly holesell." They were bona fide bargains. "Have it appraised, dahlink. Pay me later."

Leopold's relationship with the president and his circle was often baffling to outsiders, but it existed and was accepted. And Millie Tucker and Irving Leopold seemed to have zeroed right in on each other, an affinity of eccentrics.

Soon Irving Leopold was a fixture in the Tucker's immediate social circle. But then, he seemed a fixture in everybody's company. When columnists mentioned his name or his picture appeared in the paper, he was always the first to mention it but with a modest bow of the head and flush of the cheek. "Me, who vants to keep only a low provile." Even at public events, reporters approached him. "My name is anonymous, sunny girl," he would say, sure to get a mention.

"But how did you give birth to yourself?" Millie had asked him one day at a dinner party, loud enough, of course, to be heard by all within three blocks of her table.

"Vasn't easy to give myself a cesarean."

Everybody howled. Part of his charm was self-parody. He was also a raconteur and because of his large circle, ever the world's most important authority on everything. "I get it only from the donkey's mouse." He brought along his own entertainment, himself. And anybody who was anybody among Washington women wore his jewels.

He was also capable of what passed for serious conversation, especially in connection with politics. He could be a spreader of seeds on fertile ground. Harry had witnessed the procedure one evening as he and Billy sat with Irving over brandy and cigars. It was after one of the terminally boring inaugural balls, the second time around. A little round table at Pisces, men together, women apart for no apparent reason.

"Next time a free-from-all," Irving was saying.

"Free-*for*-all," Billy corrected.

"Whomever. The point is that there is no one strong. With this president, he was in position. No one is in position."

"What will it take, Irving?" Harry asked, looking pointedly at Billy, poised for potential amusement.

"Baldness," Irving said. "Ruthfulness."

"Now that's profound," Harry said.

"First you must have a type." He looked at Harry, stabbing a fat finger in Billy's direction. "Like him. Handsome." He tapped his temple. "Good whipped crim." His red moist lips formed a smile. "Not going to be like before. A regular ret race. Take millions even to begin. Especially if like you, you're a loyal object. I'm not saying you got to be a traitor. You know vy." He patted his pocket. "Gelt. Kronen. Ruples. Scrooples." He sighed. "You become nothing without pfennigs. And how can you raise this ven you are a loyal object? Even with permission." He mentioned people who had retired from public life and were already positioning themselves for the future fray. "Catch twenty," Irving said smugly.

"Catch twenty-two," Harry corrected.

"I get your drift, Irving." Billy said.

"But you got the goods, Billy," Irving said. "I watch. I see."

"You got an instink," Harry said facetiously.

"A qvestion of the right note," Irving continued, pinging his glass with his middle finger. "I read. You get mentioned. A black horse but a possibility. Unfortunately no public office. You need organization, people. Most important—"

"Moolah," Harry said.

"You've got plenty," Irving said, looking at Billy.

"Not enough for that," Billy said. He looked at Harry and raised his eyebrows. A recollection of their previous conversation, Harry knew. "Anyway money is only part of the mosaic."

"Always." There seemed something anticipatory in Leopold's remark. He paused to re-light his cigar, watching the growing ash for a moment. "You vant I should suggest how it comes?"

"The financing?" Billy asked. Harry could see that he was getting hooked.

"Vat else?" He puffed deeply on his cigar, moved his pudgy body in its chair, and lowered his voice. "Like a scena..." He stumbled, searching for the word. "A movie story. I tell a movie story. Okay?" He looked at Harry. "Good you're here, Mr. Customs. You look mostly for dope, right? Everybody looks for dope. You train dogs to sniff. You got defectors, metal defectors. All that. But vat about stones? Stones are small, compact, tiny little babies. You hide them so simple."

"Are you suggesting smuggling diamonds?" Billy said, laughing.

"A movie story, I said." His eyes seemed to jump from face to face, testing interest. He knew his customer, Harry thought, watching Billy reach out to give him credibility. "Those crazy Dutch in South Africa. They vant to hold on... how long... fifty, maybe a hundred more years. They pay for time."

He was moving fast now, talking in tones so low they had to

strain to listen. Not the court jester now, not the clown. Even the bumbling with the language seemed to recede. "They got diamonds, stones in the rock. Enough for every man, woman, and child forever. Ten, twenty each. As long as the earth is alive. For time they pay in diamonds. For the right man. For them, it's nothing."

Billy lifted his hand suddenly, moved closer in his chair.

"What are you saying?"

"They pay in diamonds. Simple. For the right man."

"And what does the man have to do?"

"Go easy, maybe. Be patient. Vatch the vords. Make a policy that's not so bad. Nudge a little. But don't push. They know the end is cominck."

"You say diamonds," Billy said, his eyes blazing with obvious interest. To Harry, his reaction seemed ominous. Warning bells went off in his head. "How do they become money?"

"A man like Irving transacts. Makes magic. Stones into a paper."

"And how do they come into the country?"

Irving suddenly looked at Harry.

"That's another business."

Harry felt a cold chill flare down his back.

"In your movie," Billy asked. "Do the people who give the diamonds know to whom?"

"Stupid they're not. But they trust an Irving, you see."

"So they don't know?"

"They are used to risks."

"But suppose the man doesn't become what they want him to become?"

"Crust on the vaters."

"And the risk to the man?"

"That's also Irving's department. Irving transacts. Makes stones into paper and delivers paper. A delivery boy."

"In the movies it might work," Harry said.

But Billy ignored the intrusion, continuing his interrogation. "What are we talking about in numbers?"

"You tell me. That's your business," Irving said.

Billy pondered, scratched his chin then lifted his brandy pony and swallowed it in one gulp. Beside them, they could hear Millie's throaty laughter. The bar was filling up with other stragglers from the various balls.

"Nine, ten mil," Billy said. "About ten percent of what it would take to mount a serious challenge."

"Only in millions he talks," Irving said. Was it Harry's imagination or did his lips seem more moist, glistening, capturing more light than the glasses on the table? "No vonder he becomes secretary of the treasury."

"Couldn't touch it for less," Billy said, straightening. Harry wondered if, once again, he had tucked away the idea.

"Not a penny less," Irving said. His cigar had gone out and he relit it. The stub in his teeth looked shredded, worn out.

"I couldn't tell from your scenario," Billy said.

"Actually, I vas tinking of that neighborhood. Excellent-grade stones.. Also maybe a *D*."

"What's a *D*?" Billy asked.

"The best. The whitest. Only maybe a hundred a year are found, maybe forty-fifty thousand a carat. But only one I can handle. The rest good but not superior jeweler quality. The idea is to carry a small package."

"Should make a helluva movie," Harry said, his eyes studying both men. He was getting little response from either of them. "But a couple of loose ends bother me. What does this character,

your character, Irving—get out of all this?" The question, as Harry
expected, had just the right spin to get them both involved.

"Like ten percent," Irving said with the lilt of expectation.

"Everything's ten percent." Harry calculated effortlessly. "A
good piece of change. Nice round figure."

"Worth every rupee," Irving said, his eyes drifting toward Billy.
"You like my movie, Mr. Treasury?"

"Who would believe it?" Harry pressed.

"It's only a movie," Irving said.

"I'm not sure… " Billy mused.

"But how does it end?" Harry asked.

Irving finally removed his cigar and put it in the ashtray. Then
he looked up and scanned both their faces.

"Happily," he said. "How else?"

V

Newton Parker looked thinner, his skin grayer than when she had seen him last. He had sculpted down his Afro, which had given him a fiercer, more intimidating look than he had now.

Through the window of the coffee shop, Elly had seen him coming, a tall figure, slightly bent. From the winds of misfortune, she decided. She hadn't known him before his arrest but those who did described him as "polished up," a snappy dresser, with enough street smarts to appear well behaved. Why then would he have been hired to man a reception desk in a swanky Washington apartment building?

She had seen him briefly at his arraignment, but the police had hurried him away, and all details to flesh out her original story were provided by a police spokesman. At that time, she was more interested in the victims than the thief, and she had played the story for its wry humor. Now, of course, she looked at things in an entirely different light.

She sat at the last booth along the wall, waving at Parker when he arrived. He pulled back his shoulders and, knowing he was being watched, swaggered forward. It wasn't quite the black dude walk, but a close facsimile that told her there was plenty of bluff left in the man.

She knew his age, twenty-eight, and his background, a familiar litany of young black manhood. Born to a fourteen-year-old schoolgirl, raised by his grandmother. His curse was, she surmised, that he was a little too intelligent for his fate, but not intelligent enough to carry through his scam unscathed. He had simply burgled one apartment too many.

"You're Eleanor Fox?" he asked. She could see what they had meant by "polished up." The accent was hip, but not street black.

"And you're Newton Parker."

She held out her hand and, after a quick wiping motion against his pants, he reached out, held it tightly, pumped. Then he slid in across from her.

"Coffee?"

He nodded, surveying her with cold, mocking eyes. His smile was tight, his expression wary. She wondered if he was struggling with his guise of humility, wanting to mock her, show the victim's brand of arrogance. Perhaps, offer her a lecture on black-white relations. Actually, she wasn't sure what to expect. A waitress approached.

"Another for me," Elly said. "And one for Mr. Parker." Now don't patronize him, she admonished herself silently. Yet, she had no alternative approach. He was alien territory. "When is the trial?"

"Next month."

"What do you think will happen?"

He blew air out of his mouth, which she took as a comment on her ignorance.

"A year at Lorton, maybe."

"You think that's fair?"

"You've got to be foolin'."

Her plan had been to gain his confidence, maybe trip him up, a long shot at best. But she hadn't been able to think of any other way to begin. She had to size him up first, see how far she could go. But first she had to gain control of her edginess.

Al had come home from Venice more difficult than ever. The tension between them had accelerated She knew she had reacted badly, grown overly excited too quickly, shown him too much obsession, too much compulsion. It only had inflamed him, made him more determined than ever to make his point, to press his case. Aborting their vacation was both a statement and a warning. But what it had done whipped her forward.

Charlie Carruthers had been less enthusiastic when she approached him again.

"Show me," he had said, throwing the Parker case in her face. "Prove it was Leopold's cash."

It had taken her two weeks to make her decision. She knew what she had to do. Besides, Al had made speed essential.

In a way she felt a kinship with this black thief. We're both out on bail, she thought. Awaiting trial. The waitress came with their coffee.

"But why this plea of innocent? They caught you red-handed."

"Not true, my lady," he said, broadening his smile, showing rows of young white teeth. Not broad enough to show the pink gums. Somewhere he had learned how to smile for whites. "They found goods. That's all."

"Stolen goods."

"Stolen? Me, I bought 'em. With my bread. My own." He emphasized the last word by tapping two fingers hard on the table. "My *own*."

"You're saying that the hundred thousand in cash found in your apartment was your own?"

"Ninety-nine thousand, three hundred."

"It's a hard one to swallow, Newton." She was careful not to mock him, wondering if she had trespassed by calling him by his first name. He gave no hint of protest.

"Hard to understand. That's me." He picked up his coffee cup. She noted the odd grace in the movement of his chocolate-colored fingers through the ring of the white cup. He had been quick to accept her invitation, which had, at first, puzzled her. Not now. His own persona was central to his life. His obsession was, quite understandably, with his own survival in a world where his species was under constant attack.

"I'm trying to make heads or tails out of it, Newton. That's my business."

"Gonna put my picture in the paper? You didn't last time."

"That upset you?"

"Wouldn't be no party without me."

"You have a point."

"So you wanna hear my side?"

"Is there one?"

He shook his head and gave her his broad smile again. He seemed to be loosening up. She could see he liked the attention, another facet of his deprivation.

"I earned this money. Made a hit on the numbers is all. Three. Three. Three."

"I thought the lottery put that racket out of business."

"Shows how much you know."

"Do you seriously believe you'll ever get your hands on that money?"

"Gonna try."

He took another deep sip from his coffee cup. There was a kind of delicacy in the way his lips touched the rim. Even in the way he sat at the table, as if his grandmother had insisted on "manners," the importance of presenting himself with "dignity." She groped for some way to break into his fantasy world.

"So you say you did not steal anything?"

"Nothing. Not the money either."

"Wasn't in the briefcase?"

"I thought you were gonna tell my side." He had slipped into street accents, saying "mah sahd."

"Okay, I'm listening."

"When I got this numbers hit happened before. I like to buy strange things. Makes me feel good. How was I to know if it was stolen or not? Just street goods. All it is."

"Six sets of silverware. Silver candlesticks. Seven television sets. Five VCRs. Twelve sets of earrings. Assorted necklaces and bracelets. Come on, Newton. I gave up fairy tales when I was five." She tried to keep her voice modulated. There was, unfortunately, no way not to be judgmental.

"So I got strange tastes. Don't make me a crook. If that stuff was stolen, I say give it back. But how would I know? Let's say everything was stolen. Everything but the money."

"Proceeds of crime, Newton. The police aren't stupid either. It's down as proceeds of crime, tagged as stolen property, and locked in their warehouse. As for the cash, you'll never see a nickel of it. Never. In seven years it will go to the District of Columbia. A nice fat gift to the government."

"It's my bread," he muttered, lifting his chin, undefeated "I know. Three. Three. Three."

"Problem is how you gonna write about my side, if you don' believe it?"

"I'd rather write the truth," Elly said.

A memory echoed in her mind. Her father's words. They were leaning on him very hard by then. Even the ads had stopped coming. Couldn't keep it going without ads. That was his mother's perpetual plaint. She knew. She sold them. Or didn't at that point, because the County Commissioners didn't like the way Tom Fox went after them, exposed corruption.

A cliché, he called himself, the quintessential two-billionth mold of the crusading weekly owner-editor fighting the corrupt small town old buddy system. "I'd rather write the truth," he had said. Didn't do the family much good, any good. It dragged Tom Fox down to an early grave and put this bit into his daughter's mouth.

She knew perfectly well who worked the reins. She didn't need the whip. But this time she was on to it. "Wrong is wrong her father's voice called down from the saddle. He had this racetrack vice that had also permeated his life. Go for the Triple Crown. The last voice was her own. Also don't get mad, get even. Al knew, too. She had said it in a hundred ways. Broken record, Elly. No more music.

"Good, then. You write my truth."

"Won't wash, Newton. We can't write tall tales. I'll tell you the story I'd rather write."

From the way he cocked his head, she could see his quickening interest. So he has painted himself into a mental corner, she decided. She wondered if he was ready to make his way out.

"You robbed Leopold's apartment. No sweat. You worked the night desk. You made copies of keys. But what you found disappointed you. It was just a pad he used to dump his hat. Nothing fancy. No goods for resale. Didn't even have a television set. His principal place was in New York, you see. Anyway, there was this briefcase. What, after all, is a briefcase worth with someone's name already embossed in gold? You opened it, saw the cash. Bonanza. A real score. Never happened before. Never will again. Odd that the briefcase was the only item taken from his place, and he hadn't even reported it missing. Imagine."

"You're crazy, woman," Newton barked, pressing his back against the rear of the booth as if he wanted to put even more distance between them. She liked the signs and pressed on.

"Then when no one came forward to make the claim, you got

this idea in your head. You put the cash into the briefcase. Look, Newton, it's a doomed idea. Better for you if you told the true story. Could maybe start a whole chain reaction of people falling, bad people, corrupt people, greedy people, like the domino theory."

She paused, watching him. Definitely on the wrong track, she decided. What the hell did the Newton Parkers of this world know or care about domino theories? Maybe they didn't even know about dominoes. Still she pressed on stubbornly, hoping to find the right note, wondering if she should invoke the name of that black hero, without whom Watergate would never have happened. Except that she had forgotten his name. Besides, he wouldn't know the man from Adam.

"And all because of you, Newton."

She watched him as he listened. Oddly she imagined that he was hanging on every word. She wasn't sure. He seemed capable of wearing several masks, especially for people who didn't understand the black idiom. People like her.

"What's in a story like that for old Newton?" he asked shrewdly, with what seemed like surprising sophistication.

"Heroism maybe."

"You jivin' me?"

"Patriotism?"

"You're jivin' now."

"How about simple notoriety? You become a celebrity. You can build on that."

Newton rubbed his chin as if he were contemplating the idea then he started to laugh, uncontrollably, the kind that shakes a fat man's belly.

"You're one foxy lady." He pointed a finger at her, like a stick of brown marble.

"I'm out ninety-nine thousand, three hundred."

"Still singing that tune?"

"You gotta better one?"

That required some heavy thinking. The idea bubbled up, but she capped it quickly. Then it was loose again like a mysterious gas leak. Pay him. That's what he wants.

She flushed with a sense of mortification. Was he tempting her to violate the vaunted journalist code? Pay money to this black Deep Throat? Then something stirred in the darkest thicket of her mind, its most private place. How did the original Deep Throat feel about not being cut in, shut out of the millions made in the giant multimedia expectoration? Deprived of the glory. Even now. How could he have missed the great opportunity of a lifetime? "I am Deep Throat." Too late now, she decided. Every year the audience diminished and the price plummets. After nearly two decades the currency was gone with the wind.

"What exactly did you have in mind?"

His pupils darted from side to side in their whites. The chocolate-colored fingers of both hands tapped the table.

"You get me off."

Obfuscate, she told herself. Go slow. You're cracking him.

"And if I do?"

"Then you do your number."

"You'll tell me the truth?"

"I didn't say nothing about that." She reached for her pocketbook, made motions to leave. He continued. "It won't matter. You write what you want."

"That the money came out of Leopold's briefcase?"

"Came outta the sky. I don't care."

"I can't make up stories. You've got to stand behind it. And it's got to be the truth."

She looked directly into his eyes, trying to hold them, trying to lock them in. But he turned away. "I'll do my best," she said. It would be none too good, she knew. Who would she ask? What would she say? This thief is helping me on my story, therefore set him free?

Newton continued to tap on the table. Then he shook his head.

"No way," he muttered. "You couldn't do shit." He pronounced it "sheet." Then he stopped tapping and scratched his head. "You give me maybe a thousand for thinking money. I'll let the idea run around in my head."

She had put down her pocketbook on the seat beside her. In it were the financial remnants of their vacation, fifteen hundred in American Express Traveler's checks. Again, this unruly thought needed capping. Paying for the truth seemed ugly, anathema, unethical, immoral. Opprobrium came down on the idea like golf ball-sized sleet. She clutched the pocketbook and slid along the seat. As she did so, she watched his hands for any sign of gesture to stop her. When it didn't come she stopped herself, barely an inch from the edge of the seat.

"Newton. There's no way to avoid jail. Sure as hell they're going to put you away. No one is going to believe your story. The truth is that it sounds ridiculous. People will laugh at you."

"You white people wouldn't believe a nigger he stood on his head."

"Total crap," Elly said.

Was it real indignation or just frustration? "Climb down from your fantasy." She started to stand up and this time he moved, touched her arm. She sat down again.

"All I need's some folding money for a while. Not too much to ask."

Under the table, she felt the tension in her thighs.

"You realize you'll have to change your plea. Probably be better off. Won't be wasting the court's time."

"So says the great lawyer they give me."

"Not bad advice.

They both waited through a long silence, like mute circling boxers. Unfortunately it was a fixed fight. Each protagonist had already surrendered something, and each knew the outcome in advance.

"Only way I do it," he said, the first to speak. It was a victory of sorts, she supposed.

"It was in Leopold's briefcase?"

"Just a thousand. Take care of a few things before I go to the place." He shook his head gloomily. "Should have taken that hundred thou, buried it somewhere," he muttered. There it was, she thought, the inference. Would it be enough for her story, an implication, a hint?

She opened her pocketbook, took out her sheaf of traveler's checks. Her hands, she noted, were shaking. He watched her fingers.

"It was in Leopold's briefcase then?" she asked, putting the traveler's checks on the table.

"What's them words you people use? No comment."

"So that's the way it's going to be?"

"Dumb shit ain't claimin' it, is he?"

"That tells you something, Newton," she said. "It's dirty money."

"Who don't know that?" Newton said, smirking, pointed with his chin at the traveler's checks on the table. "Not like what's in that."

"So you're going to stick by your story. No one is going to believe it."

"No sheet."

"All right then," she said. "I'll write it this way, quoting you."

He was silent, shrugging. Was it consent? Did it matter? She was dead certain it was the truth. She flipped through the book of traveler's checks. They were all in fifties.

Suddenly he reached out and took the book out of her trembling fingers, counting the checks.

"Fifteen hundred," he said, glancing at her, offering a twisted smile.

She shrugged.

"Okay. But don't live with the delusion that you'll ever see a dime of Leopold's money."

"One thing… it won't count against me. With nobody claimin' it, it's still circumstantial. Even if I do say, I found it in the briefcase."

Well, well, she thought, he had the makings of a jailhouse lawyer. She took out a pen and started signing the checks.

"No good to me," he said watching her count. "I try to cash them, they'd think I stole them."

"You'll have to do something about that image," she cracked. The joke fell flat. "There's a bank around the corner. I'll go. You wait outside."

Of course, she didn't feel good about paying for information. Of all the contrivances and rationalizations she used to justify the act, the most credible one, at least to herself, was time. She was simply speeding things up, rushing up the mountain.

But later, hearing it played back on her tape recorder, which sat on Charlie Carruthers' desk, she felt, if not elated, at least vindicated.

"Proof positive," she said clicking off the recorder.

"And you saw him actually get on that ship? Iraqi you said?"

She hesitated then covered it by sucking in a deep breath, a gesture of exasperation.

"I told you that."

"And your idea is to juxtapose the two elements?"

"At the beginning," she said cautiously. "Shake the coconuts."

He smiled and shook his head.

"For your sake, I hope it flies."

"My sake?"

"I don't really need it." He leaned back on his chair and crossed his arms behind his head. "I've done mine," he sighed, and she sensed that he was revealing something very precious to himself, very intimate. "But it would be nice. One more send-up."

His voice trailed off, his eyes glazed. He suddenly seemed older, more wrinkled, bent. But his message was clear—a swan song. She felt compelled to respond.

"I feel it, Charlie. I won't let you down." Us, she thought.

"Better be good," he croaked.

"A great journey begins with but a single step," she said, wondering if it sounded foolish.

"I've seen a lot of guys crawl back," he whispered, then cleared his throat. Whatever was pregnant and poignant in the moment passed.

"You want a partner on it?"

"No."

"Want it all, eh?"

He had it exactly right. If it were going to be her swan song, it would have to blaze across the sky, her name the only one in lights, big enough for Daddy to see. Perhaps Al might understand the concept of swan song and have faith in it.

"Nothing goes in without me and the lawyers. Hear?" Charlie said. "I don't want any grief."

"There will be grief somewhere," she said. Of that she was dead certain.

VI

Always the first to rise in his household, Harry muttered obscenities about the inability of the delivery people to deposit the paper on his doorstep. Slippers flapping against the wet driveway, he ran through sheets of rain, got a good grip on the paper in its plastic sleeve, and started back toward the house.

Almost to the door, he slipped, crashed a knee onto the asphalt, tore his pajamas, and came into the house feeling the beginning of nausea. Not my day, he decided rubbing his kneecap and unsheathing the paper. The plastic wrapper spread its droplets on the table and the floor.

He had already pushed the button on the coffeemaker, and the dark liquid was dripping at a steady pace through the plastic filter into the Plexiglas pitcher. While he waited, he poured Grape Nuts into a bowl, filled it with milk, and brought it to the table. He had hardly brought the first spoonful to his mouth when he saw the story. He felt the thump of his accelerating heartbeat. Sweat began to ooze out of his pores.

DID CELEBRITY JEWELER LEOPOLD HAVE ONE HUNDRED THOUSAND IN STOLEN BRIEFCASE? the headline read. It had clubbed him to attention. He read and reread the story. Front page, jumped to inside the first section. Clearly meant to demand attention. A sharp pain caught him just below the ribcage. With fingers shaking, he punched in Billy's number.

"Jogging," Millie mumbled, her voice hoarse with sleep.

"Tell him to call." He had wanted to add the word emergency but thought better of it. Calling at that hour, ten after six, was enough of a statement.

He slapped the paper down on the table and paced the kitchen. Then he came back for just one more read:

"Irving Leopold, self-styled jeweler to the stars and confirmed political groupie with connections directly into the Oval Office, might have had one hundred thousand in cash stashed in his briefcase when it was stolen from his apartment last month. This fact was broadly implied yesterday in an exclusive interview with Newton Parker, the alleged thief.

"No one else claimed the money except me. Therefore, it's mine," Parker is quoted as saying. According to the prosecutor's office, the claim by Parker that it is his money is characterized as "ludicrous.

"Leopold is missing from his residences in Washington and New York. Efforts to reach him have been futile although an eyewitness report had him purportedly on an East Iraqi freighter heading out to the Adriatic from Venice just two days ago."

He read on, mostly backfill but, nevertheless, the kind of biographical material designed to make Leopold an exotic "mystery figure." There was no mention of Billy or, for that matter, himself, but the writer spared nothing in her attempts to connect Leopold with the president, his wife and social circle, mostly material gleaned from news clips which, assembled in bulk, seemed ominous. It was the kind of story that titillated the inside-the-beltway crowd. Reading it for the umpteenth time—especially the first two paragraphs—induced in him a state of terminal bewilderment.

"Stupid bastard," Harry muttered, his eyes drifting to the

byline. "Eleanor Fox," he said aloud, summoning up a portrait of some sweaty-palmed, beady-eyed, pimple-faced, hawk-nosed woman smelling vaguely of female excretions.

Her sharp teeth, Harry was certain, could embed themselves in your ass and never let go. Never. Did she have something? Could it be that Irving was reneging on their deal to stay secluded in Venice until everything blew over? They'd even had a nice place leased out for him on the Lido. A luxurious exile. The deal was for him to stay put. Why would he want to board an Iraqi ship? It made no sense at all.

Harry went down to his study, found the number tucked into a Simenon mystery with Venice in the title and direct dialed. Only then did he calculate the time. It would be eleven in the evening in Venice. Thankfully, the answer was prompt. Only for emergencies, they had agreed. He had self-swept his own phones, and it was doubtful that Leopold's Venice line was tapped. At least he hoped not and knew he was taking a chance.

"It's me," Harry said. Just enough for Irving to recognize the voice. Also the whish in the phone assured him that it was an overseas call.

"And me." It was Irving's voice, unmistakable. It confused him further.

"You stayed put?"

"Of course, I'm put. Here is very nice."

"I think you better move on. A month maybe two. Like now. *Today.*"

"We got troubles?"

"No discussion, please."

"But today," Irving said. Harry could detect the fright.

"Please."

He hung up and tiptoed to his room, got dressed quickly

without shaving. Everyone in the house still slept. They'd be up at seven.

The telephone rang. He picked up the phone on the first ring, heard Billy's familiar voice.

"Meet me," Billy said. His mind whirled. From the beginning, they had a paranoid fear of wires, electronic ears, especially telephones. Outdoors always seemed safer when matters like these were discussed. The intrigue was tension inducing, repellent. He had hated it from day one.

"Where?"

"That place. The outfield."

"When?"

"I'm leaving now."

He hung up and went back to the bedroom. Bending over his sleeping wife, he kissed her forehead, watched her stir for a moment, then awaken. She planted a kiss on his cheek. In times of stress and uncertainty, he needed to have her administer her "lucky" kiss.

***

Because Billy lived closer to where they were meeting, he was there ahead of him. Harry could see him, a tall slender figure in his jogging clothes standing in the green behind the softball diamond.

From a vantage dead center in the field, they would have a full three-hundred-and-sixty-degree view. Nobody could sneak up on them and few could identify who they were with the naked eye. It was Billy who had said, during a staff softball game, looking far into the outfield, "Now there's a spot for secret talks away from prying ears." Odd, Harry thought, how they both knew exactly where to meet when the time came. A place waiting for its moment.

As he came forward toward the lone figure, still youthful in outline, he saw images that confused his sense of time. There was the younger Billy Tucker, backlit by the glow of the clean bright new rising sun on the dew-glistened field, a hero poised to lead and conquer. But the adolescent dream paled as Harry grew closer, saw the lines, etched deeper, the drooping crevices beside the mouth, eyes wary with fear.

Billy held the first section of the paper, rolled like a club in his hand.

"None of it makes sense," Harry said. "I called him."

"Like a deliberate lie, then?"

"Something crazy," Harry kicked the grass with the toe of his shoe. "Maybe some kind of a probe. Like a stalking horse."

"To shake things up? Get the big investigative agencies involved?"

"How else can you explain it?" Harry said.

"Then they know more than they're saying," Billy said, eyes overblinking, a nerve palpitating in his jaw.

"We mustn't overreact." They both waited through a long pause.

"Maybe he is," Billy said, searching Harry's face.

"A spy?"

"You never know. Christ, he was on the inside. You can't deny that."

"Confidante of kings," Harry said with contempt, expelling air. "Listen, if he could concoct our deal, then how can we put anything past him? All crazy games and make-believe."

"But he made it happen so easily. Nothing to it. Presto and soon there was ten million dollars. It worked."

"Wasn't quite presto, Billy."

Harry remembered his own ridiculous role, greeting Irving at Dulles, Irving dressed as an imposing orthodox rabbi, complete with beard, black shiny coat, fur hat, the very incarnation of the orthodox seer with a fortune in diamonds embedded in the forest of gray beard hair.

The Customs agents weren't going to be thorough with anyone accompanied by the boss himself, although he had made it clear that he did not want the rabbi to get any special favors. They just waved him through anyway. That second time, he had come through Kennedy in the same manner and the third time through Boston. Perhaps a rumor had started throughout the department that Harry Silver, the renegade Catholic, was about to make a conversion.

Actually it was sidesplitting, and he and Billy had howled at Harry's description of Irving's getup. "Deserved an Oscar," he had told Billy, still hating the idea and his part in it, but seeing the humor in it nonetheless—and the logic.

Tel Aviv was a great diamond-trading center these days, although the South Africans in London passed the diamonds themselves, which meant that Irving's route was London–Tel Aviv–United States.

For customs, diamonds were hardly a priority item these days. With dope, electronic equipment, and a mind-boggling array of quotas and contraband, diamonds were inconsequential. What had to be resisted was the recording of information. No matter that millions of dollars in diamonds were moved through customs surreptitiously each day, smuggled in. The issue was records, getting caught, questions. Dope surveillance was getting tighter and tighter, prompting closer and closer searches by his own department.

So real life had become a movie, then real life again, and they were standing in the middle of this green field contemplating the possibilities of extinction.

"Maybe you were right, Harry. You always said troubles come from the unlikeliest places at the least expected, most inconvenient time." He shook his head. "But this Iraqi connection. It will have to wake up the dogs. They sniff hard enough, they'll find out." He punched a fist into his palm. "Stupid egomania, grand illusions of indestructibility. Why did I listen to that asshole?"

"It's not the time to be philosophical, Billy," Harry said. "He could be into some other international scam. Might have absolutely nothing to do with us."

"Maybe all this time they were tracking him. Maybe they know everything." As he spoke, his color was draining, his ruddiness disappearing.

"We don't know that," Harry said.

"And you talked to him? Are you sure it was his voice?"

"Impossible to fake. Not his."

"So where did this woman get such a stupid fact?"

"I don't think we should call and ask her."

"What the hell do we do?"

"Worry a lot."

They had worried, of course, that the young thief would talk, which was the reason for Irving's Venetian jaunt in the first place. At least they had a modest backup position for that.

If it became serious enough and Irving was traced, a tough enough task as it was, he would merely say he was vacationing, out of touch. Then why the secret entry? Ambassador Manelli would be having a troublesome morning. And the money? A jeweler deals in cash, doesn't he?

Perhaps a media mystery would emerge. They would be

climbing all over the Iraqi thing. That was getting into deep water. Besides, it had looked as if the thief would not talk. No percentage in it. Not necessary. Too many other confirmed burglaries on his plate. Of course, that had been when scenarios could be neat and logical.

Billy began to walk in an eccentric circle then pace in crisscrosses. Not cool now. Not the Billy of home free. Then he stopped.

"They could bust us, Commissioner," Billy said, stopping suddenly. "I can see a whole line of complicating problems, the money, itself, for example. Could come under the jurisdiction of Treasury. More than just heavy irony."

"You'd be long gone, Billy. With your pants down to your ankles. Don't even think about the illegalities. Why confront the obvious? We took the chance. Simple as that."

Billy shook his head.

"I feel awful about this, Harry. Getting you involved." Harry's ears burned with the dubious sincerity, but he let it pass. "Irving made it sound so damned easy. Spilt milk. The point now is, as you say, stay cool. No panic."

His anxiety level seemed to have stabilized. No retort was necessary to the idea of getting him involved, Harry thought. He had been involved from the beginning, had wanted to be involved. No point even saying to himself that he was pushed into this screaming and kicking. And if he said it and it was true, it was too late now.

"It's one of those things that will always be there on the back burner. But that's the calculation we made earlier. We took the big risk for the largest reward."

Billy nodded. He seemed satisfied with that explanation.

"Of course, there's always Irving," Billy said. "What would happen if Irving cracks? You and I, Harry, we can trust each other.

We've got history. But Irving, he's the cipher in this." He rubbed his chin. "If the chips were down where would he stand? Then again, he has a lot to lose, too."

Billy scratched his chin and raked fingers through his hair. They seemed uncharacteristic gestures or perhaps Harry had just noticed them now, for the first time. "Not that much, really." Billy seemed to grow pensive. "Relatively speaking."

The sudden flash of haughtiness caught Harry by surprise, stirring up vague misgivings for later reflection. He made a conscious effort to ignore the reference.

"He might gain by talking." Was there a bit of malice in that? Harry wondered.

"Gain?"

"Out there in media land. Could be a good yarn. So outrageous no one would believe it."

Too late to retrieve. Again he saw the blood drain from Billy's face. Harry, of course, knew it would. How many times can people play the same song?

"I think I'll leave the nightmares to the subconscious," Billy said.

"Good idea," Harry said. No point in letting testiness and anxiety split them apart. "I told him to get lost for a while."

"I'm afraid that's not his style," Billy sighed. "And he's not living in a vacuum. Did you tell him about this piece?" He waved the club of the paper in the air.

"Not a monosyllable. I think he got the message. That's all that counted. Besides, he'll know soon enough."

"They get close to him, he'll blow us out of the water." An indistinguishable expletive cut into the air.

"We'll have to cross that bridge when we get to it," Harry said. Billy's curse had had an ominous sound.

"Then there's Manelli. He'll be having his own apoplectic attack shortly."

"Him. Supercilious ass," Harry snapped.

"But he only has a piece of it, and he's not about to sing his own song," Billy said. "Not if he can help it. He'll be in trouble himself."

"We'll just have to play it by ear. Keep in close touch. Make sure our stories are absolutely foolproof if the subject comes up, which it will. I suspect that we'll all soon be interrogated by someone, maybe even Treasury's own people."

"Who is all?" Billy asked.

"Everyone in big-time politics that ever bought one of Irving's baubles."

"Wonderful," Billy said with a smirk.

"That would mean a list as long as your arm. Maybe both your arms." An errant thought suddenly intruded. "How did you pay him? Cash or check?"

"Millie bought things out of her own money. Paid by check."

"Her check?"

"Yes."

"Well then, you could be, as they say, home free."

Billy nodded and his smile became broad enough for every part of his face to crinkle. For the first time that morning, he seemed relieved.

"You got a point there." Harry waited, wondering if Billy would now ask him the big question. When he didn't, Harry volunteered.

"I also paid by check."

"So we get the canceled checks, and if an investigation does begin, we offer them as evidence that we had nothing to do with any cash transaction."

"Speaking of cash," Harry said. A ball of phlegm formed in his throat. He cleared it, brought it up, and spat on the grass.

"Jesus. Forgot about that."

"Better remember."

Billy started his erratic pacing then stopped suddenly, his eyes caught in a spear of sunlight.

"The Amtrak run," he said, his expression noncommittal. Usually when he talked about where the money was put, he would offer a thin self-mocking smile. That was his idea. To put the money in safe-deposit boxes in banks in Baltimore, Wilmington, Philadelphia, and Trenton, stations along the path of the Amtrak run from Washington to New York. Harry had arranged for the boxes at each city, using made-up names, carrying the cash in suitcases, always in denominations of fifties and hundreds.

"We could leave it there. For the time being," Harry said. "But if things get sticky, I think we've got to consider alternatives."

"Like what?"

"I have to think about that."

"We could always have a bonfire," Billy said, a dry chuckle bubbling up from his chest.

"Problem is," Harry said. He had thought about this aspect of it long and hard. "If there's good investigative work, we'd be under surveillance. We'd have to stay away from those boxes then." Not *we*, he thought. He, Harry, was the only link to those boxes. Not Billy.

"So there may be still time to empty them. Where would you put it?"

"I really don't know. Bury it somewhere."

"Like the Pumpkin Papers," Billy mused. "Remember?"

Harry had read Whittaker Chambers' *Witness*, which recalled the events of the Hiss case. They were too young to have paid much attention when they were kids. Another Washington scandal complete with mystery, intrigue, lies, charges, and countercharges. Microfilm evidence against Hiss was hidden in a pumpkin on Chamber's farm, hence the name. Why was it, Harry thought, that such national traumas became, even in retrospect, a theater of the absurd? As now.

When this matter with Leopold had come up, Harry had wracked his brain for historical examples to counter Billy's plans. He had dredged them from memory, from the shards of other absurdist dramas filtered through media recollections of other administrations, other eras.

Even as a child, he had been a media freak, a newspaper junkie, and the oddball catchwords and catchnames had stuck in all that manure of information. General Harry Vaughn rewarded with deep freezes for political favors during Truman's time. Sherman Adams, Ike's chief of staff getting a vicuna coat from tax evader Bernard Goldfine, who needed someone to fix the IRS. Bobby Baker, the southern boy who was Lyndon Johnson's bagman, exposed and imprisoned. The burgling of Daniel Ellsberg's psychiatrist's office for records during the Nixon days. And Watergate, of course, the penultimate absurdist documentary with it's bizarre money drops in telephone booths, tape recordings, a litany of wackiness that made Woodward and Bernstein rich and everyone else it touched either famous or infamous. Then later, there was Billy Carter working for the Libyans. Iran-Contra with its bizarre exchange of monies to arm the contras. It was all madness.

None of this had made a dent in Billy's plans. "What's the ultimate downside?" Billy had asked.

"Disgrace. Maybe jail. Short sentence. White-collar crime or some such. Aggravation. Destroyed reputation. The end of dreams. To most of us that would constitute deep shit trouble," Harry had answered.

Then Billy had asked as follow-up, "But anything life threatening?"

The question had seemed curious. But wasn't it, after all, a matter of staking one's life? A biblical quotation, Harry remembered, had jumped into his head: What does it profiteth a man if he gaineth the whole world and loseth his own soul?

"Not in the sense of dying," he had answered, wondering if it had been both accurate and adequate.

There had been no need to discuss the upside, which was, of course, the ultimate, the presidency, and worth the risk. That was a given. Nor was there a need to discuss moral questions, a subject to be avoided in the context of political ambition. Moral questions were strictly for public consumption and then mostly on Sundays.

Anyway, it was too late for I-told-you-sos.

"It comes to that, I'll bury it in the yard," Harry said with a nervous giggle, but it wasn't exactly a rib tickler. "Under the old apple tree." He didn't have one, only an old chokecherry, a weed really, that messed up his lawn every spring with inedible fruit.

"All that's premature," Billy said. "We'll track it."

The encounter seemed to build confidence. The spaciousness and the autumn green grass gave the impression of serenity. "Two Men Standing in a Field" might be the title of the painting. Billy seemed to have come back from the brink, regathering the threads of leadership.

"If the story leads nowhere, it'll be scrapped," Harry said, encouraged by Billy's obvious resurrection. Even some of his facial rivulets had flattened. "It'll be yesterday's dishwater."

"May be already. That may be their full load."

"Keep talking like that, Billy. Your words to God's ears."

"Happened before," Billy said.

When? Harry wondered, not remembering.

VII

There were the four of them sitting in Charlie Carruthers small conference room just off his glass paneled office. The two men from the FBI were clones of some very neat, very clean Irishmen: light-skinned, sandy-haired, earnest, wearing vested pinstripes. Between forty and fifty, Elly guessed, new-breed types, no wasted motion.

Inspectors Rogers and McCarthy. Rogers, Elly's mental survey told her, was the one with the bushy eyebrows who spoke in bass, like someone bucking to be a radio announcer. McCarthy, despite the effort to polish himself up, was Boston Southie gone a bit plush. He would be first to draw and fire, Elly decided. Rogers was less compulsive, more likely to draw out the agony.

"Let's play with their yo-yos," Charlie had said to her before letting the men into the conference room. He had been pleased, he told her, with the way she weaved the story together with new threads and old. And he had expected the visit. "One of many," he assured her. "Wait till the spooks come in."

Two days had gone by since her first piece, and the avalanche of follow-up by other papers, television, and the wire services had begun. Most acknowledged her first story in their reports. Still others, like the New York tabloids, claimed originality, and she was dead certain that the major weekly tabloids would run screaming headlines inferring that Leopold was spotted lifting a few with Gorbachev behind the Kremlin walls.

She had expected others to fall in line with the story and start fanning out on their own. But she hadn't expected the speed with which they pursued it. As the "eyewitness" to Leopold's

East German connection, she did have an edge, but that would quickly narrow, as other journalists would open new avenues of speculation.

Her job now was to stay ahead of the pack. So far she had dealt with that without provoking inhibiting anxieties, although her sleep pattern had begun to alter considerably under the weight of imaginary nocturnal speculations.

Al, as expected, had assumed an air of icy indifference. Indeed, looking at it from his point of view, she was almost sympathetic. After all, his experience of her acknowledged that behind the facade of playing the role of "concerned and loving" wife, was the frenetic churning of words and ideas having to do with the Leopold story.

Never a very good actress, this was, nevertheless, her penultimate worst performance. Since she had no real defense for her actions, which meant long hours away from Al, she collected what was left of her attention and tried to throw the ball back in his court.

"When you're on a tough case, you also tend to be self-absorbed," she told him with a deliberate sense of calm.

"Am I interfering?" he asked with a poutiness that could strike deep into the nether regions of her own guilt. Pouting, she had learned, especially when accompanied by silence, could be a deadly combination.

"I would rather have you confrontational," she told him, hoping to engage him.

"Would it matter?" he asked gloomily.

"What is it that men want?" she asked, reaching for a little subtle humor. When that failed, she reached for something else. It was no coincidence that these set pieces took place in bed. Sex, contrary to many statistical inferences regarding marriage, had always been their best marital asset. When their relationship was otherwise frosty, like now, it made her seriously believe that, after all, that was the only true thing between them.

"You're manipulating me," he responded.

"I'm trying."

"Why does it work here and nowhere else?"

"Let's ask old faithful here. He always rises to the occasion." She put her ear to it. "No answer. All I can hear is thump-a-thump."

"He lives a life of his own. Divorced from reality."

"Precisely why I love him so much."

She showered it with her attention and, as predicted, he responded in kind. She felt her complementary reaction, which soon resulted in the usual infallible denouement, the simultaneous orgasm. Once it was their most vaunted achievement. "We could write a book," she had told him. *Coming Together* was his suggested title. "Make millions." Lately his comments were darker.

"Another wasted shot," he sighed.

"Not for me," she had murmured.

In the aftermath, the gloom had set in again, and he had moved a distance that seemed considerable, almost a full arm's-length away. Yet she had barely time to measure the distance.

Her thoughts were racing away, back to Irving Leopold. Perversely, though, she had noted the time frame. They had expended a mere fifteen minutes in the transaction. That, she decided, was worth a sharp stab of anxiety, however brief.

But, after a twisting night, she was up at dawn, rushing to put the finishing touches on her follow-up story, the result of hours of legwork, which also encompassed nonstop activity on the telephone. The story further explored Irving Leopold's astonishing circle of high-society Washington contacts. Many had, at first, tried to duck her questions in the traditional Washington way with a curt "No comment." It was a response that her tenacity would not allow. When it did occur, she offered her journalist's counterpunch.

"We'll tell it anyway. Might as well get it in the right perspective. Tell your side."

Moaning and groaning, they would be drawn in, determined to put the best face on what was decidedly negative political capital. In cold print, the possession of jewels seemed, in political terms, frivolous and slightly decadent.

"Listen," she told them. "It's a perfectly normal purchase. And what's wrong with owning beautiful things?"

When they asked for anonymity, she refused politely. "After all, you're an innocent in this," she would tell them, feeling slightly malicious, since she salivated to find a credible accomplice.

What emerged was a picture of the man as a kind of political groupie who nobody took seriously outside of his jewelry expertise. On that subject they all suggested that he was without peer. With obvious defensiveness, they expressed themselves in variations of what was wrong with purchasing beautiful jewelry with honest value? In the end it surprised her how much cooperation she had actually gotten, some inadvertent.

Even the president's wife's press secretary was amazingly forthcoming. But then she was also a lame-duck First Lady, and there was no longer any need for pretense. Cabinet people and their wives were guarded but accessible. Nobody claimed any real intimacy. Irving Leopold was simply there, as if he were hatched from an egg, a chick waddling about on the floor between their feet, hardly noticed, except when the urge to buy jewelry became manifest.

One woman, Millie Tucker, the wife of the secretary of the treasury, went slightly further than the rest characterizing him as "original" and "amusing." She expressed her own determination not to abandon the man simply because of "half-baked allegations." Definitely not, Irving Leopold could no more be a spy than Donald Duck.

Millie had also suggested that if someone had seen Irving on an Iraqi boat, he was probably on his way to sell Saddam Hussein something for his fat wife. Millie Tucker was always good for an outrageous performance.

In the current piece, Elly had decided not to serve up Millie's quotes. She made a mental note to track her down for a more in-depth interview before the other news vultures started to pick apart the carcass of her story. Besides, she had plenty of juicy stuff, including great art that she had found in the paper's library files—photos of various beneficiaries of Leopold's wholesale largesse actually wearing his baubles at various parties and balls. There was even one of the First Lady wearing a diamond bracelet at a White House state dinner. A blowup would be marvelously suggestive of conspiratorial doings in high places.

Mostly the photos were of wives of, rather than principals, although one member of the Cabinet, the secretary of health and human resources, did admit that her new husband had bought a two-carat engagement ring from Leopold.

The jeweler had come to her apartment with a large velvet-lined black-leather ring case from which, in the presence of her then husband-to-be who was an engineer from Oklahoma, she had made her selection.

"Nothing sinister in that, is there?" the woman had asked. "Of course not," Elly had replied. She had even come across male jewelry, diamond stickpins and cufflinks and a smattering of rings, mostly star sapphires and tigereyes that had been purchased by a number of senators and congressmen, although these did not come up in any photos. Nothing but class rings for the politically aware.

When the piece ran, it read more like a compendium of articles of jewelry; but with photo illustrations, it did, subliminally imply dire goings on at the top. She knew that, of course, and political people with images to protect were right to resist.

Her piece, building on descriptions such as "a flawless four-carat marquise-cut ring set in a platinum band surrounded by half-carat baguettes" invested their owners with an acquisitiveness and decadent greed more appropriate to the court of Louis XIV at Versailles than in the cradle of Jefferson's democracy.

She had also made calls to people in New York and Los Angeles to flesh out the profile of the man, the way he did business, and with whom. The only uncooperative people were the diamond merchants.

"Closed shop," one man said on the phone. "They don't talk, and when they do, don't believe a word of it. They got so much to hide in their transactions, especially those between themselves, that it would be a miracle if they say one more word after "hello.""

But she knew that she was onto something more than just titillation, although she did not eschew that aspect. Her father would have advised her to keep an open mind. "Let the story take you wherever it goes, chips falling where they may."

Of course, she loved the heft of the ax as it began to cut into the tree, spraying the chips everywhere. Sooner or later, she knew, something, someone, would surface to take a bite out of her bait. The sheer exhilaration of it kept her rolling forward, Al's inhibiting attitude notwithstanding.

"It's my shot," she had told him repeatedly, even that morning at the breakfast table. She had come to it bleary-eyed and vague, her mind still spinning with words, watching him rattle the *New York Times* as if he were deliberately calling attention to his rejection of her paper, the hated rival and enemy. She had found the Style section later near the toilet where he had thrown it, ample evidence that no one in Washington who meant anything could possibly face the day without a quick fix from its pages.

He had made a show of reading her story in her presence two days before. She had watched his face with her pulse pounding in her neck, hoping its sheer vitality would convince him that "this shot" was not a terminal threat to his version of their future together.

"Be objective," she had urged as he read. His eyes rose slowly from the pages. No smile to light up the morning.

"Good piece on such a flimsy premise."

He was being a recalcitrant bastard, she decided, spiteful and immature. Chips have to fall where they may, she assured herself, taking refuge in the old echo, wishing there were two of her, one for him and one for herself.

"You've raised some questions here of a serious nature," McCarthy said, addressing himself to the editor. Rogers did not nod in emphasis, sitting rigid and impassive. Charlie had tilted his chair back, the tips of his shoes braced against the edge of the table.

It occurred to her how accurately he fit the part, gruff-voiced, square-jawed, steel-gray straight-parted hair, puffs around light blue eyes. His clothes gave him an old-preppy air, which was quite authentic, until the words came out, streetwise and peppery, an iconoclast no longer with a need to stay in the closet. A Washington untouchable but with a skin thin enough to mock the idea.

"Name of the game," Charlie said, nodding toward Elly, who sat upright, pad and pencil laid on the table in front of her.

"We're not questioning the integrity of the story," McCarthy said. "Fact is we'd like to do some real spadework ourselves. The director wants us to get to the bottom of it."

"I'm sure he does," Charlie agreed. "It'll be a real horse race."

"Actually we'd like to avoid that," Rogers intruded in his deep bass.

"You mean you'll give us what you have so far," Elly piped up. "If anything."

Actually, not once had the men directed their questions, or interest, toward her. It was a male quirk that always offended her. She had never gotten used to it, knowing it had some peculiar connection with the concept of male bonding, although she wasn't quite sure what it meant. McCarthy turned toward her with what she took for a sneer.

"It is a matter of national security, Miss Fox," he said. "We all know what is implied in your story. A man with access is seen boarding an Iraqi boat, then disappears—"

"We know exactly what it implies," Elly said, put off by his patronizing tone. McCarthy looked helplessly at his partner, then toward Charlie.

"I'm not, repeat *not*, asking you to squelch the story. Just for cooperation."

"Meaning my sources," Elly said with some heat.

"We're the FBI, for crying out loud," McCarthy said testily. "Not the enemy."

"Who is?" Elly muttered.

"We're not here to offend anyone," McCarthy said, a tiny flush beginning at the lobe of his left ear.

"Neither are we," Charlie said with a smile. "Certainly not the

FBI. There's a story here, and we're following it up. That's our business." He had, she realized, been through this routine hundreds of times in the past twenty years. "We get something that could be of use, we'll pass it along." He paused. "Providing it's not useable, not confirmed. We don't usually make big booboos, occasional ones, yes. But most of the time, we're pretty damned good."

"We're not saying you aren't," Rogers said. "But this story, frankly, hit us unawares."

"Sure it did," Charlie said. "The man's security was cleared at all levels. Hell, he was the president's buddy. He sold him the first couple of jewels. He went to their parties. He was part of the inner social circle."

"He didn't have any access to sensitive information," McCarthy muttered.

"You don't know that for sure," Elly said. "That first bit about the cash should certainly have started the wheels of your outfit working."

"Who said it didn't?" McCarthy asked. Rogers responded with a quick cold gesture in McCarthy's direction.

Not in the protocols, Elly thought. She knew that up until the time she had her interview with Newton Parker, the FBI had not approached him. It added a bit more flesh to her story. The FBI was slow to react, too slow. Now the heat was on.

"Frankly, I don't understand the purpose of this meeting," Elly said suddenly, feeling anger building inside her.

"Well, you should," McCarthy snapped.

"Information," Charlie said, intervening.

"Well, they're not entitled to mine. They do their job. We do ours. Problem is they haven't done theirs."

She hadn't realized that her voice had risen. Charlie gestured with his hand for her to calm down.

"They just don't like to be upstaged," he said. "Bad for their image."

He turned to the two men, who were, obviously, exercising extreme control, reacting by the book. "Listen, guys, we're really adversaries. We don't trust the politicos as far as we can throw the Washington Monument. We're also not too enamored with all the bureaucratic flimflam bullshit. We don't care what you G-men do as long as it doesn't interfere with our work. Maybe you got some kind of a mole that slipped through the cracks, maybe a double agent, maybe just a horse's ass. Gives the story its thrust. You do your legwork. We'll do ours. You want to contribute, okay. But *share* is another word. What you see in print is what we share, unless we find something scary—national security scary, something so monumentally threatening that we have to get you fellows on the job fast. So far that kind of information hasn't come up."

Elly liked that and felt the urge to jump up and applaud. No question why Charlie Carruthers was the boss of bosses at the paper. Brave, tough son of a bitch.

Rogers, his features barely mobile, started to speak, his voice impeccably modulated, almost velvet.

"The basic question deals with the source of your allegation that Leopold was, in some way, connected with the East Germans."

"You know we can't give you that," Charlie said, still just one step removed from exasperation.

"We tried," McCarthy said. He had apparently reached the outer edges of his control.

She had wanted to reveal the "eyewitness" in her story, but Charlie had struck it out. "Too self-serving," he had told her. "They'll think it's manufactured. Make it anonymous. We know the source." She had, of course, looked for more confirmation. In the few hours before they left Venice, she had checked with the Venetian police. They had never even heard of Irving Leopold, although they did confirm that an Iraqi ship had docked and sailed, another fact that she had seen with her own eyes.

Nor had the Italian authorities in Rome any knowledge of Irving Leopold, even the fact of his entering the country. The paper's correspondent in Rome had reconfirmed that himself. She had even put the paper's correspondent in Iraq to work making a series of inquiries, all of which had led nowhere, which was to be expected.

"You want it. You find it," Elly said, looking toward Charlie for reaction but barely giving it enough time to register. Flimsy premise, Al had said. Then why was the FBI slopping about? More signs and symbols that she was on to something.

Rogers sucked in a deep breath and stood up. McCarthy also rose.

"Never understand you people," Rogers said with an air of futility.

"I know," Charlie said with heavy sarcasm. "We're enigmas."

"Sometimes, I think you hate America," McCarthy said.

"Sometimes, some Americans," Charlie said pointedly.

Without shaking hands, the two men left the conference room.

"I thought you were noble," Elly said when the men had gone. Her heartbeat, which had accelerated, was revving down.

Charlie slowly removed his shoes from the edge of the table, then hunched down over folded hands.

"I'm out there, Elly. Ball's over."

"Look how we've stirred them up," she said.

"That's worth dickshit. This story has to go somewhere, Elly. The climate's changed. Not with those creeps. They always felt that way. Hate America? Time was when I would have kicked their ass to kingdom come." He balled his fists, pursed his lips and shook his head. "We're not perceived as the good guys anymore. Not as we were. We're getting it from all sides. The pack is at our heels." He looked suddenly tired, daunted.

"It has the stuff, Charlie. I know it has."

"It better have."

"You're just a healthy skeptic, Charlie."

"Got to be, kiddo. In this pressure cooker all you hotshots are just itching to throw the haymaker that will knock the props out from under the asshole politicians, show 'em off to be shallow self-serving hypocrites, liars, and thieves."

His voice became scratchy like footsteps on gravel. "That's the fucking fun of it." He cleared his throat, suddenly compensating, becoming the voice of authority. His gaze bore down on her. "We're not here for search-and-destroy missions. The goods have to be there."

He looked around his little conference room. He had been editor now for more than twenty years, battle-scarred, an old warhorse. These days, plagued by his own chronology and the temporary mindset of conservative ideologues who were now very much in charge, he was fighting off rumors that he was going to be put out to pasture, that his style and focus were old hat.

But to Elly, he was still the quintessential role model, the inspiration for all journalists like her, who believed that the only thing that stood between the predatory and corrupt monsters of privilege and the voiceless, defenseless, and powerless was the pure, sweet, courageous heart of the press. Yes, she thought suddenly, Charlie did remind her of her father.

Suddenly, he stood up, and thrust his fists in front of him, miming a boxer. "Hell, there's got to be at least one more blast left in the old mitts." He turned to her and feinted a jab at her chin. "Just don't show me any glass jaws."

"Trust me, Charlie."

"Show me," he snapped, pulling a light harmless punch on her upper arm. Then he gave her a long hard look and started back to his office.

"I know I've got something," she said.

But he was already out of earshot.

VIII

"But what does it mean?" Terry asked. It was the theme she had seized upon ever since the first story had appeared two weeks ago. But this one had their name in it. Obviously Harry's explanation had not satisfied her. To make matters worse, it was raining and a heavy pale of gloom hung over the city.

Paul looked up occasionally from the Science section of the *New York Times*, clearly taking it all in. The children's presence, as always, considerably inhibited any explanations. Besides, he felt it his duty to protect them from adult unpleasantness. Thankfully, Bobbie seemed absorbed in reading the Rice Krispies box.

"It says what it means," Harry said, adopting a patient air.

"It's clear as a bell, Mom," Paul said turning toward his mother, showing the tiniest edge of exasperation. "Mr. Leopold could have been a spy for Iraq. His cover was selling jewels to the big shots."

The story listed the names of people in so-called high places who had bought jewelry from Irving Leopold, including Harry Silver.

"Don't believe everything you read," Harry muttered. The children had met Irving a number of times. More grounds for resentment, Harry thought, rebuking himself for getting the children involved.

"But your name is mentioned," Terry said.

"I'm in good company," Harry muttered. "Didn't think they'd go down so far." The light touch seemed called for. Above all, they must not see his fear, especially Paul, who had an uncanny antenna when it came to his father.

"That's not true, Dad," Paul said, offended by Harry's modesty. "The commissioner of customs is an extremely important job. Stopping drugs—what's more important than that? Not to mention the smuggling of technology and the policing of dumping."

Harry did not interrupt him. It was, surely, the same speech he had given scores of times to his school chums at Sidwell Friends where he was number one in his class. Hero worship, Harry sighed. Up to then, he had reveled in the role. Now he had all he could do to hide his feet of clay. Reaching over, Harry mussed his hair.

"Supercilious pedant," he joked.

"That still doesn't answer my question," Terry said, obviously rereading the story for the second or third time. "The story is on page one. I want to know what it means to us."

"To us?" Harry mused. Perspiration had suddenly flooded his back, moistening his shirt. He held out his hands in a gesture of innocence. "Nothing."

"Nothing? Here is our name in it." She held up the third finger of her left hand showing her rings. "And this. Price and all."

"I told them." He meant *her*, this Fox woman. "There was nothing to hide. I paid by check, fifteen hundred dollars. Your engagement ring, the one I never bought you. Nothing sinister in that."

She twisted her lips and shook her head.

"It just looks so awful in print."

"Has the life of a quick wink," Harry said, determined to appear unconcerned. But Harry knew there was genuine cause for alarm. Yet it seemed so very far from this breakfast table, from his family.

"Millie seems to have captured a great deal of space," Terry said with an obvious note of disapproval. Her private resentment of Millie was, as always, obvious. Long ago, he had given up attempts to placate her on this issue.

To him, Millie was his best friend's wife. To Terry, she was the boss's wife, loud, showy and overbearing. There was also no way Harry could stop Millie from being haughty. It was part of her persona. Even Billy had little control over her.

"Only because she bought a great deal from Irving."

"But if he is a spy, how does it reflect on all of us?" Terry asked. Her concern speared directly into his gut. It was a challenge to his role of protector. His cheeks ached with the effort to keep a smile. To make matters worse for him, outside the gray gloom made things seem even more somber and overcast. Malevolent.

"You're being a worrywart," he said gently.

"How will it effect your getting that job in the White House?"

"It won't affect anything," Harry mumbled, hoping that she would not see his lack of conviction. "Especially the White House. That was Irving's turf."

If there was a joke in it, it got no laughs. He had this sudden urge to get up and run, to run as far and fast as he could. It gave him the sense of a waking nightmare in which the more his legs moved the more they resisted movement. It was agony, and he wished he could share it with them.

Terry was silent for a while, rereading the story once again, while Harry forced himself to eat. Beneath the surface, he was seething with anxiety. Who knows where an unguided missile like this might land? He had decided not to call Billy. They'd talk later. Nor did he think it ominous that Billy did not phone him. Call it lying low, he thought. He didn't know how to proceed from here.

"You don't think it will hurt?"

"Mo-o-o-m," Paul said with obvious impatience.

"No," Harry said, controlling himself. "It will not hurt."

"Not Billy?"

"In what way?" he asked. A mistake, since it implied evasion.

"You know what I mean," Terry said with a stern glance at Paul.

"If he decides to go for the presidency?"

"It's a fair question," Terry said smugly.

"Not in the context of this story, Terry. For God's sake, this is like a pinprick on the ass of time." His voice had risen.

Bobbie giggled and ducked behind the Rice Krispies box.

"I just thought I'd ask," Terry said. She had looked up suddenly, studying him and he had turned his eyes away, a gesture that could imply guilt.

Often, he wondered how she perceived his inner life. He was, after all, sparing with his revelations. There were many things he did not share with her. He dissimulated. Could it truly be characterized as lies when he wanted to spare her mental pain and anxiety? Nor did he share with her any of the real machinations of his political life.

It always set her off about Billy. Sure it bothered him sometimes to be seen as the tail of Billy's kite, but he knew that without the kite and the uncanny winds that lifted Billy, he might have been little more than a country lawyer, still under the yoke of his mother's overbearing family.

Bobbie finished her cereal and got up from the table then hurried out of the house pursued by a flurry of cheek pecks and her mother's last-minute cautions. Paul continued to read the *Times*. Harry lingered over coffee. He did not want to appear rushed. But when Bobbie had gone, Terry returned once again to the subject of the story.

"It can't do any of us any good," she said. "We look grasping and materialistic."

"Jesus. Now we have a closet socialist in our midst," Harry said, patting his wife's hand. He felt stupid and patronizing.

"I haven't forgotten where I come from," she said pointedly.

"Ask yourself that next time you go shopping for ball gowns," Harry said, edginess, at last, breaking through the barrier of his resolve.

"I do my duty. You can't expect me to look like a frump. Part of your image, right?"

"Right," he muttered getting up from the table.

But he knew her tenacious nature would not let go of the idea, that she would invest it with ominous proportions, lose sleep, brood, and nag. He wished he could spare her that.

He put on his jacket and raincoat, picked up his briefcase and umbrella, and planted a cold kiss on her cheek. Paul looked up and smiled, and Harry bent over and planted a kiss on his head.

"Off to fight the windmills," he said, lifting the umbrella like a spear. More hypocrisy, he thought. He definitely was not, like Don Quixote, pure of heart. And it troubled him.

***

"In passing," Billy said in response to Harry's question as to whether the story in the morning paper was discussed at that morning's Cabinet meeting.

"What does that mean?"

"It means it wasn't worthy of major discussion. Only that the president said that there was not a single iota of a reason to suspect that Irving Leopold was a spy."

"That means he probably got a CIA report saying that there was nothing presently in their files to suspect Leopold. Then he told us about another harebrained suggestion of Irving's: that he take the gifts he got from foreign governments, remove the stones, replace them with fakes, and turn them out in new settings. The way he imitates Irving's accent is hilarious."

As he said this, Billy didn't crack a smile.

"He also told us about another of Irving's brilliant ideas. When the Soviets were in power, he asked that they send him to Moscow, and he'd sell the Kremlin bosses rings with hidden transmitters. It was all light touch. Not a wrinkle of anxiety. When you think about it, I suppose it is very funny."

"Then why aren't you laughing?" Harry asked.

Billy's response was a barely perceptible shrug. Because what they had done transcended funny. Others would laugh, would split their sides, howl, and sneer.

Despite the light drizzle, they strolled in leisurely fashion through Lafayette Park. Across the street, the White House looked like a glazed wedding cake. Unlike many of the other members of the Cabinet, Billy simply walked across the street from his office in the Treasury Department to attend White House meetings. They walked in silence for a time, Harry occasionally glancing over to see Billy's face, which was as somber as the weather.

"Why all the internal monologue?" Harry asked.

"Millie?"

A nightmare materializing, Harry thought, feeling the tightening down to his scrotum.

"You told her?"

"Are you crazy?"

"Then what?"

"She's consented to an interview with that Fox woman."

"Now that's brilliant," Harry said with short-lived relief.

"I thought about it. May be a good thing. She tends to enhance the human side. Nothing like a little ridicule to spice the stew. Better it comes from her than someone tight-ass and guilt-stricken. You know Millie. Loves the limelight. People do get a kick out of her. She'll be our best weapon. You'll see."

"Are you sure she knows nothing, Billy?"

"Of course, I'm sure," he said testily.

"I don't like it."

"Not to worry. Might put the topper on the whole idea. As she says, you can't help the fact that she comes from a family with money. It was her dough she used for the jewels. She thinks it would be a fun interview, make a splash. After all, she's a woman that also does good works as well. Everyone knows she's not just a lazy housewife."

"Now you're rationalizing," Harry said, understanding the taunt.

"She's been lucky for me, Harry. I think she'll put a whole different spin on it, deflect things from the target."

"I think it's nuts. Why give them something to keep it alive?"

"Because it's going to stay alive until it gets boring. After Millie, everything else will be anticlimactic."

"When is the interview?"

"They're having lunch at the Jockey Club. She likes the setting. She's color-coordinating herself with the restaurant."

"And wearing some of Irving's jewels."

"You got it."

They walked in silence, reaching the statue of a heroic Lafayette on his horse then branching off to one of the spokes of the park. Occasionally, they would pass someone who would recognize Billy, and he would nod and, ever the ingratiatory, force a toothy smile.

"I don't like it," Harry said, hardly a variation on his thoughts and words. "It could backfire."

"She knows how to handle herself," Billy said, defensively now. "If Irving is some kind of a spook, she'll make it sound funny. After all, she doesn't know any secrets." He turned toward Harry. "Not even ours."

The remark was unintentionally chilling. It recalled the problem of the money. Just thinking about all that money lying there, mute and incriminating, made his stomach do flip-flops.

They moved in tandem to the edge of the park. Billy was a head taller and, always, when they walked together, he seemed to set the pace. Crossing the street, they hurried to catch the light then parted at the entrance to the Treasury Department.

"Let's not sweat it, Harry," Billy said, giving Harry a pat on his shoulder. "The wind's blowing our way still." Harry caught the note of bravado.

He stood there and watched him go, projecting that image of strength, confidence, and courage. Where did it come from? Harry wondered. He had asked that question since they were boys.

At that moment, a ray of sunlight speared through fast-breaking clouds but just briefly. Yet even in that fleeting minisecond, it lighted on the head of the departing Billy like the finger of God validating that He was, indeed, watching one of his favorites. Harry smiled. It was the kind of image that had always sustained his hope.

It lasted until he entered the reception room to his office and saw two strange men sitting there. His secretary Mrs. Habersham stood up from behind her desk. She was a short spare woman with graying hair and a tendency to blush during moments of stress, a kind of silent signal. He received its message.

"Agents Halloran and Dolan of the FBI," she said nervously, as Harry extended a hand to each man, hoping the feel of it was crisp and officious. He knew the protocols of his domain and had carefully constructed himself in the image of a tough, no-nonsense executive always on the prowl for smugglers.

At first, he had been reluctant to accept the job, but Billy had persuaded him that it was becoming an increasingly visible position. He hadn't been certain at first.

"It'll make your reputation," Billy had argued. "A good place to stash you while I burrow in." Actually, he had grown to enjoy the job and had developed a good statistical record of drug and high-tech interventions, although he knew that, in the long run, the battle would be futile.

The men followed him into his large office, complete with the obligatory American flag in its stand and the autographed picture of the president and the secretary of the treasury. On his desk was also a picture of a smiling, somewhat younger Terry and the kids.

On the walls were performance plaques and citations and some older awards that he had received back in Omaha. Their presence told every visitor that the man who inhabited this post was a patriot with important friends, a family man, a pillar of the community. He hoped the two men from the FBI would get the message. He also wondered if they could hear the pumping of his heart, which boomed in his own ears.

"Just routine, Mr. Commissioner," one of the men said. Both of them took out notepads. He was tempted to request that he be allowed to tape-record the conversation, but he thought better of it. Make him seem as if he had something to hide.

He had already forgotten which man was which. Nor did he have any interest in distinguishing between them. "This Leopold thing. May be just some media smoke. But we've been ordered to look into it. We're talking to everybody who dealt with the man."

"Perfectly appropriate. I first met the fellow in the president's party during a campaign trip."

Was that smart? he berated himself. Volunteer nothing. Show them a razor-thin profile. Don't appear too ingratiating. It occurred to him suddenly that Billy had said nothing about an FBI investigation. Was it possible that he did not know? Was it possible that the president did not know?

"Did you see much of him?"

"How could you avoid it?"

"Can you remember dates, times, places?"

"That's a tough one. He was never in the office, and I never dealt with him on official business. Therefore, I wouldn't have it in my diary." He disliked the tone he had assumed. Was there a trace of belligerence?

"But you did purchase a ring from him."

"Yes, I did, for Mrs. Silver."

"What kind of a ring?"

"Actually an engagement ring. I never gave her one at the time of our engagement."

"A good diamond?"

"I hope."

"How many carats?"

"I don't quite remember." He was fudging now, getting into darker territory. "I think I have a paper at home."

"You had it appraised?"

"Of course." Suddenly it occurred to him that he was squeaky clean on this issue, and it relieved him somewhat. Fish long enough and you'll catch something, he thought gloomily. "Irving had the best prices for this kind of merchandise. A deal you couldn't refuse." He forced a smile but felt his upper lip stiffen and tremble.

"Had?"

He was confused. Tenses. My God you had to watch tenses.

"I doubt if high government officials will be doing business with him in the future."

"So you've read the stories in the paper?"

"Naturally."

"In your dealings with him was there ever the slightest hint that he was working for some foreign power?"

"Absolutely not. It wouldn't have even crossed my mind. He was a kind of clownish guy who hung around. The jeweler." He decided to press forward, take a more aggressive stance. "Hell, he was the president's and the First Lady's friend. One would assume from that that he was all checked out."

"Did you see Mr. Leopold socially?"

It was the other one asking the questions now. He needed time to think about that. Of course, he had seen Leopold socially. How else was one to see him?

"Would you fellows like coffee?" he asked.

"No thanks." It was the questioner answering for both of them, as if by prearrangement.

"Socially?" the questioner asked. These fellows kept their eye on the ball, he thought.

"Yes, on occasion. I think we were together at a White House dinner. Then one I remember at the house of the secretary of the treasury. Hell, he even came to my house for dinner. Other places as well. I told you. He was everywhere."

"He gave you no cause for suspicion?"

"Suspicion? Of what?"

"You never got the sense that he pumped you for information?"

"About my job?"

"That or anything else."

"You ever meet this guy?"

The men looked at each other.

"No," the questioner said.

"I tell you he was a clown. You wondered what he was doing hanging around in high places."

"But, nevertheless, you bought jewelry from him."

"If it was good enough for the president and the others, it was good enough for me."

They gave the impression that they knew a lot more than they were revealing through their questions. Standard interrogation procedure, Harry thought. Just the same he didn't like it, didn't like the feeling of paranoia or even the need to throw up defenses.

He knew he was a prime perpetrator. Indeed, one might accurately say that he had been a principal factor in causing these events to happen. He wondered if he had said anything to give himself away. Had they seen? Did they suspect? Worse, they had caught him by surprise before he had a chance to dig a deeper moat.

He watched as the men looked at each other in silence, shrugged, closed their notebooks and stood up.

"What do you think?" Harry asked. He wondered if he was being credibly casual. "You think that story had it right?"

"That's why we're here," the first man who had asked the questions said. They put out their hands and Harry shook them in turn.

When they had gone, he realized that, despite his guarded answers, he had given them the evidence of his fear. His palms were wet with sweat.

IX

Millie Tucker wore a bright red dress and turban that matched perfectly the spray of cherry red tea roses that were placed on the table. The costume also set off the exquisite diamond pendant that hung from her neck, the large emerald-cut diamond ring, and the diamond bracelet on her wrist. Elly noted how the diamonds outshone the crystal settings on the table. If she had ever had doubts about the intrinsic beauty and value of diamonds, she had none now.

"They are breathtaking," she said.

"Magnificent," Millie agreed, her bejeweled wrist blazing as she raised a hand to smooth her neck.

Elly could see that it was her favorite gesture. The woman had a smooth gazellelike neck, her best feature, although her brown eyes with the yellow flecks were interesting. She wore her hair in a bang cut, a shade youthful for her age, which was somewhere vaguely in the late-forties. Her skin was lightly freckled, which indicated that her natural hair was lighter than the dark brunette it was now. Crow's feet had begun at the edges of her eyes, but they gave her an athletic look, as if she had spent a good deal of time on sunny tennis courts. Under the clothes, Elly imagined was a tight body, small breasts, flat stomach, tight buttocks.

She had ordered a martini. A good sign, Elly thought. Not wishing to be deliberately nonalcoholic, she ordered a Campari and soda, noting that the beverage's color also went well with the decor. Elly had on a navy blue suit, a white blouse with a large bow, and costume-jewelry earrings. The only authentic jewelry she wore was her thin platinum wedding ring.

"I didn't think you were so pretty," Millie said. "Most journalist types are rather frumpy."

"I thank you for myself and take umbrage for my colleagues," Elly said brightly.

"Taking umbrage. I like that. Haven't heard it much these days."

There was no hint of belligerence. Millie Tucker liked to exhibit herself, no doubt about it. In researching the interview, Elly had checked the paper's files. Millie's media history was a compendium of one-liners and a trademark consistency in dress, particularly headwear, as if it were worn to mask some disfigurement in the scalp area. Elly attributed the contrivance to a need to be, not merely noticed, but memorable.

Millie's history was quintessential preppy. Daughter of a Wall Street broker, generations of money, peer-group schools, handsome, successful husband, a set of female twins in a Swiss boarding school. American-no-need-to-apologize aristocracy, a dark-horse possibility to reside at 1600 Pennsylvania Avenue, since a nice touch of eccentricity was no longer a barrier to such aspirations. Americans wanted entertainers as their first couples, in their news coverage as well. Elly salivated at the rare confluence of these attributes. May not be sinister, Elly thought, but surely fun to read. Her senses drank in the details.

"I really think you'd make a wonderful picture. Would you mind?"

"I have nothing to hide. What you see is what you get. Everybody knows that."

"I've taken the liberty of asking one of our photographers to arrive at about two-fifteen." There was no question in Elly's mind that the woman had come fully prepared for the eventuality and desired it.

"Would you mind if I used my tape recorder?" Elly asked cheerfully, taking out one the size of her palm.

"Now that, I mind. I hate those things."

Her refusal took Elly by surprise. A mistake, she decided. Nevertheless, she flicked the ON button and put it in her purse. She had purchased a very sensitive instrument.

"This *is* an on-the-record interview? Wasn't that our understanding?" she asked politely.

"A conversation, my dear. You're free to write what you choose. But I am paranoid about these high-tech gadgets."

"May I take notes?" Elly asked innocently.

"Don't you think that would be inhibiting? Rely on your memory, dear."

"I just want to be accurate—"

"Don't be silly."

"You don't think my stories have been accurate?" It was obvious to Elly that she was swiftly losing control of the interview.

"That business of Irving being a spy. Pure fantasy."

"How can you be so sure?"

"Scent," Millie said, tapping her left nostril. With her right hand, she lifted the stem of her glass and took a deep sip on her martini. "If he's over there—a big *if*—then, I'd keep an eye peeled, my dear. Watch Madame Hussein's wrists and fingers. But then who sees the wife of these Arab men? Philanders all of them."

"You think he's over there selling them jewelry?"

"Why not? People are people. Observe them in their walled homes where they can let their hair down. Materialists, the lot of them."

"You've been to Baghdad?"

"Yes, as a matter of fact, on a trip two years ago. Lovely warm people."

"Their leaders as well?"

"So that's it," she said. "You can't possibly quote me as saying that Iraqis, in general, are lovely warm people. The leadership is a mess, much too anal."

"Are you a Freudian?"

"Just making fun, my dear."

Elly smiled.

"Did you know Irving Leopold well?" Elly asked, hoping it would redirect the emphasis. Millie chuckled and took another sip of her martini.

"Who really knows people well in this town? You are in people's company. Everyone is guarded. All have some ax or other to grind. You see facades. You know facades well. People become labels, defined by titles, as in the courts of kings. Irving wore two labels, king's jester and jewelry salesman. That defined him. He was good for a laugh and gave excellent prices on exquisite jewelry like this." She fingered the pendant around her neck. "Everything beyond that is pure silliness on your part." Picking up her glass with a ceremonial gesture, she finished her martini.

Elly hid behind a calm smile. Facades, she thought ironically. This woman was performing, loving it, knowing she was making delicious copy, yet cautious in an odd way.

"How do you explain the cash in the briefcase?"

Millie winked.

"Nothing like cash, my dear. My father's dictum."

"You don't think it implies wrongdoing?"

"*Wrongdoing.* What a word," Millie said, laughing. "Shall we order?"

They looked over the menu.

"Everything is wonderful. They have a perfectly divine lobster salad."

"Sounds wonderful."

"And a nice cold bottle of chardonnay."

"Suits me fine."

"One thing I insist upon is that I pay the bill."

"But I invited you," Elly protested.

"My dear girl," Millie said, pausing. It was now apparent that this little pause was a quirk, a contrived timing device when the woman was about to deliver a punch line. "I can well afford it. My husband is secretary of the treasury."

It struck Elly as a much-used line, but she giggled politely.

"It would be on my expense account. Believe me, the paper can also afford it."

"I don't doubt that for a moment." She lowered her voice in a parody of intimacy. "You wouldn't be trying to buy your sources with a mere lunch? I'm far more expensive than that."

She had put on half-glasses to read the menu. Now she took them off, refolded them, and slipped them into her purse. Then she signaled to the waiter who fawned and scraped and took their order. After giving it, Millie looked around the restaurant and nodded to diners at other tables, enjoying her celebrity. Elly was fascinated. The woman was outspoken, on the verge of outrageous, clever and contrived—but not too transparently—and deliberately and authentically amusing.

"We were talking about wrongdoing," Elly said as a reminder of where the official interview had left off.

"Yes. And I called your implications silly."

"But suppose I was right?"

"What does *right* mean?"

"That Irving Leopold was using his access as a cover for spying." Elly hesitated. "Call it intelligence gathering. Collecting psychological profiles of people in the administration, for example.

Picking up bits and pieces of information, then passing them along. Using that premise, one might conclude that the cash was a payoff for services rendered."

"I do think you've seen too many movies," Millie exclaimed. "Considering what Iraq did in our desert war, one might say that, if Irving worked for them, he had gummed things up royally."

"Hussein is still in power."

"It's all so delightfully sinister."

"None of that appeared in my story."

"Now, now. Let's not be coy. It reeked of it. Guilt by innuendo."

"Well, then, why doesn't good old Irving step forward to dispel the lies?"

"He's probably scared to death."

"If he's innocent why should he be?"

Millie raised her chin, showing her long graceful neck. It reminded Elly of a beautiful horse rearing up on its hind legs.

"Because no one is innocent. Not by the standards of you journalists. Everyone is guilty until proven innocent. A kind of reverse constitutional right."

I love that, Elly thought, must use it.

She was finding the rhythm of it finally, flanking the facade. The woman was carefully weaving her image, creating herself as delightfully witty and iconoclastic, wise and provocative and marvelously quotable, working the turf for story opportunities, ways of projection and self-promotion. A "wife of" trying to cut her own swath, a perfectly legitimate Washington aspiration. She wanted to be a media "darling," to share the limelight without having paid any dues beyond sharing, or enduring, her husband's bed and board. She also reveled in titles and glory. This lady wanted, very much indeed, to be the wife of the president of the United States.

The waiter came with the salads and poured a bit of the wine in Millie's glass.

"*C'est bon,*" she said to the effusive delight of the waiter who filled both of their glasses. Elly tasted it.

"Quite right."

"Food and drink is easy. You can always tell the genuine article. Not so in people." She raised her yellow-flecked eyes and studied Elly. "What exactly are you looking for?"

"A link between Leopold and people in power. More than just the jewelry."

"But why?"

"Because it's a positively great story." She paused to wash down a bit of lobster with the wine.

"Irving must be loving it."

"But you said he was not coming forward because you thought he was afraid."

"That doesn't mean he doesn't love the publicity."

"As an end in itself?"

"Maybe that's all there is."

Despite Elly's cynicism, Millie's words did have an air of profundity, delivered effortlessly, like a languid bon mot at some Balzacian soireé. The concept of publicity being "all there is" interested her, but it would not be enough for her story to merely paint a portrait of this most unusual personality. For Charlie, she needed more substance and, from his point of view, was getting nowhere. She needed somehow to force the issue, get Millie to say something, well, "newsworthy."

"What was your husband's relationship with Irving Leopold?"

She could see the sudden flush of resentment on Millie's cheeks, the controlled anger.

"I paid for these jewels with my own money," Millie snapped.

Elly was startled by the intensity of the answer. It also excited her. She wished she had the nerve to tap her nostrils and say "scent."

"I think you've misinterpreted the question," Elly said forcefully, but with an attitude that could still be characterized as respectful.

"It is a transaction that I made with my own money, by check. If you wish, I can show you the canceled checks."

The defensiveness seemed excessive. But she was beginning to understand the subtleties embedded in Millie's attitude. When the spotlight moved out of her orbit, she bucked. She was in this by virtue of her own purchases, and she had been characterized in Elly's story as the wife of the secretary of the treasury, a title that she had, earlier, mocked. Elly enjoyed such psychological speculations. "Forget the face," her father had said. "You need the mind and motivation to get at the truth." She was getting there, she thought. Time to summon cunning.

"Were they really that much a bargain?"

"No question about it. They're appraised at twice the cost, sometimes three times. Even when one accounts for the drop in diamond prices."

"But how could he have done it?" Elly pressed. On this subject, Millie was not at all frivolous.

"He had no overhead," Millie shrugged. "One assumes his markup was small."

"Or that he deliberately kept his prices well below the market to ingratiate himself."

"I can't see the profit in that," Millie said, frowning, looking into her glass as she drank. The waiter, hovering near them, rushed to replace what had been consumed.

"Unless there was a method to his madness."

Elly felt in control now, taking her along the path of her choice.

"Your spy theory?"

"What other reason then?"

"How naive you people are," Millie said, shaking her head, as if rebuking a young child. "No business sense at all. A form of advertising. What better endorsement than having the president of the United States as a satisfied customer?" She stroked her pendant. "Not to mention the others. Maybe these little trinkets were loss leaders."

She was holding her ground. Possibilities were being explored that did not augur well for her story. It was true that Leopold had sold jewelry to other nonpolitical celebrities, but ironically, they were less forthcoming than the politicians who needed to rationalize their purchases for public consumption. Her story using their names made it inescapable. Stonewalling could mean that they had something to hide.

"But he also could have sold his jewelry to entertainment celebrities as loss leaders," Millie continued. "Trumpet them just to sell more to others." For a moment, she must have sensed she confusing herself, going too far afield.

"It's the political people that interest us, Mrs. Tucker," Elly pressed. "He could have been paid by the Iraqis to garner information."

"Well, then, we seem to be getting to the turkey stuffing. His so-called sinister motive was profit, would always be profit, a perfectly respectable American desire, not nearly as sinister as being this master spy you've portrayed him to be."

Elly allowed herself time to mull over Millie's words then she embarked on yet another path.

"But why did he hang out with the power people?"

"Chicken and egg. Publicity and business. The joy of rubbing shoulders with the high and mighty." She stroked the front of her neck again. "I must say you people have tunnel vision."

"All right, he became a kind of mascot. But why?"

"I just told you."

"You've given me your point of view. I'm interested in our friend's, Mr. Leopold's."

"Then you must ask him."

"If I asked your husband, what would he say?"

She was cautious about the delivery, hoping not to strike an irritating chord. Millie lifted her eyebrows and smiled thinly.

"Something as I have, I suppose. He was an amusement, an entertainment, a mascot. My husband was amused by him." She chuckled. "He and Harry Silver would sit for hours listening to his cutesy talk."

"Cutesy talk?" For hours? she thought.

"In his cute little accent. Thick as fleas when the three of them got together." Thick as fleas? There was a brief pause, and Elly acted to fill it, to keep things going.

"You were more interested in the possibility of good buys than his talk?"

"You might say that."

She spoke now between bites of her lobster and sips of wine. But tiny bells were tingling in Elly's brain, each summoning more questions.

"What was his conversation like?"

"Oh, the usual trivia for that type."

"What type?"

She let her fork hang in midair for a moment, then pursed her lips and waved the fork up and down in an attitude of rebuke.

"Naughty. Naughty. I'm not one for discussing other people's predilections. Nor have I any knowledge of Irving's. Out of my area, darling."

A homosexual affair had, of course, been a possibility. That was always good in spy scenarios. The Brits, though, seemed to have cornered the market on gay spies—what were they called? Moles.

So far, her investigation had turned up nothing so racy. Nor had any bitter lover turned up. There wasn't even any conclusive proof that Leopold was gay, other than the stereotype—a middle-aged bachelor who dealt in beautiful things and was slightly effeminate. There were female dates, and she had talked with them. Her conclusion was that Irving Leopold was more of a walker, an escort, a neuter.

"You mentioned Harry Silver. He's the commissioner of customs."

"As everybody knows, Billy's closest friend. They grew up together."

She gave no hint of her own feelings about that relationship. It was merely a stated fact. Nevertheless, the implication, whatever it was, seemed worth pursuing—perhaps not during this interview. She had simply triggered an idea that, even now, was beginning to nag at her.

"Would you say that the president, people in positions like your husband's liked the man?"

"I doubt if they would have him around if they didn't."

"They must have liked his jokes."

"Who knows? He could wear on you after a while. Don't get me wrong. I adored him. But sometimes he could chatter away like a little old lady. Small talk is all right in its place. With Irving it was an endless emission."

"Then why do you think they got such a kick out of his company?"

"Who?"

"Your husband and Harry Silver."

"You'd have to ask them."

The words had been ejaculated without thought, and Elly could see that Millie would have liked to retrieve them. For the first time during the luncheon, Elly detected a brief diminishment of confidence. Millie masked it nicely by putting her fork down and emptying her wine glass, unmistakably her grand finale. Elly had barely touched her food and hadn't had more than a sip of wine.

She pondered the question of what a man like Leopold could learn from the secretary of the treasury and the commissioner of customs. She would have to think about that. Might be a key link. Might be nothing.

"Have I been helpful?" Millie asked when the waiter had cleared their plates. He had quickly returned to pour their coffee. There seemed a marked reticence in her attitude.

"I'm not sure."

"I want you to know that I stand by my original perception."

"And I stand by mine."

"Well, then," Millie said. Again, Elly noted the deliberate pause. "It's what they call a standoff."

It wasn't really that clever, but Elly gave the appropriate smile of admiration. Then she asked the inevitable question.

"Is the secretary going to take a shot at the presidency?"

"He certainly would make a good one," Millie said. Elly could see the gears shifting to deliver the well-rehearsed reply. "He's doing his job for the president. And, Lord knows, there is a great deal to be done on the economic front. It's really too early for any decisions. Let's say he's keeping his options open."

The cliché of the politician hungering for higher office, Elly thought. At that moment, she saw the photographer standing in the vestibule and signaled him to wait for just a few moments. Millie asked the waiter for the check and signed it. Clearly, she was anticipating the photographer.

"Better freshen up," she said, getting up and walking toward the ladies' room. Elly watched her recede, wondering how to put her in context.

Fair game, she decided. Definitely fair game.

X

They had one of those voice-activated answering machines that they used also to send each other messages when one or the other was out of reach of a telephone. Elly had tried Al's office earlier, and was told by his secretary that he was at a meeting outside the office, in the hotel suite of a client. She called the hotel and was told that the client had instructed the operators not to put any calls through.

No good leaving an impersonal message, she decided. Not while the present level of hostilities was at such a high peak. A dinner had been scheduled for that night with an out-of-town client and his wife. Al had asked, and she had consented to be present, fearing that any protest would result in a new conflagration.

But now that the dinner hour was approaching, and she was still nowhere near finishing her story, she decided that there was little choice left to her but to cancel herself out. Too much hanging, too much on her mind, she would make a lousy, disinterested guest.

She dialed their number, waited for their cute joint dialogue, one line for him, one for her, to end then put her message into the machine.

"Al," she said to the machine, "You can't imagine how terrible I feel about this. I tried your office. Then I tried the hotel, and they were holding all calls. Could you, please, see your way clear to go yourself? I'm just up to my neck in problems and anxieties about you-know-what. So give me a break, a reprieve, if you will. I'll make it up. I promise, promise, promise."

She had opted for the cute touch, which fell flat, like telling an off-color joke at a funeral. It was all off-kilter between them, out of sync, off-center. She knew precisely how much it meant to him, to be the good "wife-of" at this dinner with a client and his "wife-of."

"Please, forgive me. Call if you can. I'll be here at the paper." She giggled nervously and added, "At the rate I'm going, probably forever."

She signed off, not knowing quite how to end it, gripped by fear, knowing that his reaction would widen the already yawning gulf between them. Always when she thought that, her mood soon turned from fear to anger, anger that she was feeling fear as well as fear that he would react to his frustration in a terrible way.

But once she had turned back to her computer, she dismissed it from her mind. Again she read over her notes. She had listened to the tape recording of her interview with Millie Tucker three times, a surprisingly clear copy considering where it had been hidden. She had spent most of the afternoon calling around. Neither Commissioner Silver nor Secretary Tucker had called back, although, their respective secretaries had suggested that she talk to the Public Information person of either Customs or Treasury, which she refused to do.

She did, however, manage to get through to a few of the prominent women who sported Leopold's jewels. They were less forthcoming now that her stories had appeared, more cautious. What she was seeking, she told them candidly, was some fix on Leopold's social habits. Who did he talk with mostly, the men or the women? What did he talk about? The women were, admittedly, confused by her questions.

All, Elly knew, carefully weighed the image consequences to their husbands and they themselves then replied with caution.

Yes, he seemed more comfortable with the women. What did they talk about? Gossipy things mostly. Was he like one of the girls? One or two ruffled feathers over that one. But yes, you might say that.

She wondered if it was too trivial a point. It sounded that way, but something compelled her forward. Why, indeed, did the secretary of the treasury and the commissioner of customs spend that much time with Leopold? She searched for that portion of the tape that had particularly jogged her interest, "—would sit for hours listening to his cutesy talk." Then forward to, "—thick as fleas when the three of them were together."

Still there weren't enough hard facts to nudge the story too far in that direction, except for the obvious subliminal suppositions and innuendo that an alert editor might catch. Nevertheless, she mused, remembering how she had obtained the information from Newton Parker.

Around her, the activity of the newsroom slowed as deadline time came and went. Through the glass of Charlie's window, she could see him reading stories on his computer. Yet, she resisted the urge to talk to him. At this hour, he would be irritable, short-tempered, as he found the usual plethora of mistakes and bad-judgment calls.

The enterprise was simply too vast and unwieldy to be properly policed by a single individual, although the staff tried their best to reflect their editor's wishes. He had to be a superman to deal with all those conflicting egos and burning ambitions. Like hers, she thought.

At that point the photographer dropped the pictures he had taken on her desk. There was Millie Tucker in all her publicity-hound magnificence. The camera had caught both the sparkle in her eyes and in the jewels. Lovely, she thought, feeling better.

The newsroom was nearly empty when she finally began to write her story. In her lead, she threw out the bone of credibility to Charlie and the editorial purists.

"The FBI has launched an investigation into the mysterious disappearance of Irving Leopold, whose high-level administration connections gave him access to some of the nation's most important decision makers."

She did a couple of paragraphs of review to jog recall, inserting the usual "the CIA has refused to comment," then launched into the Millie Tucker interview, which she hoped would open the floodgates to the real story, although she wasn't sure what that meant.

Take risks, she urged herself, as she tapped the keyboard keys at a frenzied pace. "Follow your instinct." Her father's words boomed into her consciousness along with "let the chips fall where they may" as she approached what could be, as the late Alfred Hitchcock used to say, the "MacGuffin," the linchpin that held the answer to the puzzle.

Was she too close to it? she wondered. Too panicked by fear of failure? Or challenged? By what? Why? She shrugged aside the avalanche of questions. What she was doing was fishing for the truth and she knew it. In this business, you're in a war, her father had taught. The only decent thing in a war is the right cause.

"Mrs. Tucker, although she found Leopold amusing, seemed somewhat puzzled that her husband and his boyhood friend Harry Silver, the commissioner of customs 'would sit for hours listening to his (Leopold's) cutesy talk.'

Again she listened to the quote on her recorder then went back to the keyboard.

"Mrs. Tucker also observed that they were "thick as fleas when the three of them were together."

The words were embedded in the story, like diamonds in rock, she thought, appreciating the simile. Then she went on to quote some of the women who had told her that Leopold didn't usually engage in "man-talk." The juxtaposition of these comments with the two key quotes from Millie Tucker pressed home the point that what the two men were doing with Leopold, namely being thick as fleas, had the air of conspiracy.

She stopped her typing and looked for a long time into the face of the monitor. She was in no mood to confront moral questions. There was, she knew, a subtle element here that would undoubtedly focus attention on the secretary of the treasury and his commissioner of customs. The question of guilt or innocence, whatever that meant at this point, was not the issue. Above all, the story had to be kept alive, and she needed the hook to do it—and get past her editors.

But the moral question would not stay conveniently and obediently in its place. As her fingers lightly touched the keys, she looked at them, saw them as symbols of power. It was another issue that she was in no mood to confront.

There were priorities of interest here, she told herself. No sense larding her motives with high-sounding idealistic motives. She wasn't going to deny that. Not, as they say, in her heart of hearts. Did she want only the celebrity of achievement, the notoriety and all that its fallout had to offer? Wasn't that what she meant by "her shot?" or was it vindication, revenge? What? Quickly, she aborted that line of thinking.

Her story's present dilemma, she realized, was also caused by the fact that, although it had a mystery man, it did not yet have "a whipping boy." That point was still only tentative and diffuse, although she did have vague targets in her sights, like cardboard cutouts on a pistol range.

There was, despite all her stylistic efforts, still no central focus. In rereading what she had done, she decided to change the juxtaposition. She put the woman's quotes in front of Millie's two controversial statements. The setup was more natural, flowed better, did not look contrived.

She sat back in her chair and reread the story. Then, for the first time since she had begun, she looked at the clock. She was shocked to find that it was nearly midnight.

Dialing her home, she waited as the ring began at the other end. Midnight would be late for Al, even with clients. Everyone in his orbit knew that he chose to keep regular hours. When he did not answer, she spoke the code that activated the messages. His voice came over the wires, hoarse and muffled.

"I don't think I can handle this, Elly," it began. The words seemed tentative. In the background she thought she heard music. "I don't quite know how to put it without sounding, well, maudlin." He cleared his throat. "I may be a little tipsy. I do love you. I respect you. I understand your compulsion. I really do. I'm not jealous of your work or your success. And I know you're not jealous of mine. But, Christ, Elly, there is more to marriage than work and ambition. You know what I mean? I can see us drifting into infinity, just the way we are postponing—always postponing. Can't you hear my heart crying out? I want my wife. The way we are is, well, not what we intended. Sure you might think that I merely want to replicate the way it was with my mom and dad.

You know, all the old-fashioned marriage things. So what the hell is wrong with that? Why, in the name of God, can't you do both? Others can." There was a long pause. "I feel trapped, Elly. A little lost. I want to go home, but I'm afraid you're not going to be there. God, I know I sound awful. Silly. Sitting here in this stupid bar talking to a damned machine, because I don't want to go home, and I don't want to call you at the office and be told that you're too involved, or too busy or too whatever. Now I'm getting there. Self-pity. You know how I hate that. So, I'll just sign off now." There was another long pause, an odd noise, perhaps a sob, then, "Over and out."

Her throat was dry, as if she had listened without breathing. She felt his anguish, his pain, his loneliness. Although, in one form or another she had heard similar words, their pleading tone coming out of the impersonal machine seemed pathetic and demeaning.

By the time, she had gathered her things and left the office, she was wading through a sea of ambivalence, not sure whether to be sympathetic or angry.

When she got home, the house was empty, which was worrisome. It was nearly one by then. Feeling drained, she took a long hot bubble bath and listened for his footsteps.

She lingered over an elaborate before-bed ritual of removing her makeup, smearing moisturizers on her face just to stretch the time. By two, panic began to set in, and her imagination began to assume a variety horrors. Beneath the concern, she could feel the undercurrent of anger, a kind of constant rage, as if her emotions were warring with different factions. How dare he trigger her guilt? How dare he make her worry? How dare he make her feel as if her work was less important than his?

She got into bed, but it was quickly apparent that she could not sleep. Anger stayed with her. Panic verged on hysteria. Guilt again intruded. All right, she begged herself, perhaps it is time to hold yourself up to judgment.

From the very beginning of their relationship, she was a committed journalist or an about-to-be committed journalist. She had just taken a job with Journal Newspapers, a chain of suburban papers in the Washington area, and he was a senior at Georgetown Law School. So there, she thought, considering this kernel of memory absolute proof of the integrity of their callings.

There had never been subterfuge or obfuscation. Even in her mind, the words seemed pompous and important. He knew the parameters, she told herself, confirming the righteousness of her cause. And she had never totally rejected the idea of having children. Not irrevocably. Mostly, she resented the guilt.

For a moment, her sense of logic had strayed, and she forced herself back on her original track. So he was more organized than she was, more disciplined, more skilled in the allocation of personal time. Even when he wo rked as a lawyer for the Justice Department, he had never squandered time.

He had the habits of a monk, of which he was proud. Up at six. In the office by seven, he was home never later than seven. On the other hand, her management of time was more diffuse. She blamed it on her work, which was partly true, since legwork and writing were less prone to regulation. Whatever time it takes was the watchword of journalism, just as long as the deadlines were met.

At the beginning, she was certain he understood this. It was never a matter of contention between them. Nor were there conflicts in the management of their household. Whoever got home first cooked the dinner. And they ate out a good deal. It was a policy that carried them through a series of small apartments to the big one that they now owned on Connecticut Avenue. They made enough money between them to easily afford domestic help. A maid did the nitty-gritty that neither of them wished to do. She came in three times a week.

Yet, somehow, they even had managed to synchronize their metabolic clocks. She had learned to be an early riser. Often they stole a few moments in bed for a morning "quickie." No conflict in that department. Never was. It was, she decided, given his obsession with the matter of time, the root of the problem.

He was obsessed with the idea of time running out on them, of missed opportunities for the type of life he yearned for, the role he saw for himself, the bourgeois paterfamilias. Benign wise father, devoted husband home from a day in the office, meal on the table, children scrubbed and ready to recount their day's joys and sorrows—"The Poppa."

She did not snicker at the image. Her own father was exactly in that mold. He was worshipped at home by her mother, son and daughter, especially daughter whose highlight of the day came when he would come home from his ink-stained world, briefly safe from the agonies of running a small weekly paper, recounting his struggle against the "powers-that-be."

She would listen wide-eyed and mesmerized by his sweet stentorian voice, so musical and wise in her mind's eye. Back in the mists of memory, at the very beginning of her consciousness, she had yearned to follow in this sainted man's footsteps, to take up the relay stick and run heroically into the jungle night.

Only the dream lasted; the man did not make it into her adulthood. When she was still a teenager, he lost the paper, lost his spirit then lost his life, wilting away. He died in his sleep before he was forty-five, of a heart attack, the doctors said. But she knew better. Surrender and despair had summoned the grim reaper to move up the deadline.

If only Al had known him, he would surely understand the real priorities of her life. If he had sat there at their dinner table night after night and learned what it meant to be the guardian of truth, fairness, and decency. Suddenly her whirling thoughts froze. She heard clumsy groping, a key turn in a lock, unsteady footsteps.

All anxieties gave way to relief. Only the anger endured, as it had all night, just beneath the surface. She heard him stumble forward then move unsteadily through the house. Feigning sleep, she watched him lurch through the bedroom to the bathroom. He vomited, making loud retching sounds. Serves you right, she told herself, resisting the urge to get out of bed to comfort him.

In a perverse way, his physical suffering seemed a vindication of her position. It was the kind of idea that made courage possible. He would just have to adjust to her requirements and, more specifically to this present situation. After all, he, too, would reap the benefits of her success. She felt her anger dissipate.

From the bathroom came the sound of a shower. She listened for a while, satisfied that he was fine, then slipped into a deep sleep.

XI

To avoid a scene, she left the house before Al was awake. Later she amended the reason. She wanted to be in the newsroom to field any questions about her story as it made its way up the editorial ladder. Charlie had ordered her immediate editors to give him the last look before the story continued on its journey to publication.

Nevertheless, she had, over coffee, prepared this long speech for Al, an exposition of her position. Her mind was cooler now. Her anger spent.

She truly understood his anguish, and she would beg for his patience. She would promise. No. He had heard those before. But now she had this sense of immediacy on her side, this tiger by the tail. She could not possibly let go. Not now. Give me running room, she would beg him, for the moment.

At the beginning she did harbor vague ideas that marriage would one day demand a commitment to the concept of children, parenting, nurturing, family. But the conviction, in retrospect, was never more than lukewarm. Was it? Where was the sin in not craving children? Why must she conform to what others saw as a biological imperative? Not that she had anything against children. She simply wasn't ready to bear such burdens. Not yet. Indeed, she might never be ready. To Al, such a position would be heresy, serious enough for deep speculation about the future of their marriage, despite all protestations of love to the contrary.

Why should such matters be an intrusion on her career? Was it so unnatural not to wish to propagate the species? There were plenty of other women to do that job. Did such a view make her mean-spirited and unsavory, niggardly? Was she an aberration? Born without a maternal instinct?

She wondered if she should dislike herself for thinking such thoughts. No, she decided, she had every right to debate the issue with herself, force herself to consider the pros and the cons. And if this maternal instinct suddenly materialized in her psyche and manifested itself in a craving emanating from deep within her tissues, she would know. Definitely then—she would know.

Once in the newsroom, these ruminations ceased. Well, not quite. But they could be neatly stuffed into a mental drawer, even locked up for a time. Here, she felt more alive, more significant, the matters she dealt with more compelling.

At her desk, she called up her story on the computer. She made some minor adjustments, felt reasonably pleased, quite proud, actually. The problem was what to do for an encore. What she needed now was "fallout," some hitherto unknown source that, for very private and mysterious reasons, would step forward with the elixir that would prolong the story's life.

She did not dismiss the possibility of reaction, particularly from the treasury secretary or the commissioner of customs, who were the real victims of Millie Tucker's indiscreet remarks. of course, a man like William Tucker was an old hand at dealing with the press. Surely, he knew that a reaction would just make things worse. Do exactly as she wanted, keep the story alive.

No matter, she told herself with resolve: "Where there's a will, there's a way."

But when Charlie Carruthers called her into his office at midmorning, and she saw Harlan Evans, the *Post*'s chief counsel and current scourge of the editorial department, sitting on his couch, her "way" seemed suddenly difficult.

"He thinks we got a hot potato on our hands," Charlie said. She scrutinized him, seeking some clue to his position, but couldn't find any.

"This business of these quotes and their juxtaposition. It's not a particularly good climate for innuendo."

"It's her quote," Elly snapped.

"I'm not saying it's not," Evans said. He was a large, formidable man, with a round pink face that reached far up over his forehead, almost to his crown where it culminated in a curly fringe of gray hair. When he frowned, pink wrinkles reached all the way to the fringe.

"Then what are you saying?"

She looked toward Charlie, whose expression was still noncommittal. *So he's letting me fight my own battles. They've lost their cojones,* she thought maliciously, realizing suddenly how really big a stake she had in the story.

"The entire story smacks of supposition," Evans said. For the first time, she saw a spark of pugnaciousness in Charlie's eyes. "You simply don't understand what's happening out there in the libel and slander arena. Our plate is full up to here."

He made a cutting motion with his hand across his neck, oblivious to the mixed metaphor. She and Charlie exchanged a thin smile. "Never once have you said who saw—exactly who saw this Leopold fellow board an Iraqi ship?"

So they had been reading her upstairs, in the hallowed precincts of power. She was flattered, which only increased her will to fight.

"I did. I saw him myself."

"Then you should have said so."

"Why? I was absolutely sure of the source."

"I think our readers were entitled to that fact."

She turned toward Charlie.

"Why is he complaining now?"

"Different world out there," Charlie shrugged.

"It's a natural—" Elly began.

"Could be a natural disaster," Evans said blandly, offering a broad smile. "You can't just manufacture these scandals."

She could see Charlie's face redden. About time, she decided. But he merely shrugged as if to say "Out of my hands. They're scared shitless upstairs."

"I'm not manufacturing anything."

"You could have at least got Secretary Tucker to comment. Or, at the least, Commissioner Silver."

"I tried to. They wouldn't even answer my calls."

"But can't you see, that the way it's written, it's a kind of guilt by offhand comment, a bit of sophisticated gossip."

"He's got a point," Charley sighed.

Was he cutting her loose?

"But you see," she said, making a gargantuan effort to remain calm. "The wagons have circled. Here is a man who literally has had access to the highest people in the administration. Why? Because he sells them jewelry wholesale. It defies imagination. If he is a spy, the cover is wonderful, absolutely bizarre. Readers love that."

"It is one helluva story," Charlie said.

"I don't want to comment on the editorial merits, only on the legal implications."

"You think someone will sue. The Tuckers? Or Silver, for example?"

"Anybody can sue."

"But he's a public figure."

"That criterion may be falling apart. Recent Supreme Court decisions are swinging toward deliberate malice as a test."

"Deliberate malice?" Her voice rose. "Are you suggesting—"

"Easy, lady," Charlie murmured.

Again, she forced herself under control, throwing Evans a look of rabid contempt.

"You mean we can't say anything detrimental about a public figure?"

"I didn't say that. It's a judgment call in this case, that's all I'm saying," Harlan Evans said smoothly. "And I'm basing my judgment on the way in which the story is written. It just leaves a bad impression on a purist like me. The bedrock legal basis for all libel suits is simply this: Is it fair? What was the writer's intent?"

"There it is again. You're saying that I'm deliberately maligning these men."

"Not for me to say," he said after a long pause. Then he looked at Charlie, who shrugged.

"The foxes have taken over the chicken coop," he said, but with an air of resignation. "Lawyers and cost accountants." His expression was one of unmitigated disgust. "Sheet," he said with a genuine country-boy inflection.

"Come on, Charlie," Evans said. "All this world-weary cynicism smacks of self-righteousness. You know what we're up against. Even when we're right these days, people file lawsuits. Our libel insurance premium has gone through the roof and hardly covers our exposure."

"You know what I think, Harlan," Charlie said. Evans, who obviously had been through these discussions before, seemed totally prepared for whatever was coming next. "I think you're in the wrong business. We're first and foremost a newspaper."

Evans raised his hand.

"I know—guardians of the truth."

"Bet your bippy."

"It's not a club to swing out indiscriminately, hoping the swing will catch someone in the guts," Harlan said. "I quite agree with your concept of guardian of the truth. That's the whole point of this exercise. Truth comes in lots of different shades."

"Your shade and mine," Charlie said.

"And mine," Elly said.

Charlie turned to her.

"We'll get to you in a minute," Charlie snapped.

"It's the usual dynamic tension between the strictly legal and the strictly editorial," Harlan explained, confusing her, as if this altercation was being staged for her benefit. Were these people in cahoots, Elly wondered? Or just scared, protecting their asses?

She looked at Charlie Carruthers and wondered. Had he, indeed, lost his *cojones*? A wave of sadness washed over her. Charlie had been the inspiration for a whole generation of reporters like her, who defined their profession as the only shield between good and evil left in the universe. If not us, who will hold the line against the greedy, the power hungry, the manipulators? Was it heroic music she heard in the background of her thoughts?

"What I'm saying is that we've got to be more responsible. The Watergate era is dead. It's not a free-for-all anymore. People are watching," Evans said.

"Just whose side are you on?" Charlie asked, but it seemed a mild remonstrance.

"I'm on the side of good business. And it's definitely not good business to operate this business just to break heads. We've just got to think before we leap."

Elly was getting another side of the picture, and it shocked her. Men like Evans and their ilk with their smug conservatism had always been the enemy. She imagined how he must have fumed inside from the ragging he was sure to be getting at the country club or by his friends in the hallowed private watering holes of the capital. "Goddamned media! And your paper is the worst. Always tearing people down. That's not American."

"I can back up every fact in my story," Elly said.

"Suppose she comes back at you and says your quote is inaccurate?"

"I'll shove the tape down her throat."

"You got permission to tape?"

"Did I need it?"

"It's an issue I would not want to put before a jury. Taping without permission could be a problem. Remember, in a libel suit the issue is always fairness. And intent counts."

"My word against hers."

"And the truth is?"

Elly folded her hands tightly. She looked first at Charley, then at Evans. How dare he, she thought, her mind running toward an old memory. Her father, sick and dying, broke—everything lost—shaking his fist, ranting, fulminating against the "tree swingers," the half-men, half-whatever, swinging by their ugly tails from tree to tree, dropping turds on everyone's head. Not monkeys. Not apes. In his mind, they were too good for that. These were the enemy, an aberration, a distortion of humankind, who existed to wreak havoc, destroy goodness, perpetuate evil, repress and rule. And when he rises, she thought, I'll see his tail and then I'll know.

"She didn't give her permission," Elly snapped.

"Now think about that. How does that make us look?"

"It's proof she said it."

"If there is ever a jury trial, they'll look at the tactic, not necessarily the words."

Elly shook her head, frustrated.

"I don't think I like any of this," Charlie muttered. Then addressing Evans. "What is it you would like me to do?"

"I'm not the editor, just the chief counsel. If I were editor, I'd take out the references to Tucker and Silver. Just as a precaution."

"He wants me to toe the line," Charles said to her. "It's called winning by intimidation. If we get sued, he's on record as opposing it," Charlie said. His vehemence under the calm surprised her.

Evans stood up. She craned her neck, looking for the tail, watching his back as it receded through the newsroom, dead certain that he had it wrapped around his middle, just waiting to twitch free at the first available opportunity.

"Bastard," Charlie said when he had gone. He seemed to unwind. Now he looked out of the window and tapped the desk nervously. The flush that had begun left little cherry-red circles on his cheeks and a snarl on his lips.

"Has he got that much clout?" she asked.

"For the moment. He's one of the bottom-line boys. Got the ear of the owners. Sometimes they like to play people against each other. Son of a bitch would like me deep-sixed. But he hasn't got the power. Not yet." He suddenly banged his fist on his desk. "I've still got some lead left in the old pencil."

She saw both the bravado and the impotence, and it saddened her. Once his power on the paper seemed absolute. Now it was being watered down. She wondered which way he would go on her story.

"I say screw 'em," she said, testing the waters. "They're not journalists."

"Tell me," he sighed.

"Let them try to run the show without you."

He turned to look at her.

"Sad thing is that we're all expendable. In the end, we all lose."

"That's pretty defeatist," she said, scrutinizing his reaction.

"He's right about one thing. *Times* they are a-changing."

"The more things change, the more they remain the same."

"That's a load of crap," he said, raising his voice. She wasn't sure how to proceed now. She needed an answer.

"So do we run the story as is, or knuckle under?"

She held her breath, knowing that she had loaded the question, caught him at his lowest ebb.

"Fuck 'em," he snapped. "We go." Then he added. "Let the chips fall where they may."

She wanted to spring up and kiss him on both cheeks. But she held back. He might take it as too womanly.

XII

Terry had kept him up all night. The tranquilizers nauseated her, and she had to get up numerous times to vomit. The pain in her wrist grew worse ,and when she did doze off invariably woke in a cold sweat, shaking and hysterical. When he tried to hold her in a comforting embrace, she shook him away.

Sometime toward dawn, she finally quieted down from exhaustion, but, by then, it was impossible for him to sleep. He lay in the bed, looking at the ceiling, his thoughts vague and jumbled. By sunrise, he found himself mentally chewing at a single question: How could they have possible gotten involved in such a ridiculous and threatening situation?

He dressed quietly. Outside, a heavy windswept rain was beating against the landscape. Wearing hat, raincoat, rubbers, and equipped with an umbrella, he drove to the park, waiting in the car until Billy's figure came into view. He was wearing a kind of transparent parka over his jogging clothes, cutting through the rain head down, stopping in the middle of the field. Harry got out of the car, opened the umbrella, and sloshed through the puddled grass.

"Don't you think we're carrying paranoia too far?" Harry asked as he faced Billy, his eyebrows covered with droplets and water running down the deep ruts in his face like streams noodling down a mountain.

"Better cautious than caught," Billy said. Pouches shivered under his eyes and his normal ruddy color seemed ashen, unhealthy.

"Two assholes standing in the rain," Harry muttered.

He must have felt Harry's scrutiny, speaking to deflect it.

"You look like hell," Billy said.

"You're looking into a mirror."

Billy looked down at his wet Nikes, glistening and muddy. His left foot kicked a puddle.

"Lousy time for a Cabinet meeting this morning. More jokes from the president."

"He joked last time," Harry said. "Then came the FBI."

"Nero fiddles while Rome burns," Billy mocked.

"Rome's not burning. But we might be."

"That's a very unhealthy thought."

"So what's the report from damage control?" Harry asked. A vague painful pumping began at the side of his head.

"She just went up to the spare room. That's all I know. I did call my assistant and told him to make absolutely no comment. None."

"Billy, does she know anything?"

"I promise you, nothing." With a wet plastic sleeve, he wiped moisture from his nose. "Listen, I can't control what she says. You know Millie. She sees herself as the voice of irreverence in a sea of tight asses. The public loves her. You see the hand she gets when she attends a public function. Hell, it may not be as serious as you think."

"Just good ole Millie sounding off."

"Something like that."

"The sun comes out tomorrow." He lifted his face to the rain.

"So I notice."

"I had time to think about it."

"So have I," Harry said. "And I'd say that they're going to start crawling all over us. We've become grist for the mill."

"So we just stand pat. No one ever loses in this town who just stands pat."

"Where do you get these dumdum versions of Washington historical lore?"

Billy shrugged.

"Would you rather I whistle?"

Harry watched the raindrops drip down Billy's plastic coating.

"What she's doing is stirring up hot ashes, a mess of them. Some of them are bound to burst into flame."

"Harry, I love your metaphors."

"If we don't say anything, they'll write around us. That Fox woman is not done with it. She's got the Pulitzer bug, thinks she's got something that will blow the administration apart."

"But she's got no real facts to work with."

"She's got better than facts. She's got entertainment. People love this shit. Conspiracy in high places, mysterious acquisitions of jewels, greed and decadence, irreverence and cynicism. Think of the book and movie rights. It's not going to stop now, Billy."

"Maybe we should fight back then?"

"Like how?"

"Put out a statement, hard-hitting. Accuse the writer, the paper of distortion, yellow journalism, unfair treatment of public officials. Maybe ask for a public apology. Threaten a libel suit. Something. Anything."

Such a tactic had occurred to Harry, but he had rejected it for traditional reasons. The press thrives on controversy, baiting the establishment. They attack. You defend. Parry and thrust. It becomes a fight between gladiators. A spectacle. Entertainment. Unfortunately, it's the press—not the individual—that sells the tickets. He had learned a lot about dealing with the press as commissioner of customs.

"I suppose it's an option. I think we've got to see where it goes."

"If it goes?"

"Don't hold your breath, Billy. Better just brace yourself and hope that someone doesn't step out from left field."

"Like who?"

"The South Africans, for one thing."

"They're not crazy. Besides, Leopold assured us that they did not know who was being fed the proceeds from those diamonds."

"That's his story."

"Or that smug Italian, the esteemed ambassador. The man that validated your ability to walk on water."

"He's not going to blow his career out of the water. Not now. He's less than a year from retirement."

"Or any of the people that Irving dealt with to recycle the diamonds, get cash for them. Probably some of those hot diamonds are in settings sold to people like us. Maybe even the president's wife. Or Millie." Or himself, he thought, bitterly.

What had once seemed airtight, now appeared leaking from stem to stern. "People talk. No matter why, they talk. And there are also the lesser lights, bystanders, people bribed to act, look the other way. Don't forget, these people are out there and the more the story unfolds, the more nervous they'll be getting. Like us, for starters."

"You ready to confess, Harry?"

The remark had the impact of a glancing blow. Surely, Billy could not put such a low premium on Harry's trust. He let it pass. People say things out of fear they really don't mean.

As if to confirm the truism, Billy said: "Now that's worthy of an apology. I don't know what the hell got into me. So I apologize, Harry. You've been one helluva friend all these years, one helluva friend." He punched Harry lightly on the upper arm.

"Or Irving," Harry said suddenly, conscious of a touch of

malice in the remark. Billy searched his face, puzzled.

"Irving?"

"He called, Billy. Last night. Called three times, as a matter of fact. He left no number, thank God. I don't know where the hell he is. Besides, I had my hands full with other problems. Terry cracked her wrist. We had to go to the emergency room at Holy Cross. Paul took the calls, recognized the accent, said he sounded upset. Can't imagine why."

"Trouble is like rain. When it comes, it comes in buckets."

"Now that's profound," he snapped, looking across the rain-swept field. What could be more conspicuous than two people standing in the rain?

"What do you think he wanted?" Billy asked.

More speculations, Harry thought, wet and weary and miserable and disgusted with this whole process of evasion.

"I've lots of ideas. All ominous."

"Damn," Billy said. The curse seemed all-inclusive. A gust of wind swept across the field carrying fistfuls of raindrops. Harry felt moisture seeping through the bottoms of his trousers.

"Let's get into the car. This is crazy," Harry said, meaning everything.

"Why look for trouble? Better to be wet than bugged." His glistening features suddenly rearranged themselves into a mosaic of curiosity. "You didn't tell Terry?"

"Oh, sure," Harry replied.

Billy scrutinized Harry's face, squinting through the curtain of rain.

"You think he wants to tell all?" Billy asked.

"Listen. Look at it from his point of view. He's at sixes and eights, on the run. He reads these stories. Don't think they aren't in Europe. He gets scared. He's accused of being a Goddamned spy. He's not stupid. There's an international search on, maybe Interpol, intelligence agencies of other governments. The South Africans, too."

"Oh, shit."

"To them, he's a liability. Maybe all of us."

These were new ideas that had just jumped into his head. He felt his limbs shake with fear and cold. He noted, too, that Billy's lips had begun to tremble.

"Now there's an idea that got away," Billy said.

"Just a scenario," Harry said. "Never trouble trouble until trouble troubles you."

"It's troubling me."

"You're the guy wanted to be president." Foul, Harry cried to himself. They were in it together. No denying that. Contrition came quickly, demanding a response. "I'm in it for myself, too, Billy."

Worst thing is for thieves to fall out, Harry thought suddenly. He capped an urge to giggle, wondering if it was the beginning of hysteria. Unfortunately, experience hadn't given him a map for these road conditions.

"You think we should pull the money?"

"I think I better."

He noted his own use of the first person singular. It had been Billy's idea. To put the money in safe-deposit boxes along the Amtrak line. Harry had done so under assumed names. But that did not foreclose on anyone recognizing his face.

"What will you do with it?"

The idea of burying it in his backyard had lost its allure.

"I'm not sure."

"Maybe we should wait. See what kind of reaction we get from today's story. Maybe—"

"We haven't a choice, I'm afraid."

"Could blow right over," Billy said. His lips seemed to be turning blue. "Hell, a hot story could knock it right off the front pages."

"As if an atomic bomb dropped on Baghdad?"

"Something like that."

"Billy. You know what I'm discovering? Trouble like this accelerates the disappearance of the brain cells. You lose all perspective, all proportion. We're not just two assholes standing in the rain, but two panicked, scared shitless, helpless, dumb assholes standing in the rain."

***

Harry's office was bedlam. He had forgotten that today was the start date of the new sweep of incoming plane traffic, which would surely raise the hackles of members of Congress and senators who would quickly begin to receive outraged calls from their constituents. In addition, businessmen, plagued by delays in getting various goods in and out of the country would also be raising hell.

The operation had been in the planning stages for nearly six months and had the blessings of the secretary and the president. All part of the administration's "get tough" policy, designed to show violators that America had to protect the integrity of its borders.

Everyone knew, of course, that it was strictly cosmetic, a shell game really. It was impossible to make a dent in the drug trade or prevent foreign dumping violations. But it made the administration look good and balanced off the network bad news with a touch of soft soap.

That was the public reason. The private reason was that Harry needed some favorable public exposure to grease his way into the White House staff. Billy, as always, was foursquare behind the maneuver, and it was he who had lobbied for and obtained the president's blessings.

The strategy, as outlined by Customs' young hotshot public affairs officer, Bob White, was for Harry to get "out front," make himself available for interviews for the press and electronic media.

His office had also prepared radio and television spots in which Harry explained what the Customs Office was doing and why. They ended with a burst of patriotic music and a close-up of the flag waving in the breeze against a gorgeous blue sky. There was no way to abort the effort. All the wheels were, at that very moment, in motion.

Very wet and depressed, trying desperately to wear a facade of authority, Harry, unfortunately, had to run the gauntlet of his prim middle-aged secretary and the very obviously uptight Bob White. The latter followed him into his office.

"No privacy left to a public servant," he muttered stripping off his raincoat, rubbers, and hat and wiping his face with a towel from the adjoining bathroom. A tuxedo hung behind the bathroom door. He debated changing his wet trousers to his tuxedo pants, but decided that he felt foolish enough without exposing himself to that incongruity.

His secretary, Mrs. Habersham, tension blushes mantling her cheeks, brought him a steaming cup of coffee, a gesture that put him on his guard. One of the caveats of her employment was never, ever, to provide him with coffee. That chore was always left to one of the more lowly clerks. This was, therefore, a special gesture.

"You saw the paper?" he said, sipping, bravely enduring a burnt tongue.

Mrs. Habersham and Bob White exchanged glances then nodded. Harry suspected what was going through their minds, and it prompted a sudden upsurge of philosophical musing. All bureaucrats worried about the general well-being of the superior who controlled their fate.

The nature of the apparatus required them to serve, satisfy, placate and generally brown-nose this person. If they had done their work well, and the recipient of all this ingratiation was in trouble then they, too, were either an endangered species or had little to look forward to except beginning the cycle of ass kissing all over again when a new person took over. All this, of course, had little to do with the specific mission of their employment.

Essentially, the highest priority of their job was to make their superior look good to his superiors. His job was to make his superiors look good to theirs. And so on into the stratosphere of the pecking order. If one person in the line faltered, there was an accordion effect and someone on the line got crushed between the creases.

"Only Millie Tucker shooting off her mouth," Bob White said, lowering his voice to stress the confidentiality of the remark, which signified that he felt secure in having his boss's confidence.

"You know the media rats," Mrs. Habersham said. She had strong opinions, especially when they appeared to be shared by her boss. Actually, Harry's feelings about the media were not as vitriolic as others, Billy Tucker, for example. But Mrs. Habersham assumed that, with the appearance of the Fox article, Harry's antagonism level had been significantly upgraded.

"In my opinion, it shouldn't make a particle of difference to our program," Bob White said. He wore a pinstriped suit, white shirt, and polka-dot bow tie, and although he was twenty-eight, he looked fourteen and spoke with a high-pitched prepubescent voice. The current sweep with its accompanying media campaign was, Harry knew, about to be the highlight of Bob White's exit résumé.

"And what do I say when the reporters ask me about Irving Leopold?" Harry asked.

"Just tell them the truth."

Harry could barely hold his features steady and prevent himself from laughing out loud.

"Which is?"

Bob White seemed startled by the comment.

"Well, surely you're not a spy, Commissioner." Harry noted that Bob White's comment was a bit tentative.

"I wouldn't say one word," Mrs. Habersham said. "Stupid media people love these conspiracy theories."

"It will all be forgotten in a day or two," Bob White said. Despite his youth, Harry thought, he had mastered the art of telling superiors what they wanted to hear.

"From your mouth to God's ears," Harry sighed.

"All right then, let's ignore it," Bob White said, offering an ingratiating smile. He was holding a file, which he placed on Harry's desk. "I've got a super program arranged, a press-conference launch. The spots start tonight all over the country. Coverage has got to be fabulous, especially when the jam-ups begin."

"Reports are starting to trickle in," Mrs. Habersham said.

"It's going to be real exciting."

"And the press conference?"

"*Today* at two. Just in time to make the network news."

"Thanks. All I'll get is questions about Irving Leopold," Harry sighed.

"That's a given," Bob White said. How quickly these idiots become experts, Harry thought. "Frankly, Commissioner, I think you're taking this Leopold stuff too seriously. He was only a silly little jeweler. Nobody could possibly believe that stuff about his being a spy, even Mrs. Tucker in her story pooh-poohed that. So the FBI is investigating the matter. Indeed, they should. I don't know anything about this Mr. Leopold, but it really is ludicrous. Nobody of any intelligence will give it credence. You'll see—it will seem ridiculous in a day or two."

The young flack had picked up a logical line of reasoning. Maybe Harry was too close to the situation to analyze it clearly. Certainly, Billy hadn't been much help. Actually, he was feeling better. The coffee had warmed him, and his trousers were beginning to dry. A bad night for both of them had brought on an attack of paranoia. His earlier resolution to pick up the money that morning now seemed precipitous.

"And if we cancel the press conference, it would seem as if you've got something to hide," Bob White said.

Supercilious son of a bitch has a point, Harry thought. He wondered if he should bounce it against Billy. He rejected that. Above all, they still had their jobs to do. This Leopold thing had a paralyzing effect on their reason. Maybe this press conference was a good thing, an opportunity to ridicule the reporter's implications. Put it in an entirely different context. More important, his words might give Irving the courage to keep his cool. Irving was the pressing problem, a panicked Irving, spilling his guts. Yes, he felt better.

"Okay then," Harry said. "Keep all systems on go."

"Very wise," Bob White said with relief.

"Absolutely the right thing," Mrs. Habersham said.

We'll see how it plays, Harry thought when they had gone. Still turning it over in his mind, he thought of the money, the tangible evidence. Could always pick it up tomorrow. Or leave it where it was. Or what?

Where in hell could one stash ten million dollars in fifties and hundreds? He began to sweat, which reminded him of his wet trousers. Thinking about the money was melting his sudden burst of optimism.

He suddenly wasn't feeling so good about the press conference anymore and was annoyed at his swift vacillation and uncertainty. He reached out for the phone and started to punch in Bob White's extension. Instead, he called his home. He was surprised to hear Paul's voice.

"Why are you home, son?"

"It's Mom. She feels rotten. And she can't stop crying."

"Crying?"

"She's acting funny. I was afraid to leave her."

"Why didn't you call me earlier?"

"I wanted to. But she didn't want to worry you."

"Let me talk to her."

There was a long silence. He heard movement, footsteps, muffled voices. Paul's voice came on the phone again.

"She says she's fine. She's resting." From his tone, he seemed tentative, acting in a way, for him that was against the grain.

"You're not going to school?"

"It's all right, Dad. I can get my assignments."

"And Bobbie?"

"She's in school."

"Are you sure now that you can handle things? I'll try to get home early."

"We're okay, Dad."

Hope so, he thought, without conviction. He wished this whole matter would disappear. All optimism was draining away. New worries were deepening the old. He knew Paul, an avid follower of current events, had read the morning paper. But it was not the time to discuss the matter, certainly not on the phone.

"Will you tell Mom something for me, Paul?"

"Sure, Dad."

"Tell her that everything is fine. There is no cause for concern. None at all." He spoke slowly, with emphasis, as if he were dictating a dispatch from a war zone.

"Really, Dad?"

The comment troubled him, but he ignored it.

"Absolutely," he said.

Hanging up, he noted that his palms were also wet.

XIII

All night Elly had wavered between self-pity and indignation, tossing on the empty bed like a cork on a wave. She had come home to their apartment with a mind set on reconciliation and celebration. Hadn't she gotten what every journalist craves— backing by her editor against the powers-that-be? Good old Charlie, she thought warmly. Still lead in the old pencil.

Armed with champagne, pâté, stuffed pheasant from Gourmet to Go, fresh asparagus and chocolate éclairs, she had set the table with their best china, scented candles in silver holders with a bouquet of yellow roses between them. She had not called Al during the day. Nor had he called to congratulate her on her story.

She told herself that she must understand his action, or lack of it. Besides, he was probably nursing his hangover. But someone had to make this effort at reclamation. There was, after all, a sense of stability in resolving to make no changes in one's personal life. Wasn't there? One could argue that Al was selfish, inconsiderate, and self-centered. On the other hand, she could also see how he perceived her as obsessive and equally as selfish, inconsiderate, and self-centered. Still, someone had to make the first move.

It did not occur to her, not until the table had been set, the pheasant put in the oven, the asparagus on the stove, the champagne in the refrigerator that he was considerably later coming home than was usual. Only then did she turn on the answering machine. His message was curt: "Spending the night in New York. Client business in the morning." The bastard.

If only he had known what considerable discipline had to be mustered to put aside her thoughts about the Leopold story and

tear herself away from her desk. She had spent the day worrying
that Charlie, plagued by his own private demons of insecurity
and aging and despite his agreement to back her, might have
second thoughts about letting her continue to pursue the story.
So far it was getting lots of attention, but she lived in fear that, at
any moment, Charlie would change his mind and reassign her to
the soft news of the *Style* section.

Nevertheless, she continued to relentlessly pursue the story.
Charlie's backing had buttressed her notion that she was on the
track of something big and her mind buzzed with possibilities.
She continued to call the FBI. As expected, nothing was forthcoming. Again, she called various diamond dealers in Manhattan.
As before, to a man, they denied any knowledge of Leopold's
transactions.

It occurred to her that although she had acquired some knowledge of the cost of jewelry, she had little understanding of what
being a jeweler was really all about. Little by little, her calls drew
her into the technology of precious stones and the ways in which
they were mined and marketed.

She called dealers in Tel Aviv and Antwerp, the closed little
world of the diamond dealers, cutters, and polishers. To a man,
when the subject of Leopold came up, their comments grew
tentative, then murky, ending finally in various forms of denials. Frustrated, she called London's Central Selling Office, the
principal outlet for the sorting and distribution of diamonds to
the world's dealers, a division of DeBeers, the South African diamond monopoly.

A perky man with a British accent promised to call her back
after "checking." Before hanging up, he explained the way in
which the Central Selling Office sold more than 90 percent of the
world's diamond supply, almost exclusively the products of South

Africa's eleven diamond mines. Uncut, or "rough," diamonds are separated by color, shape, weight and quality; lots are formed and "boxed" to fill the needs of each diamond dealer authorized to buy. The dealer has only two alternatives. He can accept the preselections in the box and the price quoted, or he can wait the obligatory five-week period to receive another selection.

She had listened patiently to the spokesman's explanation, wondering what happened to the other ten percent. Of course, she asked. He explained that the government held them back for tax purposes and for use by local industry. If anything, the information buttressed the notion that this was a strictly controlled industry and "wholesale" had different meanings depending on many factors.

She looked over her notes again and called various dealers to determine just how much Leopold saved his clients. As best she could reconstruct, the savings on the stones, after discounting the price of the various settings, and figuring the traditional inflated markups, tallied as much as fifty percent. No wonder, she thought, that Leopold was a smashing success.

As expected, the perky Brit at the other end had no record of a Mr. Irving Leopold, although she doubted that, even if it existed, he would confirm it. If she hadn't been so anxiety-ridden, she would have pressed the point. Instead she hung up in a huff. Perhaps it was these little frustrations that sparked her need to reach for reconciliation with Al. Nor had she expected the humiliation of his absence.

***

That morning she deliberately did not clear the table. She embellished it with the complete feast, the half-done pheasant, the pâté and crackers, the asparagus, the champagne in its silver bucket and, of course, the slowly wilting yellow roses. Let him come home to that scene, see how that little guilt-inducer grabbed him.

In the newsroom, walking the gauntlet of admiration and jealousy from fellow staffers left her curiously unmoved. Anger had taken the edge off her joy. But then Charlie had come over to her desk and whispered in her ear.

"Only praise from upstairs. No libel. No slander," Charlie said. At this point in his career, it seemed the most valued of compliments.

"And Evans?" Elly asked.

"Probably praying for incoming fire. That's his chief wish." He snickered and patted her shoulder. "What have we got for an encore?"

"Encore?" She was suddenly flustered. So now they're pressing me, she thought. "Got a couple of irons in the fire."

"Gotta keep the juice flowing."

When he had gone, she looked over her notes. They were not enough for a good follow-up. She decided to call Millie Tucker. By now, she would be deluged by requests for interviews. The *Today* show had probably already called her. She would be served up as entertainment disguised as serious current events.

The phone continued to ring, but no one answered. Then she called Secretary Tucker's office, and was politely told by his administrative assistant that the secretary was at a Cabinet meeting.

As she hung up, a copy person dropped some wire-service copy on her desk.

"Should be interested in this," the copy person said. She was a young woman with black stringy hair.

Elly read the copy:

"Harry Silver, commissioner of customs, will hold a press conference in his office today at 2 PM to discuss the launching of a sweep of incoming international airline traffic."

Incoming airline traffic—she repeated the words to herself. An idea, half-formed began to thrash around in her mind. There is a point, she knew, when a reporter's imagination became hyperactive. Go with it, she told herself. Let it happen. A new range of possibilities were opening up, more raw meat.

Up to then, she had been locked into the idea of Leopold's being a spy, a convenient motive for access. But suppose he had other fish to fry, something to do with drugs. The idea excited her. Beware the obvious. It was another lesson of her father's, absorbed and long forgotten.

But then, she thought, how does she connect her first hypothesis. A scenario presented itself. This Silver somehow is in collusion with Leopold. The secretary of the treasury is, or is not, in on it. Somehow Silver provides information, access, whatever—to drug kingpins, who may, or may not, be dealing with Leopold, whose role is to launder the profits through diamonds. A logical possibility, she decided, proud of her deduction. The face of truth has many expressions, she told herself pedantically.

A telephone's ring again interrupted her thoughts. She answered it.

"Man out here says he has something that will help you with your story," the receptionist said.

Mildly wary, she was nevertheless curious. Sometimes good sources came through the transom. Most times the people that showed up unannounced were, at best, the harmlessly loquacious and disgruntled and, at worst, sad paranoids deprived beds at mental hospitals.

"What does he look like?"

The receptionist's voice became a rush of air as she whispered into the mouthpiece.

"White socks."

"That bad?"

"What shall I tell him. In or out?"

"I'll be right out."

She took her purse, made sure the tape recorder was in it, gathered up pencil and ballpoint and went out to the reception area. A bald man, wearing a neatly pressed blue suit, brown shoes and white socks, hands folded on his lap, watched her as she approached.

"I'm Eleanor Fox," she said, offering a smile and holding out her hand.

The man stood up and took her hand. His was soft, fleshy and warm. Its touch reminded her of an eel. Thankfully, he drew it away quickly. The man's complexion was pale, his nose fleshy with red-tipped nostrils, his squirrel eyes shifty. He did not seem like a legitimate bearer of information.

"You the one writing that story about Leopold?"

"Yes. You know him?"

The man stared down at his open palms. Then looked up quickly, eyebrows raised in a gesture of surprise. A nervous tick, she observed.

"Can we go someplace?" he whispered.

She looked out over the newsroom. A row of offices lined the outside wall. She remembered that a political reporter now on the road occupied one of them. She motioned the man to follow, and they settled on a couch in the empty office.

"All right then, Mr.—"

"Jones," the man said quickly.

She didn't believe him, but let it pass.

"You have something that might interest me?"

"Maybe. Maybe not."

She noted that the man's teeth were brownish and that his darting squirrel eyes looked everywhere but at her face, for which she was grateful. He had the look of a man with bad breath.

"I saw you wrote about the commissioner of customs. Silver."

"Yes. I did mention him."

"Spent thirty years with Customs."

"Did you?"

"Retired. I'm in insurance claims now. My office is just around the corner. So I thought I'd just drop in. You know what I mean."

He was a man of habits, she observed. His responses were punctuated by looking up with surprise from a zealous inspection of his palms.

"I got something sticks in my mind. You know what I mean?"

"About the commissioner?" she prodded.

"Yeah." In the brief silence that followed, she heard his wheezing breath, as he rubbed his chin, then looked down again at his palms. "There was this Jewish rabbi. You know what I mean."

"A little redundant," she said with a chuckle she could not repress.

"What?"

"All rabbis are Jewish."

"Are you one?"

"A rabbi?" she asked innocently. It occurred to her that her initial assessment of the man had been faulty. Just another paranoid, she sighed.

"No, Jewish. You know what I mean?"

"I'm not." She looked at her watch. "I'm really quite busy, Mr.... er... Jones."

Again he studied his palms. She was growing increasingly irritated. Then he looked up quickly, as before, surprised. He seemed chummier, less wary.

"He came through at Dulles, a flight from Tel Aviv. Had this bearded Jewish rabbi with him, long gray beard. You know how they look, like the guys on the cough-drop box." He giggled maliciously at his little joke, then cleared his throat. She edged away from him. He lowered his voice.

"I was the one on duty at this station at Dulles, so I saw it. This Jew had a black leather bag. I was going to open it for inspection, but hell, the Jew boy was with the commissioner. So I didn't. You know what I mean?"

"You want the truth?" she snapped. "I don't know what you mean."

He was too lost in his own thoughts, to detect her sarcasm and irritation.

"I mean why such a special favor for this Jew? He meets the plane, walks him through. As if he was a VIP. I always remembered that one. You know what I mean? Then I read your story, and it pops back into my head." He moved closer. She noted that she had been right about his breath. "Talk about spies, selling out the U.S.A. The Jew bastards were in a conspiracy. They always are, always ready to fuck over America."

"I didn't know the commissioner was Jewish," she said, trying to keep her voice calm. From clips, she had noted that he was a Lutheran.

"Yeah. So what was he doing meeting a Goddamned rabbi coming off a plane from Tel Aviv? You tell me. Just walked in and picked him up and walked him through. What was that all about? You know what I mean?"

"You make my blood crawl," Elly said.

"I thought it would," the man said with an air of triumph. He had completely misinterpreted her remark.

She pondered getting rid of him. His blatant bigotry disgusted her. Her mind dredged up this image of a creature infested with maggots and her skin began to itch. Not professional, she decided, still unsure as to whether the man, despite his rather familiar paranoia, had anything of significance to impart. But, despite everything, the man had piqued her curiosity.

"May I use my tape recorder?"

She regretted putting his ravings on that level. Goes with the territory, she told herself, putting the tape recorder between them on the couch. He looked at it with caution.

"I don't know about that."

"That's the way we take notes."

"I don't like it."

She picked up the tape recorder and clicked it off. Then she stood up. "You want to tell me something? Or you want to play games? I haven't got time for games. You know what I mean?"

"What the hell," he shrugged. "I can't let them get away with it, can I? Next thing you know they'll hand us over to the Commies. That's their goal you know. Hand us over, then take over."

She sat down again and clicked on the tape recorder.

"When did this occur?" Elly snapped.

"The first time?"

He watched her, smiling, flaunting his brown teeth.

"How many times did it happen?"

"Only twice, a month apart. First about six months ago, give or take. Second time, I just waved 'em through. I remember I was pissed off. But hell, the bastard was the boss. Now, reading your stories I begin to see what it was all about."

"And you feel a little guilty, right?"

"Yeah. Maybe that."

"Did the commissioner ever do this before?"

"Sometimes he would tell us to go easy on certain people. You know, political types, diplomats. The usual. But this thing with the Jew, that was something else. He walked him through himself. I'm telling you there's something fishy here. You know what I mean?"

"Maybe he was extending this courtesy to an important religious leader?"

He threw his head back and showed his full set of brown teeth.

"Yeah, and the Pope's a Baptist.

"Did he tell you not to inspect the rabbi's belongings?"

"He didn't have to say that. He was there. We got the message. Move him through."

"And you did?"

"Sailed right in."

"What do you think he was carrying?"

"Something valuable. Drugs maybe. You know what I mean? It's all money with them. I got the impression, he was just doin' his job, ass kissing one of the bosses. Most of 'em work for the Jews anyway. You know that."

"Somehow it escaped me."

"That's cause they're clever bastards, these kikes. Idea is to get everybody fighting with each other then they step in. So when I saw your story, I say to myself, now I know why the bastard brought the Jew in, all part of the same conspiracy. This Leopold. What was he? Just another Jew." He tapped his temple. "You got to put two and two together."

"Do you remember the man's name?"

"Damned right. Pincus. Abraham Pincus. I don't forget things like that."

"Anybody else know about this?" she asked.

"I told some of the boys. Problem is no one sees the real truth of it."

"They thought you were crazy?"

"Sure they did. Anyway you got to watch who you talk about it to. They're everywhere. And they got their spies."

"So you're taking a real chance coming here?"

"Listen, somebody's got to stand up. You know what I mean?"

"Yeah. I know what you mean. Now you can tell me something, old buddy." She paused, watched his face, wondered if, in his twisted way, he thought he had found a sympathetic ear.

"Sure."

"I want your real name," she barked. "No bullshit."

He rubbed his chin, and his squirrel eyes blinked nervously. He did not look at his palms.

"Then they'll be after my ass."

"You mean you're afraid of them. I thought you were here because you wanted to get them. I thought you had balls." Again she stood up, picking up the tape recorder but not shutting it off.

"You want to get me killed, lady?"

"So you're a damned coward."

"I'm not stupid. You know what I mean?"

"Then I'll make a deal."

"Deal?"

"I can't use the material without corroboration. I need a source. Without it my editor will shoot me down on this. Also, I've got to check it out. What I'm saying is that what you just told me is worthless if I can't use it."

"Shit, they won't print it anyway in this Commie rag. That's the trouble with you guys. That's why you always lose. The Jews now, they're not afraid to take chances."

She felt her stomach congeal.

"That's why they got all the money."

She watched his little squirrel eyes blink. A crenulated red tongue slid out from between his brown teeth and licked his lips.

"You just don't use my name. Deal?"

"No names. Guaranteed."

"James Hopwood."

"Address and telephone number?"

She held up the tape recorder and he spoke into it.

"Good deal," she said, starting for the door. Obeying the signal, he got up. "If we need anything more, we'll call you."

"As long as you don't use my name," he said with obvious regret that he had revealed it. "Something happens to me you'll have it on your head."

I only wish, she thought, nodding a farewell and pointing the way out. She could not bear to touch his flesh.

***

They had shifted the press conference to an auditorium on the floor below. Apparently, they had not expected that many people to show up. Camera crews were setting up. Radio reporters were attaching microphones to a podium. Still photographers were checking their light meters, and reporters literally filled the room and spilled over around the rear and sides, much to the irritation of the television people.

As she walked through the room, eyes turned. She sensed herself being pointed out. She liked the feeling and the knowledge that her words had exercised this power. At home she had felt trapped, frustrated. Out here, among her peers, she knew she was the object of admiration, perhaps jealousy. To her mind, jealousy was another form of respect.

She took a seat in the center of the auditorium imagining that its vantage would give everyone a good view of her. Although it was a very private thought, she wished she could summon up a bit more humility. But how then does one revel in success?

The entrance of Commissioner Harry Silver aborted such weighty questions. It struck her first that he did not look like a Harry. She wasn't sure what that meant, only that the image in her mind of him was not of a Harry.

Perhaps she had been thinking of a Truman-like Harry. Who named their children Harry these days? Unless, it was a derivative nickname for Henry.

Then there was his appearance. She had expected someone quite different, perhaps a person with rimless spectacles, bald, paunchy, in a word, tacky. He was definitely not tacky. His black hair, speckled with gray was full and long. From where she sat, she could not see the color of his eyes, but they were set deep, with a look that was more circumspect than intense. He had a square jaw that made him appear stubborn. When he spoke, his voice was youthful. If she closed her eyes and listened to his voice, he would sound twenty or younger.

She was not surprised to view him as one sizes up an opponent. Despite the jaw, he seemed vulnerable. In her present state of pride, she felt certain she could take him.

He began the conference by explaining how the sweep would work, who would be most inconvenienced, why it was being undertaken, and its importance to the country. As he began to speak, television lights went on. Cameras whirred. She could hear the sound of pens scribbling across notebooks. She had brought along her trusty tape recorder and she clicked it on.

It had begun, she noted, as a perfectly traditional Washington press conference, a recitation of normal, bland, self-serving events. As expected, there was a youngish man in a bow tie standing a few paces to the side of the principal but obvious enough for them to know that he was the orchestrator of the enterprise.

Harry—she decided to refer to him as Harry—came armed with visual aids, statistics, and, of course, that Washington staple, handouts. She had always considered Customs no more than a minor fiefdom of little consequence. She was quickly being convinced otherwise.

A deluge of billions of dollars worth of illegally imported materials, mostly drugs, was being dumped on America. Principal among those arms of government mandated to interdict this deluge was the plucky little Customs agency. For a devious, cunning, unprincipled and greedy man, willing to take bold risks, the job of commissioner could be a license to steal. It was from that vantage, under intense scrutiny that she wanted to observe him. Guilty until proven guilty.

In keeping with the role in which she had cast him, Harry was making a reasonably good account of himself and his agency. No question, she decided, the man had all the attributes of a comer. This was good, she decided. There was nothing to be gained in knocking over a loser.

By the time he was winding up his initial presentation, she had figured out her strategy. No point in asking any questions at this press conference. Her colleagues knew what to ask. Nor did she wish them to get off the tack she had already set. More momentum would surely bring more ghouls out of the woodwork. Maybe even the illusive Leopold himself. She would pounce on him after they had roughed up his carcass a bit.

When he had finished his presentation and asked for questions, her colleagues whipped out their brickbats.

"What exactly was your relationship with the alleged spy, Irving Leopold?" a reporter for the *New York Post* asked.

"Does that have anything to do with the subject at hand?" Harry replied. A buzzing groan rustled through the audience.

"Must I repeat my question, Mr. Commissioner?" the man from the *Post* asked.

At that point the man with the bow tie stepped forward, solemn and self-important. He raised his hand to silence the rebellious crowd. When they complied after a few moments, he said: "Ground rules have been set to stick strictly to the matter at hand."

"Bullshit," a number of reporters shouted.

"We want this to be orderly," the young man with the bow tie said, clearly shaken.

"Commissioner Silver," the man from the *Post* continued, as if he were the designated spokesman for all present. He looked around him, certain that he had obtained the consent of the group. "You simply cannot deny these serious allegations. You and Secretary Tucker have been depicted as conspiring with an alleged spy."

A clamor of agreement broke out in the audience. Elly was, of course, troubled by both the accusation and the hyperbole. She had never stated, bluntly stated, that Irving Leopold was a spy. Had she?

"Time for clear-cut answers," the man from the *Post* said smugly.

The young man with the bow tie, whose complexion now matched his white shirt, started to speak again, but the reporters booed him down. Harry raised his hand to settle the crowd.

"All right," he said. "I'll answer the question this way."

The crowd grew hushed and expectant.

"I wish," the commissioner began, "that my brain was nimble enough to come up with more synonyms for *preposterous*. This innuendo—these ridiculous assumptions—are so absurd, so off-the-wall and beyond any semblance to the truth, that the only defense I can muster is to say: It's a damned lie."

His face had flushed. He had expelled the words with his jaw tipped upward in defiance. For a moment, she felt the odd sensation of wanting to get up and cheer.

"But you knew Leopold?" the man from the *Post* asked.

"So did the president."

"And you bought jewels from him."

"So did the president and half his Cabinet. My purchase was a fifteen-hundred-dollar diamond ring. I had never given my wife an engagement ring."

"Did you pay by cash or by check?" someone shouted.

"By check," Harry said with just a flash of impatience.

Although the man from the *Post* was still standing, someone else got up behind him.

"Was Leopold in a position to get any significant secrets?" the man asked.

"I doubt it," Harry said, then backtracking, "unless the secret might be who was the latest to get a face-lift or who needed one."

A few reporters snickered. Meant to be a joke, it fell flat.

"What was the treasury secretary's relationship with Leopold?"

"There wasn't any."

"But what did you talk about?"

The questions were coming thick and fast now, the reporters acting as interrogators, firing questions like a dart competition. All sense of order and procedure had vanished.

"Social chitchat," Harry said.

"Ever mention Iraq?"

"Never."

"Saddam Hussein?"

"Never."

"Do you know where Leopold is?"

"No."

"Did he know, for example, about this operation?" The woman who had stood up pointed to the easel that held the visual aids. Elly held her breath. They were set to push into her new turf.

"Of course not," Harry said with indignation. "What I can't understand is your fascination with this subject."

"Did you ever suspect he might be a spy?" someone asked from the back of the small auditorium. Since he had put on the armor of denial, Elly decided, you couldn't blame the reporters for looking for chinks.

"No more than I suspect my wife," Harry said, but instead of accompanying the remark with a smile, he frowned as if he had inadvertently opened the wrong door.

"Is your wife a spy?" one of the reporters asked with a giggle.

"I'm trying to be forthright, trying to satisfy your demands," Harry said with a bad stab at humility.

"No, you're not. You're stonewalling," one of the reporters shouted.

"Against what?" Harry asked. "There's no wall. No story. It's a nonstarter. I think one day a reporter got up from a dream and wrote it all down."

Nobody laughed. Putting me down, is he? Elly thought, sensing glances in her direction. A burst of anger erupted from the still hot ashes of the morning. As expected, her colleagues picked up the challenge. At this level, they were less cautious than their editors, the present climate notwithstanding.

"Has the FBI been around to see you?" a woman reporter asked with an obvious touch of malice. Harry, an animal of another species, was not making friends among the jackals.

"Yes," he replied.

"What did they ask you?"

"You know I can't answer that question," Harry replied.

"Why not?"

"It's an ongoing investigation."

"That old turkey."

Why doesn't he just dismiss the group, Elly thought. Call off the press conference. Why try to appear humble and innocent to this group of vultures? How different these press conferences appeared on live television, with everyone conducting themselves with polite, guarded behavior.

Harry Silver was walking farther and farther out on his limb. In a little while, she was going to saw it off. She felt no pity. Ya pays yer money, ya takes yer cherce. Go on the power trip, take the fallout, brothers and sisters. Her rule of thumb—again her father's words—a free press demands an adversarial relationship.

One of the older reporters rose to his feet, a craggy-faced man with a silver mane who wrote a syndicated column and was an occasional commentator on Public Television.

"There is some talk around town—" the man began in dulcet tones, pausing to gain everyone's attention. "—that Irving Leopold is a secret presidential emissary to Iraq."

His silken voice gave the revelation an air of authority. New wrinkle, Elly thought. She was surprised it hadn't crossed her mind before. She watched poor Harry's face. His jaunty jaw had dropped as if his mouth had fallen open. Also, the question was delivered without a questioning tone, making the remark appear like gospel truth.

"Do you seriously expect me to comment on that?" Harry asked.

"Why would I have asked the question?" the silver fox replied, looking about him for the crowd's approval, which was spotty. Somehow, they seemed to like the spy idea better.

"Beats me," Harry said. "Must be a slow news day."

A ripple of smug harrumphs rolled through the audience.

"Are you people finished?" the young man with the bow tie said, apparently recovered.

It was also obvious that the conference had lost itself in its own maze. She breathed a sigh of relief. He'd given them good copy in his denials, and the old reporter's odd question would send the pack scurrying to the White House press office and the State Department.

"Thank you all, very much," Harry said, striding off the stage. Agile as a gazelle, she bounded after him, the figurative scent of raw meat in her nostrils.

There was a back entrance to the auditorium and she caught up with him just as he and his young flack had reached the door.

"The conference is over," the young man said between clenched teeth. Harry Silver had turned to observe her. His face was flushed, and there was a rim of perspiration on his upper lip. In his eyes, she observed the pain of defeat.

"They gave you a pretty bad time," Elly said, also observing, inexplicably, that his eyes were brown.

"It's over," the young man said.

Harry turned and opened the door, obviously leaving her to be disposed of by Bow Tie. She bounded past the young man and slipped through the door behind Harry. He walked fast, but she kept up with him, Bow Tie snapping at her heels.

"I'm Eleanor Fox," she said.

He slowed down.

"Oh, Jesus," he groused.

"No. Eleanor Fox," she said, hoping he could sense the smile in her voice. His response was to speed up his pace.

"It's going to get worse before it gets better," she said, half believing it. "Might as well say it your way."

"To you?"

"Two sides are better than one. Besides, we're just the conduits."

He turned suddenly, looking at her, eyes blazing with anger and frustration. It was an attitude he had kept hidden in the conference. Only now, at this distance, could she see the truth of his expression.

"Don't you think you've gone far enough with this fairy tale?"

"That's why I'm giving you the pulpit."

"Thanks for nothing."

He turned away and started down the corridor, the Bow Tie in tandem.

"Harry," she called after him. He continued to move. "Who is Rabbi Abraham Pincus?" He hesitated, then stopped dead in his tracks, turning slowly.

"Who?"

She repeated the name. Remembering Hopwood and his ugly bigotry, her stomach knotted. She felt unclean.

"All they know is how to harass," the Bow Tie said.

"What is it that you want?" Harry asked.

"I told you. I want to give you the pulpit."

He sighed, shook his head, and looked up at the ceiling.

"All right, then, come on into my church."

XIV

Now that he had an opportunity to study her, he was confused by her appearance. He had seen her sitting there in the audience, her chin tilted upward, had sensed her scrutiny. But it was merely one face in a sea of many. He felt literally bruised by their observation. His skin ached with it. And his bones, like a defensive perimeter deployed to protect the heartland of himself, were weary with effort.

He was confused because she did not look like the enemy. She had the caste of a redhead, creamy, lightly freckled skin, auburn hair with glints of gold cut in the shape of a rather unruly bird's nest, which slightly reduced the field of vision of her green eyes, set wide. Her nose was wide as well, but her most distinguishing feature were her lips, thick and pouting, the upper lip like a wide cupid's bow, the lower lip puffed outward over a broad chin.

She wore a chunky jewelry necklace around a strong smooth neck, revealed by an open blouse with a turned up collar. She was of medium height, with a trim waist that accentuated a well-shaped upper and lower torso. It surprised him, too, that he took such pains with his observation. Know thine enemy. Was that the reason? The bitch was destroying his life. She had no business looking like that.

She sat at the side of his desk, legs primly crossed.

"I have a tape recorder," she said, pulling it from her purse. "Okay?"

"Would it matter?" Harry asked.

"Are you implying I make things up?"

"Not just implying. I'm stating it unequivocally."

"You took a drubbing out there," she said, obviously making a hundred-and-eighty-degree turn in their conversation. Obediently, he followed the trail, determined to keep up with her.

"Pretty awful, wasn't it?"

"Put you on the map. A real national figure."

"A figure of scorn, I'd say. I got the impression that no one really believed me."

"What gave you that impression?"

He began to feel more uneasy, if that was possible. He decided that this interview was definitely not a good idea. Too late now. But she had mentioned that name. Strictly Irving's idea to pose as an Orthodox rabbi and carry the diamonds hidden in his beard. Who would believe it?

"Just a feeling."

"It wouldn't be your fault if this Irving Leopold was a spy, would it? Or a presidential emissary? Or..." She paused. In the brief silence, he could hear the purr of her tape recorder. "Anything."

"As far as I know he was a jewelry salesman."

"Then why did he disappear?"

"How should I know?"

"No thoughts on the subject?"

"Believe me, I don't spend my life thinking about Irving Leopold." Oh God, he thought. Deliver me. His mouth ached now, probably from the continuing stream of obfuscation and at least one outright lie passing through it. Now look here, he wanted to say, here's the real truth. Just listen. Don't interrupt. Instead, he said: "The whole thing is off-the-wall." Watch it, he warned himself. Remember at all times that the tape is running.

"Now let's get on to Rabbi Pincus."

"Who?"

She repeated the name. With some effort, he kept his face immobile.

"The man whom you shepherded through customs at Dulles airport. And apparently elsewhere." Her cupid's bow stretched with a smile, revealing her moistened lower lip. He was stunned, blown away behind the facade of his newly contrived public face on which his life now depended. How could she know that? First show her disbelief, he decided.

"Are you serious?"

"Yes, I am."

Then ridicule.

"That's what I was afraid of."

"You never heard of this Rabbi Pincus? From Tel Aviv. Long, gray beard. Shiny black costumes that they wear. Black beaver hat." He struggled to enhance his definition of extreme puzzlement.

"Are you sure you haven't got me mixed up with some other person?"

"My information is impeccable," she said.

"May I ask from whence it came?" he asked, reaching for a light touch.

She tapped her broad chin, watching him. She seemed very calm, very assured, and he wondered, with growing panic, if he was as transparent as he felt.

"I didn't make it up," she said. "Nor can I reveal my source."

"Because there isn't one. It's pure fantasy."

With the initial shock weathered, he replayed the episode in his mind. Irving in his disguise was preposterous. The paste-on beard made him look like a cartoon caricature created by an anti-Semite.

"From the best makeup artist in Israeli theater," he whispered, as Harry had ushered him toward the "express lane" used by diplomats and selected VIP's. The whole process had taken just moments. Then he had whisked Irving to his car parked just outside the entrance, protected by his pasted windshield decal.

In the car, Irving had untied little bags secured by thin leather tongs that hung just under his beard like Christmas decorations.

"You leave it to Irving," the jeweler had said, tapping his temple. "Irving uses his *tuchas*." He hadn't understood the word, and Irving had had to explain.

"Who would believe this?" Irving had asked. Too late, he discovered that he had actually repeated these words to the Fox woman with Irving's intonation.

"In Washington, I find I am asked this question frequently," she replied. "But study recent history. An actor who plays second fiddle to a chimp in a movie becomes president. A congressional wife who scandalizes the so-called establishment by admitting to making love on the Capitol steps acts in a flick called *Return of the Zombies*. The government pays for a prominent Russian defector's love affair with a prostitute. The largest defense contractor in America charges the taxpayer for boarding the boss's dogs in a kennel. A president deliberately tapes and preserves the evidence of his own guilt. Later eighteen-and-a-half minutes mysteriously vanish from the tapes. A vice president takes cash bribes, insists he is "innocent," then surrenders to the courts in a virtual admission of guilt. A woman surfaces to accuse a man of sexual harassment alleging that he had told her there was a pubic hair on his coke can. Got a couple of months, I can give you more. And from this wacky place, we run the free world. The point is that, in that context, anything is believable. So don't ever ask "Who would believe this? Because the answer would be: "Nobody in their right mind.""

Breathless, she paused and pouted, perhaps annoyed with

herself that she had made such a long and somewhat rambling speech. He could have added a few examples of his own, he thought, which prompted a question to himself. "Why do people do these things repetitively, as if what happened before never existed?" But to her, he framed a different response.

"And those are only the things that actually come out in the wash."

"Commissioner Silver, that revelation is too detailed, too precise."

"Fantasies usually are."

"Now you are going to give me pedantic and profound bon mots. What exactly are you hiding?" He could see in her expression the rising tide of impatience. Good or bad for him? He wasn't sure.

"What do you think I'm hiding?"

"A scam of some kind."

"You think I'm a traitor?"

"No."

"Well, that's a relief. I hope you will correct the misapprehension in your next missive to the world."

"I probably will."

"Then why are you here?"

Her pause indicated that she seemed tentative on that point.

"I want to know what you and this Rabbi Pincus were up to, why you had to appear in person to usher him through customs. Then I want to know why you're denying it ever happened."

"I'm not denying it ever happened. I'm saying that the fact of it doesn't exist."

"You never walked a bearded rabbi through customs?"

"When you play that question back, you'll be hysterical with laughter."

"You never walked anyone through customs?"

"On occasion, yes. Some VIP. A service of the service. Not often. Usually, we just make arrangements for swift pass-through. Perfectly proper and legitimate."

"Suppose I told you that I had an eye witness?"

"Produce him."

He had determined to give her a fast response. Now he regretted it.

"Why do you say "him"?"

"A generic term." He coughed, hoping he would mask a sudden discomfort.

"I really don't believe you, Harry."

This blatant attack on his credibility stunned him, adding to his feeling of helplessness, as if he were a butterfly stuck on a pin. "You're torturing me, lady," he muttered in his mind.

"Well," he said with sarcasm. "We seem to be developing a relationship." He wished for the phone's ring. But he had instructed Mrs. Habersham to hold all calls. Every move that day, he decided, had been a mistake. Why was he giving this woman so much time? Why didn't he throw her out? Perhaps she was wondering the same thing.

"You're a very evasive man."

"Because I don't want to play the role you've cast me in."

"What role is that?"

"Some evil villain."

She shook her head vigorously.

"Not really. I'm just intrigued."

"Obsessed, you mean."

"That's what my husband says," she whispered.

"Listen to him." He was tempted to tell her about how the stories she was writing were affecting Terry.

"Why won't you tell me about the rabbi?" she asked suddenly.

"Why all this hocus-pocus about Leopold? Maybe he wasn't a spy after all. Maybe he smuggled drugs." She paused, as if to let the words sink in. "Maybe you greased the way for him. Maybe—"

"I'd suggest you reread the laws of libel and slander."

It was, he realized, a shot in the dark, the final threat. Threats, he knew, had a life of their own. Unless you were prepared to back them up, they were merely expressions of haughty bravado. Occasionally they worked, like a bluff in poker. Watching her, though, her expression indicated that perhaps this type of intimidation had an effect.

"Could be this whole drug screening at airports is a ploy to keep attention away from the real story. Hell, considering all your bragging about interdictions, you could be one of the biggest drug kingpins in the country."

"Tell me how," he said coolly. "I'll cut you in."

"Well," she said, lowering her eyes. "Perhaps I *have* gone too far." She paused and nodded her head as if in acknowledgment. "Then tell me about Secretary Tucker. You and he are buddies?"

"Good friends, yes."

"Both of you thick as fleas with Leopold."

"Still on that kick."

"Let's face it. The man's close to the president, real close."

"And extremely able."

"A possible presidential contender."

"So they say."

"Then what the hell is he doing with Leopold?"

"Which is also true of the president and others."

"In high places."

"That sounds so sinister."

"Yes, it does. Do I have to go through the litany of associations?"

"Spare me."

"I may not be able to, not if you won't cooperate."

"Listen," he said in a conciliatory tone, reaching for a resonance of absolute sincerity. "I really want to answer your questions to the best of my ability. I can't. I can make up answers, of course, but what would be the point of that. I don't know where you've got any of your information. Rabbis with long gray beards. Spies. Now drug smuggling. And you did fall for Millie Tucker's shock-value routine—"

Then he remembered that the tape recorder was running. "She likes hyperbole, especially when it comes to the press. Doesn't mean you have to fall for it hook, line, and sinker. Look, I can't stop you from writing about anything you wish. All I ask is that you check your facts. Double- and triple-check them."

Again he resisted the temptation to talk about Terry's reaction. And Paul's. Even Billy's and Millie's. He felt himself sinking under the weight of a self-imposed mudslide. He looked at the woman, searching for a target. "You should consider how your stories affect other people's lives, the pain they inflict."

"I can't consider that." Her reply indicated a possible vulnerability.

"Reckless accusations could backfire."

"You have access to the courts."

"And your bosses would have to defend. Have you any idea of the costs, both monetary and psychic? I don't think that these days your owners will welcome any kind of libel action against them."

He seemed to have made some headway on that point. Time to try blatant intimidation, he decided. Hell, he felt he was fighting for his survival. Worse, he was not without guilt.

"We can help other media find ways to discredit your facts."

"That's your prerogative," she replied.

Am I chipping away at her resolve? he wondered.

"I'm not just going to stand here and get pilloried for no reason. I think I'm doing a pretty damned good job as commissioner of customs. Within the limits of what is possible. I'm not bragging. But just remember. I'm a public servant, a citizen on temporary duty, making his contribution."

Was he going too far? Patriotism and self-sacrifice, he could tell by her expression, weren't the ticket here. The real danger, he decided, lay in talking too fucking much, he rebuked, himself.

He slapped his desk and stood up. "Defense is very strenuous," he said, forcing a smile. "I've got a very busy day ahead of me."

She clicked off her tape recorder and stood up. He noted that she was also tall, graceful. A viper, to be sure, manipulative and dangerous. Then why couldn't he bring himself to hate her?

Facing him, she put out her hand. He took it, felt the warm flesh, the odd thrill, pumped then released it.

"I'm not going to go away, Harry," she said, her eyes staring into his.

"I don't expect so," he muttered, watching her walk away, her movement fluid, undulating, feminine.

He stood by his desk for a long time pondering her wake. So he was no longer merely adrift in shark-infested waters. A school of them had caught the scent of blood, his blood.

***

A chill wind rolled in from the river. They were walking along the footpath of the C&O Canal. A blazing setting autumn sun shot spears through the almost leafless trees. Harry had tried to give Billy a verbatim account of his day, but the sentences became tangled and the chronology out of sequence.

At this moment, Harry knew, the word, as they say, was going out through the land. He had already determined that it was pointless to watch the network news. Even more pointless to read the Fox story in tomorrow's paper. With so many anxieties crowding in, it was difficult to set priorities of worry.

"I guess it just got away from us," Harry said, disturbed at his own tone of contrition. "It's out of control."

"You should never have held that press conference," Billy said, for what seemed like the tenth time.

"No point in going over that one, Billy," Harry said. "Toss of the coin."

"You should have postponed it."

"I don't think we should continue to dwell on 'should haves', Billy. I've got a few 'should haves' of my own." No sense beating that dead horse, Harry thought. "Anyway, you should be relieved. I'm the one in the spotlight. I'm the star."

"But it's crazy. The whole thing is crazy."

"Alice on the other side of the mirror. And I'm the Mad Hatter."

"Do you really think she's got something with that rabbi thing?" He had asked that question repetitively as well.

"She's got it."

"But from where?"

"Is it important? She's got the name. Who would have thought that stupid agent would have made a big deal about it." He shook his head. Maybe, he told himself, there just are no secrets, ever, not in this company town. "How do you suppose we got sucked in like that? Now what? Irving said that this Pincus rabbi was dead. He'd bought the passport from a man who said he bought it from the family. He assured us the passport would be good for the time needed. Sounded like a good choice at the time. An Orthodox Jew with a gray beard. In Israel there are thousands of them. Where was the risk? I shouldn't have gone, shouldn't have called attention to him."

"That was your idea," Billy said with a faint mocking tone. "In your own instructions to customs agents, remember. In a strip search, check all body orifices. Look inside hair, under beards. You were pushing for the little busts then. Let's face it. You had to go just in case. They wouldn't pull anybody out of the line with you beside them." The mocking tone had evolved into sarcasm.

"The arrogance of power," Harry said.

"No philosophy. Please, Harry."

"Why did he have to go to Israel to get the diamonds cut and polished? He could have done it right here in this country."

"According to Irving it was less traceable," Harry said, an explanation that triggered in Billy a wry chuckle. They were picking at scabs now. "Anyway, the whole episode is a comedy of errors. The thing has taken on a life of its own. Of course, I denied the whole thing to that woman. Deny, deny. Believe me, Billy, it was against the grain for me. Who could believe a turkey story like that? It's laughable. Irving a spy for Iraq? So I drowned her questions with ridicule."

"Did she buy it?"

"Who knows? Probably not. She was all business. Dead serious. Even brought out a tape recorder. I let her." He blew air out through his teeth. "Not only is the story unlikely. She is a real knockout. Which only increases the feeling of unreality. What she's doing is hanging us—me—for the wrong crime. As if I was a serial killer instead of a petty thief."

"Let's say she has the rabbi thing right," Billy mused aloud. "She can't know it was Irving."

"Not unless he told her."

"Who?"

"Irving himself."

"You mean just picked up the phone and told all."

"Look at it from his point of view. He's holed up somewhere, scared shitless. He's read bits and pieces. He has no support system. Alone and afraid, one lousy combination."

"Funny he didn't call again."

"Maybe we should ask the Italian to make some inquiries?"

"Him?" Billy snarled with contempt. "Best thing he can do is crawl into a hole and stay there."

"Not a bad idea."

They continued to walk but in silence.

"What we need now," Billy said, "is a monumental international or national disaster, like the Kennedy assassination, something to crowd everything else out of the media. It's all a function of space."

"Maybe you should have shot the president this morning. What's Irving disguised as a rabbi against that?"

Billy stopped suddenly and shook his head.

"You're going round the bend, Harry," he muttered.

"It's no joke," Harry said. "That's why I'm not laughing. Worse, how am I going to explain any of it to Terry? And Paul? I might tell them that the media is blowing smoke. Would they believe me? Hell, no. Terry's at the edge with worry, and Paul is confused and wary."

"Listen, no matter what she writes, she has to print your denial. Think about it. What's so terrible about accompanying a religious leader through customs? You've done nothing wrong."

Harry stopped abruptly.

"Nothing wrong? Aiding and abetting a diamond smuggling

operation, hot cash in strongboxes, potential political favors for foreigners, bribing a foreign ambassador, lying and illegalities. Are you living in a dream world? And that's just for openers."

"Nothing can be proven," Billy mumbled.

"Not yet."

"Maybe never."

"Billy, they're breathing down our necks. Can't you sniff it? If she has the rabbi thing, she could have everything else, the passport of a dead man. Come on. She could be paying it out, little by little, like a suspense thriller."

"Dumb idea," Billy mumbled. He stopped, kicked a stone then turned an ashen face to Harry. "Where did we get the idea we were invincible?"

The question prompted memory, and Harry was suddenly seeing old images through the tunnel of time. Billy Tucker, golden hair glinting in the sun, tanned legs, muscles taut, jumping hurdles with the ease of a gazelle on the college track.

Harry had been a lone spectator in the stands watching and thinking the word—invincible. The image etched itself in his mind, became the matrix for what success meant. Billy jumping hurdle after hurdle, not once did a leg or foot catch the wooden barrier. Up and over, one after another in a puddle of golden light, Harry following with his eyes, as if he were right behind him on the track, tagging along.

"I'm going to pull out the money tomorrow, Billy, first thing. They find that, it's the hottest log on the pyre," Harry said.

"Maybe so. At least we'll keep it in play." He giggled suddenly. "Might need it for our defense fund." The giggle seemed to end in a choking hack.

They walked for a long time in silence. The sun began to slip beneath the horizon, and they headed back toward Georgetown.

"Millie has gone up to the country house," Billy said suddenly.

"Probably a good thing."

"And I'm off to Asia tomorrow."

"Tomorrow? I didn't know."

"Just China and Japan, marching orders from the boss. Be back in a couple of weeks."

"Jumping ship, eh?"

It was purely a reflex, a half wise crack that under other circumstances would elicit a mild laugh. Instead, Billy stopped abruptly, turning toward him. Harry recognized the expression. He had seen it the other night when Billy had berated Millie.

"I don't know what that implies, but I sure don't like it."

"Wasn't meant to—"

"The hell it wasn't. And don't think I'll escape the press. They'll be yapping at my heels. I'm in it with you up to my ass, and you know it."

"You've got it all mixed up, Billy."

"Have I? I'll tell you who's mixed up. Throwing that dumb press conference today. That was a mix-up. Talking with that reporter. That wasn't too smart either. God knows what will come out tomorrow. Who knows just how I'll be dragged into it? I mean that one was really stupid. You should have called it off. The hell with that damned sweep. You won't catch flies, and you know it. It's all cosmetics, a little frosting on the cake. I think it stinks."

Saliva flecked Billy's lips. Harry was stunned. He wasn't prepared, hadn't expected the attack. His reaction was a kind of sputtering confusion. "Listen," Billy continued. "I can't control you, and I can't control this situation."

Still fuming, he turned and left a stunned Harry to watch him walk swiftly down the path toward Georgetown.

XV

If you do not read it, listen to it or watch it, then, Harry reasoned, it does not exist. Right? He had spent the entire night assuring himself that it was possible to create a communications vacuum in his mind, to cut the rope that held this little dingy of himself to media earth, and to bob listlessly on calm waters in a cocoon of silent fog.

To achieve such a condition, he detached all plastic jacks that connected his phones, removed the connecting wires to the four television sets in his home, eliminated batteries from all portable radios.

With Terry immobilized in their bedroom by a sedative administered by a doctor, Harry and the kids scrounged some TV dinners from the freezer and baked potatoes in the microwave oven.

"But why can't I watch TV?" Bobbie asked, mashing her fork into a compartment of gelatinous Swedish pot roast.

"Because it will make your brains scrambled eggs," Harry replied.

"Not *Cheers.* You said yourself that *Cheers* was intelligent."

"It used to be intelligent. Before the reruns."

"They're the same programs," Bobbie whined.

"That's the point," Harry sighed. He glanced at Paul, who sat beside him, eating with little relish, quiet and morose.

"I think it stinks," Bobbie said.

"It's the enemy, you stupid little nerd," Paul said suddenly, pushing away his tray.

"How can it be our enemy? We got four of them," Bobbie replied.

It was the kind of remark that they had once characterized as precocious. Now Harry was getting a different message. Bobbie was recycling wisecracks picked up from the tube. His own daughter, "Made in Media." The government should require labels on all human goods produced by media.

"The TV is saying bad things about Dad," Paul said.

"I never heard that," Bobbie pouted. "About Daddy?"

"It's not on *Cheers*," Harry muttered.

"I'm right, though, aren't I, Dad?"

"The TV doesn't say things. It only sits there, the conduit," Harry corrected, wondering if he was being accurate, remembering Marshall McLuhan. The medium is the message. It all seemed too overwhelming to understand.

"You know what I mean," Paul said gloomily.

Harry felt more scrutinized by his son than by the others, the media, the FBI. Every look became a barb. Falling from that pedestal would be an endless drop into a dark, bleak, bottomless pit. Now that is truly shame, he thought.

"What's it saying then?" Bobbie asked.

"Things you shouldn't know about," Paul said.

"They're all lies anyway," Harry said, forcing a smile. "Pay no attention to them." In some ways, he was technically correct.

"I'm sure they are, Dad," Paul nodded. A hopeful sign, Harry decided.

"Irving Leopold is not a spy," Harry said, benignly. "They got that wrong."

"But the FBI is investigating you. Right?" Harry detected Paul's tone of belligerence.

"They're looking into everybody who ever had any dealings with Irving Leopold. Including the president. So you see, I'm in good company."

"So why can't I watch *Cheers?*"

"Because they still may say bad things. Right, Dad? There'll be more coming. Things that are bad."

"They won't be right," Harry mumbled.

"But they'll say them?" Paul asked.

"The point is that they won't be right. They won't be telling the truth."

"Will you sue them then?"

"Sue them? I haven't got that kind of money. Anyway, you can't win."

"Even if you're right and they're wrong?"

"Why are you being such a question box, Paul?" Harry asked impatiently. "Maybe you believe them?"

Paul looked blankly at the tray. Grease was beginning to congeal on the microwaved meat.

"I believe you, Dad," Paul said. But he seemed tentative.

Harry felt his stomach churn. In the strictest sense of his own rationale, he had not lied. That did not mean that he was truthful, either. What was that word? Obfuscation. Using that on his own children. He pushed his tray away and reached for the ice cream, dipping his spoon into the half-melted scoop.

"Look, kids, I'm not perfect. But in public life, you have to expect criticism. It has to do with politics, power, media, differing priorities, ambitions. You need a strong stomach to be in this business." He brought a spoonful of ice cream to his mouth. It tasted waxy and unpleasant.

"I still don't see why I can't watch television," Bobbie said.

"Will you stop whining," Paul rebuked sharply. He got up from the table and rushed away to his room.

"He's just worried about Mom," Harry said.

"He's just an old worrywart," Bobbie pouted. She, too, got up from the table. Still sitting, he turned in his chair.

"Come here, kitten."

She obeyed, climbing up on his lap. Soon, he thought, she'd be too old for that. He stroked her hair and kissed her on the cheek.

"Do you believe your old Dad?"

"Sure do," she said, kissing him on his nose. In the end, it comes down to this, Harry thought. You built your fortress, and you dug a moat around it, and inside was the core of you. They could never touch that. Never. He hugged his daughter to him.

"It will all be fine. You'll see," he whispered, knowing she did not understand.

"Can I watch *Cheers?*" she pleaded. He pushed her gently off his lap.

"Not tonight," he said.

"Tomorrow?"

"We'll see."

Tomorrow could be worse, he thought, watching her bound up the stairs into her room. He sat at the table for a long time, making an effort to abort a tidal wave of depression that was crashing over him. Too late.

It was one thing for him to go through the ordeal, quite another to put his family through it. If there was a chief regret among the many, it was that he had not even considered their reaction. But then, neither he nor Billy had fully calculated the effects of failure. They had considered them coldly, analytically, with all the logic and reason they could muster, but it had been bloodless, unemotional and, therefore, inaccurate.

It proved, beyond the shadow of doubt, what others had only learned by experience, that human events were never predictable and human behavior was even less so. Case in point: Billy

Tucker, the great God Billy, idol and mentor, a quarter century's observation down the rat hole. When rattled, what does he do? Kick the dog.

"Woof, woof," he muttered, going up to his bedroom.

In the soft light of a single lamp, he saw Terry's eyes. They were open, glazed. Her jaw was slack, her hair spread out awry on the pillow, her hands were clasped tightly over her stomach.

"How do you feel, baby?" he asked.

"Fine," she whispered, offering a thin smile.

"That's great."

"I guess I'm just not built for… " She seemed to be searching her mind for a word. "Adversity."

"Your imagination just ran away with you."

"I'm supposed to come from hardy pioneer stock."

So much for genetics, he thought, wishing suddenly that he had inherited his father's penchant for silent observation and deliberate withdrawal. He could use some of those traits now.

Changing into pajamas, he got in beside her.

"You don't see me worrying about anything, do you, darling?" he said. More lies. The chickens were coming home to roost. Hadn't he wanted an old-fashioned girl, someone with no illusions about her place within the family, dependent, devoted, wifely, motherly, someone to be shielded and protected?

"I want to go home, Harry," Terry whispered.

"Home?" Where is that? he wondered.

She was silent for a long time and from hearing her shallow breathing, he thought she had fallen asleep.

"Why are we here, Harry?" she asked suddenly, her voice hoarse and trembling as if she were crying deep inside herself.

He pondered the question, turning it over carefully in his mind as if it were a delicate porcelain figure. He wanted the answer to be precise, but all he could string together were unrelated words like ambition, devotion, loyalty, power, revenge, mattering, becoming. At least Billy knew what he wanted. Billy?

In his mind he hummed something about hitching his wagon to a star. Even that was off-key.

                              ***

In the morning, he waited in the stillness, watching for the paperboy. He saw him come down the street in the ice blue light of presunrise, waited for him to fling the paper into the driveway then dashed out to get it.

His original intention was to carry it to the yard, bury it like some dead skunk. But as he carried it, he could not resist a peak into its transparent plastic wrapper.

CUSTOMS STARTS DRUG SWEEP. AIRPORT DELAYS STAGGERING.

The headline's connotation startled him. He had expected the worst. *Today* is the day you worried about yesterday and all is well, he told himself, his heart beating with elation and relief. He removed the paper from its wrapper, opened it and instantly regretted his action. Another headline just below the fold read: BUT THE COMMISSIONER CAN GET YOU THROUGH IN SECONDS. Without reading beyond that, he flung the paper to the ground and stomped on it. Then, angry, but feeling foolish, he carried it to the yard and buried it under a layer of fallen dead leaves.

Dressing quickly and silently, he went into a storage room in the basement and got two large suitcases and a smaller leather one, an oversized briefcase really, bought specifically for this purpose. He put the leather case inside one of the suitcases and walked up the basement stairs.

"Dad?"

It was Paul's voice. He was standing in his pajamas rubbing sleep out of his eyes. There was no way to avoid his seeing the suitcases. "Going on a trip?"

"Not really," Harry said, floundering.

"Then why are you carrying those?"

There was simply no way to counter his suspicions and no way to tell him the truth.

"I… ah… promised to lend them to someone in the office."

"Oh."

He looked at the boy—pale, quizzical, obviously confused, unbelieving. Trust me, son, he begged, hating himself. The boy was no fool. What must he think of his father?

"Just keep the TVs and the phones disconnected."

"Sure, Dad."

"And don't answer the door."

The boy nodded.

"And keep an eye on Mom."

"I will, Dad."

He started toward the door.

"Dad—"

Harry turned, saw the boy's misted eyes.

"You'll tell me, won't you?"

"Tell you?"

"The truth," the boy said haltingly.

It felt like a blow to his midsection.

"Of course," he muttered in dismissal.

It was a discussion he did not wish to pursue. He let himself into the garage, threw the two large suitcases into the back seat of his car, and eased it out of the garage. Then he drove around the beltway to Amtrak's suburban station.

He made it to the seven ten just as the doors were closing. Was it a sign of changing luck? But half an hour out, he was suddenly assailed by a galloping attack of paranoia. Was he being followed? He looked around the car for signs of some sinister presence. How could one tell?

Then it occurred to him that he had left his car at the parking lot next to the station, a dead giveaway. They could have agents pick him up at any of the stops along the way, follow him to the banks, dangle him between them like a children's toy acrobat manipulated by squeezing wooden slats together.

Sometime later, he got panic under control. If he was being followed, then he'd have to give them the slip somehow. He also had to get at the money, collect it from the safety-deposit boxes of the three banks then hide it. After all, without the tangible evidence of the money, everything else was speculation. Accusations could be flung from here to Friday, but without the proof of money passed, which was the money itself, all investigations would lead to dead ends.

The problem was to get at the money unobserved and, if observed, to get away. He felt like a criminal. Therefore, he reasoned, he was a criminal. Now he saw the true lure of it as a profession. It wasn't just the profit. It had to be the excitement.

All senses alert, he got off at Baltimore. Removing the large leather briefcases, he put the two suitcases in two large boxes at the station, put in his coins, and removed the keys. The action was the replay of his first sortie, getting the money into the banks.

Briefcase in hand, looking much like any other businessman on his way to work, Harry walked toward the bank, which was deliberately chosen for it's proximity to the station. It was he, Harry, who had carefully worked out every detail of the action. The money had been delivered to him in thirds, and he had pursued his own operation in thirds. How clever he had thought himself. Then he had felt like a political bagman, which had it's own unpleasant stigma. But this time around he was feeling more like a thief and self-disgust had gripped him, punishing him, like a cramp in his gut.

Still too early for the bank's opening, he stopped at a drug store and made a call to his office. Mrs. Habersham always arrived before the rest of the staff.

"My God, Mr. Silver, the phone is ringing off the hook," Mrs. Habersham said. "I'm going crazy. They say they can't get through to your home."

"What have you told them?"

"That you're on your way to the office."

"Good. Keep saying that."

"Where are you?"

Harry hesitated.

"I'll be in later, Mrs. Habersham."

"Are you all right?"

"Fine."

"I assume you saw the paper and the television."

"Sure," he muttered.

"That Fox woman was very nasty. You shouldn't have talked to her yesterday."

"Touché."

Waiting, he sensed that Mrs. Habersham wanted to respond, but she was too dignified for that, and he let the moment pass.

"Mr. Silver, what shall I tell Bob White to say?" she asked.

"Nothing," he sighed. "No comment. We should have done that yesterday."

"Have you a number where I can reach you?"

"I'll call you."

He hung up the phone.

By the time he reached the bank, it had just opened. First customer of the day, he thought. Not a good idea. "Oh yes, I remember him. He was the first customer of the day." He had used a fictitious name at each bank, but he had not taken the trouble to attempt to alter his handwriting. No retrospection, he admonished. He'd just have to take his chances.

Surprisingly, everything went smoother than anticipated. He had signed the name Bob Martin, short and sweet. No suspicious eyes scrutinized him. Just a nice gray-haired lady offering him a pleasant smile, ushering him into the vaults, and putting a key in one of the twin locks. He nodded to her but said nothing as they turned the two keys simultaneously.

The objective here was to give no clue, no sense of individuality. Be anonymous. When the woman had gone, he took the oversized box to one of the private rooms nearby and quickly transferred the shiny plastic wrapped and pressed bricks of hundred dollar bills to the leather briefcase.

He brought the box back to the vault, motioned for the woman to join him, and inserted the box. They turned their keys simultaneously again, and he was quickly off on a walk back to the station. The briefcase was extraordinarily heavy, and he had to switch arms periodically. But he would not take a taxi, especially this short distance. The less people involved, the better.

Approximately an hour later, he was in Wilmington repeating the operation, soon after that in Philadelphia then in Trenton. It amazed him. It was demonic. To be standing on the Trenton railroad platform with suitcases loaded with five million each. He had disposed of the leather briefcase. Ten million dollars in cash. Few people in the world, excluding people who worked in the mint or in banks, had ever been in such proximity to so much cash.

He looked up and down the platform, watching people plying their daily trade, living out quiet uneventful lives, pounding out their substance in exchange for—for what he had sitting there beside him. None of them, he was certain, would come close to that sum in a lifetime, ten lifetimes.

In that context, he could understand both the risk and enormity of the amount. And it had been earmarked for an equally enormous task, to help make Billy Tucker president of the United States, such a lofty aspiration. Here were the seeds, on this spittle-stained concrete platform of an aging railroad station. But they were also the seeds to grow new life for himself. He could buy himself another identity, disappear, actualize a whole other life for himself. Ten million offered limitless possibilities. it was not something to be considered lightly. Later he could send for Terry, Paul, Bobbie. Or not. He shivered with expectation, anticipation, infinite possibilities.

Beside him was a pay phone. Last link, he thought. One more time. He put a quarter into the telephone and called his office.

"Where are you?" Mrs. Habersham whispered.

"I'm on my way," he said, thinking that he was technically correct since he stood on the platform heading toward Washington.

"Some of the natives are getting restless." From her tone it was obvious that media people were in her office.

"Suppose I said never." He chuckled deliberately so that she would understand it as a joke. Was it really? His throat tightened.

"Then you'd be one very smart man." She lowered her voice. "They're now implying that you're a drug dealer, that Leopold was into drugs. I mean it's getting wild. There are TV cameras camped on our doorstep."

"Just tell them I'm dancing as fast as I can."

"What does that mean?"

"I'm not sure."

"I think maybe I should go home. I'm not good at holding forts."

"Go then, my child. Far."

"Are you all right, Mr. Silver?"

Oddly, with the ten million beside him, he felt untouched by her sense of panic and harassment.

"Right as rain."

"I *am* going home, Mr. Silver," she said firmly.

He hung up, trying to make sense out of what was happening, including his own reactions. With effort, he picked up the suitcases, and caught a glimpse of his reflection in the waiting-room glass. Willy Loman with his smile and his shoeshine, he thought, contemplating the image of himself. Time to find a new territory. Maybe head west where all new things were supposed to begin.

Good idea, he thought, wondering on which platform one boarded western trains.

XVI

She had left Al a series of messages on their answering machine. When she called his secretary, Elly was told that she hadn't heard from him, that as far as she knew, he was still in New York. No, she didn't know which hotel. Was he scheduled to return today? She wasn't sure.

"You're not telling me the truth," she blurted. Secretaries were always lying for their bosses. Yet, she had always seemed so friendly and trustworthy. "All right," Elly told her coldly. "If he calls, would you have him call me at the paper." She hung up without waiting for a response.

Last night had been worse than the night before. To get her through it, she had taken two sleeping pills and spun off into a dead dreamless torpor. She deserved the interlude, she told herself. If she didn't shut her mind off, she was convinced her brain would overheat and self-destruct.

Al's childish emotional tantrum was squeezing the joy out of her success, taking the sweetness out of the honey. She was the paper's golden-haired girl with her teeth in the tail of a running story of mysterious chicanery in high places, every journalist's dream. Who knew where it would lead?

Buoyed by the owner's support and a chance to give Evans a drubbing in the boardroom, Charlie was ecstatic and had given her carte blanche. Well, almost.

"Just don't fuck it up with hyperbole," he had warned with a smile.

He had termed her new twist on the rabbi, the drug implication, the idea of special customs' favors "delicious stuff." She had used Hopwood's quotes, keeping her promise to withhold his name. She had also eliminated his vicious and irrelevant anti-Semitism. But she had opened up a Pandora's box of sinister possibilities.

Harry Silver's denial added spice and titillation, leaving the "rabbi" as "Mystery Man," a pervasive and exciting image. The story, she knew, offered a vast array of subliminal intrigue. Spies. Drugs. Smuggling. Favoritism. Access to the greatest power figures in the land.

It begged questions of impropriety. Poor old Harry, she thought. But he had lied blatantly, balls out. He deserved the pummeling. Best of all, she wasn't sharing bylines with anyone. Charlie had asked if she needed help. "No way," she had replied.

She was, of course, still pushing the snowball up the mountain, gathering heft and size. The competition on the tube and other city papers had jumped onto the track, and she knew she had to move with superhuman effort to stay in front.

Which was why flashes of anger and frustration interrupted the thunder of recognition and success. Al had no right to do this, none at all. It was better shared, savored. Her offstage life, as the kids say, sucked. With two strong sleeping pills in her, she pulled down the curtain and shut off the lights.

It left her with a foggy-headed lethargy that didn't wear off until midday. Again, she had walked the gauntlet of congratulations. Other media outlets were rehashing her stuff for their own front pages, quoting her piece with acknowledgment. The traffic between her and the paper's correspondents had begun to accelerate. She had called Bob Robbins, their Israel correspondent, to check on the identity of the mysterious rabbi, and she put out lines to their people in Europe, Africa, and other parts of the Middle East.

One paper, she had learned, carried a report spotting Leopold in Austria. Another put him on his way to South America. Still another had him in Baghdad visiting with Hussein. Another had him boarding an airliner for Japan. Japan? It wasn't as far fetched as it sounded. The first stop of Secretary Tucker's Asian trip was Japan. Perhaps Leopold and the treasury secretary would secretly meet, strike a deal. Leopold would give himself up in exchange for leniency. Possibilities. Possibilities.

Laced through all this reportorial mud was the odd role of Harry Silver, the customs man. Cool as a cucumber, she had observed, but intriguing, more to him than met the eye. She had, of course, carried his denial, a perfect setup to crush his credibility, like squashing an insect. What was he hiding? Pressed to the wall, they always made mistakes.

Hopwood called in the afternoon to thank her for keeping her word. Despite his revelations and his linchpin role in her story, his voice made her uncomfortable.

"We'll get the bastards," he said. She resented the collective pronoun. We, indeed.

Overhanging her day was a desire to get a reaction from Harry Silver. She had checked repeatedly with his office. "On his way," she had been told, an obvious ploy.

The phone at his home did not answer. A friend at the networks told her that the front of Silver's house in Chevy Chase was buzzing with television crews and reporters.

Mrs. Silver, badly shaken up and looking like the wrath of God, had opened the door and told them that as far as she knew her husband had gone to work. The paper's photographer had been in the forefront of the pack and had gotten a picture. He was rushing back to get it developed.

She checked on the status of the drug sweep, finally reaching the supercilious Customs Department PR man who told her that it was going "splendidly," although he could not specify what that really meant. A contact at the Drug Enforcement Agency had told her it was, despite all the hoopla, going nowhere. And the stories about long delays and disgruntled passengers were building. Countries, airlines, and passengers were all complaining vociferously. Things were definitely not going well for Harry Silver. In an odd way, she wished she had never met him, had done her interview on the telephone.

But the frosting on the cake arrived very late in the day, just after the first edition had gone to bed. No sense doing an immediate investigative follow-up, Charlie had advised unless she could come up with another firecracker. There were plenty of people to do the routine stuff.

Bob Robbins called from Tel Aviv with the startling news that a Rabbi Abraham Pincus had, indeed, existed, but he had died suddenly eight months ago. A persistent reporter, who she knew well from her days on the Metro desk, Robbins visited the family of the deceased who were puzzled that a man bearing the same name and description had passed through customs in the United States. To their knowledge, he had never been to the States.

Baffled at first, Robbins started on the trail of the man's visa, discovering it had been issued at the U.S. Embassy two months after he had died. Yes, this rabbi had appeared at the embassy, shown his Israeli passport, filled out the proper papers, and was granted a visa.

"Someone found a bureaucratic hole," Robbins said, adding with a wry laugh. "We have here a living ghost."

"That's a conflict in terms," Elly joked, elated with the information.

"There's more."

"I can't stand it."

"Your friend Leopold was in the country at approximately the same time."

"Where did you get that?"

"Diamond cutters. Business stinks, and they're fighting over crumbs. The word is that Leopold came in with a sack full of raw stones. Came in twice. Once, a few weeks later."

"And came out with rocks, cut and polished."

"Presumably. The trail ends with the raw stones."

"Is there something fishy in that?"

"Not here. It's a way of life. This is Israel, hard up for hard currency. They wink. They do business. They wink."

"Someone was winking here as well. As my story says, the customs commissioner himself walked him in. Wink. Wink. And no records of diamonds passing through." Another thought suddenly struck her.

"Where do you suppose he got the raw stones?"

"He probably bought his box at the London Clearing House."

"I checked. They never heard of Irving Leopold."

"Then he had to have bought them from a middleman."

"That would cost more, wouldn't it?"

"Considerably more, I'd say."

"Then how could he afford to sell the finished product for under the market price?"

"You're making me fantasize," Parker said.

"Fantasize then."

"Your Mr. Leopold came in with hot stones, got them cut and polished, then moved them to the States as Rabbi Abraham Pincus under the direct sponsorship and protection of the commissioner of customs. Probably did it twice."

"I can't print that. No proof that the man in the rabbi suit was Leopold."

"Who then?"

"I wish he would surface," Elly mused. "Clear it up."

"If he didn't buy the stones from a middleman, didn't get them from the London Clearing House, then what?" Bob Robbins speculated aloud. As all good reporters, he relished the mystery.

She paused a moment, her mind racing.

"He probably stole them," she said firmly. "Or he got them from the source, South Africa."

"Where they hold out ten percent of the raw stones for local consumption—or whatever." He waited for a reaction.

"Pie-in-the-sky speculation," she said. It was time to surround her information with covered wagons.

"You mean they were stolen or transferred?" Robbins asked, obviously hoping that the speculation would keep the story in play.

"I won't breathe a word of what I'm thinking, even to myself," Elly said, mostly to emphasize their camaraderie. "At this point, it's strictly what Onan did."

"He spilt his seed upon the ground. Wasted it."

She laughed, feeling the giddiness of excitement. The fog was lifting. Bits and piece were forming themselves into a recognizable pattern.

"Not me," she joked. "I'm freezing it for later use."

"God, Elly. I'm salivating."

She was just about wrapping things up, when the telephone rang. It was Al.

"I was just so damned busy, Elly. This case has got me hopping."

"When will you be home?"

"I'll keep in touch."

"Al, am I still being punished?"

She had listened carefully for any sign of contrition or apology. Neither appeared evident in his tone.

"Maybe I just overreacted." His tone was oddly flat, noncommittal.

"No," she protested. "You had every right."

"We'll get on it just as soon as I can get control of this case."

"And as soon as I finish this story, I'll be ready for all kinds of resolutions." She wondered if she meant it.

"Sure," he said.

"I'll make it up," she said, wondering what she meant. Then she decided to test the waters, confront a subject that could not be avoided. No way, she thought, sensing the old anger. "Have you been seeing my pieces?"

"Jesus, Elly. I haven't been able to get to a paper."

"You haven't seen the TV either?"

"I've been so damned busy."

"Al, it's everywhere. You have to be deaf, dumb, and blind to miss it. I'm hotter than a pistol. Charlie Carruthers is ecstatic. This is big-time stuff. Really."

"I'm sure it is, Elly. I've just got my own fish to fry."

She felt hurt, disappointed. He was trying a different tack now, eschewing anger and recrimination. This was less direct and hurt more.

"Well, when are you coming home?"

"I told you, I'll call."

"Al—"

"Yes?" he asked flatly, without curiosity.

No, she decided. No time for a confrontation. She'd just have to ride it out.

"Keep in touch," she said.

"Sure."

*Post*ponement had its virtues, she assured herself, massing all her powers of concentration, determined to shift gears, veer off in the direction of the story. The story! It frightened her to discover how quickly she could dismiss Al, husband, lover, friend, family, rock, mooring. And yet, when she was alone, literally alone, longing began again, the craving. To keep that at bay, she worked at polishing the story until she was sure it would hold its bite. The trick was to keep the language neutral enough, to seem objective, to hide the bared fangs, and to keep a strong enough pull on the line. Above all, the story had to stay alive, promote the thirst for further installments.

The reader had to say to himself: Where there's smoke there's fire. And she had to bury the hook of curiosity in the proverbial craw. Why had the commissioner of customs blatantly offered his protection to this man, obviously disguised as an Orthodox rabbi using the credentials and name of someone who had died? Who was this mysterious man? Why had Harry Silver denied having done this? Why was he avoiding comment? Indeed, where was Harry Silver? Why did the secretary of the treasury pick this moment for his Asian trip? Where was Irving Leopold? Was Irving Leopold a spy, drug or diamond courier, a mastermind, a double agent, a secret presidential emissary? Were any state secrets revealed? Who was guilty? Of what? How high up did it go? At this point, scenarios were infinite, imagination rampant. What was her own emotional life against that?

It was nearly two when she finally shut down the computer. The newsroom, except for the usual skeleton night staff was practically deserted. She waved good-bye to the night editors and left the building, walking past the guard to the adjacent parking lot.

She picked up her car and drove toward home. But as she neared her building, the prospect of confronting emptiness assailed her. After seven years of marriage, she was conditioned to Al's presence beside her, his sounds, scent, and feel, the counterbalance of his weight on the mattress, the knowledge of his presence.

Such images only exacerbated her sense of deprivation, the delicious comfort of knowing his flesh was available for her comfort and her frequent orgasmic joy. For some mysterious reason, biological, psychological, anatomical, she had the gift of sexual sensitivity. It was a discovery made with only the tiniest of guilt stirrings when she was ten. Only later, when she was old enough to understand, she had realized how rich and wonderful her autoerotic life had been and how easily it had made the transition from pure imagination to the enjoyment of the male, at first generically and then specifically. Only in her mind, during that time, had she been promiscuous.

Of course, there had been men before. Luckily her initiation had been kindly. A forty-year-old reporter, who worked with her father at the paper, had done the messy job of rupture, at her insistence. She was eighteen then. Considering the times, she was actually late for such a procedure.

Not that she had deprived herself or her teenage dates, but had never, as they say, gone all the way. Her initiator was married to boot, and the deed was done in her own bed in her parents' house while they were out of town. Who could ask for anything better than that? The comfort and security of your own bed, the experience and expertise of a happily married man who knew the value of gentle patience—for this she owed him a debt of gratitude for making that first time a joy rather than an ordeal. How many females came that first time, making it well worth the brief pain? She remembered having thanked him.

For seven years Al had satisfied these impulses, had joined her in the sexual feast that had been so much a part of their marriage, channeling emotional energy, validating their sense of sharing in this most intimate exchange. Surely this tension between her and Al would pass.

It annoyed her to be wasting her substance on such matters when she needed every atom of thought and concentration to be focused on her work. Such reflections were turning craving into frustration, frustration into anger, anger into rage. Why had everything else gone awry?

Then suddenly she was thinking of Harry Silver, who must also be asking himself a similar question. Yet she felt less animosity toward Harry than she felt for Al, which seemed strangely incongruous. And she was destroying Harry Silver with the cold calculation of a killer. In the distance she felt it coming. Was it a sudden wave of compassion? She became confused, disoriented. She gunned the motor, and zipped past her apartment building, heading toward Maryland.

She moved up Connecticut Avenue toward Chevy Chase Circle, intersected by the demarcation line between Maryland and the District of Columbia. She slowed with the traffic lights, as she passed over the line to this green and prosperous minisuburb that was once "the country" for affluent District residents wishing to escape the scorching swamp heat of the capital in the days before air-conditioning. The action, she knew, preceded the understanding of where she was headed.

There was this sudden compulsion to explain herself to Harry Silver, to assure him that he was simply a chess piece in a very personal and private game, that he had to be taken out for the sake of her winning, that an occasional deceitful double move was a strategic necessity. Nor was there any way for it to be stopped. Besides, this game would carry her to the Mount Olympus of journalism, wherever that was.

It was this deceit that intrigued her, obsessed her now. She felt a kinship with it, a part of it. Yet, in his eyes, where such qualities were naturally revealed, she had received no message like that. Not fear, either—perhaps a mocking irony.

Had he been laughing at her? Not that either. Calculation? That was the closest she could come to it. She wondered, too, what he saw when he looked at her. A reporter wielding a stiletto behind a contrived facade? A professional adversary? Or merely a woman with a paper heart? No. A paper sword.

She knew she had an odd look for such work. Pretty, some said, although she wished her lower lip did not pout so much, and the cupid's bow was not so pronounced, the nose above not as wide, the eyes closer spaced. She liked being a semi redhead, although the freckles proliferated too much in the sun, and her skin blistered if she wasn't careful.

She was considerably more comfortable with elements of her body peculiar to her gender, breasts firm, nipples pink, quick to stand, stomach flat, pubic bush full, more golden than carroty, and the other parts tight and easily primed. Good legs, too, with sturdy-looking muscle definition, thighs that tapered from the hips. Built for strong, sometimes contorted, embracing.

Now she was confusing the personal with the public, clashing images. Was her mind just too tired to discriminate? Or was some autoerotic fantasy beginning to take hold in her imagination?

But she did not turn back. She knew vaguely where he lived. Al had colleagues there. She remembered little maps they sent with their cocktail and dinner invitations. Left on Leland, right on Taylor, three lights from the circle. Pulling over, she opened her purse and consulted her notebook, memorized his street and number, then made the appropriate turns through the streets.

She drove slowly. It was often impossible to see the numbers, and she had to backtrack to find a visible number and then follow the sequences to the correct address. The street was deserted, and she shut the motor, doused the lights, and observed the Silver residence.

Bastardized Tudor, two stories, a garage with a basketball hoop over the door, a yellow light on the brick beside the main entrance. On the driveway, crinkled leaves from two tall tulip oaks in the front yard. A low light showed in an upstairs window. Fear of darkness or beacon? she wondered. On the street, she saw the inevitable signs of the impatient bullying press, Styrofoam cups, discarded photo boxes, hamburger wrappers, waxy Coke containers.

The man had a wife and two children—older boy, younger girl. She had gotten bits and pieces of their history from old clips in the paper's library. Theresa, a farmer's daughter; Paul, an honor student; Roberta, Bobbie to her friends. Somewhere it said her favorite singer now was Prince.

And Harry, whose rabbi (the cheap irony did not escape her) was William Tucker, star quality, with a wife who had created her own mold of the political spouse. What struck her was this mundane suburban scene, so ordinary, so familiar, so secure on its surface, so far from the cauldron of intrigue, mystery, and chicanery that seeped like hot lava from her story.

Was he frightened, skewered on the bytes of her computer? Did he see himself as the small fry, the expendable rear guard put on the line while the real big fish ran for cover? Was he just that? She sent tiny antennae out from her mind, from her skin, from her heart trying to pick up signals from that darkened house of troubles. But nothing stirred in the air except a signal from within, her father's voice, lamenting. "Death to tyrants. Down with corruption. The center must hold, and we are its guardians." It came to her as the voice of justification. She could feel the warm pat on the head, the soft words of approval.

Finally, she felt spent. It was a futile exercise to look into an antagonist's heart. The enemy must be seen as a cardboard cutout, bloodless, above all, not a victim but a perpetrator. She stirred suddenly, reacting to the hum of an oncoming motor. In the puddle of streetlights, she saw it, moving cautiously. She lowered herself below the dashboard, listening. The car was moving toward her, slowing just as it drew up beside her car. She stiffened, her breath shallow. She heard the pad of tires as the wheels turned, and the sound of the motor changed its pitch.

Looking up cautiously, she saw the garage door open slowly. The car moved within. Then the motor stilled. The garage door began to descend. But in the brief light, she saw the man emerge from the car's door. Harry Silver.

Where had he been? She looked at her watch. It was after three. None but the bad tooled around in the dead of night, she thought, turning the ignition key.

Like her? She shivered and stepped on the gas.

XVII

It was not as if he was consciously aware of making a decision. The train, like some giant reptile, had slithered into the station. The doors opened. People got out. People entered. Others watched from the interior of the train. Some glanced his way. It was difficult to assess what their eyes saw, certainly not a man with ten million dollars in untraceable cash at his feet. Nor a man on the verge of unzipping his skin, stepping out of the costume he had worn for forty-two years, contemplating the purchase of a new one, entirely different from that which he presently wore.

At that moment the old skin broke out into a river of sweat. The conductor looked at him. A loudspeaker blared the train's destination, Washington with stops in Philadelphia, Wilmington, and Baltimore. The conductor looked up and down the station, then at him.

"We're leaving now," the conductor said.

Was it an invitation? A threat?

Before he could protest, a black man in uniform appeared, grabbed the handles of his two bags and carried them onto the train. Harry shrugged and followed. Always at the mercy of others, he rebuked himself. Resigned, he let the black man put the bags on the rack above his head. He gave him a dollar, then settled back into his seat as the train pulled out of the station.

So once again he had gone along, stayed on the track. He contemplated the symbolism, then he looked up at the innocuous looking baggage on the rack above his head. Had he been left holding the bags? He smiled, chuckled sardonically at his little joke.

He was taking—had taken—most of the risks. Why? From

the beginning he had assessed the danger, championed doubt, shown reluctance, allowed himself to be manipulated by Billy, flattered. It struck him now that his own motives for having entangled himself seemed pallid against those of Billy and Irving. Billy hungered to be president, the leader. His whole life had been programmed in that direction. The ultimate leader. The Pied Piper. And he, Harry, had heard the tune as a child, had blindly followed, trusting, because he did not have the will to be himself, whoever that was.

Hi, Dad, he called silently, hearing the echo.

"He hasn't the will," his mother had said. By then, she was saying it in front of them, father and son. "You need the will to succeed. It can only come from inside."

His father had looked at her impassively, rooted to his chair. Always, as long as Harry could remember, this was where he spent his evenings, chin eventually drooping to his chest, which rose and fell evenly with the shallow breathing of sleep. Sometimes Harry would sit for hours watching the phenomenon, the slack-jawed posture of surrender.

"Let that be a lesson," his mother had told him, pointing to his sleeping father.

"What do you suppose he thinks about?" he had once asked his mother.

"Nothing," she snapped, with an air of complete authority.

Harry had reflected upon her answer, viewing his father with the kind of scrutiny one reserved for animals locked in their cages at the zoo. It was as if he had asked: What does that sleeping lion think about? What are his dreams? He had spent a lifetime inventing answers, assuring himself that they were true, but never certain, not beyond the shadow of a doubt. His father's inner life was rich and varied, he had assured himself. His dreams ranged over all possibilities. In the core of the man's self, he had remained true, had, above all else, preserved his dignity. Hadn't he?

So where was the dignity in this little caper, Harry thought, imagining how his son would see him. It had all the elements of sleaze. A sleazy group of bigots is determined to stall change, to drag their heels and continue to maintain an offensive system of one racial group profiting by the repression and exploitation of another racial group.

A sleazy jeweler sees a way to marry the designs of this government with his own plan for personal delusion and enrichment. A sleazy politician (how else to describe him) sells himself to this idea in exchange for seed money to help satisfy a hungering, limitless ambition. A sleazy flunky, himself, goaded by his own paltry need to prove a vague and still undefined something to—to whom?—lends himself to the sleazy enterprise.

Had it seemed so from the beginning? Enter Eleanor Fox. A picture of her leaped into his mind. He had been disturbed by his inability to detest her, by her insidious sensuality, by her having built this battering ram out of false materials.

Of course, he had lied to her. Lied to survive. Like people who ate their dead companions to survive. There. That surely rationalized any venality. It also gave a certain balance to the running story, a basketful of untruths and inaccuracies.

He had a mind to tell her the absolute truth, watch her squirm, force the paper to confront the dilemma of its own credibility or lack thereof. Irving Leopold, you idiots, was in Venice for crying out loud. Of course, to tell the truth now would hold him up to ridicule. Just another damned liar, they would say. Was he?

So everything starts to unravel. Even the unravelers are sleazy. He was certain that everyone involved operated out of his or her own sleazy motives. Sleaze begets sleaze.

He looked around him, suddenly wondering if he had said this aloud. No one had turned. It gave him an opportunity to inspect everyone in this particular car. Again he wondered if he was being followed, if they had stood their distance and watched him and were waiting for the appropriate time to move in. At that point his thoughts drifted to Terry, already falling apart because of mere hints of impropriety and danger.

He sighed, looked up at the baggage rack with disgust then turned to watch the passing landmarks of another, older, America. For some reason scenes next to railroad tracks remained static, locked in time, perhaps a half century from the present. From the vantage of a passing train, America seemed frozen in the Great Depression.

It grew darker. The passing scenes faded. Soon all he could see was his own image. Not a pretty sight. He slouched in his seat then attempted to sleep, but his thoughts continued to race then became repetitive.

At the suburban station on the Maryland outskirts of Washington he got off, baggage in hand and loaded it into the backseat of his car. A few people got off with him. Again, he wondered if he was being followed. By then, he had a clear idea of what had to be done. He felt chills of expectation.

"It is a far, far better thing that I do, than I have ever done." He whispered the words Dickens had put into the mouth of Sydney Carton in *A Tale of Two Cities*. Then, turning the ignition, he chuckled aloud. Old Sydney was saying the words on the guillotine, just before the blade was to fall.

He drove out of the parking lot, started toward Washington, then backtracked, got off the main road, stopped at a gas station to fill up. Using a self-serve pump, he peered at the passing cars, wondering if he was being followed.

When he went to pay, he discovered he hadn't enough cash and had to use a credit card. The irony of that threw him into a paroxysm of silent hysterics. With ten million in the backseat of his car?

Heading east toward Annapolis, he stopped at a MacDonald's, bought some hamburgers from a girl at an outside window, ate them silently in the parking lot and washed them down with Coke. He did not drive swiftly, letting cars pass, getting horn blasts of frustration. With relief, he noted that no car held back behind him.

Not far from the tollgates to the Bay Bridge, he pulled over to a Wendy's, bought a large container of coffee, and then sat in the car for a long time drinking it, waiting.

Traffic thinned as the time passed. By one o'clock few cars were on the road. He pulled out of the lot. Fed with caffeine, his mind felt trigger-sharp, alert. He paid his toll, then started the drive over the high bridge, watching the sparse traffic from both ends. Passing over to the Eastern Shore, he stopped again, pulled into a closed used-car lot, parked, doused his lights, and waited.

Getting out of the car, he transferred the suitcases to the front seat, got in again, turned into the lanes leading back toward Washington, and moved slowly toward the Bay Bridge again. The traffic coming from the Eastern Shore had practically ceased. But there was still an occasional car coming from the other end.

A car came up behind him. He let it pass. As he ascended the hump to the bridge's highest point, he began to get a clear view of the road in either direction. The bridge was deserted.

As he reached the pinnacle of the hump, he doused his lights, pulled close to the bridge railing, jumped out of the door, crossed in front of the car, then opened the door on the other side.

Grabbing the handle of one of the large suitcase, he swung

back, and in a quick movement hefted it over the railing. He repeated the operation with the other one then jumped into the open door and gunned the motor. A moment later, he clicked on the lights.

"Now there's a first," he said aloud. He was dead certain that no human being had ever performed such an original act. Someday he would have to tell this to his children. Would they believe it? No way.

For the first time in his life, he had a clear view of what *rightness* meant, acting in perfect moral harmony. He felt emptied of all conflict, cleansed. Was this sensation what was meant by deliverance? It was as if all of his life's journey, all the convoluted paths and strange detours and meanderings were meant to culminate at this moment in time and space, on the bridge. He had confronted his destiny. He had made his statement. He had accounted to himself. From here on in, he feared nothing.

He approached his house cautiously. The streets were deserted. He slowed down to a snail's pace, squinted into the darkness ahead. Although he sensed a presence, he saw nothing. He stopped the car, inspected the black night, and moved on. Then suddenly, he accelerated and drove swiftly up the driveway, flicked on the automatic garage opener, heard the door lumber and creak upward, then drove in, pressing the control to close the door almost at the same moment as he had crossed the garage's threshold.

Paul, in robe and pajamas, opened the door to the kitchen and came forward. Bobbie, her eyes red and swollen, dashed toward him, and he stopped to embrace her. She clung to his neck, her heart beating furiously.

"Oh, Daddy," she whimpered. "Oh, Daddy. We were so worried about you."

He patted her back.

"It's all going to be fine now," he told her, squeezing a tear out of his eye. It slowly dripped down his cheek. Raising his eyes, he saw Paul through the mist. Dark patches seemed to have grown under his eyes. His face seemed gaunt.

"It's okay now," Harry said. "I promise you."

He patted Bobbie's back, carried her to the kitchen, and sat on a chair. She sat on his lap.

"Those people beat on the door all day," Paul said, slumping on a chair opposite Harry, the table between them.

"I can imagine," Harry said, kissing Bobbie's smooth cheek.

"How is your mother?"

"Still freaked out," Paul said.

"Did you call the doctor?"

Paul shrugged.

"I was afraid to do anything, Dad."

"Believe me, it's gonna be fine." Harry sighed. The sight of his anxious children had considerably diluted his euphoria.

"I listened to the TV," Paul confessed. "I had to."

"Me, too, Daddy," Bobbie sniffled. "But not *Cheers*."

"It's all right, baby," Harry said.

"But we kept the phones off," Paul said.

"Good."

"They're talking about investigations, bad things," Paul whispered. "A couple of senators said they were going to hold hearings."

Bobby wiped her eyes.

"Are you a criminal, Daddy?"

He did not answer immediately, embracing the child, not knowing how to respond to the question and still be technically accurate and truthful. It was, he knew, impossible. Instead, he chose evasion.

"Do I look like a criminal?"

"Oh, no, Daddy."

"Then what is it all about, Dad? They had this strange story about you helping some rabbi. I don't understand any of it, Dad."

"It's all a misunderstanding, Paul." In that, he was sure he was reasonably accurate.

"I hope so, Dad. It's been pretty hairy, what with Mom's reaction and all those people trying to get into the house. But what I want to know... " The boy hesitated. The media had made his father a suspicious character, had painted a picture of an unknown man. Not the father-protector he had known all his life. "What I want to know... ," Paul repeated. Am I guilty or not? Harry thought, wondering how to reply to that question. But the boy did not ask that. "Where were you all day? That's what I want to know." So it had become the unaskable, Harry thought with sorrow. Yet he yearned to tell them what he had done, convey to them this monumental experience of deliverance and fulfillment. Some day, he sighed.

"I saw Mr. Tucker on the television, too," Bobbie said.

Billy? How would he explain what he had done to Billy, both the fact and the feeling? If all this did blow over, then Billy, the ever resourceful, would simply put together another plan. Maybe it would even succeed. One never knew with Billy and his charmed life. And if it didn't blow over, if the worst-case scenario became reality, if Irving Leopold confessed, if the South Africans confirmed, it would simply be talk without the evidence, words and speculation.

"He was in Tokyo. He said he couldn't believe these stories about you."

"Did he?"

"He called them prep something," Bobbie said.

"Preposterous," Paul said.

"He is right. They are." Weren't they? Spies, drug dealing, mumbo jumbo. He wished he could scream out his rage at all these absurdities and lies. At least, he told himself, hang the bastard for the crime he did commit.

"He really defended you, Dad. At least it shows one thing. You got a very loyal friend in Mr. Tucker."

"Great to have friends," Harry said, gently putting Bobbie aside. His children followed him upstairs. Terry was lying in bed with the light on. She looked up at him with a blank, dazed expression. Sitting down on the bed, he kissed her forehead. It was ice cold.

"It's going to be fine now, Terry."

Tears streamed out of her eyes.

"I know it's all very confusing," he told her. "Just hang in there. It will eventually run out of steam."

"I just don't know what to say," Terry whined.

He turned to Paul.

"Did she see the television?"

Paul looked down sheepishly, and he turned back to Terry.

"It's all lies, Terry," he said. "Dirty rotten lies."

She shrugged and looked at him aimlessly. He wondered if she comprehended.

"I know this is a trial for us," Harry said, turning toward the children. "I hope you won't doubt me." He wanted to say more, to tell them the truth. But how much of that would they understand? he wondered. "Now I want you all to go to sleep," he said. "It's been a long day. And tomorrow we go on about our lives, business as usual. No restrictions. We're going to plug ourselves back in. Whatever they say about old Dad, they say. There's just

nothing we can do about it. All I ask from you is your support."
It sounded like a political speech. Glassy-eyed, Terry looked at
the ceiling. Paul seemed uncertain and turned his eyes away.

Bobbie came over to him, and he embraced her once again.
Then he carried her to her room and put her into bed, tucking
the covers under her chin.

"So tomorrow I can watch *Cheers*? All Paul would let me watch
was the news."

"Anything you want, baby."

He decided then that he would not be going to the office.
He'd stay home, watch the home front, reconnect the telephones.
Fear had disappeared.

She closed her eyes, and he kissed the lids. It was a gesture he
suddenly remembered in another context, in another time. He
had done it over his father's dead face.

He heard the door to Paul's room slam shut. The boy was wary,
disappointed, holding back. Could he blame him? The respect
of his children had been an important goal of his life, and he
had cultivated it with great care following the immutable laws of
action and reaction. His own father had been held up to ridicule
and contempt, forced into his secret life behind the facade of
feigned sleep. Because of this the door had been shut between
father and son, and what communication there was came only
through the senses, mysteriously and clandestinely. I know what
is behind your mask, he had assured himself, loving his father.
But he had also pitied him.

Back in the bedroom, Terry continued to stare through the
film of her eyes. He undressed and got into bed. Still, his mind
could not stop turning over. So Billy had defended him, he
thought, had cut him adrift to fend for himself depending on the
old tie. The old tie, Harry mused, whatever that was. Admiration

seemed to have evaporated over the last twenty-four hours. Love? Loyalty? Devotion? These, too, seemed pallid and exhausted clichés.

What then? He drifted off. Doors and windows were closing. Shutters were snapping shut. A curtain was going down in his mind. Only the tiniest sliver of light showed somewhere in the totality of the darkness. His last conscious thoughts had to do with honor, courage, dignity. But he was not sure what they meant.

XVIII

"A helluva story. A helluva story," Charlie said, flipping a handful of peanuts into his mouth like buckshot, then washing down the mash with a slug from his second martini. They were sitting in the swanky lounge in one of the city's best hotels across the street from the paper. "Reads like Ludlum."

Elly nursed her second white wine, loving Charlie's display of enthusiasm, especially since at that hour a number of the paper's brass were present, including Evans, Charlie's archenemy of the boardroom. Upon arriving Charlie had nodded in his direction, muttering through his smile: "Ass-kissing shit."

"I really appreciate this, Charlie. Giving me all this free reign."

"You earned it, baby. We got a live one here. Did you see that guy Silver on the boob this morning? Denying everything. Dumb shit. Deny. Deny. Deny. Won't these asshole politicians ever learn. He's hanging out there all by his lonesome. It's a cover-up. I feel it in my fillings. He's just the fall guy. The truth is higher up. Always is. Someone will goof. Hang in there, someone will goof. Squeeze this Silver, squeeze hard and out will come the gumballs."

"I'm squeezing as hard as I can."

"Harder. Harder."

He opened and closed his palms, pumping up the veins on the back of his hand.

"You really think it doesn't stop there?"

"Never does."

"You mean there's another smoking gun?" Elly asked.

"Always is."

"Suppose he keeps it to himself?"

"They never do. Not when their back is to the wall."

"You think it goes up to his buddy Tucker?"

"Maybe higher."

"The president?"

"Happened before."

"How long do you think before he folds his hand?" Elly asked.

"Up to you." Charlie took another sip of his martini. "Chutzpah is what the schmuck has. You know what chutzpah means?"

"Roughly," Elly said.

"Balls. *Cojones.* Like the pair you wear, only you know where you're going. He doesn't. He's walking right into the lion's jaws. Hasn't got a prayer. Is it as we figured it, you think? I love it. They smuggle out stolen diamonds from South Africa. Polish them up in Israel. Smuggle them into the States, a rabbi yet. It's wonderful. Wonderful! Now the question is who gets the jack? And why? Never know what kind of deals they make on the inside. Maybe they are into the spy thing. Use the money to buy information. What an access ploy. He sells the stuff all gussied up in fancy settings to the people they're screwing. Irving. Irving. You're beautiful, baby. I love that scenario. And with the head of Customs as a confederate, all bases are covered. Beautiful."

"All fits together. Problem is our South African correspondent is being fluffed around," Elly said. "On the one hand, they say the smuggling thing is fantasy. On the other, that it was probable but not possible. Then they tell him to leave it alone. He was going to take one more pass at it and call me tonight."

"That's them. Scared shitless."

"But why tell him to leave it alone?"

"Looks bad for them all ways," Charlie said. He had the cynic's contempt for all governments and their spokespeople. "First, they don't like to call attention to their diamond monopoly or the mines where they exploit blacks. Second, their control is tight and efficient, and they don't want others to think that people can get away with smuggling their most important crop. Third, they don't want to show a connection high up in the American government. Looks like play for pay. A little grease in the right places, just to insure the little winky game they play with Uncle Sam. Good stuff for your next installment."

"So we have deny, deny, deny again."

"The more they deny, the better the story."

"The lady doth protest too much."

"That's a story."

"Or the lady says nothing."

"That, too, is a story."

"The lady runs."

"Another story."

"The lady stays, offers herself."

"More story."

"The lady balks, confesses."

"Better yet."

"So the confession is the end of the story."

"Hell, no. The end of the story is the truth. That's thirty, baby. The truth."

"You're confusing me. Suppose the truth never comes?"

"Then the story dies of boredom. Call it olds, not news. We're not an *old*spaper."

He laughed and, with his fingers, he dived for the olive in his martini then popped it in his mouth. That was it, she thought, the fear that the story would get tiresome, lose the power of "what happens next." It had to have an end, a logical denouement. "All we need is proof, proof positive. It'll come." He patted her hand.

"Pop to the surface like a cork."

"I just hope that when it does come, it doesn't disappoint."

"Like what?"

 She tapped her chin.

"Maybe they did it just for the money," Elly said.

"Who are they?"

"Silver. Leopold."

"Small fry. We want the big bananas. Like last time."

"Suppose it doesn't go that far?"

"That's defeatist, baby." He raised his arm as if he were carrying a sword.

"Charge," he said loudly. "Maybe the bucks are so big, they'll blow your mind away."

"Like millions?"

"Multi. In a great scam. Like we're talking about—spies, drugs, big government, international intrigue. We need a few dollops of chicanery and double-cross, then a good moniker: Diamondgate maybe. Yuk. I'm fed up with gates. How about Silverstone? Make the poor bastard immortal." He was feeling good. He signaled the waiter for another round. "Haven't had so much fun in years. And just when they were beginning to write off old Charlie." He looked toward Evans, who looked up. He gave him the finger, but with a broad smile. "Just a little joke, prick," he whispered. Evans shook his head, as a father might rebuke a child.

"And you nearly muffed the chance," Elly said, certain that she had reached that level of intimacy.

"I forget sometimes how these things begin. I really do. So you see this crazy jeweler get on a boat heading east from Venice. A coincidence. Like a guy walking in Manhattan, first day on a new job. Kisses the wife and kids. Wears a new suit, fancy tie, shiny shoes, Calvin Klein undies. Big smile. Sun shining. Air crisp.

Glad-to-be-alive feeling. Then a man drops a screwdriver from the sixtieth floor, and it goes right through this schnook's brain."

"Difference is that my antennae are always out there looking for signals."

"Looking for glory."

"Looking for truth."

"Bullshit."

No point in pursuing that, she decided. Keep this up, and they might get really philosophical and start discussing ends justifying means or other weighty moral issues. Better stay off that one, she thought, remembering what she had given Newton Parker and other little so-called ethical lapses. The drinks came along with another bowl of peanuts.

"Take away these mothers," Charlie barked at the waiter, who quickly removed them.

"Al, my husband, is really pissed off. He thinks I'm devoting too much time—" Her words trailed off. She wondered if she was crossing some fine line.

"One of those, eh." Charlie took a deep sip of his martini. "They don't understand. These civilians. They don't know what it means to be a journalist, to get your teeth into the tiger's tail. They don't understand that. Never will." He raised his glass to her. "You got the calling, baby. It's a talent." He tapped his nose. "The scent. Sixth sense." He shook his head. "God, I love this business. The joy of it."

He put an outstretched finger under her nose. "Never, never, never let the bastards get away with it. They think they got it made. They come here, they think they can get away with anything, all kinds of shit. Love to see the bastards get their comeuppance, love to hear them scream bloody murder at their innocence. Bullshit. They come here, they better not fuck around. Not while we're looking. Hey, kid? Not while we're looking." He had wandered. Now he pulled back, found his place again. "I don't want to butt in. But this I know. The civilian had better back down. He's gonna lose."

"I think you're right about that. I just hope I don't lose him."

"Can't be helped," Charlie muttered. "Besides you're on the verge, baby."

Just today, she had gotten a call from a New York literary agent. He told her that her story had the makings of a great book, maybe a movie. She hadn't told anyone as yet. Besides, she didn't have an ending. She sipped her wine, felt the beginnings of a buzz. Maybe that would be a good thing, she thought.

Al had called earlier and told her he wouldn't be home before the weekend, maybe not even then. But he was surprisingly pleasant if not affectionate. Too much work. Big case. Big bucks. Naturally, she couldn't protest even if it was just punishment, tit for tat.

She did ask if she might come up and join him, but he must have caught her sense of reluctance. There were no vacations from a story like this. She didn't want to be caught napping. Other reporters had jumped into the fray. News organizations had committed troops, which meant she would have to do double time to stay ahead.

"I sure wish that Leopold would surface," she said. "Put the frosting on the cake."

"He'll show up somehow. Won't let you down. I guaranfuckingtee it." His speech had thickened, but he wasn't drunk, not yet. "He's one of your partners."

"Partners?"

"Sure. Takes two to tango. In your case, three, a regular ménage à trois. Forgot about old Harry?"

"That's an odd concept," she said.

"You're in it together is all. What would you be without them? What you have here is a relationship." He laughed again and signaled to the waiter. "Where the hell are the peanuts?"

She started on her third glass of wine. It disturbed her to look at things in that light. Was there such a thing as being too wise, too honest? What constituted a relationship? She took a deep pull on the wine. The waiter came with another bowl of peanuts, and Charlie scooped up a handful and stuffed them into his mouth. Then he pushed the bowl away and finished his martini while standing.

"You go get us an encore," he said, putting his hand on her shoulder, like the laying on of hands. His hand was heavy, his grasp hard. "Your job is to squeeze. Keep squeezing."

"Ouch," she cried.

People had turned to watch them. He loosened his grip. Despite the brief stab of pain, she liked the attention. She was entering star territory, she thought. The idea set off a surge of adrenaline. Go get 'em, tiger. The words popped into her head. Was it the voice of her father? She wasn't sure. Not anymore.

***

It might have been the wine. Its effect often made her exaggerate, elevate a nuance to a fact. Squeeze, he had said. It stuck in her mind, along with "oldspaper." It was true that the South African connection would be good for her next piece. As Charlie said, it would work any which way. And after that? Now that the great dinosaur of suspicious Washington had stirred, she could expect a crowded field of players.

Kevin Broderick called from Johannesburg about eight, and she snapped on her tape recorder.

"They're angry here," he said. "Very angry."

"Good."

"I had the temerity to ask them if they were buying Washington favors with diamonds."

"Who is 'them'?"

"The director of information. Man name of David Bancham."

"He denied everything?"

"They always do that."

"So how do you read things?"

"I like the premise. But the facts are rather sketchy."

"You don't think you can pick up any connection?"

"Elly, I tried. If there's anything to it, it's kept close to the vest."

"But do you think there is any truth to it?"

"Maybe, yes. Maybe, no."

"Where does that leave me?"

"At the when-did-you-stop-beating-your-wife stage."

"I am a wife."

"Then make it vice versa."

She hung up angry. Denial, she knew, was always good for a story, if couched in the correct terms. Charlie had said so. She turned on her computer and tried a lead.

"The South African government today vehemently denied that they had traded diamonds for political favors through the good offices of jeweler Irving Leopold." No. She rewrote. "The South African government today officially denied that they had participated in a scheme to trade diamonds for political favors. Through a middleman, the missing jeweler Irving Leopold, and allegedly with the collusion of Commissioner of Customs Harry Silver, millions of dollars worth of diamonds were smuggled from South Africa through Israel to the States." It sounded like an indictment of the entire administration. She stopped, reread the copy then shut off the computer.

Too many holes in the story. Surely, officials of the South African government would not be stupid enough to do something so obviously ridiculous. Private citizens might, but not the government. And none of the recipients of the jewelry had offered any explanation for their purchase except pure price. South Africa with all its problems was, she was certain, light years from their consciousness. Problem is, she thought, once you started, there was only a finite amount of backtracking allotted. You had to move ahead. Keep fishing upstream.

She opened a drawer and took out her file of stories. She had also clipped a number from the other papers. She reread them. The writing was good, clever, supple. It was inescapable. Irving Leopold was hiding something. Harry Silver was hiding something. Maybe everybody was hiding something. Odd how the roles had been reversed, now it was Charlie screaming for more. Go get 'em.

She put the stories aside, tried to penetrate the morass of her thoughts. Charlie wanted encores. Soon she would have to write the South African story, connection or concoction. It didn't matter. And the encore after that? All roads led to Harry Silver. Squeeze as hard as you can.

She found his home number and dialed, surprised to get a ring then an answer.

"Yes?" The voice was clipped, flat, and furtive. It was as if he was waiting by the phone, challenging it to ring.

"This is Eleanor Fox."

"So?"

"We really should sit down and talk," she said.

"About what?"

"I'm kicking your ass to hell," she said. "There's got to be your side."

"We tried that once." His voice was noncommittal, bored. She detected no fear.

"I'm about to write a piece about a South African connection."

"Your prerogative. Freedom of the press."

"You don't care?"

"Why should I care?"

"I'm going to imply that you helped Irving Leopold smuggle diamonds into the States."

"Why would I do that?"

"I'm not sure. Maybe to buy political favors for South Africa."

"What could I do for South Africa?"

"Not you. Someone higher up."

"That should upset the South Africans."

"And you still deny that you had anything to do with it?"

"Why should I deny anything? You'll publish it anyway."

"You mean you won't deny it?"

"I've been answering questions like that. Most of them make no sense at all."

"That's the point, I'm trying to make sense out of it all."

"Not with all those half-truths."

"So now I'm half right," she snapped back.

In the long pause that followed, she could hear him breathe. She listened for signs of agitation. Then suddenly, she heard nothing, as if he had put his hand over the mouthpiece.

"Are you there?"

She waited, hearing his breath again. Her heart pounded in her chest.

"All right," he said.

"Now? Tonight?"

"No."

"Then in the morning. Maybe breakfast?"

"No. Lunch. Where?"

Actually, he had caught her off-guard. She hadn't expected such a quick and positive response. Her mind buzzed with possibilities. Maybe he was going to split the whole thing wide open. Like a diamond. She smiled at the example then let her thoughts catch up with her excitement.

"Virginia. I know a place. Very discreet. I'll pick you up at noon. Corner of Connecticut and K."

"I like that. Hush-hush and mysterious." He seemed to be mocking her.

She let it pass, afraid to rock the boat. She said good-bye and hung up. But her excitement did not subside. Not even later as she lay in bed, alone, unable to sleep, her mind crowded with questions she must remember to ask him. There was also something else, somewhere out there in the darkness, like distant trumpets. She strained to hear. Were they coming closer? She wasn't certain, although she could not deny the compelling signals, the excitement of anticipation.

XIX

He was remembering the toy. It was shaped like a telescope and when you turned the end of the tube furthest from the eye and held it up to the light, the bits and pieces of colored paper rearranged themselves into new patterns. He had had such a toy when he was a child and had bought similar toys for his children. Now it was suddenly the metaphor for his life. From moment to moment, at each turn of the tube, the pattern changed. All earlier systems of logic disappeared. Everything was instantly new, rearranged, profoundly changed.

The best tactic, he supposed, was to keep the kaleidoscope turning, encourage the process of rearranging. Like a camp follower servicing an army division just called off the line from combat, he made himself available to all comers.

And like a good whore, he had even invented a special technique for fast turnover. Crisp repartee, service with a smile, illusion and evasion. Are you a spy? For which country, the Principality of Monaco? Are you a drug dealer? Would you like some aspirin? What did you get from Irving Leopold? Political herpes. How can you be seen with a man who was legally dead? I think the fellow needs the ghost busters. Why was Leopold leaving Venice for Iraq? They wouldn't let him into the gondola union? Have you been asked to resign? My standing resignation letter is on file. How high up does this corruption go? Right to the pearly gates, pearls supplied by Irving Leopold. On and on, the drumbeat of questions was relentless, as were his answers. He was, after all, practicing for the big leagues. A congressional investigation was in the works.

And yet, considering all the publicity, Irving Leopold had not called again, which seemed strange. Billy hadn't called either, but that was understandable in the light of his paranoia about listening bugs. Disposing of the money, of course, had made all the difference. However the offense was measured in legal terms, he had considerably reduced the category of risk.

Whatever the consequences, one thing was apparent. His reputation was tainted forever. His credibility was under suspicion. Any chance of further advancement in government was finished. Billy had cut him loose. Whatever verbal support he might get from those in high places was purely lip service. He was a walking political corpse.

"I want to know what it means, Dad, that's all I want to know," Paul asked as he drove him to his school. Running the gauntlet of all those media people was bad enough for him, let alone Paul and Bobbie. He had just dropped Bobbie off.

"It means that your old man is odd man out. Patsy of the month."

"I understand that, Dad. I just want to know if it's true."

"That I lie, that I could be a spy, a drug dealer, a thief, a conspiring sinister character?"

It was awful, he knew, using this tactic on his son. Unfortunately, to tell him the truth was impossible. Not now. He had already made that decision. He could never betray Billy, no matter how things had changed between them. Never. Someday, of course, he would have to tell Paul, explain to him about the meaning of personal honor and the mystical bond of true friendship. He made that commitment to himself firmly, irrevocably. But not now. Honor was an admirable trait to be revered, not trashed.

"I just can't believe any of that, Dad. No way."

"Then shut your eyes and ears and hang on," he said with

bravado. Courage, too, was an admirable trait. And good humor in the face of disaster. Paul would have to see those things for himself.

"I'll try, Dad."

He slowed the car, turned off into a quiet street and stopped, cutting off the motor. He looked at his son. He seemed pale, uncertain, and confused. God, he loved the boy.

"I'm not perfect, son. Also—well, the truth is I *am* holding things back."

"So it's true then?" Paul asked, agitated.

"It's impossible to explain." He scrutinized his son's face. "What I want is your trust and respect, son. That's the main game between fathers and sons, Paul. I'm not a saint, but I'm not a villain either." Harry shook his head and slapped the shelf on top of the dashboard. "Damn."

Then he turned to his son, valiantly trying to cap a burst of anger. "Listen, it's your choice. If you want to lose confidence in me, then you're just hurting yourself *and me*. I mean the wrong is not monumental in this case. I'm not different in any way. What you thought of me and felt for me before these damned stories came out should remain the same. You're my son, for Chrissakes, and I love you." Paul's face was impassive, and he glanced away. "You can't make judgments based on what the press says. It's superficial. It doesn't explain character. And in this case, it's all confused." He studied his son's somber expression.

"Nothing's changed, Paul. Just give me the benefit of the doubt."

"I'm trying, Dad."

"I know, son."

"I promise that someday, you'll know everything."

"Sure, Dad."

"It's not a question of trust, either," he said, feeling foolish. Could he explain that it was for the boy's own protection, in case he was interrogated? Was it really?

"I'm sure you know what's best," Paul said. Did he detect an air of doubt?

"I promise," Harry said, restarting the motor.

Silently, he drove Paul to school then headed back to the house. The press swarmed around his closed car. Lips compressed, he looked at them with annoyance, saying nothing as he edged the car into the garage.

Inside, he was surprised to find Terry up and around. She had combed her hair, put on some makeup, and was wearing her best dressing gown. He kissed her on the forehead.

"Good for you," he said.

Up close, he wasn't so sure. Her eyes were not clear and alert, and her smile seemed forced, hollow.

"I drove the kids to school," he said. "Moved them through the wall of vultures."

She sat down at the table and looked out the bow window to the backyard.

"Better get the lawn raked. There are so many leaves."

"Good chore for the weekend," he said.

"Got to clean up the vegetable garden, too."

"Next year you should make it bigger."

She paused and continued to look out of the window, her eyes glazed. He wondered what she saw.

"I used to have this goat. Won the 4H prize year after year. His name was Huckleberry."

"After Huckleberry Finn."

"No after the huckleberry. We had a patch of huckleberries on the farm. Dark blue, but not blueberries. They came from a different shrub. People forget that. A huckleberry is a huckle-berry." Her face flushed suddenly.

"I do know the difference, Terry."

He watched her face. A nerve palpitated in her jaw, and her lips trembled.

"It's going to be fine, Terry. I promise you." The refrain seemed meaningless. It wasn't all right, not at all. "It's all a misunder-standing." Surely, he should tell her. He owed it to her. "They got it all twisted, a crazy misperception. I don't know how it hap-pened or how to explain it. It wasn't that big a deal."

Stop there, you lying son of a bitch. Ten million. Smuggled diamonds. A blatant political payoff, however you slice it. "Sometimes you take chances, depending on the risk to success ratio—" He watched her, still looking into the yard. She wasn't listening. She had blocked that all out. "I mean things are still the same between us. So what's a little public humiliation? Can't stand the heat, get out of the kitchen." She still wasn't listening, and it was pointless to continue. Besides, he had to go.

The phone rang. The jangle bit into his nerves. It was Jeff Bilton, the president's chief of staff.

"I think we better see you first thing, Harry," Bilton said. There was no salutation. No preliminaries. The missing ritual was preg-nant with meaning. Harry was quickly becoming a political liability. They had undoubtedly been figuring out how to excise him without things getting messy. Not so easy, he thought, offer-ing the mouthpiece a wry smile.

"I'll be there in half an hour."

"And, Harry, no press please."

"I understand."

"Got to go, Terry," he said, bending over to kiss her cheek. "White House." She continued to look out of the window. "Will you be all right?" When she didn't respond, he repeated it louder and got a desultory nod. He stroked her hair. "Just take it easy."

He unplugged the phones assuring her that if she needed to dial out, all she had to do was reconnect them again. He worried about leaving her alone.

"Will you be okay?" he asked.

"Of course," she said vaguely.

"Sure?"

She nodded.

"Just don't answer the phones. Do you hear me?" He got another vague nod. He got to the outside door, turned and shouted back into the kitchen.

"It's gonna be fine, Terry, just fine."

***

Jeff Bilton was a severe young man who wore little round rimless spectacles. This made him appear even more severe. His hawk face also embellished that image, although his short weak chin softened it somewhat. He was, everybody acknowledged, an expert political tactician and an efficient administrator, a very rare combination of talents.

He came out from behind his desk to shake hands with Harry and lead him to facing chairs in front of a cocktail table. The atmosphere was ominous. No others were present. Bilton crossed his long legs and peered through his rimless glasses, which made his look penetrating, beady-eyed.

"What the hell is going on?" Bilton asked.

"I haven't got the faintest idea," Harry said blandly.

"How can you say that? This rabbi thing. They have a witness."

"My word against his."

"You think this is some kind of a plot against you?"

"Could be. Maybe I've been too aggressive on this drug business. Who knows?"

"So you deny everything?"

"Of course."

"No deals with Leopold?"

"I bought a ring. Hell, everybody bought something."

Bilton patted the air with his right hand.

"You don't have to say it." He looked at Harry and shook his head. "The FBI has got you dead to rights on the rabbi thing, Harry. The witness is absolutely certain."

Harry said nothing. Deny, deny, he told himself. Lie like hell.

"The guy was dead, Harry. Dead. Who was the man, Harry?"

"Fiction," Harry said. The less said the better, he decided.

"Then we've got this new thing with the South Africans. The CIA checked in with that last night. The newshounds are smelling around. It goes something like this—the Dutchmen paying off in diamonds for potential political favors. The stuff carried to Israel, cut and polished, brought into the States, then converted into cash."

"That's science fiction."

"Tell you the truth, I don't understand it either. We called the treasury secretary." Harry's heart began to pound. "He's puzzled, too. Says as far as he knows you're straight. Except for this business of bringing this rabbi through customs."

"I told you it wasn't true."

"And I heard it. Turns out the witness is a known anti-Semite, a real flake. But that doesn't mean he didn't see what he said he saw."

"I'm not even Jewish."

"I know that, Harry. I just don't understand any of it, these stories in the papers and that stuff on television. It smells bad. And it can't go on, even if you're clean as a whistle. As for the possibility the drug boys are showing some muscle, why you? This country is leaking like a sieve, despite all the visible action."

Harry welcomed the sudden deflection.

"There's no way to stop it, Jeff. You know that. It'll take billions. An army. A navy."

"That's not the point. What I mean is, why you?" He tilted his head. His nostrils flared as if Harry was emitting some obnoxious odor.

"Slow news, I guess. They needed someone to kick around."

"I frankly don't know what the hell to do. I've been trying since yesterday to head off a congressional investigation. And there's this crazy Irving. Where the hell is Irving? At first it was just a joke. Now it's serious. Maybe he was a spook?"

"What do our spooks say?"

"They don't know. Nobody knows. Not one single intelligence agency knows. Not in our country. Not in any other. Maybe he was what he was."

"And decided to get away from it all," Harry said innocently.

"To Iraq?"

"Only if you believe it."

"It's not what *I* believe. It's in the papers, on the tube, it becomes a fact."

"Like the big lie. Say it over and over again, and it becomes the truth."

Bilton tilted his head to the side, watching Harry obliquely.

"What about that hundred thousand?" Bilton asked cautiously. "The money found in his briefcase."

Appear quizzical and perplexed, Harry urged himself.

"Beats the shit out of me," he said.

"Up here we don't know whether to laugh or cry."

"All I know is that somebody has decided to hang me up by the thumbs."

"People are saying, where there's smoke there's fire."

"I smell only smoke," Harry said. He had already learned one thing from this little meeting. They were very far from knowing the truth.

"The point is that we have to accept what the media is saying."

"Even if it's full of bull?"

"In this business we must deal in perceptions. In this case someone is manipulating perceptions. True or not, it's reality."

"How can what is false be reality?"

"Because the medium is the message."

"That old turkey."

Bilton got up from his chair and paced the room. A window looked out on the green south lawn. He walked toward it, peered out.

"It's what they believe out there that counts," Bilton said.

"I don't see anyone," Harry said, deliberately facetious. He had no defense. No real offense either. All he had was the core of himself, hidden deep inside. They would not get a crack at that, he vowed.

"The strategy is this," Bilton said, turning to face Harry. He had moved forward and was standing above him. Harry was sorry he had gotten into that position. There was something to height in a situation like this. "We're going to put out a statement backing you to the hilt. We're going to throw you orchids."

So it would be a modern version of a gangster's funeral, Harry thought.

"Then I commit hara-kiri," he said.

"Hey, good play on words, Harry," Bilton said, smiling for the first time that morning. It was tepid, without warmth.

"I step down for the good of the administration. Too controversial, inhibiting to the great patriotic work of Customs. Et cetera. Et cetera. Blah, blah, blah."

"You got the routine, Harry. Very bright guy. You could have written the damned thing yourself." He took an envelope out of an inner pocket, opened it, and drew out a neatly folded letter. "Got it on your own stationery. Office of the Commissioner."

"I appreciate that."

"We'll give it out a couple of days after our statement. Maybe sooner. Even kept the date blank," Bilton said. He had come back to the chair and sat down again, pushing the letter forward across a little table to Harry, handing him a pen from an inside pocket.

"That long?" Harry asked sarcastically, looking blankly at the letter, refusing to read it. He took the pen by rote and signed it.

"Hell, Harry, you're a lawyer," Bilton said, refolding the letter and putting it back into the envelope. "Three hundred bucks an hour. Get rich. Maybe you'll get lucky and pick up some of the drug families as clients. After all, you know the game plan. Harry, I think we're doing you a favor." He slapped his thighs, a clear signal of dismissal, then stood up.

"What about the congressional investigation, if they do go ahead?"

"We might be able to head it off." He had put the letter back into its envelope and on the table between them. "If you have to testify, that rabbi business may get sticky. Hell, get yourself a good lawyer. Take the fifth if you have to. Just remember, keep the boss out of it. And Tucker, keep him out of it. You wouldn't want to appear ungrateful." Bilton put out his hand. Harry looked at it curiously, not knowing what to do with it. "Nothing personal, Harry. You were a good soldier."

When Harry didn't take his hand, Bilton put it on his shoulder. With the other, he grasped his upper arm then winked through his rimless spectacles. "What you're going to do will seem like an act of courage and patriotism. Give them something to chew on out there."

"Resignation under fire could seem more like a confession of guilt," Harry said.

"Depends on where you sit," Bilton said.

Harry shrugged and began to leave the office. He paused at the door then turned. Bilton had already gone back to his desk and was preparing to use the phone. He looked up wearing a carefully contrived "case dismissed" look.

"Yes?"

"Did Secretary Tucker—" A lump suddenly formed in Harry's throat.

"Did we discuss it?"

Harry nodded.

"Actually we did. I'll tell you this. He really is in your corner. He used every argument in the book with the president and with me. Called all the way from Tokyo. I want you to know that having a friend like that is really, well, inspirational."

"So he fought to keep me on," Harry murmured. Billy hadn't cut him loose after all.

Bilton raised his eyebrows. The skin rippled in his forehead.

"Other way around, Harry. He wanted you out of the line of fire."

XX

She had maneuvered him to take the inside seat, looking out, which was where she usually sat in a restaurant when she went with Al. It gave her more to see. In that kind of setting, people could be considered entertainment. But this was business. What she wanted here was to focus, fully and completely, on Harry Silver. She had left word at the paper where she would be lunching.

In the car, they had chatted aimlessly. Occasionally, she would turn to take in a quick look, a snapshot really. He looked paler than when she had seen him last. In the revealing daylight, she could see strands of gray in his black hair. From the side, his lashes looked longer, darker, hiding darting eyes, which caught her swiftly, clandestinely, whenever she was forced to concentrate on the road.

Mostly she had led the conversation into the banal. Hometowns. Schools. Studies.

"But surely you know all that," he told her, after he had politely provided her with the relevant facts of his early life.

"It's not the same when people tell it," she said amiably. She had volunteered a bit of her own history, but he hadn't responded, hadn't shown much interest. Of course it had to be awkward, she assured herself. Yet she threw at him all the charm and ingratiation she could muster, speaking through a broad smile, pumping out lots of "reallys" and "wonderfuls" at, she hoped, appropriate moments. During the ride, his attention had a tendency to slip away. She wasn't sure whether this was natural or deliberate. One gesture, however, seemed deliberate. He sat at the absolute outer edge of the front seat, a message with undeniable implications.

In the restaurant, he had ordered a Perrier and lime. A bad sign, she thought. She had ordered a white wine, planning to nurse it.

"All right," he said, when he had settled and suffered through what must have seemed to him a blatantly intrusive inspection. "I'm here."

"And I appreciate that. I really wasn't sure you'd show."

"I was. I always keep my word. One of my most consistent faults." He did not smile. Before he had made a modest effort to be ingratiating. Now he was simply correct. She had expected more hostility, but for some reason he seemed subdued.

"You must think I'm an awful bitch," she said. She had decided upon humility as an opening tactic.

"What I think about you is irrelevant."

Actually, she felt a slight disappointment at his lukewarm attitude toward her. After all, she had studied him with obvious intensity. She had thought a great deal about him. She took a deep sip of wine. One of his hands, she noted, lay idly on the table, fingers caressing a spoon. The hand was smooth, veinless, with jet black hair along the finger's ridges to the knuckles then continuing in a patch to the wrist. The finger's tips traveled toward the bowl of the spoon, a movement that arrested her attention. She felt an odd stirring deep inside her and had to force herself to raise her eyes. Again she was disappointed. He was looking beyond her, over her shoulder, vague and indifferent.

"Above all, in this business, you want to be fair. You worry about being fair."

She searched his face for some reaction. It remained impassive, although his eyes drifted briefly to meet hers then moved away. Was he lying back deliberately? On the phone yesterday, he had seemed much more involved.

"A question of morality, ethics, and conscience, no doubt?" he asked. So at least he was listening. It was a hopeful response, especially the sarcasm.

"Something like that. Yes." She waited for more words to come from him. When none came, she asked:

"Would you like me to use my tape recorder?"

"Your option," he shrugged.

"But you see." She felt awkward, stumbling. "I want your side. I thought you understood that. It's an opportunity. We can even make a dub, just to be sure you're not misquoted. Above all, I want to be fair. I mean—certain conclusions are inescapable in my stories."

"In everybody's," he said. "You've started an avalanche."

"Look I—"

"Just doing your job."

"That's exactly right," she snapped. She took another sip of wine, surprised at her nervousness. Then she dipped into her purse and took out the tape recorder. "Well, what will it be?"

"Doesn't matter," he said.

"Well then, I won't use it." She hadn't planned to respond that way. She wanted to use the tape recorder. Instead, she put it back in her purse then clasped her hands. "But it won't mean that I won't be listening."

He looked into his glass of Perrier but didn't lift it. His fingers still caressed the bowl of the spoon. She felt a sudden urge to touch its handle, to participate with him, as if by the act she could share his thoughts. Was he conscious of how this was affecting her?

"What you have to understand is that there are people out there. They react. They tell secrets. Sometimes they're accurate, sometimes not. Sometimes they want their pound of flesh. In this business you dig deep enough, everybody is vulnerable. Take this thing with the rabbi, for example. This fellow volunteered information. We checked it out. It's undeniable. Undeniable. Then why do you continue to deny it? Don't you see? It makes you automatically suspect."

"Of what?" he asked softly.

"When you say things like that, you just sound as if you're hiding something." A note of exasperation had crept into her voice. "Or covering something up for someone else."

"Don't you think I'm capable of perpetrating my own crimes?" He smiled—or smirked. She wasn't sure which.

"I'm trying to help you, you know."

"You've been a fabulous help." He picked up his glass and raised it. "I toast your help." He drank.

"This is not going well, is it?" She finished her wine. "Would you like to order?" She motioned for the waiter. He ordered a shrimp cocktail. "That it?" He nodded. "Bring two," she said to the waiter. "And another white."

Then she turned to him again. "Look, Harry." She paused. "You don't mind if I call you Harry? You can call me Elly." His response was to remain impassive. "Whatever you're involved in, it can't be hidden forever. I'm here because I'm paranoid about the possibility that you may be an innocent."

"An unwitting pawn?"

"Something like that."

"In other words—stupid."

His eyes were drifting less. Perhaps she had begun to engage him, had opened a path?

"Maybe naive," she said cautiously. He raised his eyes to hers, searching. After a brief moment, she turned away and found herself watching his hand again. The caress of the spoon's bowl was rhythmic. It seemed to have gained momentum.

"A fool? An instrument for spies."

"Like Irving Leopold?"

He smiled and shook his head.

"It has all the logic in the world." She hesitated for a moment, contemplated telling him, then did: "I saw him board that Iraqi boat with my own eyes."

She watched him carefully, and he did react. His eyes narrowed to a squint, then blinked, a clear gesture of doubt. Where else could he have gone? she thought, suddenly, seeing the picture in her mind, the soft Venetian air, the speedboat moving into the darkness, leaving its wake.

"I would not have trusted anyone else on that point. And I'm sure it was Leopold, dead sure. The rest, as they say, is history." She paused, watched his lips form a wry smile. "You don't believe me, do you?"

"I don't doubt you for a minute," Harry said, too quickly.

"One of these days, he's going to turn up and tell the truth."

"Now wouldn't that be an embarrassment."

"There is an implication there," she snapped.

"I hope so."

The waiter came with their shrimp cocktails and her glass of white wine. He looked at the large fat shrimps with indifference.

"You really don't want to tell your side, do you?"

"I've already been hung. Why tighten the noose after the fact?"

"I'm trying to help you, Harry." She felt a flash of anger. "Why did you agree to meet me then?"

"I'm not sure," he said. For the first time, she felt he was offering her a degree of contact.

"You can't just keep on denying everything."

"Yes, I can," he said, looking away suddenly. She had the

impression that he was resisting the urge to say more.

"It's so obvious, Harry. There's smoke here." She watched his face. "We think the South Africans are in it, too." She paused. "It will all be in tomorrow's papers. Would you like to hear what it's about?"

"Not particularly."

"Because you already know about it?"

"Because I'm not interested."

He had not touched his shrimp cocktail. She ate hers to mask her exasperation. He started to drift away again. Was he someone on the razor's edge of indecision? Had he wanted to tell her things, then changed his mind? Suddenly, she remembered Charlie's words. The real guilt was higher up.

"Are you protecting William Tucker, Harry?" she asked.

For a moment, he seemed startled. His jaw fell open, and his eyes narrowed. She sensed that it might be the time to press forward.

"Someone else then? Someone higher? Harry, something is going on. It's there. You know it, and I know it." She paused, assessing him. Again, she saw his hand toying with the spoon. She reached out, touched his flesh, felt the strange transmittal of energy, a pulsating electric thrill, which startled her. "Maybe it's time we work together," she said haltingly, confused by her reactions. You have a relationship, Charlie had said. He withdrew his hand, but not before it had lingered longer, she imagined, than might have been appropriate. Yet she had not calculated on making the gesture. It had been mindless, compulsive.

He was silent for an inordinately long time, but she was determined to wait for his response, to let his mind soak up the consequences of what she was saying, offering. She had entered unfamiliar territory. That much she knew. She would have to work through it, digest it, understand it.

"It's like a computer gone amuck," he said finally.

He seemed calm, in control, thoughtful. He wasn't addressing her. That much was apparent. He was speaking to some unseen audience known only to himself. "Like all those little bytes were getting signals that were oblique, once removed. All that's coming up on the screen is slightly off. Words are missing suffixes or prefixes, sentences hang in space, meaning is distorted, awry. It's like you're looking into one of those distorted mirrors in a funhouse, and it's throwing back false images."

"I don't understand."

"That's the point."

"So you're just going to sit back and let me do this to you?" It was, of course, the ultimate question, the one she had kept in reserve for just this moment.

"That may be my only defense," he said. He wasn't drifting now. His full attention was engaged. He just wasn't making sense. Or she wasn't understanding him. Or they were transmitting messages to each other on different wavelengths.

"I don't know what you're trying to prove," she said. "You haven't got a prayer. You'll go down in flames."

"Good for your side," he said.

"I'm not on any side, Harry."

He was playing with her. She was sure of it. For him this little exercise was to show her his sardonic side, to bait her, corrode her judgment, play with her head and her emotions. His hand was back on the table now, toying with the spoon. There.

"All you have given me today, Harry, is nonsensical abstractions." Bubbles of boiling anger seemed to erupt inside her. "Just remember, I tried to help, tried to get your side. You're mixed up in something pretty rotten, and I can smell it." She tapped her nose. "I've got the scent. When I get through with you, they'll chew you up and spit you out. You people come here and you forget that you're just public servants—"

Suddenly he raised his palm like a traffic cop.

"Spare me," he said. "Let's just quit while we're behind."

"You're behind," she snapped. "I'm winning."

"So far," he said.

At the moment, as if on cue, the headwaiter came up to them.

"Are you Eleanor Fox?"

She nodded.

"Good description. The big clue was redhead," the headwaiter said smiling. "Telephone."

She welcomed the interruption. The interview was going nowhere.

"Here's Elly," she said into the phone.

"What the hell are you doing out there?" Charlie asked.

"You said squeeze. I'm out here squeezing." And getting nowhere, she told herself.

"You're with Silver?" His voice grew lower. "Shit." The sibilance grated in her ears.

"What is it, Charlie?"

"Just got a call."

"About what, for crying out loud?"

"It's Mrs. Silver. She's cracked up her car."

"Is she all right?"

"Afraid not. Report says she's at Holy Cross Hospital in a coma."

***

She weaved in and out of the beltway traffic, doing seventy. At intervals, Elly would turn to him. "She'll be fine. You'll see."

She had not had the courage to tell him the real extent of her condition, only that she was in this terrible accident. His skin had turned dead white and his expression stony and inert.

"I should never have left her alone today," he whispered, stifling a sob. The sound was like a dagger in her heart.

"Is there anything I can do?"

"Bobbie and Paul. Our kids—" He sucked in deep breaths.

"Tell me, Harry."

"They're in school." He took out a pen and paper and wrote down the names of the schools in a faltering hand.

"Get them home," he said, swallowing hard. "When I see how things are, I'll call. Okay?"

"Sure, Harry."

She pulled up to the entrance of the emergency room, and he dashed out. It had been a mistake. Reporters and camera crews blocked his way. He waded through them, saying nothing. Ghouls, she mumbled, as if she had suddenly distanced herself.

"What happened?" she called to one of the reporters she knew, a young man from one of the television stations.

"Wrapped the damned thing around a tree in Rock Creek Park."

"What's the status?"

"Dead. Probably knew too much."

He was heavyset, and a rim of beaded perspiration covered his upper lip. She felt his scrutiny. It made her uncomfortable. "You really got something goin' here, Elly. They must be jumpin' up and down in the newsroom."

"Yeah. Jumping."

She made a grimace of disgust and gunned the motor. Inside herself, she felt churned up, unable to fully comprehend the degree of her own culpability. It was an issue that she would have to confront. Was she to blame? The question angered her, and she tried unsuccessfully to block that path of consideration.

The schools were not far apart. She explained to each principal why she was there, and they quickly fetched the children. To each of them she introduced herself only as Eleanor, a colleague of their father's, telling them that their mother had been in an automobile accident, had been taken to the hospital, and their father had asked that they be taken home.

"But will she be all right?" Bobbie asked for the third or fourth time as they drove toward the Silver home. Her eyes were misty and her voice trembling. Paul, on the other hand, was stoic. He sat beside her saying little.

"I should never have gone to school today," Paul said. "I should have stayed with her." An echo of his father.

"Wasn't she well?"

"You've seen what the papers and television have been saying about my father. Terrible things. They upset her."

"May have been something completely different. Purely an accident." It might have sounded sincere, but she knew it lacked conviction.

"I know better," Paul said. He grew quiet again, then as they neared their house, he cried out: "They lied about Dad. They lied." He clenched and unclenched his fists, pounding them into his thighs. "It's just not fair."

She wanted to explain and offer him comfort at the same time. Yet she could do neither. She felt disoriented, cold, and alone. What was she doing here?

Parking the car in the driveway, they went into the house. It struck her as well cared for, cozy, lived in. Theresa Silver, she had learned in her research, was considered a good wife and mother. Not colorful or overly bright, but stable and devoted exclusively to her husband and children.

Bobbie suddenly started to cry hysterically, and Elly, helped by Paul, brought her up to her room. Wailing, she threw herself on the bed. Shoulders shaking, she buried her head in a pillow and cried uncontrollably. Elly held her in a tight embrace, patted her back, and kissed her hair. She quieted down and fell asleep. They left her. Paul went into his room. When he had gone, she called Charlie.

"Where the hell are you?" he asked.

"At the Silver home," she whispered.

"Inside?"

"I'm taking care of the kids."

"Are you crazy? Getting yourself involved like that."

"He asked me." Was that a reason, she wondered?

She could hear Charlie's labored breathing.

"There's a helluva sidebar in that," Charlie said.

"Sidebar?" From Bobbie's room came the sound of whimpering. Apparently, she had awakened.

Elly was standing in the kitchen using a wall phone. Beside it was a bulletin board on which pink slips of paper were pinned. In the bottom right-hand corner was the familiar sketch of the round happy face. "Orthodontist, Bobbie. Friday, 2 p.m.," one read. "Harry's dress shirt and tuxedo, cleaners," another read. And another, "Bobbie's dance lesson. Monday, 3 p.m." There was one in a child's scrawl. "Going to Mary's house after school. Love you, Mommy. Bobbie." Mommy! The word jumped out at her. Mommy! There were lists of food, lists of things to do. "Call plumber for leaky toilet." Bits and pieces of ordinary family life. She felt suddenly deprived, envious.

"Are you there, Elly?"

"Yes."

"You know what I mean, Elly. The human side. The domino effect. A family devastated. You know what I mean. You've got a unique vantage."

"Jesus, Charlie."

She had the sensation of being cleaved, split in two, each side an enemy of the other. She was mad at Charlie, mad at herself, mad at Harry. It was like being stuck helplessly in a whirlpool, struggling against the suction. Words began in her head then faltered. She had no idea which part of her was supposed to speak.

"Don't lose your objectivity," Charlie said softly. "Keep your eye on the ball."

"I'm not sure—" she began. Her eye caught a faded child's drawing, a crude picture of a house. In one of the windows of the house a woman's face had been drawn. "Happy Mommy's Day." Her lower lip trembled, and tears spilled over her eyelids and ran down her cheeks. A sob bubbled out of her mouth then a sniffle.

"I know the feeling, Elly," he said. "Like covering wars, seeing death. Gets to you. I understand. It's all right. Make them feel what you feel. Get it out. But don't let your involvement get in the way of your work."

His tone was gentle. Obviously, he had been through this before, perhaps many times. She kept swallowing, tamping down sobs. She put a hand over the mouthpiece, took deep breaths, wiped away the tears, which continued to come. Stop this, she admonished, pinching her forearm, hoping the pain would shock her into control. Sisterhood demanded it, she rebuked. The bastards waited for you to fall apart, reveled in it, as if it validated their emotional superiority. She was not, under any circumstances, a participator. No. No. No. She was an observer, a fly on the wall.

"Skip the hearts and flowers, Charlie," she said through clenched teeth. "I know my job."

"Hell, Elly, we're only human."

"That good or bad?"

She had begun to feel better.

"And by the by," Charlie said. "The South Africans are raising holy hell. Love it."

He hung up, and she washed her eyes in the sink. Then she went into Bobbie's room. The girl had gone back to sleep, her face still puffed from crying. She smoothed her hair and kissed her on the forehead. Then she knocked softly on Paul's door.

"Anything I can get you?" she asked.

She listened, heard a grunt, which she assumed was meant to be a negative response, then went back to the kitchen and made herself a cup of coffee. Suddenly the phone rang.

"Mrs. Silver? Terry?" the voice asked. She heard the whooshing sound peculiar to overseas calls. "Can you hear me?" The man's English seemed accented.

"Yes, I can hear you," Elly said.

"It's Irving Leopold," the man said. She was too stunned to respond.

"Who?" she asked stupidly.

"Irving Leopold. I must speak to Harry. I called his office, but I could not get through." The tone of panic was inescapable. "Where is he?"

"He'll be home in a little while."

"How long? I got no time. I got to leave here. It's terrible what's happening. I'm so afraid. They're following me."

"Where are you?" Elly asked.

"Vienna," Leopold said. "I don't know what to do. You say how long before he comes home?"

"Soon, maybe a half hour, an hour." She wasn't sure. How long would he stay with his dead wife?

"All right, then. I'll call back. I can't believe all this is happening. The things I see they write." His voice broke. "Please." He hung up.

Elly stood for a long moment with the phone in her ear. Irving Leopold in Vienna. She looked at the clock on the wall. Mickey Mouse wearing boxing gloves. It was ten minutes after four. No sooner had she hung up than the phone rang again. "This is AP," a voice said.

"No one home," she said, hanging up. Then it rang again, three times in succession. Each time, she broke the connection with the same answer. "No one home."

Then it quieted, and she heard a sound coming from below her, an automated garage door. She listened for his steps. Wearily, he came up the stairs. Standing by the kitchen door, she moved forward, then stopped. Paul came out of his room.

"Dad?"

Father and son exchanged glances. Harry's face was haggard, ashen. Paul ran down the steps into his father's arms. It was too painful to watch. She turned away, tried to lift the coffee cup. Her fingers shook, spilling the black liquid into the saucer. She put the cup down with a clatter. It was all wrong, she decided, miscalibrated. She had accidentally walked into someone else's nightmare. Her resolve of moments ago seemed to have slipped away. Listening, she heard low sobs then footsteps moving upstairs. In the sudden quiet, she felt the full impact of aloneness, of limbo, the void. Where was Al? Why wasn't Al here? He had pulled up the anchor of her life, sailed away.

The phone's ring jangled in her head. She started to reach for it then held back. Surely, there were other phones in the house. The phone rang again. Two, three times, then four. She looked at the clock. Four forty-five. More than a half hour had passed since

Leopold's call. Her arm, as if independent of her will reached out, picked up the phone.

"Is this the Silver household?"

"Yes."

"This is Jeff Bilton, chief of staff at the White House."

"Just a moment."

She put down the phone and ran up the stairs. They were sitting on Bobbie's bed, arms wrapped around each other, locked in a grief so personal and compelling, she couldn't bear to disturb them. She ran downstairs again.

"I'm terribly sorry," she said, her voice trembling. "He just can't come to the phone."

"Whom am I talking to?"

"A neighbor," she said, haltingly.

"Oh. Well then, I'm sure I can give you this message," Bilton said, his voice cool. She had the impression that he was relieved. "Would you tell him that the president sends his earnest and most heartfelt condolences."

"Of course."

"And tell him also that we have just released a statement to the press. The president has, in effect, given Mr. Silver a vote of confidence, dismissing the allegations in the media."

"Well, I—" Again she felt split in two. Perhaps three. She cleared her throat. "I'm sure he'll be glad to hear that," she muttered. He thanked her and hung up.

She continued to sit in the kitchen. She looked at the clock, at Mickey Mouse's gloves punching away the minutes. Of her life as well? Shadows lengthened. It began to grow dark. She wondered why Irving Leopold had not called back.

"I appreciate this." Harry's voice startled her. She turned, saw his forlorn look as he shook his head. "Tough on the kids."

"Can I make some dinner?" she asked.

"We'll send for something."

He sighed and turned away.

"Nothing I can do?"

He shook his head. She watched him as he looked out of the window into the darkening street. Words caught in her throat.

"I want you to know—" Meaning became garbled. She wanted to crawl into his mind, see it from his point of view, slip into his heart, feel the pain, the anguish. But he turned too quickly, showing her his grave face.

"Please," he said. "Can we be alone?"

"Of... of course," she stammered, hesitated, turned, then came back. There was this message she had to give him. Irving Leopold. Not now, she told herself. Not now. They wanted to be alone. Alone? As she left the house, she knew that, of all things, she couldn't bear the thought of being alone.

***

The plane banked and from her window seat she could see the light show of New York, a vast eye-boggling exhibit, pulsating with life. She was impatient to be part of it, not merely an observer, a voyeur.

Watching the city move closer, she could feel the connections begin, the sensation of joining the great amorphous glob of humanity. All the old priorities had suddenly aborted. If there was a single enemy in her life now, it was aloneness. She envied Harry his grief, its depth and anguish. The image of the three of them, Harry, Paul, and Bobbie embracing, connected, had made her feel inconsequential, irrelevant.

She would surprise Al. They would feast on each other. She

would prove her contrition, pledge herself. She had felt this concept beginning to emerge inside her, this idea of family, emotionally, intellectually.

She could not be sure whether it was simply envy or some deeper, more compelling instinctive need. For what? Conception and birth? Did she want to suckle babies on her breast, to love and nurture and worry and, above all, feel?

She knew that she wanted to feel hard male arms around her, the press of a hair fringed body, the hard smooth probing stick of erected manhood. God, what was happening to her? Was it lust, desire, something beyond that? She pressed her thighs together, felt the ooze of expectation, the hint of joyous release. Was this reality and the story she was working on, obsessed with, merely myth, unreal, outside life, a surreal dream? Was it time to put it out of your mind? Answer me, she demanded.

Tomorrow she would tell Charlie, she told herself. Tell Charlie what? That she did not have any fire left in the belly, that she had changed her life, reordered priorities, that ambition had died, that she had lost her desire to poke around the garbage dump of greed and chicanery. Had she? Had she really? Tell me, she cried to herself.

She was the first one out of her seat, violating the caveat to remain seated "until the aircraft comes to a complete stop." Without the encumbrance of baggage, she was also the first out of the entrance, the first on the taxi line.

The driver was gabby, but she ignored him, concentrating on what lay ahead. She looked at her watch. It was just seven. She had proceeded directly from Harry's house to the airport, had called Al's office and demanded, absolutely demanded to know where he was, then intimidated and threatened his secretary with dire consequences unless she told where he was staying.

"The Plaza," she said finally, "And please don't say I told you," his secretary whined. "Fuck you," Elly said, slamming down the phone, dashing off just in time to catch the six o'clock shuttle.

She resisted calling him from LaGuardia. What she needed was, once and for all, to prove her credibility, to underline her commitment with her presence, her physical self, not a disembodied voice on a telephone. It was no longer a time for promises. It was a time for action, proof positive, immediacy.

She would present herself, with nothing more than the clothes on her back. Back home, her first act would be to throw away her birth control pills. It would be done in his presence, a solemn ritual marking the end of an era. He would, of course, remember the other time, but that was different, a kind of white lie. She was ready now, ready to prove her commitment.

The Plaza, as always, looked elegant, lovely. She dashed up the steps and strode boldly up to the desk.

"The name is Brian. I forgot my number."

She rarely used her married name. The officious young desk clerk assessed her, satisfied himself then checked the computer and handed her the key. Going up the elevator, she felt giddy with excitement, hoping that Al had the good sense to choose a room overlooking the park.

She found the number, listened at the door, heard nothing. Quietly, she slipped the key in the lock, turned it, and opened the door with a flourish. The room was dark, and she flicked on the lights.

What struck her first was that the king-sized bed was unmade. At that hour it seemed incongruous. Papers cluttered the desk, his briefcase opened beside it. There was a towel on the floor. She giggled. "Slob," she said aloud.

Then she saw it, tangled in the folds of the bedspread, a pair of panties. She felt a strong beat in her head. Picking it up, she held it at arm's length like week-old fish. Then she flung it away.

Repugnance gave way to indignation, which forced her sense of caution. No, she told herself, she would not assume the role of outraged wife. There were varying degrees of unfaithfulness and betrayal. Perhaps he was entitled to a quick roll in the hay. He was lonely, upset. He missed her. He was a sexy man. He needed relief. She was not immune herself to such needs. No, she decided, she would accept this revelation as punishment due. He was entitled. She would dismiss the discovery. Indignation paled, became understanding.

Nor did she speculate on other episodes. He did travel, although not extensively. Wouldn't be surprised, she told herself. For years they had made it a practice of calling each other every night if they were apart. Sometimes they would talk themselves into an autoerotic orgasm. Nothing harmful in that, she remembered.

Catching her reflection in the mirror, she saw a smile on her face. Besides, a little strange sex might be helpful, make him appreciate her more. After all, she had no peer in the sack. Hadn't he said that time and time again?

She picked up the towel and went into the bathroom. One look crushed all her self-deceptions. Beside his toiletries were vials of makeup. In a little duffel bag on a table next to the bathtub was a diaphragm.

She rushed back into the room, opened the closet, saw a woman's suit, two dresses, shoes. Real cozy. Beside it his gray pinstripe, the one she had picked out for him at Woodies. For a moment she was stunned, sitting down on the edge of the bed. She made a valiant effort to work through her humiliation. After all, it was her fault. Hadn't he given her fair warning?

For a moment she studied the room and its details with her trained reportorial eye. There was something easy and familiar here. An intimacy that was not clandestine. She fought down an urge to search further, to identify the woman, to picture her.

Once again, for the second time that day, she fell apart, the little match girl with her nose pressed against the glass. Suddenly it became too unbearable. She was confronting the failure of her marriage, and it filled her with sadness. Perhaps, she thought, she might fight her, prevent this woman from taking her husband. The truth was that she had given him away. Her epiphany, she knew, had come too late.

She let herself out of the room. Downstairs, she slipped the key in the slot at the desk and walked quickly out of the lobby. She was back at the newsroom by ten.

XXI

The graveside service, as Harry had specified, was a simple one. They stood together, the three of them, holding hands; Paul in his best suit, Bobbie wearing the velvet dress Terry had made.

Harry had told them both to "be brave," not sure what that meant, wondering if his child ren knew. Aside from the reporters, who were kept at a distance, the mourners were comparatively few. Mrs. Habersham had come and Bob White, along with a sprinkling of executives and secretaries of the agency.

There were some neighbors, parents of Bobbie's friends. Paul did not have any close friends. There were also some women who Harry recognized as casual acquaintances of Terry. Vague faces and names. Part of Terry's daily round, reports of which he had listened to with half an ear.

Harry had realized that he had taken Terry for granted, that she had created his world of creature comfort and had demanded little of him. Had she been happy? He suspected that there were patches of that, various entertainments and excitements. He knew he had failed her.

Billy Tucker, without Millie, had arrived late. He had returned from Asia the night before and had called to offer Harry condolences. He had sounded exactly like a Hallmark card and Harry had responded in kind.

Grief had forced his reflection. His job had absorbed most of his life, and Billy took up most of what remained. Terry had been merely an appendage. And, yet, he wondered if that was the way she perceived herself. Wife. Mother. In the context of family, it struck him that maybe he was the appendage. While she lived, he could blame it on Washington, the greasy pole of Washington where one was forced to climb hand over hand, hanging on, bracing oneself not only against the pole but on the person above and the person below. Only at the very pinnacle was there even the possibility of comfort.

With her death, he saw things from other perspectives. Washington was a city of masked figures, where people carried labels in a rainbow of colors pasted on figurative lapels. One knew what the labels stood for. There were ample job descriptions and information and a pecking order of protocol based on power, both visible and invisible. Behind the masks, carefully fashioned from snippets of bland amiability and ingratiation, were hidden personalities fearful of confronting their real selves. A mask torn away was a ticket to oblivion. The object was to keep the mask intact at all times.

Being philosophical, he knew, was an indulgence. Except, perhaps, at funerals. Too late for him, the only metaphor now was combat, and his side had already taken casualties. One dead, three wounded. His thoughts drifted. He listened to the minister's words. They were filled with platitudes. Washington was a city of platitudes. The idiom was platitudes, ground out from language like hamburger.

People lived with the illusion of communication by trading platitudes back and forth, like currency. Billy's presence here was a platitude. Who really knows anyone? Who was Billy? His mentor, his idol, his role model, his friend? Billy, for whom he gave his substance and to whom he had pledged fealty, loyalty, devotion. Billy, to whose star he had hitched his wagon. Billy, the blessed, for whom the waters opened.

Somewhere out there as they were crossing the heavens, Billy had reached out and cut the wagon loose, with Harry in it, and it had crash-landed into a swamp of quicksand.

Beyond the rope that contained the reporters, he had caught a glimpse of Eleanor Fox. She had nodded her head to acknowledge herself to him, and he had waved tentatively, embarrassed by the gesture. Was she really the Eleanor Fox who had been the instrument of his destruction? Was he really the man named Harry Silver mentioned in her stories? Even the children had waved.

That morning a story carrying her byline had appeared under the headline A FAMILY DEVASTATED—A WASHINGTON STORY. Compelling reading, he had decided. But who was it about? It was a first person account of the reactions of a man whose wife had been killed.

As all the stories allegedly about him, or a man with his name, this one, too, seemed to be talking about someone else, another family. She had done considerable research about a woman named Theresa, describing Terry's kitchen, even the familiar lists and reminders that hung on the bulletin board. Indeed, it seemed as if she had all the outward details correct, the grief, the sense of loss, speculating how much this man named Harry must have regretted their move to Washington, how providence had intervened to make a hell out of the family's existence.

> "One sensed his deep guilt feelings. However his public life has developed, he revels in his family life and has the absolute support of his son and daughter. Devoted wife and mother, Terry Silver was clearly an innocent, an outsider in the mysterious underground that connected her husband with the fugitive figure of Irving Leopold."

No doubt she had wrestled with methods of presentation. As

the protagonist of the story, Harry Silver came off a lot better than he might have expected. Not that it mattered to the real Harry Silver at this point. All the wheels were in motion for his official destruction. There was little to do in the face of it. Now that he could glimpse the parameters of his demise, he was losing interest in the subject matter.

Such intense reflection carried him through the minister's eulogy, to which he could not connect emotionally. When he was finished, the tiny cluster of mourners lowered their heads in prayer, and he and the two children threw handfuls of freshly turned earth over the coffin of the dead mother and wife. That done, he looked back at the group, shook hands, and listened to condolences. Suddenly Billy was in front of him, squeezing his forearm, his handsome craggy face somber, lips pursed, eyes gleaming.

"Got to talk. Say the ball field, couple of hours." The words were whispered, furtive, urgent. He turned his eyes away and kicked his toe in the grass. "Okay?"

"Sure, Billy."

At that moment, someone else, a friend of Terry's, grabbed his hand and spoke words of sympathy. He nodded, half-smiled, turned away. Billy had disappeared. Then he looked over at the penned reporters. Cameras clicked. TV cameras were activated. He saw Eleanor Fox. Their eyes met briefly, then he moved with the children into their rented limousine.

***

They stood at the edge of the field. A soccer game was in progress. Most of the players appeared foreign, a rainbow of skin tones. It was odd seeing their meeting place populated. Billy was waiting at the edge of the field under a tree, wearing his jogging clothes.

"I feel like crud, Harry," Billy said. "I feel it's all my fault."

Harry deliberately did not respond, letting the matter hang in the air. Consent by silence, he thought. Billy looked tired. Bags of flesh had puffed out further from under his eyes.

"Was it really an accident?" Billy asked.

"She was very depressed. Who knows?"

"You've been taking one hell of a beating Harry. The damned vultures are tearing you apart. It's not right. It's not fair." He jammed a fist into his palm. "I'm the guy that should be taking it on the chin." He shook his head, looked around him, and lowered his voice. "Now this other thing," he whispered.

"What other thing?"

"We weren't supposed to come home until today. We flew all night. Went right to the White House."

Another illusion shattered. Harry had thought he had come home for Terry's funeral.

"What are you talking about?"

"It's supposed to be top secret. This is a real violation. I want you to know that, Harry. That's important. Our relationship goes beyond such things. You know that?"

"You're going to have to make yourself clearer, Billy."

Again he looked around him. Harry had never seen him so frightened.

"It's Leopold. They fished him out of a lake outside of Vienna yesterday."

"My God!"

"Their spooks notified our spooks."

"Suicide or murder?" The irony galled him.

"No one knows."

Harry noted that Billy could or would not hold his glance.

"You know, Billy."

"Me? Are you crazy?" He looked around him again, and the color had drained from his face.

"I don't think you can keep it from me, Billy. Not now."

"I'm between a rock and a hard place, Harry."

"I'm touched."

His arm reached out, and he slapped the trunk of the tree.

"It's *Alice in Wonderland*, Billy. That's what it is. Now they're really beginning to believe he was some kind of a foreign agent. But they're not sure for whom or why. What bugs them is the access. Now everyone is suspicious of everyone else. It's out of hand."

"One misperception piled on another."

"Something like that."

"Are they close to the truth, Billy?"

"The truth? What the hell is that?"

"Somebody must have ideas. About Leopold, for example."

"Yes. I've got ideas." He sighed, paused, swallowed with difficulty. "The Afrikaners. No question. It was easier to dump him into the river than let him run around loose. That way speculation could never be proof. They're cutting their losses. It's the only theory that makes sense."

"But do they know who the money was earmarked for?"

Billy shrugged.

"I hope not."

"So they know only what they read in the media?"

"But it's garbage. All mixed up. He wasn't an agent for an enemy, for crying out loud. It's all wrong."

"Did my name come up?" Harry asked.

"Damn it, Harry. of course, it came up. Hell, it's all over the press. You're connected. The link. Harry, they know who the rabbi was. The Israelis got it." He looked around him once again. "I'm afraid you're going to be in for it. They're going to try to head off a congressional investigation. The president's really pissed. It's really out of hand, Harry."

Harry felt his lips curl into a cold smile. "I saw him with my own eyes," Eleanor Fox had said. Because she had wanted to see it, he thought. Everyone saw only his or her own truth. She needed to see that.

"You can clear it all up in ten minutes," Harry said, watching Billy. His nostrils twitched, and a nerve began to palpitate along his jawline.

"I thought of that," Billy said.

"For how long?"

"I've given it a lot of thought, Harry. I really have. The thing is—with Irving gone—it sounds ghoulish and all that. But there's nobody that now knows the real truth but you and I."

"And maybe a couple of Afrikaners," Harry muttered. "And if they knocked off Irving to save their ass, how safe are we?"

"All right, let's assume that they do know who we are."

"Bet your bippy," Harry said. "Nobody gives away ten million without knowing to whom and why, despite Irving's assurances to the contrary. We were living in a dream world on that one."

"So let's say we were then," Billy snapped, showing a brief burst of frustration. It seemed to Harry an odd response. "Without the man in the middle, the thing must appear manageable for them." He paused and expelled his breath through his teeth. "Depending, of course, on how we react. Right?"

The odd question had an ominous ring to it, and Harry was certain that it was, for the moment, purely rhetorical.

"As long as you maintain your innocence, what can they prove?

All they have is you helping Leopold get into the country in a disguise. They don't know why. Not for sure. Comes down to a question of who believes what. You can always deny it. Then there's the money." Harry felt Billy's eyes scrutinize his face. "I assume you've got that hidden in a safe place. I don't want to know where. The point is that it might be better in the long run to take your chances. Let the string run out. The press will get bored with it."

"What about the congressional hearing?"

"Let's hope we can head that off. Besides, if things get too hot, you can always take the fifth." He had blurted the words too fast, and his face wore an air of surprise. "But only as a last resort."

"You're big on advice today, Billy."

"Look, Harry. I'm looking at it from both our points of view. This whole experience has kind of soured my taste for the presidency. Who needs it? Millie goes a little ape-shit when she steps into the limelight. And when you get down to it, when you really look at it objectively, what is it but an ego trip? Hell, I haven't got any great ideas to make this country better."

"Since when was that a criterion?" Harry asked.

"It's just an ego trip," Billy shrugged. "Would have been fun to try."

There was a note of sadness in his voice. In an odd way, Harry felt pity for him, the golden boy, the blessed one, admitting to himself finally that he had feet of clay. Or was this more sop, more baloney? This is bullshit, he assured himself. This man had given up nothing.

"The truth is that what we did here wasn't such a big deal. No security was compromised. And even if, by some fluke, I had become the president, I wouldn't have had to do anything special about South Africa. Nature would take its course there anyway.

Hell, I don't give a flying fuck about South Africa, black, white, or pink." He put his hand on Harry's arm and squeezed. "Above all I don't want to see you go down, old buddy. You mean too damned much to me. You've been a helluva friend, one helluva friend. In the end it will work out right for both of us. That's why I've—well, I've got this idea—and I hope you'll give it lots of thought. Sure I could tell them everything. Make a clean breast of it. Take the consequences. But when you get right down to it, what's the point? Why sacrifice both of us? What I say is this: Take the ten million, Harry. It's yours. There's lots of ways to launder it. Hell, when things blow over, I'll help all I can. I didn't become secretary of the treasury for nothing." Suddenly, he smiled brightly. "Think of the kids. No more money worries. Me? I got plenty, and Millie's loaded. I'm not saying it's without risks. But you're one clever guy, Harry. You'll find the way out."

He had spoken quickly, the words flashing across Harry's mind like ticker tape.

"That's very generous," Harry said. He wasn't sure whether to laugh or cry. He decided to do neither. He remembered Billy's earlier reference to *Alice in Wonderland.* So this is life on the other side of the mirror, he thought. He wished suddenly that Eleanor Fox were with them, her little tape recorder running. Make something out of that one, lady. Take the money. Take the rap.

"Least I could do, Harry." Stupid bastard hadn't even picked up the sarcasm, Harry thought.

"And when they call you, Billy? When and if you're up there on the Hill or talking to the FBI, what do you say?"

"No sweat there, Harry. I'll never run you down. I'll say it over and over again. It's all a mistake. It can't be true. Simple as that." You stupid bastard, Harry thought. It's for me that I will do this, for me.

"Of course, I won't be able to escape scot-free. People know we've been friends, that I've been a kind of sponsor. I'll have to come up with a routine, myself."

"Hell, you know the script—all a mistake, all a surprise. Harry Silver? No way Harry Silver could be involved in something like that. Harry's no crook or spy. Harry's a loyal American. Frankly, I'm shocked and disheartened by all these revelations."

"Something like that, Harry. It'll go something like that."

"Good wholesome lies," Harry mocked.

"Harsh word, Harry. But if we're careful—"

"We?"

"If you're careful, cautious. Trick is to watch those questions. I think we might head off the congressional hearing. We do that you could be in good shape. But the downside is a trial. Perjury, the big P. That's the one they could hang you on. That happens, one thing you've got to do is get the best lawyer you can. Spence, Bailey, somebody like that. Hell, you can afford it now." He managed a wan smile.

"Thanks."

"No big deal. Even if there is a conviction, there are appeals. And the worst would be a couple of years, counting time off for good behavior."

"That all?"

"It's only the worst-case scenario, Harry. You come out with a fortune."

Slime, Harry thought. It was a word seeking an image, an image seeking an illustration. He was a pig wallowing in muck. To escape from this, he could find only one door, so deep in the dark tunnel of himself; he could not find it except by feeling. He stretched out imaginary finger pads.

"And suppose I tell them the truth?" Harry asked. Billy's

response was surprisingly quick.

"Your prerogative, Harry. In that case, we all go down in flames."

"All?"

"As I told the president," Billy said. His neck swiveled. "One thing leads to another."

"What the hell does that mean?"

He was, obviously, sorry he had slipped into it.

"Listen Harry. He knows I've been your buddy. Hell, I've been pushing you for his staff. He's one shrewd bastard. Also he doesn't need this shit in his administration. He's home free. All he wants now is to play to the historians."

"And he thinks I'm fucking things up for him."

"Not you per se, Harry. The damned media."

"So he's asked you to handle it. Get rid of the problem."

"More or less."

"Does he know you're in it?"

"Are you crazy? He knows only what the media tells him. He's only interested in proximity."

"Because if it slops over to you, it slops over to him. Dominoes, right?"

"I've lent him money for years," Billy said. "You know that. They'll think I bought my job. And he'll be in deep shit."

"So I'm the first domino. You want me to fall sideways."

"That's a good image, Harry."

"Are you going to whistle 'The Star Spangled Banner' now, Billy?"

"If I thought it would help."

"A lot of good men have gone down with that song ringing in their ears."

He had the sensation of receiving and sending scrambled

signals. The meanings of words were awry, off-kilter, distorting his thought processes, skewering logic.

"See my point?" Billy asked.

Harry looked over Billy's shoulder. A roar went up from the soccer players. Someone had scored a goal. He had, of course, heard the question, but he was busy elsewhere. There was only one point in all this, to preserve himself, the idea of himself, his ultimate moral identity. Nor could it be articulated to anyone but himself. It had suddenly become necessary to declare Billy a stranger.

"Clear as a bell," Harry said calmly. The signals suddenly unscrambled. Billy's hidden words echoed in his mind. Survival was the first law of life. He could see Billy's face relax. His skin sank back into its crags, the color returned to the leathery parchment of his skin, and his lips curled upward in a broad toothy smile. He punched Harry playfully on the upper arm.

"Trust me," Billy said.

Watching him, Harry thought he seemed to be receding in proximity, shrinking, disappearing. Somewhere in another time, on another landscape was another Billy. It felt better to know this, Harry decided. The voice, it was true, was still familiar, but only vaguely.

"Haven't I always?" Harry said.

"So this is a kind of temporary good-bye," Billy said. "Best we steer clear of each other until this blows over. Soon as the sky clears we'll pick up the strings, try another deal. Hell, this country is the land of opportunity."

He put out his hand. Harry took it, squeezed, felt the warm flesh, unfamiliar now, and then watched as Billy moved away along the edge of the field. Then suddenly he began to jog.

Harry continued to watch as his figure became smaller and smaller, then disappeared completely.

XXII

Elly observed Charlie watering his scotch with Perrier, an unusual gesture. He was taking no chances with his brain cells. Besides, it was late in the evening and, despite the natural adrenaline, a tired mind needed care and respect.

"Notice I'm not begging you for a pledge of confidence," Jeff Bilton said. "There are no ground rules here. I'm just going to trust your good sense."

Late that afternoon a messenger had appeared at Charlie's office with an envelope. In it, on blank stationery, was a note.

> "Please meet me at my apartment. Watergate. South Building. Apartment 605. Ten tonight. Bring Eleanor Fox."

His name, Jeff Bilton, was scrawled at the bottom of the note.

"It's a summons, not a request," Charlie said.

"Unofficial. No White House stationery," Elly observed.

"He thinks all we do now is drop everything and appear for the command performance."

They would, of course. Perhaps she had been nibbling around the edges of something beyond even her own speculations, speculations inhibited by emotional complications. Standing across from the graveside earlier that day, she could identify her sense of compassion. It was awful watching this family suddenly deprived of wife and mother.

Writing that story had been deeply affecting. Tears had

streamed down her cheeks, and she could barely see the screen of her computer. At the funeral, tears had engulfed her once again, and she had to summon a superhuman effort to hide these feelings. But it was impossible to hide them from herself. Poor Harry. Poor Paul and Bobbie.

Later, back at the paper, compassion gave way to guilt, then anger, then rage, mostly at herself, that she should be feeling anything. It was so unprofessional. Wasn't it? To further stir the pot, Al had called her at home, detonating her out of a pill-induced semicoma of sleep.

All she could remember of the conversation was that he would be in late tomorrow, and they had matters to discuss. Matters? She could not even find the time to consider the problem. Rejection or contrition? Al, as husband and concept, suddenly seemed far away. She realized that she had dismissed him on both counts. She decided she had a real talent for dismissal. Except that she could not dismiss Harry. Damn him. How dare he spring suddenly to life, flesh, blood, tissue, and mind?

Squeeze him, Charlie had said. For his own good as well, she had added. It was a nuance in her thoughts that surprised and disturbed her. She had called their correspondent in Vienna who was checking out Irving Leopold.

Now that he was back from Asia, she had also pressed hard for an interview with Tucker, but his secretary was fending off all her advances. But she had seen him at the funeral. Close buddy. Family friend. Surely, he could not let his friend go down in flames without some rescue effort. People at the top were good at protecting themselves. They had an army of cannon fodder to take the brunt of the attack.

Which is why her hostility to Jeff Bilton was endemic. With his bow tie riding up and down his Adam's apple, his weak chin and round glasses, he looked mechanical and humorless, therefore, dangerous.

He began with an apology for the White House's lack of cooperation. These private little sessions, Charlie told her, always began in the same way. When they needed something from the media, they were contrite as hell, he pointed out.

"We were remiss," Bilton said blandly. Behind his glasses were little mouse eyes with pink rims that barely blinked. His face was difficult to read, a barren landscape. "We should have responded to your inquiries."

"No shit," Elly said. Charlie looked at her and frowned.

"But now this whole thing is out of control."

"Whose fault is that?" Elly asked.

"There're errors on both sides," Bilton said.

"Granted," Charlie said.

He had assumed the air of an elder statesman, a natural consequence of the differences in their ages. Bilton was barely forty. Elly didn't like either Charlie's assumed role or his response.

"Believe me when I say that we're as interested in the truth as you are."

"Then why has it been so hard to get at?" Elly asked.

"Because it is hard to get at," Bilton said. "Leopold was nothing but a damned jewelry salesman, for crying out loud. He was part of the scene."

She caught the tense, but let it pass. He had a reputation as a man who never wasted time, and she could sense that he was quickly coming to the point.

"And you're here because it's become a nuisance," Bilton continued. "One of those things that deflects concentration from the real issues. I've been authorized by the president to tell you everything we know. Everything. We have nothing to hide. Your stories imply that there is some sort of cover-up. Nothing could be further from the truth. All this implication and innuendo. Take this South African crap. Everyone knows how we stand on the issue. Apartheid is dead. This is not to say that dear old Irving might not have found a way to pick up a few bucks from them. They're gullible as hell. They think you can spread money around like horseshit and fertilize the soil. The problem is that we can't confirm it. The South Africans deny it. Not just for media consumption. They really deny it, and there's no way we can check beyond that. Now for the spy allegations: The FBI, the CIA, you name it, the whole government investigating apparatus is looking at it. Comes up lemons. We've talked with every government with a first-rate intelligence operation. Third parties have even talked to the Iraqis."

"Sorry to have put you to all that trouble," Charlie said with obvious relish.

"Power of the press," Bilton said through a sly smile.

"Glad you got the message," Charlie said.

"Remains to be seen," Elly said with obvious skepticism.

"What I need from both of you," Bilton said, glancing from one to the other, "is confidence. I need you to believe me. The president needs it as well. We're innocents. I swear to you." He turned to Elly. "Your stories reek with intimations of cover-up, secret conspiracies, hints of duplicity. Problem is nobody knows exactly what the hell you're talking about."

"Maybe you haven't looked hard enough," Elly said. She felt a surge of secret enjoyment. Nice seeing him squirm. Nice knowing that she had stuck a needle up his ass.

"The thing is we have tried, and we're still looking. That is the point of this exercise." He paused and blinked his little pink mouse eyes. "All we have is Harry Silver. And we've got him dead to rights on that rabbi thing. The Israelis have confirmed it."

"So we were right," Charlie said. He turned to Elly and winked.

"On the money," Bilton said. "The name of their little game."

"Money?" Charlie asked.

"What else?" Bilton said. "A lousy little smuggling scam. Just the two of them, Leopold and Silver. Motive profit. The only possible explanation."

"Which takes everybody off the hook," Elly said coldly. "Including William Tucker."

"An innocent bystander. I can tell you he feels sick about all this. He was, as you know, a close friend and sponsor of Harry Silver. His mentor."

"What makes you think he's not part of it?" Elly asked.

"Tucker? Of all people in this administration, the Tuckers don't need money," Bilton said indignantly.

"Mrs. Tucker wasn't averse to a little wholesale," Elly snapped.

"Even the rich like bargains."

"How profound."

"You know—" Bilton looked at Elly. "I'll never be able to understand your attitude. It's so—so confrontational. You know, there's a human side to power. Relationships get tested every day, even in the stratosphere of the White House. How would you feel if your best friend turned out to be a crook, betrayed a trust?"

"Heavy stuff," Elly said.

"You're looking for something that just isn't there. As far as we can tell, this matter involves only two men." Bilton's little eyes narrowed to slits. "Now only one."

Charlie and Elly exchanged stunned glances. Up to then, the interview had amounted to what seemed like elaborate obfuscation. They waited for Bilton's denouement. He seemed to be enjoying the suspense.

"Leopold's dead," Bilton said, watching their faces through a long pause. Elly felt her insides lurch. "Fished out of a lake outside Vienna yesterday." Only two days ago, she had heard his panicked voice. "You have it exclusive," Bilton said.

"How generous," Elly said contemptuously.

"I don't detect any gratitude," Bilton said snidely, shifting his gaze to Charlie's face. Elly had expected it to register outrage. Instead she saw contemplation, which troubled her.

"It's a lynch party," Elly said, directing her attention to Charlie. "They're throwing Harry to the wolves."

"So it's Harry?" Bilton asked smiling.

Elly felt a hot blush rise to her cheeks.

"Are you saying that Irving Leopold was murdered?" Charlie asked with surprising calm.

"More like suicide. The truth is we don't know. Death by drowning. That was the Viennese police's autopsy report."

"Always the truth—" Elly began. Charlie lifted his hand, and frowned in her direction. Words bubbled helplessly in her throat.

"That doesn't necessarily rule out foul play," Charlie said.

"No, it doesn't," Bilton admitted. "Except that the autopsy report shows no sign of violence."

"Which is what they want us to think," Elly blurted.

"That's precisely one of the reasons for this little visit," Bilton said. "You have every right to call it murder if you wish. We can't stop you. But where's the percentage for you? There are no guilty parties, not where you're looking. No secret tapes. No presidential complicity. None of those goodies you pant for. And your Mr. Leopold was found in Austria. Not Iraq."

Charlie grew thoughtful.

"They never stop," Elly muttered. "Spend their lives figuring out ways to weasel out."

"I can't understand why your attitude is so lousy," Bilton said with an air of incredulity. "Always looking for the rotten side of things. All I'm saying is—as far as we know." He shook his head looking, even she had to admit, genuinely perplexed. "Christ, I have torn the place apart. That's not to say I couldn't be wrong, couldn't have overlooked something. What I'm trying to convey is that there is nothing here. Nothing." He paused, his eyes roaming their faces. "Except—"

"Harry Silver," Elly hissed.

"Sorry, folks. But that's all there is."

"Because that Harry Silver is happily available about midway up the totem. No real clout. No muss, no fuss, no bother. It's all become annoying, counterproductive." She heard her voice rise. "Throw us Silver, his raw meat, and we'll be off the scent."

"That's ridiculous," Bilton said indignantly. "May I remind you that you started everything? Has it ever occurred to you that all that coverage may have driven Leopold to suicide? It's already claimed the wife of Harry Silver."

"Now that's out of line," Charlie said. She felt only partially relieved. He seemed to be buying Bilton's story.

"Maybe so. But there's no evidence of anything more to this. For crying out loud—" Bilton paced the length of the living room, then came back to where they were sitting. Palms out, he spread his arms waist high. "Look at it from my point of view. I have the president's permission to tell you this. I am here naked and alone and appealing to your common sense and good offices. We are very sensitive to any hint of internal cover-up. That tactic, to say the least, has been severely discredited. Now I know the media never trusts the administration. That's a given, right? I also know that you, Mr. Carruthers, are the ultimate curmudgeon in this town, the unbeliever, the pinpricker of the bloated bags of the pompous, especially the people in power. You are the enemy. We're as frightened of you and your paper as we are of Hussein getting the bomb. Okay? By a process of elimination, there appears to me one motive and now one culprit. I'm not begging you to lay off the president on this one. There is, after all, a natural tendency to want to lay all blame on those closest to the throne, if not the king himself. Look at it from his point of view. He's got just a couple more years to be presidential. He's writing history now—above the fray. He doesn't need this. And he stands foursquare behind William Tucker. He commiserates. He knows what it means to be betrayed by friends. You can even quote me on everything I've said."

"He's very convincing," Charlie said, turning to Elly.

"That's his job."

"Christ," Bilton's voice rose to this side of shrill. "Be skeptical. Be cynical. Hate us. But Jesus Q. Christ, we are just people trying to be reasonably honest, reasonably sincere, reasonably sensible. Even beyond the power trip, the ambition, the obsessions, the conflicting egos, the foibles, mistakes, and stupidities, even us, the guys with the fingers on the buttons, are just plain dumb folks. Give us credit for an occasional kernel of truth."

"This guy's a poet," Charlie said. Unfortunately, she detected belief beneath the ridicule. He turned to Elly. "What he's saying is that we still got a story, but with a different twist. A sort of Raffles caper right under the president's nose."

"Isn't that enough of an administration embarrassment to satisfy you?"

"We'll take all we can get," Charlie said. He stood up, walked to the bar, and poured himself a fresh scotch, sipping it straight.

"What about the noise they're making on the Hill about a congressional hearing?"

"Where's the politics in it?" Bilton asked innocently. "No point to it. Strictly a criminal case—a guy betraying public trust for profit."

"It's a con job, Charlie," Elly said.

"A good one," Charlie said raising his glass in Bilton's direction.

"I can't believe this, Charlie. You were the one who said Harry was holding back. Squeeze, remember?"

"Hey, who said stop squeezing? There's still a lot to wrap up here."

"I'm all for squeezing the son of a bitch. Push him. Maybe he'll resign," Bilton said. "Hell, we got G-men looking for the money."

"Do you?" Elly asked with some contempt. "And what have you found?"

"They've just begun."

"What makes you so sure there's money to be found?"

"Might solve everybody's problem is all."

"Suppose there is no money? Suppose he's really innocent?" Elly asked.

"Innocent? Is the Pope a Catholic? That's not the way you portrayed him," Bilton said. "Anyway, a resignation will confirm his guilt in the public mind. That's all we care about. Leave the rest to the investigators and the courts. We've got a country to run. Hell, I've given you a scoop." He smiled.

"And we better get it written," Charlie said with a nod toward Elly. He looked at his watch. "Still time for tomorrow."

"Push him hard enough, maybe he'll confess," Bilton said.

***

"A comer, that kid," Charlie said in the car as they drove toward the paper.

"So you did believe him?"

"Believe? That's an ambiguous condition. What I did believe was his assessment that the stream in which we were fishing has no big fish running."

"That's believing," she said cautiously.

"Hate to admit it," he sighed. "He's saying that there's no big payoff following the present line. No smoking gun. Maybe a little dumbness, but no sinister intent. So all we got left is Harry Silver."

"To flush down the toilet," she said flatly.

"Good. Might be interesting to see, tell our readers about it."

"I just can't see him as a jewel thief."

She forced herself to remain calm, remembering again her conversation with the now-late Irving Leopold. Why then did he call? It troubled her.

"Therein is the nub, lady. You made the fatal error."

"I am not emotionally involved," she countered, too defensive for credibility.

"It's why doctors never operate on members of their family."

"I am completely objective." But the words seemed self-serving and hollow. Just like the others, she thought. Everyone was speaking at cross-purposes, not communicating. There was no common ground. Even the language seemed distorted.

"Bullshit."

"What you're doing," she said, holding back anger, "is telling me that I'm incompetent to pursue the story."

"You said it."

"I've made an assessment of the man, Charlie."

"Instinctively," Charlie mocked.

"That's a perfectly proper tool of the investigative journalist."

"And you think he's the innocent one, a victim?"

"The word is patsy."

"Him or you?"

She felt the dikes of control give way.

"I think that's crap," she said. "You're all playing assy-savey."

"Hey, that's good."

"You especially," she said, knowing she was going too far, unable to stop herself. "Backing off because that stupid little prick tells you that all the big boys are innocent. You just don't have the balls to probe any deeper, afraid you'll make a mistake, come up with a dry hole, too much of a buildup but no payoff, not a big one like Watergate, because you're scared of those bastards in the boardroom, scared that you won't deliver a big one, scared and old—Jesus." She was out of control, panicked by her own language, frightened by its intensity. She fiddled with the door lock. "I have to get out of here."

He stopped the car along the curb, sucking in a deep breath, looking straight ahead.

"Just don't make me take away your badge, baby," he said.

"I have to get out of here," she cried.

He leaned over and worked the latch opening the door. Then he looked at his watch.

"You got about two hours to work off the tantrum," Charlie said. "I'm a little rusty, but if I have to, I can write it."

"Good," she snapped, getting out of the car, walking swiftly, hearing the tap-tap of her heels along the pavement. She hailed a passing cab and got in.

***

"I'm sorry," she said, as Harry let her in the front door. "I didn't have time to call first."

"It's all right."

She followed him into what apparently was his den, a paneled room with a large desk off to one side and bookshelves filled with books. Papers were scattered helter-skelter over the desktop. Obviously, he had been working at his desk, but he did not sit down behind it. His arm swept toward a brown leather couch and she sank into it.

"Coffee?"

She shook her head, wondering if she appeared agitated. She felt it subsiding.

"The children?"

"Sleeping, I hope."

"It's been tough on them, hasn't it?" she asked stupidly.

She felt awkward, unstable. Why had she come? He settled himself just across from her in a matching leather chair. As if she were a child bent on impressing him with her posture, she sat stiffly, thighs pressed together, hands folded on her knees, chin up. She avoided his eyes, although she could not ignore his scrutiny. Her eyes wandered to the desk.

"Terry did the household stuff," he said noting her attention. "I thought I might pull it together, before it gets out of hand."

"Hard to know the extent of the loss until it happens," she said, hoping her comment would seem wise.

"Life goes on," he said. It occurred to her that he was as awkward as she. Two fumblers. She took in a gasp of air, hoping it might further calm her. She wished she could escape the memory of Charlie's accusations.

"Terry could never balance the checkbook. I thought that would be a good starting point."

He sounded so sensible, so clearly logical. Did he realize what was happening to him? Did this sound like a man who had made millions? No way.

"I haven't got much time," she said.

"Oh." He seemed puzzled.

"Deadlines," she said. "We're slaves to these deadlines." She looked at her watch. "The best I can do is the last edition now."

His fingers were clasped around his knees. Again, her attention was drawn to them. They seemed strong, the clasp tight and sure. Was he curious, she wondered? Surely in his position, she would be curious.

"Actually," she said, continuing the thought. "The story that I'm going to write will only make the last edition. The point is that we'll be on the record. Get the jump. We're a very competitive business. The thing is—" She was starting to get agitated again. "Damn."

"Sure I can't get you a drink?"

Was her nervousness so transparent? Or was this all in her own mind? Perhaps the color had drained from her face. When she didn't answer, he got up and poured her a drink from a bottle of scotch. As he offered the glass, she noted that his hands were steady. Not hers. She needed both of them to hold the glass. After a deep swallow, she felt the trail of heat the liquor made going down. It did shock her system, calm her down, but her hands continued to shake. Reaching out, he took the glass from her and set it aside on a table beside the couch.

"What I'm looking for is something, well, strongly positive. Some explanation." She sucked in a deep breath. "Damn it, Harry. Irving Leopold was found dead in Vienna. Drowned."

His reaction was a resigned shrug.

"Does it mean anything to you?"

"Of course it does," he said, a mild remonstrance.

"Your reaction is so—so restrained."

"I find the best way to cope with what is happening is to put everything out of my mind as quickly as it comes into it."

"Harry." She sat forward on the couch, her eyes seeking his. "I was here in your house, the day your wife died, remember? Irving Leopold called from Vienna. He wanted to speak to you. He said he would call back in an hour. While I was here, he never did call back. Did he ever?"

"You must be mistaken," he said blandly. For a brief moment, he had locked into her gaze. As quickly, he turned away.

"You're not that good a liar, Harry."

"You were mistaken."

"I did not imagine it. Like the thing with the rabbi. In the face of proof positive, Harry, you can't just stonewall on everything. Certainly not on this. I heard his voice with my own ears. I knew the man. I recognized the voice. No question about it. He also said he was in Vienna. I did not dream it. He died in Vienna." She reached out and touched his arm. "Harry, I did not write about it. Deliberately. I withheld it. I can't now. Don't you see?"

"I didn't ask you to."

"In other words, you're just going to let it happen. No explanation."

He looked at her and shrugged.

"Is it possible that you don't know what's happening to you?"

"Does it matter if I do?" he said blandly.

"I think so. After all, I'm here trying to look at it from your point of view. They've decided, no, decreed, that you and Irving Leopold had this scam going, that you were a couple of jewel thieves. That the noose was getting tighter, that Irving couldn't take it and committed suicide. Jeff Bilton himself provided my editor and me with this scenario. I don't buy it. I mean I started it, Harry. I think you're taking the rap, covering up. I don't know the reasons. I'm more confused than ever. Harry, I feel so damned helpless. I don't believe any of this. I don't even know why I don't believe it. All I know is that I've started something that is going to burn you into a cinder. And you're letting it happen. Cheering it on. I wish I could shake it out of you. For crying out loud, you've lost your wife, you've as good as lost your job, your reputation. God knows what else. What I'm saying to you is save yourself. Let me help you save yourself." She had this urge to reach out and shake him by the shoulders, shake some sense into him.

"Maybe I am saving myself, Ms. Fox," he said after a long contemplative pause.

"Can't you even call me Elly?"

"All right, Elly."

"I'm sorry I even started this," she sighed.

"Too late for that, I'm afraid."

"Don't you want to save yourself?" she asked.

"Of course, I do," he said.

"Now we're getting somewhere," she said. "I've got the power to do that." She reached into her purse, took out her tape recorder, turned it on. "Shoot."

"That's not what I mean."

"You are an exasperation, Harry. Look, everybody has some justification for their actions. Maybe if I put it in that context—"

She could tell he wasn't listening. He had unclasped his hands and was stroking his chin contemplatively. "Haven't you any regard for yourself as a person?" she said. The words tumbled out in a shrill plaint. "Nobody can stop this but yourself. Hell, they think you've stashed millions."

"Why are you so bothered by this? As far as I can see no one is questioning the veracity of your reporting. Not even me. I haven't even complained. What makes you so sure I'm such an innocent?"

"So that's it," Elly said.

"That's what?"

"The deeper it gets, the more you stand to get out of it. More profitable to be a bad boy." She was instantly sorry. "Strike that," she said. "I don't believe a word of it."

"Why not?"

She tried to create a logical answer in her mind. Was he seeking a kind of martyrdom? Or punishment? Protecting some noble instinct within himself? Testing the limits of personal courage? Had he actualized a romantic fantasy of himself as lone ranger? Or was it fear, ordinary bone-rattling fear that he would meet the same fate as Irving Leopold?

"How do you think Irving died?"

"You just told me. Drowning."

"Was he murdered?"

"I have no idea."

"Does it make you afraid?"

"Of what?"

"Can't you see I'm trying to help you?"

"A little late for that, don't you think?"

"Are you covering up for anyone? For William Tucker?"

"Covering up what?"

"I'm not sure. They say he feels betrayed, disgusted."

"Who are they?"

"Bilton."

"Maybe he's right. He ought to know."

She stood up, exasperated, looked at her watch, felt the panic of helplessness.

"I haven't got any more time."

The den was comparatively small and when he stood up, the distance between them narrowed. He wasn't that much taller than her, but she had the odd impression that she was standing in his shadow. Nor could she deny the excitement that the proximity generated. Before, she had seemed to linger at the edge of the feeling, as if it were a moat between them. Now she found herself trying to define it.

"You're an enigma, Harry," she said. "I wish I knew you." Suddenly, she felt very foolish. But when her hand closed around his, she knew exactly what she had meant.

XXIII

He had the sensation of suspension, half asleep, half awake. Slivers of light from the venetian blinds filtered through dust-laden air. He was sure he had been in that state all night.

Somewhere he had read about people who slept with one eye open, guarding something. He knew what that meant. Day and night now one eye was always open, guarding something. He had, at the moment, the vaguest outline of what he was guarding, but he was certain that it was the most precious possession he possessed.

Earlier he had heard the outside door open and close. Paul going out to get the papers. There was, of course, no defense against that. The purveyors of information were ubiquitous. By now, they would have begun to gather outside with their notebooks and their cameras, seeking crumbs to flesh out the stories and give them immediacy and, they hoped, believability.

He no longer read or watched or listened. His main job was to guard this most valuable and not-quite-defined treasure. There was a kind of ironic logic in Eleanor Fox coming to look for it. Of all the people in the world, he was certain that she would be the only one to whom the value of this treasure could be explained and understood.

It would not, of course, prevent her from using the surface facts for her so-called journalistic endeavors. Yet these surface facts were part of his own defense as well, his special strategy for personal survival.

"Dad?" Paul whispered. He had walked soundlessly into his father's bedroom.

"Yes, Paul." He raised himself on his elbows, watching his son come forward in the half-light. He saw him go to the windows and reach for the pulley to draw the blinds.

"Not now," Harry said. At that moment, he preferred the darkness.

"Thought you might want to read the papers, Dad."

Since the funeral, the boy had been very quiet, reflective, perhaps too reflective. It was, Harry knew, also for Paul, perhaps especially for Paul, that the treasure must be preserved. Tell him, a voice inside him begged. No, Harry protested, brushing aside all temptation to explain himself to the boy. Not now. Someday. Not now.

"Have you read it?"

"Yes, Dad."

"What do you think?"

"I don't know what to think. Shall I read it to you?"

"No. But I'd like to hear your impressions."

"It's says Mr. Leopold committed suicide in Vienna."

"I heard."

"And that you and he might have smuggled diamonds into the country."

"Is that all?"

"No. It also says that you resigned effective today."

"Slow news day, I guess."

"There's a picture of you, too."

"That makes me a celebrity."

"They say you could be hiding millions."

"You believe that?"

"No."

Paul sat at the foot of the bed looking down at him. In the semidarkness he looked older, more mature.

"Elly Fox wrote the story, Dad."

"That's her job."

"To write lies?"

"She doesn't think they're lies."

He felt Paul searching his face, looking for some sign that was not there. Not to be shown.

"What happens now, Dad?"

"Investigations, probably. Lots of people will be around asking questions."

"Will you go to jail?"

"Maybe."

There was a long silence.

"Will they ask me a lot of questions, too?"

"Probably."

He shrugged.

"Bobbie, too."

"Maybe."

"What should I say?"

"Tell them the truth."

"I don't know the truth."

"What do you know?"

He wasn't certain that he had actually uttered the words, posed the question. He heard this voice saying the words, recognized it, but it displaced his sense of present reality. Time was flip-flopping, going backwards and forwards, like a film editor's machine, showing bits and pieces of recorded events. Was he inside his father's mind? A younger Harry Silver, for this was the voice he had heard, had posed the question and his own father, hidden as always behind the silent facade, was pondering the question. Was there more to convey through continued silence or through speech?

The man, his father, lay dying, beaten. He had every reason
to welcome death. Life had been a humiliation. He could not
remember any kind word his mother had ever said to him. Or
his uncles. He was the failed brother-in-law, the failed husband,
although Harry was never sure, even now, what that meant. It
was true that he had failed at various business ventures. Harry
remembered a haberdashery, a real estate office, a furniture store.
Then sleep, mostly sleep, a living death. Evenings, he slept on the
chair in the living room, mouth open, gulping air, snoring, the
butt of ridicule and contempt.

In the eighteen years Harry had lived at home, it was his most
compelling memory of his father. Silence and sleep. He would
watch him at times, resentful and ashamed. Even his last illness
had changed nothing. He slept. Then he died. And it had left his
son with a mystery that could never be solved. For this reason he
had once promised never to hide himself from his own son. Now
he was going against this promise, and it hurt like hell. But what
choice was there?

"What I want to know, Dad—" Paul began.

"Better if you don't know now, Paul," Harry said, interrupting,
resisting the temptation to say, "Trust me." It was a phrase that
had lost its currency.

"So all this is true?" Paul asked.

"Don't push it, please," Harry said. He looked at the troubled
face of his son, reached out his hand, and touched his shoulder.
The boy recoiled, stepped back.

"You don't think I can keep secrets?"

"That's exactly the point, Paul. If you don't know any secrets
you don't have to keep them."

"So you are afraid I'm going to tell?"

"You've got it all backwards."

Harry got out of bed and drew the blinds. No sense keeping out the daylight now. The sudden blast of bright sunlight reassured him. He had felt himself faltering.

In the light, Paul's face showed his strain. Always thin, he seemed gaunt now, spindly, his face a map of confusion and despair. Seeing him, Harry wanted to reach out and hold the boy in his arms, comfort him. But he held off, afraid the boy would reject him.

"In the end," he whispered, then his voice trailed off and he spoke only to himself. "In the end, I'm going to need your respect and Bobbie's. But first I have to keep my own." It was getting clearer now, the vague outlines becoming sharper, more defined. "This is a hard choice," he said aloud. The wall between the conscious and the subconscious collapsed. He saw his course clearly, understood it implicitly. He was not a man who could live with betrayal. It was as simple as that. It had nothing to do with fear or guilt. He did fear the possibility of assassination, and he could not deny being tortured by a sense of guilt over Terry's death.

It was awful, and he knew he would pay the price for a lifetime. Whatever had motivated him to commit or participate or conspire in this bizarre subterfuge, whether it was zeal, loyalty, ambition or stupidity, he knew that the only expiation for him lay in preserving his bedrock sense of morality, his code of inviolate personal ethics in which betrayal was a high crime. He would not, could not, betray Billy Tucker.

Was it a taste for martyrdom? He was sure not. He also hoped that it had its pragmatic side. Silence was "golden," because gold was the most valuable metal on earth. Now that all this was out in the open, he felt relieved.

"I know it's tough for you to understand, son. But I've got to go my way on it."

"But all I asked—" The boy hesitated, swallowed, pursed his lips as if holding back words, or tears. "Just tell me, Dad," he blurted.

"I know you're part of it, son. I know that. I also know it's not going to get any easier on you and Bobbie. Not right away. I have to think of the long run for all of us."

Paul shook his head then, when it was obvious he was not going to hold back his tears, he ran out of the room.

There was nothing to do now, but wait.

XXIV

She had stalked Charlie Carruthers all day. In the morning she saw him in his glass-walled office, busy on the phone, talking to editors, reading stories, the picture of the busy newspaper executive. Midmorning she had appeared at his office door, but he had waved her away with a curt "later," as he picked up the phone.

No wonder he was pissed. He was right, of course. She had gotten emotionally involved. Worse than that, zeal and ambition had distorted her objectivity, and she was ashamed.

Back at her desk, she noted that his conversation had been a brief one. He was avoiding her. Twice she had followed him through the newsroom. Once he had disappeared into the men's room. The other time he had ducked into an elevator. The door had closed before she could get into it.

He was gone most of the afternoon, during which time she tried to keep herself focused. She couldn't seem to summon any more investigative energy. Not on this story. For her it was done. A true thirty. She hadn't the stomach for it any more. The pot was still boiling. She felt enervated, unable to function.

She blamed part of her lethargy on the sleeping pills she had taken when she got back to her apartment. Leaving a trail of discarded clothes from front door to bathroom to bedroom, she had dropped into bed and disappeared into a drugged fog.

But it had kept her from thinking about Al, turning his betrayal over in her mind, facing her detonated marriage and the necessity of a final confrontation. And Harry. More and more, his presence loomed in her thoughts, confusing her. In the morning her action had been purely mechanical, and it had taken her some time to find her way back to reality. She wished she hadn't.

Her first deliberate act was to call Harry Silver. A compelling need, she wondered. Then why? Soon an avalanche of questions was sure to begin in her mind for which there would be no apparent answers.

After a score of rings it was apparent that he had disconnected his phone. She couldn't blame him. But hadn't she given him his chance to defend himself? Self-righteousness as a rationale was a lot less effective than it had been last night.

How dare he be so calm and unruffled in the face of her agitation. It wasn't fair, wasn't honest. Couldn't she see how much she cared? If he insisted on being squeezed, then by God she would squeeze him. Every tap of her finger on the keyboard was a dart aimed in Harry's direction.

A good little soldier, she knew what Charlie expected, and she was determined to give him what he wanted. It wasn't Harry Silver who handed out the perks in her life. Besides, she began to feel that perhaps she had overreacted. Charlie's instincts had brought him a long way, and if they were counter to hers then perhaps she was at fault. It was quite possible that Bilton was not lying. From memory she had even reconstructed paraphrases that, she was sure, caught the essence of his denials. The result was a story that could effectively torpedo the career of one Harry Silver. Well, that was exactly what he wanted. Wasn't it?

With shaking fingers, she had picked up the paper from outside her door. They had slotted the story above the fold, which gave it considerable status, but reading the headline made her suddenly queasy and she flung the paper away from her. CUSTOMS COMMISSIONER RESIGNS UNDER DIAMOND SMUGGLING CLOUD, the headline read. The horror of it was that it did accurately reflect what she had written, although Charlie had judiciously edited it.

In the office she tried Harry's number again. No answer, which further fueled her resentment and recalled the image of his calm exterior. Last night she wanted to shake it out of him. Now she wanted to choke it out of him. Wire-service copy was dumped on her desk. The telephone rang. She did not answer. Others took her messages. Nor could she summon up the courage to reread her story, to consult her notes. She wished she could shut down her thoughts, hang up a sign in her mind that read OUT TO LUNCH.

Charlie didn't return to his office until late afternoon. She contemplated him at a distance but was unable to catch his eye. She wasn't even sure why she felt compelled to see him. What she really wanted, needed, was to see Harry Silver, to listen to his true confession, to savor his sweet innocence, to provide him with the succor of herself, mind and body.

The thought shocked her and she rose from her desk and barreled into Charlie's office. He made no effort to resist, watching her with wry amusement. For some reason, she hadn't expected the visage he presented. He was surprisingly calm. The deep lines of the night before had flattened. He rolled his eyes upward.

"They loved it," he said.

"Loved it?" She was momentarily confused.

"The whole shtick. Beginning to end. Even Evans acknowledged it was clever stuff. I'm laying another ten thou a year on your nose, Elly. Starting with your next check." He winked and his face crinkled.

"But it's not over."

"Hell, no. But what'll come down now will be more mainstream." He looked down at his desk and picked up a piece of copy. "Then this Wilmington thing... "

She took the copy from him and read it. Her heart leaped. A bank clerk in Wilmington had recognized Harry's picture.

"Says he had a safe-deposit box. Came in with a suitcase, both times, first to open the box—sometime after that rabbi thing—then a few weeks ago. After your story began. Probably got cold feet. Came to remove the cash. Hide it somewhere."

"Hide the cash?" Her throat went dry.

"Hell, they'll find it. Probably buried somewhere. A helluva caper story. But you can see that we're really no longer in charge. The bloom is off the rose in terms of exclusivity. You cracked it, Elly. No question about that. Fact is that upstairs there's a sigh of relief. They had no stomach for the blood of our leaders. Not these days. Emphasis is on ad lineage, not poison ink."

"And you?"

"Me?" He laughed, showing a row of gold fillings. "I'm ready to coast."

"You believe Harry Silver was in it only with Leopold?"

He pointed to the wire story.

"In the face of that?"

"You believe everything you read?" she asked facetiously, hoping her attitude might ridicule the idea. There's more to it, she insisted to herself. I know the man.

"Got your spoon in the wrong stew, Elly," Charlie said gently.

"Something wrong in believing there might be another explanation?"

"Show me proof, absolute eighteen-carat proof," Charlie said firmly.

"All right, I will," Elly snapped.

"And we'll run it in big black headlines."

"He's hiding something, protecting people upstairs. Probably Tucker. I feel it in my gut."

"So he'll confess. Make a deal. Plea bargain. After all, he's not crazy. And we'll report it down the line. Every gory detail."

"You don't want to go after it, is that what you're saying?"

"It's a pig in a poke, Elly."

"It's over then?" she asked, holding in anger, feeling the burn begin in the mythical gut.

"Look, Elly, we dug up a sensational story. Good. Well done, lady. To go beyond that makes us look like we're leaning hard. Things change. Upstairs they don't want to look like that any more. Okay, maybe it is a business decision. You don't have to understand it." He lowered his voice. "I'm not sure I do. But this I know, the courts, maybe the whole country, is in a get-the-media-fuckers phase. Won't last forever. But it's beginning to cost. Maybe it is a cover-up and this poor bastard is taking the rap for somebody way up. Maybe they're paying him to take the fall. Maybe the president is up to his ass in it. Lotta maybes. It becomes a question of tone. How do we want to look?"

"Responsible," she mocked.

"Go strictly by the book. Wave the flag of journalistic ethics. Lots of who, what, where, when."

"And we let the bastards get away with it?"

"A little recess is all. So we hang the muckrake up for a year or two."

You can't do that. She wanted to scream out the words. "I think it stinks," she hissed.

"Yours is not to reason why, lady. That's why I'm taking you off the case."

Her mind stammered to find a response. She mounted an effort to resist the panic. Her body stiffened as she sat on the edge of her chair like a bird tensing its muscles for flight, ready to rise. He held up both his palms.

"Not worth the vituperation, Elly, okay? However you want to put it, it will probably come out something terrible like old Charlie losing his edge, getting soft and flabby. So don't push it. I've got to live with that for the present. I've rationalized my position. I'm not comfortable with it, and I'm not sure I can live it for long. But sometimes retreat is the best defense. Timing is everything in life. So maybe we'll be letting them get away with it, whatever it is. I'm not sure I believe it. But it's beside the point. I'm content with the jewel-thief solution. I don't feel any remorse for old Harry Silver. He's probably got a piss pot full of dough salted away. As for you, hell you're a goddamned journalistic heroine. What the hell more do you want?"

"The truth," she said pontifically.

"Oh, Jesus." He swatted his head with the heel of his hand.

Perhaps the idea had begun to form earlier. She wasn't sure. She hoped that she would have the courage to say it with just the right tone in perfect tempo. She tried to summon up a sense of the heroic, but it fell flat.

"I'm not going to retreat," she said, her cadence measured. His head cocked, turned slightly in disbelief.

"You got a choice?"

"Not a choice. Just a little yellowmail."

"What the hell is that?"

Her breathing accelerated. It surprised her that it had not loomed as something beyond the pale when she had done it, offered Parker money for information, paid for it as if it were a chocolate bar. Then, in the light of her ambition, of means satisfying ends, she hadn't given a thought to how it might look upon reflection. Indeed, she had never intended reflection or considered consequences. But somewhere between that act and now, the circumstances and the motivation had changed. Under the sunlight of exposure, that act would stink like dead fish in the heat.

"I paid Newton Parker for the information about the money in Irving Leopold's briefcase."

A flush leaped to his cheeks. His jaw fell open. When he could muster the coordination to speak, he said one word.

"Dollars?"

"That's the usual method of currency exchange in this country."

It took all her inner resources to keep calm. Yet, at the same time, this admission confused her. Why was she taking such a risk?

"So it's yellowmail, is it?" His eyes had narrowed, but she could still see the pain in it. She had socked him in the belly, knocking out the wind. "Sounds like blackmail to me."

"I'm dead serious, Charlie," she said. It was, she knew, ugly business. For Harry? Was he worth the candle?

"And if I say bug off, you're going to chew a hole in my ass."

"I don't think it would look very good for us." She raised her eyes. "Not upstairs. Not in the media community. Isn't it one of the great no-nos of the profession? One of those closet things."

He slumped in his chair. She felt genuinely sorry for him. It was an awful thing she was doing, malicious. She supposed she could work up a good case of self-hate without trying too hard.

"You know, I was a great defender of your sex," he said, his dejection profound. "Yet, deep inside, I've always sensed this very fundamental female flaw. Emotional instability. A chemical thing triggered by an ovarian electrical discharge."

"Genderphobia," she mocked, glad that he had said it. It seemed to balance the seesaw. She could now transfer some of her self-hate to him.

"The son of a bitch has gotten under your skin."

She sucked in a deep breath. She was in no mood for analysis.

"You said we had a relationship."

He clasped his hands and looked down at them. She understood his sense of entrapment, and it genuinely hurt to know it. Look at it from my point of view, she begged him silently. I've risked everything on gut feeling. Suddenly, he looked up.

"You'd bite if you had to?"

"I think I would, Charlie."

"So what would you do if you were me?"

"Just don't take me off it. I don't care who covers the present follow-up, but I want to continue digging. Just digging. I won't gum up the works. I promise that. Let me try for the truth, the eighteen-carat variety. Proof positive. You still have the power to say no go. Just keep me in the loop."

"That important?" he said gently.

She shrugged.

"Guess so."

He contemplated her for a moment, lips curling a thin smile.

"Used your own money?"

She nodded.

"A good reporter would find a way to put it on the swindle sheet," he said with a smirk.

***

She had calmed down but was still deep in the tunnel of her own thoughts when she opened the door of her apartment. It was the earliest she had come home in weeks. She was surprised to find Al sitting in the living room. He was wearing jeans and a polo shirt and was surrounded by suitcases, obviously packed. When he saw her, he looked at his watch.

"Banker's hours," he said.

It took her a few moments to absorb the situation. Without responding, she sank into the couch, waiting for her mind to clear. Was her life exploding before her eyes?

Al waved his hand in the air, taking in the suitcases.

"Somebody had to make the move," he said. "No point to it, Elly. Our trains are running on different tracks."

"That's a nice metaphor," she said. She had the sensation of her train, ramshackle vintage steam, chugging uphill, huffing and groaning.

"I was saying to myself," Al said. "If she doesn't come soon, I'll write a note. But that wouldn't be right, would it? I mean after all these years. So I was going to wait as long as it took."

"And here I am," Elly said, not with sarcasm.

"It's over when it's over," Al said, clearing a sudden catch in his throat. This was, she knew, one of life's events that had to be endured. Her own detachment surprised her. There was sentiment, she assured herself, but it bore the tranquillity of nostalgia. Her sense of the present had changed radically in the past few days.

Apparently Al's had, as well. She wanted to tell him to skip the protocol, but he was a man of conventions. He needed the ritual and all its attendant emotions. Besides, he was filled with guilt and remorse. Her train puffed uphill, further away from him. She had the sense of watching him diminish in the distance.

"You gotta do what you gotta do, Al." She hadn't meant it to be sarcastic. But she could tell he welcomed that interpretation. He needed her to be haughty and contentious. Make it easier for him to rationalize this act of personal defense. She went along with it. Be easier for her as well.

"Maybe I should put it in writing." He stood up, started to pick up the suitcases, then put them down again. They made an angry thud as they fell to the floor. "I promised myself I wouldn't get angry, that I would remain calm. I didn't want the final curtain speech to spoil the first two acts."

"Stop being hip and colorful, Al." She was fully alert to her role now, surprisingly objective. She felt no anger, certainly no rage. The man was swimming toward his own version of the shore, and she had no reason to stop him. Everyone must save themselves in their own way, she thought.

Watching him, old memories fused. She saw the young man and his dreams, images played back in her mind now. He had been totally consistent. What he wanted from the very beginning had been clearly stated, then restated *ad infinitum*. There had never been subterfuge. She knew, too, that this last scene, the betrayal of their marriage vows, disturbed him. His ultimate pride had been in the value of his word.

"No sense going over it. Is there?" he asked. He seemed relieved. Perhaps he had expected hysteria and tears.

"Not again," she said, determined to keep her voice steady and hard.

"It's not easy to do this, Elly."

"What's easy?"

"We'll split everything down the middle."

"Haven't we always?"

The less said the better. Silently, they had both agreed.

He watched her and shrugged. Actually, she admired him for this act of severance. Earlier, she had admired his forbearance. He had every right to save himself. His picture of a successful life was clearly drawn. A Norman Rockwell cover. A family cozy and secure. She was certain she saw him now as he wanted himself to be one day, every detail clear. He, white-haired Grampa looking over his specs at two generations of his progeny, carving implements poised to cut the glazed brown turkey. At the other end of the table is Gramma, glowing with satisfaction and pride, mother of the earth. All eyes are lovingly focused on the progenitor, waiting for this symbolic act of paterfamilias to begin, the sharing of life's sustenance. Outside, moonlight caresses the snow crystals. The sound of sleigh bells tinkles in the air. Stars sparkle in the sweet, clear night.

"Hope you get what you want, Al," she said, wondering if her implication was clear. He seemed to wince, catching the barb. They were slipping into a gray area now. One thing she did not want was to hear a confession. Not now.

"No point in prolonging this," she said, her lips tight.

"None at all."

Was she keeping to his script? She searched her mind for a good exit line. She was impatient for him to leave.

"We did have a good run."

"Great while it lasted," he said.

She was certain he hadn't wanted it to end in a conflagration, just a slight edge to it to chase debilitating sentiment, to defang the guilt. Relationships end, relationships begin, she thought. It surprised her to see how easily he had slipped into her past. He was already well outside her orbit.

He took a step forward then stopped. No point, he must have decided. She knew he wanted the ending to seem gallant, graceful. There was, she felt, a simultaneous conversation going on in her mind as they moved through these motions of parting. "The sex was good," she heard herself say in her head. She had never been unfaithful. "Great," was his imaginary response. "But it's not an exclusive resource. Might be found elsewhere." She was sure he had.

"You're one helluva journalist, Elly," she heard him say. The remark revealed the ultimate way in which he now defined her. Sometime in the past she had shed the role of wife in his eyes, become a journalist. So typically Washington, she thought, defined by a label. Was this also the way Harry perceived her?

She nodded, watching him pick up his suitcases. He began to walk toward the door. Don't turn, she begged. Don't. She could tell he was resisting the urge. She shut her eyes then heard the door close. She waited for the moment of panic. It never came.

No point dwelling on it, she told herself belligerently, turning the hot water spigot with her toes as she soaked in the bubble bath. By then, all the bubbles had exploded, and the surface of the water looked scummy, like flat beer.

She had hoped it might soak away the day's emotional residue. It had simply removed the surface grime. The beast inside, under the smooth clean skin, was a filthy slut. She ticked off the litany of sins, both of omission and commission, that could be laid at the slut's feet.

Thirst for recognition or revenge or spite had turned the muck rake into a scythe. Harry Silver was impaled on its sharp point. Charlie Carruthers had felt the cold edge of its cutting side against his—well, in this context it was perfectly appropriate to be obscene—considerably shrunken *cojones*. Al had gingerly side-stepped its stroke. And these, in her mind, were the good guys. The bad guys were watching the proceedings from the safety of their closed circuit TV. This slut deserved everything she was getting, the cunt.

The apartment buzzer temporarily aborted the accelerating slide of her self-image. She debated getting out of the tub. Despite the pummeling she was giving her ego, she felt safer here. Even predators had predatory enemies. Reluctantly, she got out of the tub, put on a terry cloth robe, and dripped her way to the door, checking her visitor in the security peephole. She opened the door to a pale and agitated Paul Silver.

"Paul, my God."

She waved him in. He was perspiring, his curly hair matted, his brown eyes blinking with nervousness. He stood in the center of the living room, awkward and uncertain. "You walked. I'll bet you walked."

He nodded sheepishly, then shrugged. His eyes moved everywhere but to meet hers.

"I was in the tub," she said, patting her towel turban. "Please sit down. I'll only be a minute."

She went back to the bathroom, dried herself more thoroughly and exchanged her terry cloth robe for a quilted one, ran a brush through her hair and came out to the living room again. He was sitting stiffly on the edge of one of her upholstered chairs, hands folded on his knees, looking very much like what he was, the hurt child.

"Can I get you some milk and cookies?" Paul shook his head.

It occurred to her that none of these items were presently in the house. A picture of his mother's neat functional kitchen flashed through her mind. She watched him without speaking, waiting, not quite knowing how to act herself.

"He doesn't know I'm here," Paul said, the words rushing out. She wondered if they were meant to be conspiratorial.

"Won't he be worried?"

"He's not home yet. He went away early with those men."

She knew what he meant. The FBI was questioning him.

"And Bobbie?"

"She's staying over the Perkins'."

He inspected his hands. His eyes blinked nervously then he looked up suddenly, and when he spoke it was as if he had begun the conversation in his thoughts.

"They came and dug up the whole yard with this machine. It made this terrible noise. I didn't know what to do."

She made some quick assumptions. Since someone at this bank in Wilmington had identified Harry, it was logical for them to be seeking physical evidence. She waited for Paul to answer the unspoken question, until she realized that he did not have the information she possessed. Poor child, she thought. Caught in the middle of perplexing events. Compassion quickly became anger until she remembered what had triggered these events.

"I know what they were looking for," he said with quiet authority, devoid of youthful arrogance. He was, she decided, banging on the doors of the adult world. It hurt her to know that his youth had suddenly become truncated, aborted. In her heart, she cried for him, daring not to show him her tears. Despite the loss of his mother and the danger of losing faith in his father, she was certain that he did not want her pity. "Diamonds or cash, that's what. You said in your story that he might be a smuggler."

He was only vaguely accusatory, and she was grateful for that. Nor did he appear to be questioning the obvious implication. For her the matter became doubly confusing, another strange turn in this emotional maze in which she was trapped. Harry, quite obviously, was not entirely innocent.

Then why all this fuss and bother? Hang him by the toes, and hook him on the meat rack. Except that being innocent and an innocent were two completely different issues. She wondered if this half man, half boy also sensed the difference. It became important to her suddenly to find out.

"Do you think he is?"

"A smuggler?"

"Yes."

The boy blew out air through puffed cheeks. It was another adult reaction.

"He's my dad… " For a brief moment he slipped back to childhood, the blind faith in the progenitor. She knew such feelings well, how fragile they are, how they falter at times and how little they had to do with events outside the primal relationship. But then he stiffened, tightened his grip on his knees. His knuckles grew white. "He won't tell me anything."

"That's because he doesn't want you to be involved."

"You think I don't know that?" he snapped, suddenly belligerent, obviously defending his right to be taken seriously.

"No mystery, Paul. People have a tendency to protect the people they love."

"He has no right to keep it to himself. Not from his son."

Now there was a heavy dose of maturity, she thought. She noted that a red flush had appeared on the boy's cheekbones, like dabs of rouge. She could tell he wasn't finished expressing the thought and waited. "He didn't tell Mom either." His resentment was palpable. "What are families for?"

It was a question beyond answering, pushing her further into the maze, remembering Al and his unfulfilled need.

"So did they find anything?" she asked gently.

"I don't think so. They were still working when I left."

"Do you think they will find anything?"

"No."

"Why not?"

The boy shrugged.

"But the facts have to be faced," Elly said. What facts did she mean, she wondered? In a way, the thought challenged her training. Collecting and presenting facts often lent themselves to different interpretations. Facts never sat still long enough, they changed like chameleons.

"Dad says not to believe everything I read or see in the media," Paul said, with some embarrassment. "He says that sometimes they get their facts wrong."

"We're only human," she said, immediately defensive, a knee-jerk reaction.

"He says that you were wrong about Mr. Leopold being a spy, going to Iraq."

"Now that's one thing that I saw with my own eyes." Did she really? Would Harry have lied to his own son?

"What else was I wrong about?"

"He didn't say."

"But he did tell you that I was wrong about Mr. Leopold." She paused. "How could he be so sure?"

"He said he talked to him in Venice right after your story."

For the first time she allowed herself to glimpse the possibility of her being mistaken, which meant that the story had begun on a false assumption. It did not, of course, negate the validity of what had come next. Was it really all a plot in her subconscious then? It was a possibility that she didn't dare face. Not now.

"But it doesn't follow that everything else was wrong, does it?"

"No."

"Paul, I want to ask you a question, and I want you to answer it very carefully."

"Only if you promise *me* something," Paul said.

"Of course."

"That you won't use it to hurt my dad."

Carefully, she considered her answer. It was important now to plumb the depths of her own motives. In the past, she had been perfectly capable of making promises meant to be broken, especially when they concerned information, the commodity of her trade. Honor could never be a consideration if it prevented truth—echoes of her father. She felt Charlie's presence in the room as well. And Harry's, who had his own confusing values.

"I promise."

It was a violation of a lifetime's obligation, a promise that she meant to keep under any and all circumstances. Not a simple "off the record" caveat that was always honored in the breach, but invariably led to an untraced set of similar facts. This was a promise to herself, in her heart, a solemn pledge. In it was the recognition of how much Harry meant to her, something still intangible, as yet undefined. And this boy sitting there must have sensed this. Why else, then, would he be here?

"So what was the question?"

"Do you believe your dad did the things my story has accused him of doing?"

Paul lowered his eyes and studied his fingers. But he seemed considerably more relaxed than when he had first entered the apartment.

"Yes," he said, lip trembling. "But—"

"But what?"

"He would have a good reason, and it wouldn't be for himself."

"Why do you think that?"

"Because I know my dad."

"And what reason do you suspect?"

"I don't know. Maybe Uncle Billy knows."

She felt the heat of the chase now, the thrill of following the rabbit. Little rabbit, she thought looking at the boy, curly hair pasted down like some pocket Caesar, brown eyes intense. In her did he see the potential of hope, of saving his father?

Somewhere, deep in the valley of herself, she felt the stirrings of possibility.

"You mean William Tucker, secretary of the treasury?"

He nodded.

"And I suppose they did a great deal for each other?"

"Dad and Uncle Billy?" It was a question that, at this stage, defied an answer. Like a cute puppy, he cocked an ear showing her that he was open to her questions, that he was putting himself in her hands.

"Did your mother like Mr. Tucker?"

A quick jab, based on the assumption that a wife might resent such closeness between male friends. He looked down at his tapping fingers, hesitating. She knew she had twanged a chord.

"I don't think Mom liked Uncle Billy."

"Did you?"

The boy widened his eyes and offered a reverse smile, the lips turned down. Mixed feelings, Elly saw. An unresolved personal ambivalence.

"He did a lot for Dad."

"So why didn't your mom like him?"

"She said that when Uncle Billy snapped his fingers, Dad jumped."

"Was she right?"

"Well, he was good to us—" The boy wavered. "Dad got this good appointment and—"

"And what?"

"Dad said that maybe some day Uncle Billy would be president."

It was, of course, a reasonably well-known possibility. The man had all the attributes and credentials.

"And they go back a long way? Mr. Tucker and your dad?"

"Since they were kids together," Paul said.

She contemplated him for a long moment. It was obvious that

his mother had not quite broken down his feelings of admiration for Uncle Billy as hero, friend of father, protector of the family. So how come you're not sitting in Uncle Billy's living room? she thought maliciously. Because that logic had not occurred to his semimature mind? Because his dad was, in no shape, manner, or form, a thief. Not for himself. In her mind, the possibility had always existed, but only now had it become an urgent consideration.

"Do you think your dad is protecting Mr. Tucker?"

The boy shrugged. It was, she saw, the heart of his agony. Then he shook his head in the negative.

"Uncle Billy wouldn't let dad go to jail," he said, unable to control a shudder. She felt the impact bridge the distance between them.

"Of course not," she said without conviction, her mind still chasing the illusive rabbit. Yet she felt that without any measure of proof, she was gaining on the little bugger. Lighten the load. Get rid of the heavy baggage, she urged herself.

"I think maybe it's all a mix-up." He raised his eyes, in which she could see a flash of rebuke.

"Maybe so," she sighed. "But I wouldn't count on it." She found herself wishing it were true. She hadn't realized the cruelty of her comment until she saw the boy's eyes fill with tears. His nose reddened, and he sniffled, wiping it with his sleeve.

"He should tell me—" Paul began, then coughed to mask a sob.

"Yes, he should."

It was beginning. She felt it, the exercise of the journalist's art of interrogation and manipulation. The idea had bubbled up, sprung full-grown from the boiling muck. The ironic image warmed her, gave her confidence.

"We'll do it then," she said.

"Do what?"

"Get him to tell us the truth."

The boy's eyes, still shining, seemed to fill with hope.

"How do we do that?"

His use of "we" bolstered her courage. Going to be rough on you, kid, she told him silently—me, too.

"We're going to play with his head. Maybe his heart as well." It came out as a stage whisper, but the boy had heard. His forehead wrinkled in confusion. "You think you can trust me?"

He lowered his head and shrugged.

"I think he is being a lamb led to the slaughter," she said cautiously watching his face. His eyes showed her that he understood what she meant.

"I think so, too," Paul said.

Good answer, she thought. She thought suddenly of Charlie. *Bring me absolute eighteen-carat proof,* he had said.

"Now, hear this..." she began.

XXV

It was quite possible, Harry discovered, to respond to questions by assuming an imaginative identity, becoming a different person with a different history, and to convince yourself that you are telling the absolute truth. His interrogators were relentless, pummeling him with an avalanche of carefully conceived questions designed to reveal what was, to them, allegedly hidden.

They had pressed him to take a lie detector test, which he refused as demeaning to his integrity. Worse, it would destroy the identity of his imagined doppelganger and leave his real self vulnerable and endangered.

But fencing off the truth from strangers was one thing. Segregating it from Paul was a challenge far more difficult to meet. Bobbie was still too young to fully comprehend, but Paul was another matter.

He found a note on the kitchen bulletin board from Paul saying that Bobbie had gone to stay with the Perkins. But the note screamed out another message. Why a note? Where was Paul?

He walked quickly through the house calling his name, his heart leaping with a brief stab of panic at every interval. The boy was worrisome. He had managed, but just barely, to chase from his thoughts the consequences of a jail term on the children. There were always his cousins, progeny of his mother's brothers, who could be expected to "rally round," if merely to appear concerned. Nevertheless, he dreaded the prospect.

Take it one day at a time, he had urged himself. Extrication from these circumstances, he had calculated, would take time, perhaps two or three years. He might stall even further through judicial appeals if he was convicted.

Once more, he tried to put it out of his mind, but he was sagging with fatigue and his defenses were definitely down. He was relieved to hear the front door open.

"Paul?"

"Yes, Dad."

He came into the kitchen where Harry was seated, nursing a cup of tepid coffee. He was surprised to see Eleanor Fox coming up behind him.

"He just showed up at my place," she said with a shrug. He noted that she wore little makeup, and her skin was clear and creamy. It struck him that she added a note of color to the general gloom. Harry felt himself looking archly at his son, perhaps frowning.

"Happens sometimes," Elly said. "Like going to the source. He walked all the way." She seemed vaguely uncomfortable. "I drove him home."

"We stopped at Roy Rogers," Paul said.

"A note of thanks is in order," Harry said, adding, "I suppose," as if to show his reluctance. In his fatigued state, his relationship with this woman seemed bizarre, an aberration. Worse, in spite of being tired, he felt the heat of his attraction to her.

"We had a nice talk," Elly said, putting a hand on his shoulder. Paul nodded. A brief smile had lit his face. Then it was gone as quickly at it had come. Harry saw his embarrassment and decided to make it a joke.

"Beard the fox in her lair."

Elly's chuckle made him aware of the pun. The idea also troubled him.

"You should get to your homework, son," Harry said. Paul obeyed and began to leave the room, then stopped to address Elly.

"Thanks—" he began, then hesitated. "For the hamburgers."

"Anytime, kiddo," she said, saluting. He detected the revelation of relationship, and it troubled him.

"Why you?" Harry asked when he had gone.

"That requires a coffee answer," Elly said.

"I'm sorry." He felt oddly flustered.

"No, I'll do it."

She seemed to know where the makings were and soon brewed coffee was dripping through a paper cone. She laid out cups and spoons and poured. Two blacks. It struck him as strange that she should know his coffee preference.

"He doesn't want to be kept in the dark," she said.

"And you enlightened him?"

"No, I couldn't. I only confirmed what I had written."

"My epitaph."

"I told you where I stood, Harry. The offer is still open."

He smiled, felt his chest heave with a wry chuckle, remembering his session with the FBI.

"God knows what we'll see tomorrow. I guess I'm front-page news."

"Not for me." She paused watching him. Their eyes met, disengaged. He could not deny their pulling power. "I've been yanked off your case, with honors, no less. They gave me a raise."

"Congratulations."

"So you see. I am in your debt."

"I'll remember that someday." He sighed. There was a long pause. Through it, they looked at each other furtively then away. It seemed to Harry like some kind of a game. "So what did you guys talk about?"

"Who else?"

"I wish you wouldn't."

"Talk to Paul?"

"About me."

"It was his idea, Harry. I told you he walked all the way. He's scared, upset, confused. He's lost his mother. His father is not leveling with him. He sees bad things about the old man everywhere."

"No thanks to you."

"So can you blame him?"

It was, Harry knew, the area of his greatest vulnerability.

"Can we change the subject? I've had a rather trying day."

"Tell you the truth, I haven't followed it. They've put another man on your tail."

Be wary, he urged himself through his fatigue. Yet he did not want her to go. Not yet.

"I can't seem to make them believe me." His hand waved through the air toward the yard. "They've ripped up my yard." She turned toward it.

Through the kitchen's bow window she could see the wreck of the yard in the moonlight. He followed her gaze.

"Looks like they left no stone unturned." He shook his head. "What a silly idea." of course, he felt responsible, but only partially.

"Washington is full of silly ideas. I've been doing research."

"Bet you have."

"They all have these odd little descriptions, media labels, sometimes real names, trigger mechanisms for the memory." Her eyes drifted back to the yard. "Like a game of Washington corruption trivia. Old hands are good at it. Word association. Take deep freeze."

"Harry Vaughan, Truman's military adviser."

"Not bad," she said with mock awe. "How about vicuña coats?"

"Sherman Adams, Ike's administrative assistant."

"Very good."

"Political science minor," Harry said. "Eighteen-and-a-half minutes?"

"Rosemary Wood, Nixon's secretary," she responded without missing a beat.

"Chappaquiddick?"

"Not fair. Too easy."

"Ellsberg's psychiatrist?"

"John Ehrlichman. The break-in," she said.

"Bobby Baker?"

"Lyndon Johnson's man Friday."

"Amaretto and cream?"

"Hamilton Jordan, Carter's number-one boy."

"The Nixon pardon?"

"Jerry Ford."

"Elizabeth Ray?"

"Wayne Hayes."

"Rita Jenrette?"

"Screwing on the Capitol steps."

"Ollie North."

"Paper shredder."

"Senator Cranston."

"Keating."

"Brock Adams."

"Sexual harassment."

"Now there's an enduring image for you," he said.

"All part of the craziness, like Harry Silver."

"So I'll be part of the game."

"And the answer is?" She paused, watching him.

He considered the answer, unable to disengage.

"Miscarriage of media," he said, surprised that he was smiling.
"How about cover-up?"

"Has no pizzazz, too pedestrian, not individual enough."

"All right then. Here's one for the history books. How about
Silvergate?"

"Ridiculous."

"No more ridiculous than smuggled diamonds, a rabbi in disguise, Irving Leopold, jeweler to the political stars, a body in a
Vienna river." She was abruptly silent. "A woman's suicide." He
felt his gut wrench. Not fair, he thought. Out of context. But
he let her continue. "Missing money." Still he did not respond.
"William Tucker." He let it pass. "A troubled child."

"No longer trivia. I can tell," he said, holding himself together,
conscious of her scrutiny. "I thought you said you were off my
case."

"I did." She continued her scrutiny. "What's this miscarriage
of media?"

He pointed a finger at her.

"See. You're all so thin-skinned. Doesn't matter who you
kick. When the shoe is on the other foot, you can't take it." She
seemed poised to respond, then she looked around the kitchen
as if searching there for adequate words. Finally she said nothing.
"Who made you all such judges?"

"The Constitution," she snapped. "The fourth check and
balance."

"I'll go with the check, but the balance is worrisome. Behind
the type are human beings."

"So I've discovered," she said. She lowered her eyes. Did she
feel guilt? Did she know she had it partly wrong?

Odd, he thought, as he inspected her. She seemed vulnerable
and had no right to be. Disturbing images popped into his mind,

a concentration camp guard going home to Christmas dinner at a compound just outside the killing camp after shepherding a trainload of victims to the gas chambers, a headless corpse embracing the man operating the guillotine, Ann Boleyn blowing a kiss to her executioner in the black mask.

The tension in the room grew palpable. Between them there seemed a thick vibrating silence. He felt this urge to touch her flesh. His own skin grew hot and a film of perspiration began to soak his back. Body signs of desire flooded through him. Then, as if to taunt him, she put her hand on his left hand that lay inert on the table beside the coffee cup. Her touch was soft, cool, a dip in a mountain stream on a blazing day.

"I wish I could help," she whispered.

It was an anomaly. Intellectually, he wanted to lash out with something sarcastic, expressing his contempt. Here in full-bodied living color was the architect of his ruin. Oddly, the hyperbole in his thoughts sobered him. Two wrongs do not make one right. The old homily resonated in his mind. Harry Silver was, after all, merely a name in a story, a configuration of Roman letters. And Eleanor Fox was a byline. No flesh and tissue there. No mind and heart. But this Eleanor Fox. That was a different story.

"There's absolutely nothing you can do, Elly," he said quietly.

"I can try. Maybe reverse the process."

The offer confused him. It was irreversible. All he needed to do was to contain it. Even betrayal, if he were so inclined, would offer no solution. There was no escape from public humiliation now.

Perhaps, if they knew about what had happened to the ten million, he would be certified and committed. He continued to feel the presence of her hand, the transmission of attraction. He wanted to cover her flesh with his, his right hand. He resisted. No, he thought, reversal was impossible in many ways. He extracted his hand from under hers and stood up, pacing the room, saying nothing.

"Would you like me to go?"

He did not answer because he could not bear to tell her the truth. No, he did not want her to go.

"Maybe you'd better," he said, after a while.

She got up, and they faced each other. His eyes found hers, locked, explored. He wanted to jump inside them, to see what lay behind them.

"In the end, you'll have to justify yourself to the people you love." She hesitated. "And who love you." Again she paused. "Paul, for example. And, when she gets old enough to understand, Bobbie." His eyes continued to probe hers. She did not turn away. "And yourself."

Danger, he decided, pulling his gaze away. Emotion was the enemy. Desire was clearly an aberration, a perversity. Once again, he was being manipulated. Was she really off his case?

"My problem," he said, suddenly feeling open, vulnerable.

"I'll say good-bye to Paul," she whispered.

He watched her go upstairs to Paul's room. Then he looked at the backyard again.

"Pumpkin papers," he whispered. He wondered if she would know the association.

A light breeze had come up, causing a brief shower of autumn leaves, which glowed with a silvery shimmer as they followed the moonbeams to the ruined ground. Silvergate, he thought. A cloud suddenly blocked out the moon and the silvery shimmer disappeared. He shivered, turning away from the desolate landscape, and his heart ached.

XXVI

Charlie assigned Brent Hargrove to the story. A good choice, Elly thought. Brent was pushing sixty, conservative and cautious. It sent the appropriate message to all interested parties that the Silver–Leopold imbroglio was no longer investigative from the paper's point of view.

Other media took the hint, and the story merely became one of justice and retribution, traditional news. The FBI continued it's probe with dogged diligence, and the fickle audience for Washington scandal began to look elsewhere for their titillation.

As Elly had expected, Charlie turned cool and formal toward her. She still held the whip hand, but each passing day seemed to diminish her power over him. Her colleagues wondered what she was working on. Her response was to give them the impression that it was too hush-hush to be discussed openly, which was true. It became apparent, also, that Charlie's response to her yellowmail was to let her drown in it.

He never inquired as to her progress. He rarely talked to her, nothing more than a nod and an occasional disinterested wave. After a while, it became apparent to everyone that she had been exiled, was being left to rot in the Siberia of his indifference.

She deliberately stayed away from Harry's house, although she and Paul continued to meet clandestinely. A plan had emerged in her mind based upon certain inescapable conclusions. Harry Silver was determined to stonewall and take the consequences. He had apparently made peace with that thought, a silent pact with himself that, she believed, could not be broken. Except in a special way.

"I know it's cruel work, Paul. But he has got to feel that your well-being is more important than anything else."

It was, she decided, Harry's only chance. Naturally, Paul had been confused. It was a distortion of his values. But how else could they fight back? The real truth was the only effective weapon against the guns of ambition and hypocrisy pointed in his direction.

It was Paul's job to extract it from his father, her job to teach Paul how to do it, a grim business. What did he know about subterfuge, manipulation and guilt? Teaching him how to use the tape recorder was the easiest part.

"You must present yourself as his victim at all times."

The instruction, often went over his head, which sometimes led her to the edge of exasperation.

"Put it another way. Does it hurt to have him not confide in you, not tell you the truth?"

"Yes, it does."

"Then show it to him, damn it. Exaggerate it. Show him depression, sadness, even disgust. Make him feel that he is letting you down, hurting you. Try to focus his pity and guilt. Make it seem like his action will ruin your life." She could see the boy slip further and further from childhood. "And well it might."

"But suppose it doesn't work?"

"It will, if you make it work. Everybody has a button."

She had no illusions as to the button that Harry Silver had pressed in her.

***

The Tuckers, Elly noted from items in the paper, were back in circulation, and prognosticators in the national media were beginning to suggest that William Tucker just might have the right stuff for a run for the presidency. Earlier, the president had announced his neutrality, although more and more he seemed to be photographed with his treasury secretary. The Tuckers had also spent time with the presidential couple at Camp David.

She continued to try to get an interview with Tucker and, despite the fact that the story itself was fading, he continued to resist. His press secretary always politely refused. A machine answered a call to his home. But she would not give up. She needed to confront him.

Finally, she resorted to crashing a social event, a black-tie ball to benefit juvenile diabetes. As press, suitably dressed in an evening gown and carrying a pad and pencil for legitimacy, she was able to roam freely during the cocktail hour, the only time during which the guests mixed before the dinner began in the ballroom.

Millie, as always, was dressed in her trademark turban. Observing her from afar, Elly thought she seemed more subdued. Even her voice, which normally carried over the hum of the crowd, was decibels lower. Good trouper-politicians, Elly noted. They worked the room separately. Deftly moving through the crowd, Elly maneuvered herself into a spot where a confrontation with Millie was unavoidable.

"Good evening, Mrs. Tucker," Elly said politely.

"You." Millie stared at her with wide-eyed contempt.

"Looks like you hit the nail partially on the head about Harry Silver and Irving Leopold," Elly said. She had positioned herself in such a way as to block off any path of immediate escape.

The chords in Millie Tucker's neck stood out. Her cheeks flushed. She looked around her helplessly, but kept her cool.

"Awful thing for Harry," Millie said, an obviously well-rehearsed remark. Elly searched her face looking for genuine compassion.

There wasn't any. Resisting further comment, Millie, who was obviously more adept at social maneuvering, cleverly extricated herself by feigning interest in someone across the room.

The brief confrontation whetted her reportorial aggression, and she moved foreword toward Tucker who scampered about the room with the agility of a rooster in a chicken coop. A natural, Elly observed—handsome, charismatic, armed with the sincere "burn-in" gaze that made people believe, for one intense moment, that they had captured the man's total attention. It was, she knew, a sure sign of candidacy, the well-honed "eye-fuck."

Introducing herself, she saw it quickly lose its potency, flicker and sag. Only his handshake, a disembodied gesture maintained its firmness.

"I'm Eleanor Fox, Mr. Secretary. I've been trying to interview you," she said politely, holding back from extricating her hand. She had taken him by surprise.

"Be great," he said. She saw a tiny tremor at the edge of his smile.

"When?" she asked.

"Catch my press secretary in the morning."

"I've talked with him on numerous occasions."

"You have?" The effort at sincerity seemed genuine, the quintessential requirement of the political persona. "We'll have to give him hell, won't we? To turn down such an attractive news hen." His smile broadened, showing even white teeth.

"I'll want to talk about Harry Silver."

He had to purse his lips tightly to stop the tremor.

"Poor Harry," he said, shaking his head. This time, she could almost see the stage directions: "Show compassion and pity. Summon up a tear." He reacted on cue.

"You think he's guilty?" she thought.

"Harry Silver is my closest friend."

Evasion and obfuscation, she thought, another master of the art. She extricated her hand, feeling disgust. She knew from Paul that this so-called "closest friend" had not been in touch with his father for weeks since her last story had appeared.

"Did it bother him?" she had asked Paul. It was one of the questions she had insisted that he ask.

"He's very busy," Harry had responded, according to Paul. Some friend.

"Have you seen him or talked to him since—?"

"Of course."

"That's not what I hear," Elly snapped.

"You people." Tucker shook his head treating her like a rebuked child.

"No. You people," she said, feeling the heat rise to her cheeks.

He smiled blandly and turned away. As his wife, he had learned the physical ritual of social evasion, an arm maneuver accompanied by eye contact toward a distant point. She did not follow him. There will come a time, she vowed, when he cannot avoid me.

***

She kept tabs on the official investigation through Hargrove, whom she approached obliquely, and Paul, whom she approached directly. They met periodically after school, going over the strategies and tactics of their campaign to get Harry to talk.

According to Hargrove, the FBI had interviewed all the top government figures that had bought jewelry from Irving Leopold. They also had found no sign of any money transferred to Harry, only the testimony of three bank employees who had identified

Harry as the person who had rented a large safe-deposit box in their respective banks and had made two trips to each. None could say for certain what he had carried in the suitcase during his visits, although the clerk from Wilmington insisted that "it had to be cash."

She learned from Paul that Harry had engaged a lawyer, but that his principal defense was to continue to deny everything. It became increasingly frustrating for both her and Paul.

"He just won't say," Paul told her with accelerating nervousness. The strain was telling. The boy had grown pale and thin.

"We may have to get tougher."

She wasn't quite sure what that meant. She was certain that the boy didn't. It took all of her willpower to resist seeing Harry. Part of the plan, she told herself. Occasionally on some pretext or other, he had left messages on her answering machine, but she had not returned the call. She feared that any contact with him would reveal what she was up to with Paul. It did not keep her from probing Paul about him.

"Does he talk at all?"

"Only to ask Bobbie and me about school, homework, stuff like that."

"Does he eat?"

"Not much."

"Is he getting thin?" She had looked at him and pinched his ribs. "You are. We can't have that, mister." She meant it, knowing how important his appearance was to her plan. In that sense wan and pale were good. For such ideas, she despised herself. Ends and means, she thought sadly. Platitudes or bedrock truths? The borders had become blurred.

"I'm trying," he would protest.

"Does he look bad?"

"Not bad exactly. Distant. Far away."

"And you keep pressing him to tell you the truth."

"He says to just have patience, that everything will be all right. Not to worry."

Answers like that were troubling. They were getting nowhere. She felt trapped, impotent. And because it absorbed her so thoroughly, her mind ran the gamut of possibilities, especially at night, as she lay alone in her bed. Was it conscience that drove her? Remorse? Such thoughts heightened her sense of urgency. Was it impossible to reverse? Why hadn't she found the philosophic balance—as Harry had?

One day Charlie Carruthers, breaking his long silence, accosted her in the hallway. She had the impression that he had followed her.

"Looks like old Bilton had it down right," he said.

"How so?"

It was, of course, a lame response, and she knew he was savoring the information that he was about to impart.

"Turned out that everybody upstairs was clean. They went through everybody with a fine-toothed comb."

"Tucker, too?"

"As a whistle." He seemed joyful, happily belligerent. "I'd say it's time to come down to earth, Elly." It was a blatant pitch at reconciliation, which tempted her. But just for a moment. It made her aware of how completely she had switched allegiances, changed commitments.

"I don't believe any of it," she said, noting the quiver in her voice.

"Look, the man's not talking because he's got nothing to talk about. Except to confess. Sooner or later, they'll break him."

"Not him," she whispered.

He shook his head sadly.

"Classic case. She finds the pearl, then swallows it."

"Bad metaphor," she said. "It'll come out. You know where."

"It can just go so far," he muttered.

"And I'm going to take it as far as it goes."

"Your nickel," he said, shrugging and walking off. The confrontation had made her weak in the knees. And mad, mad enough to move in another direction, long contemplated. Once again, he had laid down the gauntlet. So they had laundered all the bigwigs, she thought, kept the dominoes in place. Except for poor Harry, who was participating in his own extinction. The situation was getting urgent.

Time, she decided, to throw the gears into reverse.

***

She waited for Newton Parker in the waiting room of the Lorton Reformatory, which the District of Columbia operated in Virginia. He came in swaggering, his Afro cut gone, his tight hair down to the skin, wearing a look of bemusement. Prison had roughened him. It wasn't only the prison work clothes he had exchanged for his neat conservative suits, he seemed more mocking, more contemptuous.

"Social or business, lady," he said with a lascivious wink.

"Business," she said hastily, hoping to foreclose on the cruel fun she was sure he was contemplating at her expense.

"Little honky pink wants to play more jive."

"Talk English for Chrissakes," she snapped, surprised to see her edginess erupt. Her sudden air of authority quieted him, made him study her.

"I didn't invite you. We made a deal, and I kept my side."

She lowered her voice.

"They've been out to see you?"

"You know they have," he said. "And I play the same old record."

"That's why I'm here."

He was suddenly furtive, glancing over his shoulder at the guard that stood at one end of the long room. She was conscious of lowering her voice, moving her head closer to his. He smelled musky, different.

"I want you to change the record," she said. "Go back to the original."

"You think I'm just a dumb nigger?"

His lips curved over his teeth in a joyless expression that resembled a smile.

"They won't be able to prove it either way," she whispered, talking swiftly. "The man you stole it from is dead."

"No shit."

"You're serving your time." She grew thoughtful. "Just tell them you got scared. Thought no one would believe you." She noted that he didn't seem too happy about the idea. "Or you can just say you made a mistake, that you want to clear the record. That the money wasn't in that briefcase after all, that you got mixed up."

"Lady, you put it in the paper."

"I said 'implied,' remember?"

"Yeah. But I told the judge I wasn't sure."

"So what's the downside now? Just say you're sure now, it wasn't in the briefcase."

"Who do I tell that to?"

"The authorities. Then the press."

She chuckled nervously, feeling his inspection. He was sitting in a chair opposite her in tight jeans directing her attention—deliberately, she was certain—to the big lump between his legs, which he periodically cupped with his hand. Macho display, she supposed, was his only refuge.

"You ain't got the number for such an enterprise," he said. She had to think about the language for a moment. She had not expected it to arrive in quite that fashion. But she knew what he meant.

"Five big ones," she said. She had earmarked twenty thousand, her share of Al's and her joint account.

"Thou?"

She nodded in confirmation. His eyes opened wide, showing red around the rims. Then he cupped his lump and scrutinized her.

"Double trouble, lady. Double trouble means double."

"You're driving a hard bargain," she said.

"I figure you want this bad. Real bad."

He was more tragic than sinister, and she had planned for the eventuality. He had, of course, nowhere to go. His credibility had already been tainted, although he had provided the authentic springboard for her story. In her mind, she had already rejected what she thought she had seen in Venice. She had not seen it or only partially seen it or merely imagined it. Perhaps it was a trick of the night tides or of the night itself or of her mind or an honest misinterpretation. It hadn't been deliberately malicious. Had it? To err is human. To persuade, cajole, manipulate is human.

"Five now. Five after," she said.

"All now, lady."

"In here?"

He thought about that. Then shook his head.

"Maybe, Mama—" he began. "No way." He scratched his scalp

and rubbed his chin. "Got nobody in this world I can trust." He banged his fist onto his thighs in a gesture of frustration.

"You got me," Elly said. He raised his dark eyes to her.

"Yeah, you," he said, shrugging. "Payin' me to tell the truth. Payin' me to lie. Tell you this. Lyin' pays better." He began to laugh, softly at first, then with belly-shaking guffaws. The guard at the other end of the room turned around.

"Tell you what," she said. "I'll hold it until you get out. Give you maybe three, four hundred now." She looked around her. "From the looks of things around here, nothing's really safe."

His laugh had tapered off to a chuckle, then a grunt, finally a nod.

"They'll think I'm crazy," he said.

"I wouldn't worry about appearances, Newton. You're just a little cog in their machine. A voice. They don't care anything about you."

"You either," he said, with what seemed like a sigh.

Me, she thought, enduring a sudden wave of self-disgust rolling over her, cresting, dissipating but leaving its moist residue. Charlie Carruthers' words pounded in her ears. "You got a relationship." Even now with Newton, participating in this surreal transaction. Zeroing in on his need, she had touched the exposed nerve, the vulnerability in herself.

"There are lots of ways to put that," she said slowly. "I certainly care about what you've agreed to do." It sounded like justification, and she quickly changed the subject. "All you do is tell them that you want to change your statement. Simple."

"They'll push," he said. "You know that."

"Doesn't matter. Who's to say no? Just you and me now."

"You gonna write it up."

"Not me. Someone else will."

He grew thoughtful, then he lifted sad eyes and watched her. "Fifteen thou," he said. "To pay for all the wear and tear."

She hesitated, frowned, waited through what she felt was the appropriate time, then she put out her hand. He reached out and took it, holding her flesh for a long moment. She looked down at the clasped fingers, black and white, bonding in fragile trust. She had the urge to give up the extra five thousand. That would be a gift, beyond the transaction. But then he stood up, and the moment was lost. He cupped his crotch and smiled broadly.

"Made my day, mama," he said, swaggering toward the door. Before he went a few paces, he turned, and pointed his finger.

"First day out, right?"

"Don't you trust me?" she said, smiling.

He smiled back at her, turned and swaggered toward the door.

XXVII

That day the interrogation had been relentless. They seemed to be working in teams. Every few hours a fresh team, like a pony express. Carter Baker, his lawyer, had been tenacious in his objections, sometimes strident.

"Something's changed," Carter said later over lunch near the FBI building. They had been having lunch at this particular place because the tables were far enough apart for them to talk freely. Harry, too, had noticed it. "They seemed less sure somehow."

Harry liked his lawyer, a big man with a shock of curly hair that fell over a large forehead and a large black mustache that drooped at the corners. He seemed inundated with black curly hair. It spilled thickly out of his cuffs to his hands and over his shirt collar upwards over his Adam's apple. Toward the end of the day, it seemed he had a five-day growth of beard. At times, especially when he sprang out of his chair to raise an objection or lecture the clean-shaven government interrogators, he seemed like some ape that had wandered out of the jungle to make his case on a matter of principle.

Harry knew the man was frustrated, not by his persistent denials, but because Harry simply refused to confide in him. Harry had made that quite clear from the beginning.

"These are the parameters," he had told Carter. "I intend to deny all allegations. If it goes beyond this stage, make the best deal you can."

"A plea bargain?"

"No, because I don't intend to tell them anything. Nothing."

"A lawyer's dream," Carter sighed. "An uncooperative client."

"So it will all be legal maneuver. Classic legal stuff."

"They'll make a case, get an indictment. You could go to jail."

"No kidding."

"They'll say you're covering up, protecting someone at the top."

"They've already said that. In that arena, I've been accused, tried, and convicted."

"What about the money?"

"What money?"

"The diamonds then?"

"That's another thing. I don't need it from you."

"You could get five years for perjury."

"Out in less than two. Right?"

"Right, but what about your kids? Doesn't that bother you?"

"More and more."

They had gone round and round. Carter had persisted. He was a man who liked near impossible challenges. Harry had been made to order.

"It's gonna cost," Carter said.

"I know."

It had been the subject of intense calculation. If, as was predicted, an indictment were inevitable, his legal expenses would come to more than a quarter million dollars, the full extent of Harry's net worth, after liquidation and including his house. Once it had seemed a fairly respectable sum, all self-made, a matter of some pride. But ever since he had tossed away the ten million, money had lost its mystique, its value for him. It was a necessity, but had no meaning. To pursue it as a reward in itself seemed demeaning. Yet it was the kind of statement that one could make only to himself.

He watched Carter across the table, sipping the first of his daily two martinis that preceded his normally heavy lunch.

"Something has changed. I can't put my finger on it." He sighed and shook his head.

Harry, too, had felt it. But he was too preoccupied to analyze what it meant. Suddenly, they had come back to the original question of the hundred thousand found in Leopold's stolen briefcase. Of course, all they got from Harry was the regular menu of denials. Those had taken some extra effort on his part. He was preoccupied. Paul was becoming more and more worrisome.

The boy was losing weight, paying no attention to his schooling. Harry had been summoned to the principal's office and warned that something was going on inside Paul that needed attention. The principal had been polite and diplomatic. Notoriety, he had said, a clear euphemism for the public disgrace of a parent, could have severe repercussions for a child, especially a sensitive teen-ager like Paul.

Bobbie, on the other hand, was coping well, an argument he used on the principal. Kids were different, the principal had pointed out. Maybe Bobbie would have a delayed reaction, maybe none at all. Besides, the children had lost their mother.

Clearly, according to the principal, Paul needed psychiatric help, an alarming suggestion. He did not, of course, tell the principal what might be the most important reason for Paul's conduct. Had it become an obsession of the boy?

"You've got to tell me, Dad."

It was relentless, a litany. He could not be in the boy's presence without the pleading beginning. He felt helpless. Didn't the boy realize that such knowledge could be deadly, that knowing the truth would not be an asset? Was, in fact, downright dangerous. The boy was not immune to interrogation by the authorities.

Worse, he might feel that it was his duty to tell to protect his father. Besides, would the boy understand that not betraying a

friend was an act of nobility? Indeed in the face of Billy's prov-
ocation, it was also an act of courage. Could Paul understand
that? Wasn't there also the shame of it? He had violated his office,
had lied and deceived. To understand that required worldliness,
maturity.

But fatherhood also had its imperative and values. There was
the boy's suffering to consider. Harry did not live in a vacuum.
He loved his children. He wondered how other fathers handled
these things, the murderer, the thief, others publicly disgraced.
Did they plead for understanding? Did the children turn against
them? Hate them?

"Tell me the truth," the boy had pleaded with tears in his eyes.
"Tell me the truth."

He could see the agony in the boy's eyes. He might have made
up some story, but he could not bring himself to lie to his son.
Silence was not a lie or was it? He had opted for postponement,
but the boy would not wait.

His own father had hidden everything away from his son,
everything, and Harry had lived with the expectation that some
day this magic moment would arrive and his father would emerge
from his lifetime cocoon and tell his son—what? He was never
certain. Only that it was important, essential, some secret passed
from father to son that would change everything.

***

He had sought out Eleanor Fox. She and the boy seemed to
have developed a relationship. Hadn't Paul come to her that one
time? Then, abruptly, she seemed to have withdrawn. Had she
merely used him and tossed him away like a candy wrapper? She
had told him she was no longer working on the story. Nor was it

front-page news anymore. He supposed he should be grateful.

Yet he felt an odd void in his life as well. He thought of Elly Fox often, saw her in his mind. He had tried to reach her, had left messages on her machine, but she had never returned the calls. Sometimes an odd feeling came over him when he thought of her, a strange sense of need.

It made him feel guilty, as if he were unfaithful to Terry. But Terry had slipped out of his life so effortlessly, as if she had merely left a train that had reached her destination. She was gone now, had disappeared. Death, contrary to belief, was not final. People existed in memory, permanent apparitions for the living to contemplate. But Eleanor Fox was not an apparition, definitely not an apparition.

Since she was not returning his messages, he had to take the bull by the horns. Hadn't he? He had already arrived at a point beyond rationalization. For Paul, he had decided. Why else?

He arrived at her apartment building late in the evening, a time when he assumed she would be at home. She was and when she saw him at her door, she seemed flustered, surprised by his presence. On his part, his heart pounded in his ribcage, muffling his words as he spoke them.

"It's Paul," he blurted.

Surely she must not think of this visit in any other context? She was wearing a dressing gown of smooth satiny material that showed off the provocative curves of her body. He sensed that he looked strung out, frantic. He certainly was ill at ease. She offered him a drink and he watched her move around the room, making the drinks, come back.

"What about Paul?" she asked.

She seemed strangely cold, avoiding his eyes. The visit, suddenly, did not seem like a good idea. He drank his drink quickly.

He had decided to leave as soon as he could.

"He's becoming, well, morose. Depressed."

"Can you blame him?"

He shook his head.

"Suppose not." She watched him but said nothing. Forced to speak, he said: "I'm really worried about him."

"Well, you should be," she said with an air of rebuke, her eyes narrowing. Her tone suggested something ominous, foreboding.

"You've talked to him?"

"Yes, he calls me."

It seemed more like a confession than a statement. He waited for her to continue.

"What does he talk about?"

"You, mostly."

Her comments seemed deliberately clipped, foreshortened, as if she were waiting for him to say more, to fill in the blanks.

"Do you think he knows how difficult he's making it for me?"

"All he wants is your trust."

"He has that."

"Does he?"

He got up, still holding his empty glass and paced the room.

"It's not as simple as one might think. He simply cannot be involved."

"But he already is."

"He won't understand."

"Try him."

It occurred to him suddenly that he was going too far, laying out elaborate hints. How she would love to know, he thought. He got up and moved restlessly around the room. He wanted to trust her, which confused him further.

Stopping in front of a window, he looked out at a truncated

view of Connecticut Avenue. Below, life seemed normal, unpressured. Behind him, he sensed her movement. His nostrils caught the scent of her perfume. It was familiar, having lingered in his memory. She had apparently come close to him, too close. But when he turned and tried to sidestep her, he discovered that the wall blocked his retreat.

"Someday," she said softly, gentler now. "You're going to ask yourself if it was all worth it."

"You can't undo what's been done," he said. His eyes sought hers then, with effort, swept away.

"You can try."

Her remark confused him. She was, he knew, waiting for his response. Was theirs a mutual need to communicate, to confide? Or was he superimposing his own compulsion on her? Something, he sensed, was collapsing inside him, beyond his ability to avert.

"It's not as simple as you might think," he whispered.

"So you are hiding something?"

He felt as if the center of gravity were changing, growing stronger, magnetizing him to the ground. Feeling its pull, he was afraid it would carry him down, deep into the earth. He wanted to reach out, grasp her, hold on.

"It's not what you think," he said, haltingly. His throat had gone dry.

"You don't know what I think," she said.

"I've got to do it my way."

"Then I'll have to do it mine."

"Do what?"

Their responses seemed miscued, as if they were giving answers to questions not asked. Questions like, what is the time? Answer, six feel tall. Gibberish.

"I told you. I'm off your case."

"Won't matter. Not with you people."

"You people?"

"The story is everything."

There seemed something relentless about her, single-minded, pressing. He felt as if he were slipping away.

"There is no story, Harry. Not for me. Not anymore. It's you I'm thinking about. Why can't you look at me as a human being first?"

It was not merely a suggestion, but more like a pleading. He felt himself under attack by a force too compelling to resist. His body's response humiliated his sense of logic and dignity.

Something was happening beyond mind, beyond his ability to understand or react logically to it. Wasn't it she who had changed his life, redirected all his priorities, destroyed a lifetime's focus? He felt himself trying to mount a futile defense, but her persona, like some magnetic force, seemed to propel him toward her. Resist, he begged himself. But he could not suit the words to the action. Quickly the space between them disappeared, the movement mutual.

Their embrace seemed instinctive and inevitable, an explosion of sexuality and need. Compulsive, driven, he tore away her flimsy gown, and she was naked in his arms, her body shivering, her breath coming fast and short as he moved to cover her mouth with his. Vaguely conscious of his own frenzy, he removed his clothes and soon they were flesh to flesh, bodies writhing in a paroxysm of ecstatic necessity.

There was no thought of comfort or contrivance. The thing between them was swift and basic, a hungry coupling. As he entered her, he felt her body's vibration as her hips rose to meet his, a sexual bout of equals. At first it frightened him with its newness, and a note of comparison pressed on his memory. Terry had been passive, yielding. Elly was aggressively determined, formidable, fighting to demand and give at her own pace, forcing him to fight for himself, his own male turf, like a duel between them. Perhaps that was what it had always been. The idea of it surprised and spurred his excitement. He wondered suddenly who had won.

After, they lay on the floor in sticky repose, clinging together. She had pulled pillows off the couch and they shared one for their heads, the other for their feet. His fingers played lightly with her nipples while she lay in the crook of his arm looking up at the ceiling.

"Like kissing the sword before your head is lopped off," he said, laughing. It had been an image trying to find words, which came to him now. It did not surprise him that he feared her, still feared her.

"And who would be the executioner?" she asked, indicating that they were still communicating at cross-purposes. As if to illustrate the confusion of definitions, she bent over him and kissed his penis.

"We seem to be reversing roles," he said. Her kiss lingered, and he was soon hard again.

"Yours is not the only exploded life in this room," she said. "I've lost a husband and possibly a career on your account."

He did not press her for an explanation, which seemed self-apparent. She had gotten involved with her target. No mystery there. His problem was understanding how the target had gotten enmeshed with the weapon.

"You won't get any apologies from me," he said.

"Nor you from me. I did my job. Shook up the bad guys." He started to say something and she put a finger on his lips. "Don't say it. I don't want to pry it out of you. Not this way."

"You won't."

"There it is again."

"What is?"

"This passion to become a victim."

"Actually, I was minding my own business until you came along."

"Not true, Harry. You were minding the public business. And because you were minding the public business, you became my business."

"So this is still business?"

"My business."

"But what if I told you. Not that there is anything to tell. But if there was?" He paused, watching her face to determine if she understood. Her eyes flickered, which he took to mean that she did.

He knew he was in a minefield. Be cautious, he urged himself. This is a dangerous moment.

"I would not like to be tested on that," she said.

"Case closed," he said, relieved.

She turned her body, leaned on an elbow and watched him. "The problem with you Harry, from the beginning, is that you defy all the clichés. You are involved in some sleazy operation. I'm pretty sure of that. And I just know, feel it in my bones, that you're taking all the guilt on yourself. Protecting others. I don't believe you're doing it out of fear. Not for yourself. I don't believe you're doing it out of financial gain. No way. I just can't put my finger on it."

"Why must you?"

"I want to know." She grew silent. Her hand made circles on his chest, reached down his stomach tracing the hairline as if it were leading to further knowledge. "Maybe if I know what's going on with you, I'll know what's going on with me."

"You can see pretty clearly what's going on with me."

"Evasions. Always evasions."

"As you can see, it is impossible to evade the central issue. Not now."

They made love again, this time a slow sensual savoring, the bartering of pleasure. Yet it frightened him, because he wanted more, he wanted the bonding to be not only of flesh, but also of heart and psyche. He had this massive urge to declare himself, to free himself of carrying the burden alone. It meant that, didn't it? Otherwise it, this utterly unforeseen sense of commitment, was counterfeit. But had it been unforeseen? he wondered. It was a mystery to contemplate forever.

"Would you like to be tested, Elly?" he asked later. The drying perspiration was cooling and she had had to take a comforter from the linen closet to throw over them. Neither of them made the suggestion to go to bed as if this place on the floor was now hallowed ground.

"I'm not sure."

"Why?"

"Because I've discovered that I care too much, that I'll be forced to choose, betray one part of myself."

"Which part? The journalist or the woman?"

"My mind would tell me to betray the woman."

"And your heart?"

She reached out and clenched him in a tight embrace, which he returned.

"Don't tell me, Harry."

He started to talk, but she closed his mouth with her kisses.

When they disengaged, she said, "Tell Paul."

XXVIII

As she came up to the front door, she sensed that she was being observed. She deliberately kept her eyes away from the window behind which she sensed that James Hopwood was watching her.

"No phones," he had said, a good sign. A paranoid was easy. If there was one thing she had learned in the newspaper business, it was how to deal with paranoids.

Before she could ring the bell, Hopwood opened the door, waved her in, and then closed it behind her. Beside the door was the blinking red eye of an electronic security system. The man was pasty-faced and squint-eyed and looked nervous and uncertain as he scrutinized her.

The interior of the house was dark and her nostrils twitched with the effluvia of dankness that infected the air. A heavy-set woman wearing a flowered housedress and curlers sat in the living room, her eyes furtive and suspicious.

"This is the Fox woman, Gladys," Hopwood said, pointing to her as if she were an inanimate object. The woman grunted an acknowledgment. He led her through a dark corridor to a small kitchen where he motioned her to sit at a booth, obviously a commercial restaurant fixture, circa 1950.

He did not offer her anything to drink and sat down across the chipped Formica table, folding chubby hands.

"Looks like we got the son of a bitch dead to rights," Hopwood said, eyes flitting from side to side.

"The FBI treat you all right?"

His eyes narrowed even further. She knew he had been

interrogated. On his guard before bureaucratic officialdom, he would have been cautious about revealing his true feelings out of fear that he would be the object of reprisals from these nefarious Jews, who in his fantasies, controlled all things.

If his interrogators had sensed his bigotry, Hopwood knew from experience, they would have redirected their questions. Can't build a case for a sympathetic jury on hate. Every prosecutor knew that. On the other hand, Elly knew hate could be a useful lever in manipulating a person.

"They're good boys. Silver deserves what he's gonna get."

"They go to trial, you'll have to testify."

"Just doin' my civic duty."

"You're one brave guy, Mr. Hopwood."

Brave confused him, emphasizing his own sense of danger. She could tell he was already halfway there, scared out of his skull.

"Anybody comes this way, I'll blow 'em right out of the water. Got a twelve gauge loaded and ready. And Gladys knows how to use it"

"Takes a lot of courage," Elly said.

"More people spoke up, we'd put all them people six feet under. Guys like Silver, who help, are just as guilty. Ya know what I mean. They're everywhere trying to corrupt people. Ya gotta be strong. Silver was red meat to them, red meat."

She looked down at her hands, acting out what she hoped was a credible version of agreement. She detested the man and his cramped hating spirit.

"Listen, Mr. Hopwood. Jimmy. I'm here because I owe you one. You really helped me with my story. Now I'm going to help you."

"Yeah."

His eyes, which had been avoiding meeting hers, now honed

in on them. His fear was palpable, and his hands before him on the table began to tremble. She lowered her voice.

"I wouldn't even tell this to Gladys. Would upset her too much."

"It would."

"You know what they're capable of."

"Betta believe."

"It's going to take all the guts you ever had."

"Something pretty heavy, huh."

"As I said, I owe you one."

The man fidgeted and she could see his neck muscles working as if he were having difficulty swallowing. His skin turned the sickly color of moist alabaster. She wondered if he was ready. In her scenario for the undoing, Hopwood's recantation was crucial.

"The problem is, Jimmy—" She looked down at her hands and made a cathedral out of her fingers. She heard his wheezy breath accelerate. "They got the power. You know that, Jimmy, they're everywhere. They own everything so they move at will. It's worse than you think." She lowered her voice to a whisper. "They got people everywhere. Judges, politicians, cops. Even in my business. Lots of them there."

"Bastards."

"I can't tell you how I found out." She lifted her eyes and locked into his. Ready now, she decided. "They're going to get you, Jimmy, you and Gladys."

He seemed to lurch forward as if he had just received a blow to the back. The plastic table cut into a fold of body fat around his middle.

"I'll blow them apart."

"You won't see them coming, Jimmy. They don't work like that.

You think they're just going to ring the bell, come to the house like the man who reads the gas meter. What they'll do is come sneaking, the way you least expect."

She paused and watched the changing expressions of fear on his face, conscious of pushing exactly the right buttons in this sad and now frantic little man. It did not take much of an effort of will to hold back her pity.

"Maybe put a charge in the house or in your car. Maybe a little push at the right time so that it will look like an accident. They want you, they get you."

"Maybe I should ask the FBI for protection?" Hopwood asked haltingly, his throat raspy and constricted. He was shaking perceptibly, vibrating the table.

"You've got one choice, Jimmy." She shook her head from side to side. "And believe me, it hurts me as well. I'm here as a fellow human being. Look at it from my point of view. I could blow my whole career. But I've got this conscience, and it drove me here. Just as it drove me to confront them."

She had every ounce of his alertness. Trapped and thoroughly demoralized by fear, he watched her face, silently pleading for mercy. "You've got to tell them that you were mistaken, that your memory of the incident was fuzzy, that you weren't sure it was Silver, that you might have gotten it mixed up. Just enough doubt for them to know they can't make a case on your testimony. That kind of thing."

"They'll think I'm a damned asshole," Jimmy snarled.

"Better an asshole than a corpse."

"How do I know you're not bullshitting me?"

His fear, she could see, was congealing into nastiness and bravado. She wondered if she had failed.

"Your choice. Not mine. I'm just here to give you the options.

It's only a matter of life and death for you and Gladys."

She started to slide out of the booth, but he reached out and grabbed her upper arm.

"That would be telling a lie."

The man's moral dilemma seemed a cruel joke. Yet, she felt no great moral superiority. There were many ways to rationalize a lie and she knew, illustrated by present experience, at least one of them.

"It's not George and the cherry tree, pal," she said ominously.

"They'll put me through the ringer," he said, still resisting surrender.

"Listen, you had the courage to step forward and tell me the truth. Surely, you've got the courage to tell them a lie." She watched him trying to absorb her convoluted reasoning, knowing that it was necessary for him to come to the same conclusion, even after mulling it over, sleeping on it, convincing not only himself but Gladys.

"You think if I do this, they'll take away my pension?"

"Pension?" She wanted to laugh out loud. "If you don't do this, they surely will take away your pension, all right. They don't usually continue paying beyond the grave. And Gladys won't be around to get her widow's pension."

She could see that of all the arrows in her quiver, these were the most effective, paranoia and pensions. She felt a sudden attack of claustrophobia. The space in which she sat was shrinking. The smallness of everything in the house, including the human beings that inhabited it, repelled her.

"I've done what I had to do," she said, swallowing to put down a wave of nausea, sliding out of the booth.

This time he made no move to stop her but sat hunched over the table, beaten by hate and insecurity. Moving swiftly, she passed

Gladys still sitting in the living room. Gladys hadn't moved from where she sat, mesmerized by the images on the TV screen. It took her the entire ride home to rid herself of the nausea.

***

It was still dark when the telephone's ring stabbed into her consciousness. She wasn't dreaming. It surprised her to discover that she was asleep. The sheets were twisted around her legs, and the covers had slipped to the floor. Apparently she had thrashed around like a trapped snake.

The undoing, she was discovering, was far worse than the doing. It was as if her value system had exploded. Rights and wrongs interchanged. The rules were being redrafted on the run. Now she was embarked on a plan to peel away her own credibility, layer by layer. Was it simply for the love of a man? Simply that? Nothing more?

"Elly?"

Harry's voice had the roughness of sandpaper. She acknowledged herself.

"It's Paul." He seemed out of breath. "He's gone."

She looked at the red numbers on her digital clock. It was a little after four. His panic was quickly transmitted to her.

"He's not here."

"I'm worried, Elly."

"Of course, you are."

There was a long silence. It was a fuzzy connection, and she could barely hear his breathing.

"I told him, Elly."

"You did?"

"We talked all evening. He got it all. Both barrels. Everything.

It felt good, too. Right. Right for both of us, I think. Now I'm not so sure."

She waited for the accusation. When it didn't come from him, she made it against herself. She had been callous to set such a plan in motion, to use the child. Paul was still half-formed, unable yet to comprehend how adults could corrupt his world. Harry's revelation should have been received as a victory for her instincts. She had, indeed, pressed the right buttons in him. But she felt drained, depressed, and she shared his fear. Perhaps it was too much for Paul to bear.

"Maybe he just needs to sort it out in his own way."

Above all, she no longer wanted to be privy to it. Perhaps, too, it was irrelevant. If Hopwood acted as she hoped he would, the case against Harry would be further weakened. If not, it might all backfire, blow up in their faces.

"Yet—telling it, Elly—it felt right, somehow," Harry sighed.

Of course, it did. The Catholics were onto that eons ago. But priests in the confessional were not emotionally involved. Not fathers or sons. Or lovers. She had the urge to confess to him now what she had done with Parker and Hopwood, and with Paul. She summoned all her willpower to resist. But self-doubt was pursuing her relentlessly now.

"I don't think I can hack it if anything happens to Paul." A sob rolled over the wire.

"Please, Harry—"

"I could have done it on my own," he said, recovering. But there was still a quiver in his voice.

"Nobody does it on her own."

It surprised her, the sudden switch in genders.

"If he comes there, Elly—"

"I think I should be with you, Harry," she whispered.

"I'd like you here, but if Paul should come there, I want him to find you home. And I better not tie up the line."

"Sure, Harry."

"And Elly—"

"Yes."

"Whatever was said was between us. Him and me—."

"Of course," Elly said. "Besides, Paul would never betray his father."

He hung up at his end first. She had no illusions where her self-doubt was leading. There was no way to escape the responsibilities of her actions. She knew she was caught between a rock and a hard place.

She spent the next hour castigating herself, her selfishness, her ignorance, her hypocrisy. She had violated all the rules. She had betrayed Al by lying about her real intentions, leading him to believe that she would bear his children, raise a family. She had betrayed Charlie's trust, then used the betrayal to blackmail him. She had betrayed Harry by manipulating him to confess the truth to his son. Perhaps now she was getting ready to betray Paul by using the information for her own personal ambition.

What in the name of God is the highest good here, she cried in her heart? Who am I to play with all these lives? "Daddy, what the hell should I do?" She heard her voice clearly. If any answer was forthcoming, the door buzzer interrupted it.

It was Paul. Not a gloomy, broken Paul, but a Paul who was animated, smiling, excited.

"I took a cab," he said. "It's waiting."

"Your father is worried sick."

"I thought I sneaked out pretty quiet."

"Not quiet enough."

He took the tape recorder out of his jacket pocket.

"And I got it all down, right there. I played it back. You want to hear it?"

"Not now, Paul."

"I got the greatest father in the world," Paul said.

So it was not the confession but the act, she thought. He had told him and that was enough. Would it be enough for her? She looked at the tape recorder on the table. It seemed ugly, offensive.

He came toward her, and they embraced. She kissed his hair, felt his cool breath, and his happiness.

"My dad is something else," he said. People were always surprising, never quite doing what they were supposed to. She had expected Paul to lose his innocence. It seemed now as if he not only had a firm grasp on it, but had enhanced it.

"Are you going to tell your dad that you were here?"

The boy shook his head.

"No way."

He was untroubled, anxiety-free, moving in an aura of trust and love. Before he left the room, he stood in the doorway.

"It's all there, Elly. You'll know what to do."

Then he was gone.

***

By midmorning she had cleaned every inch of her apartment. From time to time, she would go into the kitchen and look at the tape recorder, but she could not bring herself to touch it.

Earlier she had called the paper and told them that she was working on something and would not be into the office until later. She was not questioned. It was obvious to everyone that she was in limbo, although no one quite knew why. Then she had turned on her answering machine. She could not bear to talk to anyone. The telephone rang twice, but she let the answering machine respond.

She took a hot shower and washed her hair then filed and polished her nails, anything to fill up time. Periodically, she would go into the kitchen and look at the tape recorder, not simply look, contemplate it, speculate about the revelations it contained, then try to shake them out of her mind.

Early in the afternoon, the telephone rang again, and again she let the machine answer. She told herself it was all a game called "ignore," and the challenge of the game was to withdraw from this moment of personal existence. It was not an easy game to play. It required constant monitoring, forcing oneself not to think about anything that would cause her to confront present reality.

She had to invent strategies, like postponement and evasion, telling herself lies. Imagining herself as someone different from who she was—a housewife, a mother, a supermarket-checkout-counter clerk, a prostitute, a policewoman, a convict—anything to avoid confronting herself.

When she looked at the tape recorder, she tried to imagine it as something other than the recorder, a bowl of soup, for example—a banana, a plant, a dog—anything but a machine, anything but a tape recorder.

At midafternoon, she knew she was beginning to lose the game. The telephone rang again, then again. Outside, she could hear the sounds of automobiles, tires squeaking, horns blaring. She became anxious, and suddenly past anxieties crept through her defenses, old worries. Harry began to intrude, his face, then his body, then the memory of his touch.

In despair, conscious of her imminent surrender, she rewound the tape of her answering machine and played it back. Harry had called to tell her that Paul was back at home "none the worse for wear." The other calls were from the paper, Charlie's secretary, then Charlie himself, twice, the third time angry. "Get your ass down here," he had shouted into the phone.

Like a dam bursting, reality crashed through all barriers. Now she knew better than to look at the tape recorder on the kitchen table. Too tempting. She hadn't the will to resist. The only defense she could think of was to get out of the house, to get to the paper.

By the time she arrived the early deadline had passed. Through the glass panel of his office, Charlie saw her, glared angrily, shook his head and dialed the phone. He talked briefly, hung up and waved her to come forward. When she did, he moved into the private conference room behind his office, and she followed.

He sat at one end of the table hands clasped, knuckles white, obviously trying to control his temper. Nodding toward a seat at the other end of the table, he waited until she obeyed. Then he looked at his watch.

"They were here all day. The fuckers."

"Who?"

"Our old FBI buddies Rogers and McCarthy. I can tell you that they're pretty pissed off."

With an effort, she kept her features frozen.

"Why?" she asked innocently.

"You've remade me a new asshole, Elly." His eyes seemed to have sunk into their sockets. She started to speak, then thought better of it. What was there to say? "We're not in the fiction business. Your little black buddy recanted, then today that Hopwood guy, the former customs man changed his story. And Italian intelligence has discovered that Leopold never left Venice on that

Iraqi ship you saw with your own eyes. Great stuff and I fell for
it." He shook his head, and she could see the sadness beneath the
anger. "You've given them the club they needed, kiddo." His eyes
moved upward. She knew what he meant.

"Finished me off. When it comes out, I'm dead in the water.
Day or so they'll have to break it. Nothing there. They apparently haven't found any money and no diamonds, which means
that either Silver hid it too well or it's all a load of hubris. No
spooks, just lots of loose ends leading nowhere and doo-doo all
over the paper. Just what they want, especially that fuck Evans.
Hell, you'll be the heroine of the media haters. They'll sculpt your
head and stick it over my gravestone. Epitaph: Here was a prick
that listened to some paper doll with a hard-on for immortality."

It seemed like a swan song speech, spoken swiftly with a tone
of bravado salted with resignation and mockery. He was not a
man unwilling to go out quietly. Elly felt for him. And herself.

"But you can't be blamed—"

He put up his hands.

"Stop with blame. Blame doesn't matter. Your little yellowmail
caper doesn't matter. We printed shit, and *that's* what matters.
And *I* let it happen. Five years ago, I might have weaseled out.
Not now. Worst part is that I trusted you. A great way to cap a
career, don't you think?"

His pause demanded an answer.

"I did my best," she said lamely, her voice barely audible.

"Best? Shit in. Shit out. Kills me, I didn't smell it." He shook
his head and his body slumped. "Hell, maybe I am over the hill.
But the paper, the whole idea of what journalism means. You let
us all down. The way I see it this black dude conned some dough
out of you. And how much did the ex-Customs man cost? What
the hell do they have at stake? No perjury involved in jerking off

a newspaperman. And this bullshit about Leopold getting on an Iraqi—"

"I made a mistake," she whispered.

"Doesn't matter anymore. They hold the club now. They're the ones that can burn us. Bunch of fucking media haters. They're going to love doing this to me. Love it. You'll see. Have me dead to rights."

"You can always fire me—" she began. No matter what she did, she had hurt someone, betrayed someone.

"That's a given. But what happens to me? Forty years in this fucking business. Everybody will be around to piss on old Charlie's grave. Damned fool I was. I wanted the topper, the last punch. Nobody to trust any more around here. All you yuppie assholes out for yourselves."

"It's my responsibility. I'm the guilty party."

"Sure, your responsibility. Next thing you know you're on Donahue, and you got a book contract to tell your side, whatever the fuck that is."

He grew suddenly silent, although his nostrils still quivered with anger, but he was winding down. It was awful watching him, the legend, the great and courageous Charlie Carruthers, inspiration and role model to a generation of reporters, the seeker of truth, enemy of the manipulators and the entrenched. It was unbearable to watch his fear and his suffering. And her hand brought him down. Surely, she could not abdicate her responsibility to him, to herself, to the press. Not for love. Was it that? Really that? The words echoed and reechoed in her mind.

"There must be a way," she said, unable to mask her inner trembling.

"Why must?" He cocked his head like a suspicious dog.

"I could be on to something to change—" Her voice trailed off.

She wasn't quite certain how to put it or, for that matter, how to do it.

"You mean you still want me to believe that you can pull a rabbit out of the hat."

"I hadn't meant for you to be hurt." For anyone to be hurt, she thought.

"What kind of crap is that? In this business, someone always gets hurt." He looked at her, his mouth curling in contempt. "Usually the bad guys."

He leaned back in his chair, his anger spent. His eyes had glazed over. "Hell, I had a good run," he muttered. "In the end nobody goes out gracefully. Age votes everybody out of office."

He seemed to be talking to himself now, unaware of her presence. "Maybe things changed when I wasn't looking. Used to be a clear demarcation between good and evil. Now you can't tell anymore. It's ambition, blurs the border. Snot-nose kids want to make their name, kill for a story that'll topple the brass. But that era's gone, dead and gone. It's time for the politicians to grow horns. No one is going to cut them off. Not now." He looked at her, and his eyes cleared. "I want you to know, Elly. I believed in your instincts. Unfortunately right or wrong doesn't matter. They'll do whatever they can get away with."

His sudden tack face confused her.

"You mean you do believe I had it right? In the face of what's come down."

"In my gut, Elly. Bottom line. Even beneath your own stink. Never been any other way."

"But I thought you bought what Bilton had to say."

"All he said was that he looked and didn't find anything. I believed the bastard. He probably did look. Probably didn't find anything. The boys on top, way at the top are getting smarter is all. We taught them to keep their cards closer to the vest."

"So you challenged me. Made me think I shoved it down your throat."

"You might say that."

"You weren't bothered by me buying that information from Parker."

"Sure it bothered me. But you weren't supposed to say. You weren't supposed to admit it."

"You said you were going to take me off it."

"I wanted to see what you would risk."

"And you saw me getting involved with Harry Silver."

"I've got eyes."

"And you hoped that I would shoehorn the real story out of him?"

"By hook or crook," he sighed. "Above all, I expected the story to stand up. I figured you for a great investigative reporter. Guess I was wrong."

She did not know how to respond. Wrong? Was he coming at her from another way now, challenging her pride? Was this his desperation ploy, a last ditch stand. Did he really have a clue as to what she had done with Newton and Hopwood? No, nothing was as it seemed. Not in Washington. There was never only one truth in Washington.

"You're doing it again, aren't you?" she asked.

"Trying. Better than going down in flames."

"You think I have something?"

"I've always dreamed of happy endings, Elly. Frankly, this one looks like Greek tragedy." He sucked in a deep breath. "I can see the Parker thing, a con job. Maybe some more dough passed. I can smell the Hopwood thing, power of suggestion. You found his weak spot."

She let his speculation stand. No perfect insights, she thought, because there were no perfect people. Besides, she knew he was now playing with her head.

"But the Iraqi German thing bugs me."

"Me, too. I made a judgment based on a presumption that was wrong."

"Okay, let's call that a write-off." He bit his lip. "Still, there is smoke here. Leopold dead, maybe murdered." He tapped his teeth. "You know about Tucker?"

"No."

"Big press conference Friday morning. Our White House man says he's going to announce with the president's blessing." As he said it, he watched her, searching her face with his tense blood-shot eyes. "So you see, he's not afraid. He couldn't possibly be worried about your boy upsetting the apple cart."

He was tempting her now. Sixth sense, more like seventh. Human relations in Washington operated on instinct, the unspoken, a kind of gamesmanship. He knew he was backed against the wall, and now he was playing with her obvious involvement with Harry. Playing assy-savey, are you? Perhaps she did owe him that. And herself. But what did she owe to Harry? She thought of the tape recorder lying on her kitchen table. She felt Charlie's scrutiny. He hadn't taken his eyes off her. What was he seeing, she wondered?

"He knows the truth, Elly," Charlie said with surprising gentleness. "We could use a little of that now. Both of us."

"He hasn't told me anything, Charlie," she said, a clear admission of involvement and, at least technically, the absolute truth.

"I'm dancing as hard as I can, kiddo," Charlie sighed.

"I pushed him as hard as I could."

"Sure you did."

"Listen, Charlie. You know I don't want to see you hurt. Considering all you've done."

"You saying I have chits to call?" he said suddenly alert.

"But he'll never tell me anything. Hell, I'm the cause of his troubles. He doesn't have to. Not with the FBI off his back."

"Win some. Lose some," he grunted. He slapped both palms on the table and stood up. She remained seated, watching him. Above all, grace mattered. He could never stoop to begging. But she hated the idea of him kowtowing, going down.

"They can't do that to you. You made this paper. You're the greatest newspaperman—"

"Only as good as the troops," he said, watching her.

"But I'm not giving up on it, Charlie. I intend to keep at him," she said.

"Hold my breath long enough, I'll be dead. Either way."

"I'll get it, Charlie. I swear, I will."

"No oaths, please. Town is choked with them. They don't mean shit."

Long after he had left the room, she continued to sit there. These were not the kind of choices they taught little girls, she thought bitterly.

XXIX

She lay on the floor, propped against the couch pillows, in the same spot where she and Harry had made love. Beside her was the tape recorder. Her eyelids trembled. She had closed them against the shadows that played along the ceiling, specters caused by the breeze from the sliver of open window that rustled the curtains.

She could imagine the boy, Paul, sitting stiffly on a chair, the tape recorder hidden from his father's view. They would be in that cozy, organized, motherly kitchen, she decided. They were sitting at the table, and the tape recorder was placed on the chair between Paul's thighs. His father, Harry, would be sitting directly across from him, elbows on the table, hands supporting his chin.

She could not be certain whether they looked at each other, maintained eye contact. Certainly Paul's eyes would be on his father. But Harry might be looking away or through or around his son, inspiration and memory coming from within, not wishing quite yet to assess his son's reaction.

It was important, she thought, to set this scene in her mind, to imagine it down to the most-minute detail. The time: evening. The place: the kitchen. Bobbie would be doing homework in her room, perhaps talking to a friend on the phone. They would be able to hear her voice, her occasional laughter in the distance. She flicked on the recorder.

The words, Harry's words came, not in a torrent nor haltingly, but in measured cadences, the father feeding his son in a rhythm that could be digested and remembered. She knew her mind was not absorbing it verbatim, as if she were trying to absolve herself from this violation of such a solemn and germinal exchange between a father and a son. She had no rights here. She was an invader, an alien. No amount of rationalization could ever absolve her. She was guilty, and she knew it.

"Elly was right," the father's voice said. Perhaps it was somewhere at the beginning of their talk. She wasn't sure. "A father, well, the head of a family—no, not head, because your mother could also lay claim to that title. There are confidences that families owe each other, secrets that cannot be kept.

"I may tell you why I did these things because by the time I finish telling you I may figure it out for myself. It's not that I'm going like some stupid lamb to the slaughter. But the facts are these. No, not facts, really. The events are these. William Tucker, Billy, was always, in my mind, a man of destiny.

"Early on, he was my trail blazer, friend, model, the anointed one. Always, I trusted in the surety of fate that he would carry me along, bring me to places that I, either for lack of talent or charisma or even ambition, was not capable of getting to myself.

"I've explained that before. Maybe I loved the man in a brotherly way, worshipped him. Men follow men. Billy was a natural leader. I fell into line. And I liked the role of trusted lieutenant. There was something noble about it. Wasn't there?"

"Well, not exactly noble," Harry admitted, and then plunged forward to speak flatly about Billy's interest in running for the presidency, and the president himself telling him that, in addition to all the other human attributes, he had to have the wherewithal to get the jump on his opponents—and not just his own money or his wife's.

Billy had lent the president money over the years, although it sounded to her like paying for his affection and life style. But these little favors gave him, Billy, the inside track. After all, lending, probably giving, money creates a great bond between people in high places, especially in this atmosphere of suspended morality. That, she knew, would be a tough concept for Paul to grasp.

Politics in Washington was not just the art of the possible, but required the art of subterfuge, the art of and style of hypocrisy and the very basic and fundamental art of not getting caught. This meant not letting the media close enough to sniff your dirty underwear.

She wasn't sure of the chronology and, after a while, she was not sure that she was listening for the revelation of simple facts. They came over quite clearly: Irving Leopold's suggestion that he could get ten million from the South Africans, Harry's reluctance, Billy's acquiescence, Harry's final surrender to the idea.

It was, he admitted, ridiculous, a comedy of errors, compounded by stupidity. He emphasized that aspect of it, not sparing himself. He spoke of Leopold's method of converting the diamonds into cash, of how he had put the cash in safety-deposit boxes along the route of the Washington to New York Amtrak.

In the telling, she could detect his own reaction to the humor of it, how generations from now, when the truth were finally told, people might tell the story and howl with laughter over the sheer stupidity of it.

He mocked himself and his part in it, telling his son that perhaps he would have a good laugh about it with his grandchildren. Except that, because of what had happened to Paul's mother, it would not be a laughing matter. Never. He would always carry the shame around with him.

Harry was not asking his son for forgiveness—only for understanding.

She imagined the boy's dilemma. He would not quite know

how to react, how to understand. Not yet.

Harry told him about the burglary of Irving's hotel room, the bribe to the Italian ambassador, the attempt to keep Leopold hidden in Venice, then the unraveling of events based upon Elly's wrong assumption that Irving had been heading to Iraq. He told him about how he had helped Irving bring the diamonds into the United States. He had been dressed as an orthodox rabbi, and he had carried the diamonds under his false beard, the stuff of comedy.

Then had come Millie's casual remark to Elly during their interview, Billy's fear of discovery. He tried to explain Billy's paranoia about bugs and telephones and tape recorders, which must have made Paul stiffen with fear, certainly shame.

She felt this shame herself, reached out, touched the machine but could not bring herself to turn it off. He was telling now about the ten million, ten million dollars, how he had gathered it up, collected it in two suitcases. Riches. And how he had chosen to dispose of it and by what method.

He had paused, perhaps studying Paul, the hesitation revealing an uncertainty. The act had an air of incredulity about it, and her reporter's instincts made her wrinkle her nose with skepticism. Throw away ten million? Just like that, over the bridge's rail? Come on, Harry.

His voice, as if it were reacting to her as well, continued full of rationalizing explanation. He told of its practical side. By destroying the evidence, he was foreclosing on any further revelations as to its origin. The money, by then, had become a burden, a kind of disease that had to be cured.

Then Paul had interrupted with a question: "What did it look like, all that money?" It was a question she had just asked herself, although she had also wanted to know what it felt like.

"Like a pile of paper," Harry had answered, and then answering her question, "and it felt great throwing it away." Meaning, she knew, an act of supreme uniqueness and individuality.

"Proud of you, baby," she whispered then laughed out loud, a belly shaker. She actually had to hold her stomach to keep it from hurting. Even Harry joined in on the tape and, listening hard, she could detect a low giggle from Paul. It came at that point when he told about the gift of the ten million that Billy had proffered—after the fact.

A tale like that, Elly knew, was the most priceless Washington story in a decade, maybe a century. It had everything. She felt suddenly like a hawker selling a shell game. Her pulse quickened. Humor and pathos, bravery and betrayal, the rich and powerful, presidential politics, bribery, international intrigue, bizarre disguises, anti-Semites, burglary, suicide, perhaps murder. A story like that! My God. Charlie would bay at the moon for the sheer joy of it. The powers-that-be would be shaken to their roots.

From somewhere deep in the recesses of her psyche, a poltergeist boiling to be heard, she heard her father's voice goading her on, rattling the rafters of her soul. "Go get 'em," the poltergeist thundered.

But Harry's voice was relentless, distracting her. Details continued to spill out, putting more flesh on the story. The business of the president wanting Billy to succeed him, the fact that Billy had lent the president money for years. Wheels within wheels. She wondered if Paul had grasped the political subtleties going on here. Her journalist's mind began constructing it. Words in neat battalions fell into line, forming marching sentences.

Reaching out her arm, she touched the tape recorder, caressed it with her fingers. Then silence. She wondered if the recorder had run out of tape. She checked it. No. The tape continued to pass through the heads. Listening carefully, she imagined she could hear breathing, movement, sounds of life. Perhaps they sat watching each other now, father and son. She wasn't clear on exactly what kind of human engineering was going on.

"So now you're wondering, Paul, why I've chosen to say nothing about all this. Knowing that my old friend William Tucker has cut me loose, set me adrift, faced political realities and abandoned me. Of course, it is insulting to know that, in his mind, I have been expendable, able to be bought, sold or bartered. I'm not sure I'm surprised. By all rights, I should be reveling in revenge. I am worried about going to prison, leaving you and Bobbie. It would be awful losing my freedom, too."

He hesitated and she wondered if another long silence was beginning. "Everything I've done in this thing, Paul, has been against the grain, except maybe dumping the ten million and not selling myself out. I've done wrong, and I'll pay for it. That doesn't mean I've got to sell out Billy. No way. Do you know what I'm trying to say, son? It's about honor, a man's pride, his own soul. Do you know what I mean?"

She listened, waiting for Paul's answer. It never came. In a burst of anger, she reached out to the tape recorder and tapped the off button. Then she smashed the heel of her fist on the floor and pushed herself up.

It did not take her long to discover the heart of her rage.

"By hook or by crook," Charlie had said.

So what did that make her?

XXX

William Tucker came around from behind his desk to greet her, his smile crinkling his tanned, weathered skin. Sandy-gray hair tumbled over his forehead. A tweed sport jacket hung open, showing her his flat stomach and small waist. In this big, impressive office with its flags, large sitting area, and autographed pictures in frames and on the walls, Tucker looked comfortable, relaxed, at home.

If he was worried in the slightest, he did not show it. Indeed, Elly thought, he had good reason to feel secure.

Although the FBI had not announced that they had ceased their investigation of the Leopold–Silver episode, Elly was certain that Tucker knew all about it.

That morning she had called in sick. She did not reconnect the telephone. Sometime in the wee hours of the morning, she had come to a clear resolution. It had been agony, but she knew what she must do. Her life had come down to this moment.

Brimming with charm and assurance, he led her to a chair and sat down beside her. He was the cat that had swallowed the canary, and he had agreed to see her knowing that he was, in his own mind, out of danger.

After all, he was a man who had been born under a lucky star. Why question good fortune? She had hoped he would consent to this meeting without any harassment on her part. Perhaps at this point, he was merely curious. But he had agreed. She supposed he had decided that it would be a gesture, a base to touch, a sense of noblesse oblige. He had bested them, or so it had seemed. He was the winner and champion. Now that he was about to run for president, he knew the value of ingratiation with members of the press. From now on, she knew, he would be Mr. Accessible, sweetness and light, the "candidate."

She declined coffee. A night of coffee drinking to keep her awake and alert had taken its toll. She knew her fingers trembled, and she kept them clasped on her lap.

"I appreciate your seeing me, Mr. Secretary."

"A time for everything," he said. "Millie sends her regards." Millie would be "managed" now, briefed frequently, carefully monitored. She was probably taking lessons in public speaking.

"I had originally been trying to see you to gain some further insight into your relationship with Harry Silver."

"Ah, yes, dear Harry," he said, offering a twinkle and a sigh. She wondered where he had learned that.

"You and he go back a long way."

"From the beginning. He came to town because of me. I put him in Customs. A good man, salt of the earth. It's been a terrible ordeal for him."

"You've been in touch with him?"

She could see the slight changing of gears, the sudden gauzy film of wariness that faded the twinkle.

"The man's my friend."

Evasion, she thought, persisting.

"So you've been a comfort to him during this ordeal."

"Of course, I have."

Ten million could, in his mind, be characterized as a comfort.

"And you feel he will be vindicated?"

"Absolutely."

He had recovered the twinkle. Now, she supposed, he thought he could toy with her.

"You don't think there's anything there?"

"Not a thing." He arranged his lips, in what she decided was a sly smile. He was good. No question about that. A good choice for a candidate in a visually oriented world. She let him work through his pause, sensing that there was more he wanted to say. "A concoction of the media. Nothing more. Not that you all don't try to do an honest job. Unfortunately, you're not infallible. As we on the other side, you occasionally make mistakes. This one was a real boo-boo, I'm afraid."

"You think we had it all wrong?"

"You certainly did. In a way I feel rather sorry for you. Not that you won't recover. You certainly look strapping and resilient."

"Wrong about everything?"

"Afraid so." He smiled broadly now. "None of us were remotely frightened. We figured the press is always looking for adversarial issues. Believe me, none of us lost sleep."

"I wish I could say the same."

"Breaks of the game. Bygones be bygones. Harry will be fine."

She scrutinized him. He was awesome in the way he contrived himself, the quintessential public figure, showing her only what he wished to reveal. In looks and manner, he was the ultimate cliché of an American politician, blessed by good looks and circumstances, articulate, intelligent, and willing to recreate himself at will.

It was marvelous, even amazing how he was able to mask the sweaty-palmed ambition, the moral and ethical slippage, the hypocrisy and, worse, the criminality. She wondered how he rationalized it, squared it with traditional values of right and wrong. She was fascinated and disgusted. Was it possible that only she stood before him and his dream to be—God help us—leader of the free world?

"Yes," she said, "Harry will be fine." I'll see to that, she thought.

She waited, watched, saw him nod and smile, relaxed. "Quite a haul, ten million."

There was no escaping her fixed gaze. He was nailed into it, hammered in. His tan receded. A flush rolled over his cheeks. His eyelids fluttered. But there was no way he could hide the sudden fear.

"What are you talking about?"

"The ten million dollars that you got from the conversion of Irving Leopold's diamond haul out of South Africa."

He stood up suddenly as if yanked straight by manipulated puppet strings.

"I don't have to accept that kind of accusation." It came out like a rattlesnake's hiss, but without the rattle.

"Yes, you do," she said calmly. "And I advise you to sit down."

"I'm not going to take this—"

"You have no choice, Mr. Secretary," she said calmly. She made an imaginary gun out of her fingers and pointed it at him. "Gotcha."

He strode angrily toward his desk, opened a drawer and brought out a cassette recorder, then came back and sat down in his former seat.

"I want this down," he said angrily. "Because you and your paper are going to have one helluva suit on your hands, one helluva suit."

"This is between me and you," she said, watching his face. "But I don't mind if you record it, not at all. I've got it down myself."

He reached out and smashed his finger on the button to shut off the machine.

"What the hell do you mean? Between me and you?"

"And Harry," she said.

"That stupid little bastard," he snapped. "He's off the hook. He doesn't need this. The FBI is dropping the investigation. He's home free. It's over."

He stopped abruptly. She could sense his mind turning over, looking for the angle, the way out. He was wily, resourceful and lucky, she thought, suddenly curious as to what his strategy might be. Calm, she saw. Step one. He was determined to get his emotions under control and having a difficult time of it.

"I know everything," she said slowly. He sat stony-faced, tight-lipped as she recounted from memory what she had heard on Harry's tape.

She spoke flatly, perhaps monotonously. Little bubbles of perspiration broke over his upper lip. He put his fingers through his hair, mussing the carefully contrived shaggy look. Of course, her presentation was scrupulously edited.

She did not tell him about what Harry had done with the ten million, or how she had gotten the information, or why Harry would never personally betray him. It might have taken ten or fifteen minutes to tell her story, a few minutes more of silence as she watched his reaction, knowing that his thoughts were out ahead of hers as he squirmed to spring loose from her grip.

"You said between you and me," he whispered, his eyes suddenly seemed furtive as they inspected his office.

"Not for publication."

He flicked off some moisture from his upper lip.

"So it's money then?" He chuckled bitterly. "Why not get it from Harry? He's in it up to his ass as well."

"It's not money," she said.

"Then what?" he asked. "Don't take me for a fool."

She cautioned herself not to grow too anxious.

"Protection," she said.

"Protection?" His eyes blazed, but she knew she had thrown a match to dry tinder.

"From what happened to Leopold."

She watched his neck muscles work as he swallowed, saw the rise and fall of his chest as he breathed with difficulty.

"What do you take me for?" he asked, his words barely audible.

"For what you are," she said.

He began to rub his palms together, and his legs moved in a rhythmic, nervous, repetitive motion.

"Are you suggesting that I had anything to do with Leopold's death?"

"I'm accusing you," she said calmly. Instinct, she thought. His reaction made her dead certain.

"That can't stand up. You know that."

"I said it was between you and me."

Again, his eyes roamed his office. Suddenly, his arm lashed out, and he grabbed her pocketbook, which lay on the chair beside her. The action surprised her, but she let him rifle through it.

"There's a bug on you. I'm sure of it."

"You're welcome to do a strip search," Elly said, offering a mocking belligerent smile. "In today's climate, might be seen as sexual harassment." He sat back in the chair and leaned his head against the back of it.

"I'll do what I can," he whispered, telling her what she needed to know.

"For all of us. You can tell them that we have insurance. Tapes. Transcripts. We've thought of everything." It had, she knew, remained unsaid to Paul, but it was also part of it. Not that Harry feared for himself, but certainly for his children. "In fact, you might tell your South African friends that we can be equally destructive dead."

"Believe me, I had nothing to do with that."

"I believe you," she said casually as if it were chitchat at a cocktail party.

"Governments must take steps in their own self-protection. Believe me, they probably agonized over it. They're not monsters. We live in a dangerous world and—"

She lifted one hand.

"Please. No lectures."

He backed off swiftly as if scalded, nodding as a gesture of grudging respect. She suspected that he had already deduced her motives. Okay, she thought, that one's for Harry, me, and the kids. Family, she thought, satisfied with the image.

"I understand," he said, quick to agree, too quick. He was fawning now, following a strategy of humility. "And no publication. Is that the tradeoff?"

"For Harry, yes."

A frown passed over his face. He wasn't sure what to make of it. She imagined that the wheels were turning in his head like a slot machine, undoubtedly wondering why it was her he was confronting, not Harry.

"He probably never had anything to worry about," he said blandly. "Harry is a man of honor."

"You've got that right."

Give him credit, she thought. He was not surrendering easily, thinking, she was certain, that a bargain had been struck. And now one for Daddy, she thought.

"That's it, then?" he asked hopefully.

"Almost," she said. "I wonder where you and Millie intend to spend the rest of your lives."

He had again begun to sink back in his chair. Now he sat bolt upright as if a ghost had frightened him. He started to say something, sputtering to a halt before he got started. His eyes probed her, looking for meaning.

"Be glad to compose your letter of resignation," she said. "I'm considered a pretty good writer for a journalist. As for that presidential thing, I think a terse thank you, no thank you will do. Blame it on personal reasons. Yes, I'd say that would be quite appropriate."

She knew it was particularly venomous and melodramatic, but she reveled in it. He slid back in the chair, his tanned face as transparent as parchment.

"I won't do it," he mumbled, but it was clear that he was flustered, flogging himself to show indignation. "The president is endorsing me."

"Can't stop him from that. After all, it's bought and paid for. The real grace will be in your declination."

She watched it all sink in, like a swift process of corrosion. His leathery skin grew slack, his face suddenly jowly. She sensed in herself a sudden flash of compassion, perhaps a motherly instinct for a hurt child. He did seem helpless now, pitiful.

Against such an image, Harry was indeed noble, and she felt an urgent pride, a validation. Well, Daddy, she thought, here's one bastard that won't get away with it. But there was something more, wasn't there? Something for Elly and, maybe, all the sisters who needed to know that powerlessness wasn't something loose in the gender like a bad gene.

"For now, it's all between us, Mr. Secretary, but I assure you that what I have is a media bonanza that will make you a historical boogey man of gargantuan proportions. If you've really got an itch for immortality, then just tempt me. Believe me, it won't take much." She thought suddenly of Charlie. Was there anything left for Charlie? "And one thing more." She paused and watched him. He sat crumpled in his chair, all the fight gone. In his eyes she caught a tiny flicker of curiosity.

"The reason for your dropping out of the race," she said it slowly. "You are to call Charlie Carruthers at my paper."

"Don't you think—"

"And you are to give it to him or any reporter he assigns, an exclusive. Before anyone else gets it. No press conferences."

He shrugged and seemed to be rapidly losing interest, already deep into his own reflections.

"And you are to tell them that you are declining on the grounds of—what shall we call it—ethical considerations."

Again, she saw the flicker of curiosity, and this time, the beginning of panic.

"You will say that you don't think it would be appropriate, especially to get the presidential endorsement if you did choose to run—in the light of the fact that you have been lending the president money for years."

"You expect me to tell Carruthers that?" His eyes glazed over, and he shook his head. "No way."

"Your option. It's either that or the other."

"But you said that was between us." His voice had become a whimper.

"That was. This isn't."

She stood up. Her knees felt shaky, but she had the consolation of being in better shape than the crestfallen Secretary Tucker. Had she squared all accounts? She wasn't sure. Before she left, she glanced back at Tucker. He seemed on the verge of a question, like a bird in flight. Then, suddenly, the bird seemed to deflate, grounded.

But the question was still in his eyes. Why? She felt certain that he was asking himself that question. He would have a lifetime to find the answer.

XXXI

Harry had tried all night to call her. Then he had tried all morning. Finally, he had gone to her apartment building, but she had been out. He had called the paper, and someone there said that she had not been to the office.

Back at his house, he spent the rest of the day worrying about her. In the late afternoon, he had gotten a call from his lawyers telling him that the FBI had dropped its investigation.

"You're one lucky son of a bitch," his lawyer said.

"Guess so," he responded, knowing he was supposed to be feeling elation.

"That's all you've got to say for yourself?"

"Thankful, too."

Inside he felt a general flatness. He wanted Elly to be here.

"Seems the principal witness against you reneged, and the burglar who rifled Leopold's apartment says that his testimony was a crock. And they haven't found any alleged loot. Without that, they got nothing."

"So that's it?" Harry asked.

"It means that you don't get to see the inside of America's white-collar jails."

"I was nearly getting used to the idea," Harry said.

"I wish I knew what all this was about," the lawyer sighed. "I have to admit that I don't understand a thing about it."

"You're not alone," Harry said.

"That's Washington. A puzzle wrapped in an enigma. Only thing I can think is that you just know too much, Harry. That someone put the fix in."

"Lawyers," Harry sighed. Yet he liked Carter. "Just send me your bill."

There was a long pause, then a low chuckle.

"Trade you that for the truth," Carter said. Harry knew he was sincere but offered no response.

Yet when the lawyer hung up, he began to feel the full impact of the decision. He was, as Billy might have said, home free. He couldn't understand why. When Paul and Bobbie came home from school, Harry told them that it was all over. Bobbie kissed him on both cheeks. Paul shook his hand, and they both exchanged winks.

"Does Elly know?" Paul asked.

"Don't know," Harry answered. "I've been trying to reach her."

He noted a shadow of uncertainty cross Paul's face.

"She'll know," he said.

The telephone rang again. It was a reporter from the *Associated Press* asking for his reaction. What was there to say?

"Thankful," he said, sure that was what they expected him to say. He couldn't, of course, say vindicated or confused. Perhaps powerless would be more to the point. When other reporters called, he also offered them "thankful."

He expected that soon there would be television reporters. He'd be thankful for them, as well. He supposed that, in his heart, he might call it a victory, although he was not quite sure what he had won, perhaps a form of self-respect. It certainly wasn't any vindication. Both witnesses had spoken the truth in the first place. So it wasn't a victory for truth. Truth, he knew, would never be a winner in Washington.

He went into the kitchen and looked into the refrigerator. In the end life always returns to the prosaic. It all boiled down to "What's for dinner?"

"I called her again. No answer," Paul said as he came into the kitchen.

"She'll be fine, Paul," Harry said. "She knows how to take care of herself."

"Wouldn't be a bad idea for her to take care of us," Paul said.

Harry looked at him, cocking his head and exploring his son's face. What did he know? But now that the story had ended, did a relationship continue to exist between them?

He heard the buzzer ring, then Paul's footsteps, the door opening. He wondered if there were more reporters.

"Is it reporters?" he called.

"Only one on leave." When he turned, he saw Elly carrying brown bags. Paul came in behind her, cradling more brown bags in his arms.

"On leave?"

"Sort of sabbatical," Elly said. "Got some ideas I want to work out."

"Write a book, maybe?" Harry asked.

"Not sure. I'll play it by ear."

"Me, too." He paused and smiled, "Now that I'm, as they say, at liberty."

She put down the bags on the countertops, leaned against it, and watched him.

"There's more in the car, Paul," Elly said. The boy left the room.

"You know about the investigation?" Paul asked.

"Heard it on the radio," she said, unpacking the bags, not looking at him.

"I don't understand it."

"Why bother?" Elly asked, opening cupboards. "Nothing in this town is ever as it seems." She turned, and he watched her as she offered a cryptic smile. "In my stories either. Nobody ever hits a bull's eye when it comes to the truth. I was off by a mile."

"Not really," he said. He had the urge to say more, tell her everything. He wondered if she sensed it.

"Where is the sugar jar hidden?" she asked suddenly.

The question confused him. He looked toward the cupboards. He wasn't certain. He scratched his head.

"You know. I don't know."

"I'll find it," she said. Especially if it's hidden, she thought. She turned suddenly to find him directly behind her, almost touching. At that moment, Paul came in, holding still more brown bags.

"You must have bought out the store," Harry said.

"When you make camp," Elly said. "You need lots of supplies."

Then she busied herself putting things in their proper place. Pausing suddenly, she turned to Paul.

"You like lamb chops?"

Paul nodded.

"Me, too," Harry said.

"Figures," Elly said, winking at Paul.

The complete works of Warren Adler are available in all formats. Please visit www.WarrenAdler.com for more information.

NOVELS

The David Embrace. An ambitious second-in-command to a billionaire plans to take over the man's business empire by hiring an assassin to kill him. The assassin, part of a worldwide ring does the deed. In the process of escape, he encounters the wife of the man who has set up the hit. They fall in love. This erotic action thriller is set in the south of France and Italy, with the famed Michelangelo statue in Florence figuring prominently in the plot.

The Womanizer. A respected family man with an adulterous past is offered the presidency of a major university. The former president has been fired for sexual misconduct with a student. The potential new president is to be subjected to a thorough vetting by a wily investigator hired by the university board. He attempts to erase his past by finding his past lovers, with startling results.

Residue. The firebombing of a former synagogue in Brooklyn, which has been converted to a black church, uncovers a startling discovery of enormous value hidden in the basement of the church. A young lawyer is assigned to help the pastor with insurance claims only to be sucked into a dangerous intrigue involving the source of the treasure from the distant past.

Flanagan's Dolls. A couple in their forties have chosen semiretirement in their hometown in upper Michigan and open a funky antique store. A man seeking a specific antique doll as a gift for his ailing granddaughter sets off a mysterious murder that rocks the town. The couple who solve the crime have marked similarities to Nick and Nora Charles created by Dashiell Hammett.

Empty Treasures. A female reporter for a Washington newspaper uncovers a plot to surreptitiously finance a presidential campaign. Exploring the dark side of politics and its tantalizing, corruptive power, this fast-paced story reveals how obsessive ambition and ethical violation can impact the lives and loves of the people caught in its entrails.

The War of the Roses. The Roses thought they had a perfect marriage, but discover that their relationship is barely skin deep. This is the acclaimed and best-selling novel that became the classic divorce movie starring Michael Douglas and Kathleen Turner.

Random Hearts. Two survivors of a tragic plane crash discover their dead spouses' infidelity. This best-selling novel of love, passion and forgiveness became a major motion picture with Harrison Ford.

Funny Boys. A wannabe comedian is hired by a catskill mountain hotel to entertain guests, circa 1937, in the heyday of the Jewish mountain resorts. The hotel is where the killers of famed Murder Inc. send their wives and girlfriends for the summer. Murder and mayhem ensue when the young comedian falls in love with the hit man's girlfriend.

Trans-Siberian Express. American doctor Alex Cousins knows a dark and dangerous secret, and the Soviet Union will stop at nothing to keep him in Siberia on the world's longest and most exotic train ride to prevent him from revealing it.

Mourning Glory. A down on her luck 38-year-old single mother with a dysfunctional teen- age daughter snares a rich widower in Palm Beach. But her cynical scheme unravels and she finds herself enmeshed in a self-spun web of deception and danger that threatens to rob her of everything she holds dear.

The Children of the Roses. Ever wonder what happened to the two children of the destructive Mr. and Mrs. Rose whose story in The War of the Roses has become a worldwide classic illustrating the perils of a marriage gone awry? In this novel, the children are adults coping with the residual trauma of their parent's lives as they impact on yet another generation.

Cult. A novel of brainwashing and death. The suspenseful story of a man's increasingly desperate attempt to rescue his brainwashed wife from a religious death cult. A thriller with a chilling climax that shows how the power of sinister forces using mind control techniques can turn innocent people into weapons of destruction.

The Casanova Embrace. In this explicit and erotic thriller, a charismatic Latin diplomat cynically seduces three lonely women and uses them as pawns in international terrorism. Discovering his ruthless manipulation and betrayal, they plot every woman's revenge fantasy.

Blood Ties. During a family reunion at their ancestral castle, the famed Von Kassel family—arms dealers for over a hundred years—suddenly find themselves in possession of stolen plutonium capable of creating the most destructive weapon on earth. Secret revelations erupt into violence as the family is torn apart by their acquisition's deadly potential.

Natural Enemies. Pursued by human predators, a young urban couple becomes lost in the Colorado wilderness and is forced to confront the chilling and impersonal wrath of nature in this taut and acclaimed novel.

The Housewife Blues. An innocent and naïve young woman marries to escape from her small mid-western town. But her controlling husband moves her to an apartment in New York City and keeps her a virtual prisoner. Her journey of self-discovery from naiveté through disenchantment and eventual wisdom makes for a suspenseful story with explosive consequences.

Banquet Before Dawn. After serving his Brooklyn district for many years, an Irish Congressman is challenged by a youthful and more liberal opponent. In this remarkable novel full of unforgettable characters, the last hurrah becomes a poignant and seething masterwork.

Madeline's Miracles. A young family falls prey to a woman who convinces them that she is a psychic and can foresee their future in this critically acclaimed and chilling bestseller about brainwashing and superstition.

We Are Holding the President Hostage. When terrorists capture the daughter and grandson of a Mafia Don in Egypt, the angry Godfather insinuates himself into the White House and teaches the President some lessons of the mob. This classic confrontation between two men on utterly opposite sides of the law is laced with humor and illustrates how fierce paternal love can motivate even the most ruthless of gangsters into reckless acts of courage and bravery.

Private Lies. Two Manhattan couples are caught in a complex and emotional web of adultery, sexual obsession and deception that turns deadly on an African safari.

The Henderson Equation. The people who run the influential newspaper the Washington Chronicle have just brought down a President through their damning investigative reports. Now they want to create their own choice for Chief Executive! The power of the press to manipulate comes under the microscope in this tense exploration of the media and the thirst for power.

Twilight Child. Readers Digest originally published this acclaimed, heart wrenching novel about the visitation rights of grandparents and the terrible ordeal that ensues between generations locked in a bitter struggle for a child's love.

Undertow. After the beautiful black aide and lover of a woman-izing married Senator accidentally drowns, the Senator mounts a massive cover-up of cynical lies designed to deflect the potential damage to his career in this suspenseful tale of adultery, media manipulation, and political chicanery.

MYSTERIES

American Quartet. This is the first book in the popular Fiona FitzGerald mystery series. Fiona is a senator's daughter turned Washington, D.C. homicide detective. Four seemingly uncon-nected murders stimulate Fiona's sense of history as she delves into our country's dark past. In her effort to solve the crimes, she uncovers the twisted sexual and homicidal obsessions of a socially prominent but failed Washington politician. Named by the *New York Times* as one of the top ten crime novels of the year.

The Witch of Watergate. When an infamous and unpopular Washington *Post* reporter whose poison pen has destroyed many careers is found hanging in her Watergate apartment, suicide is the logical explanation. But Fiona won't stop investigating until she uncovers the truth, even as it leads to the corridors of power on Capitol Hill.

Senator Love. A seductive and philandering Senator is the prime suspect when bodies begin turning up buried in an upscale Washington neighborhood. Besides solving the mystery, will Fiona submit to the powerful sexual charm of "Senator Love?"

American Sextet. Fiona takes us behind the scenes of power and unravels a massive political sex scandal that shakes the Washington establishment to its core. As Fiona investigates, she uncovers a conspiracy involving six men from the highest offices in the country—a great American Sextet!

Immaculate Deception. The clock is ticking both figuratively and biologically. During Fiona's pursuit to conceive a child, a powerful female pro-life Senator is found dead. The case gets even more baffling when one shocking clue contradicts the entire investigation.

The Ties That Bind. The daughter of a prominent lawyer is found murdered, and a Supreme Court Justice with a sadomasochistic fetish is the target of Fiona's investigation. This is a case that truly brings Fiona to the dark side of the Washington scene.

Death of a Washington Madame. The death of a famous Washington hostess long past her prime reveals political and social secrets that test the investigative skills of Detective Fiona FitzGerald as she goes about unlocking the old traumas that impact on the contemporary political and social lives of the woman's progeny and survivors.

SHORT STORIES

Never Too Late for Love. The intrepid crew from Sunset Village is back! With sensitivity and humor, these brilliant stories depict the lives, loves, conflicts and trials of the modern senior citizen. This is the complete collection of the classic Sunset Gang stories.

Jackson Hole, Uneasy Eden. These acclaimed stories capture the truth, warts and all, of how modern life can both corrupt and enhance a traditional environment. Based on the author's experience as a long-time resident of this pristine valley in Wyoming nestled in the heart of the Grand Tetons, America's most beautiful mountain range.

The Sunset Gang. With time running short, the retired residents of Sunset Village in Florida continue to thirst for life, love and happiness. In the process, they teach us all a lot about living—a subject on which they are, after all, experts. These critically acclaimed short stories were adapted into a PBS trilogy that won worldwide recognition for its wonderful insights into the aging process.

Warren Adler Short Story Contest Winners. This book contains all the winners of the Warren Adler Short Story Contest, which has attracted thousands of worldwide submissions. The contest is designed to encourage writers to employ this mode of fictional expression that has been eclipsed in the last few years by the long form of the novel. These stories by extraordinarily talented writers will inspire, delight, and enlighten the reader with their skillful telling and insights.

New York Echoes. A collection of short stories by Warren Adler inspired by a return to his beloved city after an absence of forty years. These stories reflect a mature writer's insight into the way in which this multifaceted urban landscape affects those who live in New York's ever-churning and exciting environment. It will make readers laugh, cry, and ponder life in an urban pressure cooker.

The Washington Dossier Stories. In the seventies and eighties, Warren Adler wrote a series of stories for the Washington Dossier, a magazine that chronicled the lives and contemporary doings of the capital's social and political elite. These stories reflect what life was like in this unique environment where ambition and status are the motivating force of all those who live there.

Available in all formats as eBooks and Print on Demand wherever books are sold online and off.

For more information visit www.WarrenAdler.com

3449282R00232

Printed in Great Britain
by Amazon.co.uk, Ltd.,
Marston Gate.